THE INTERESTINGS

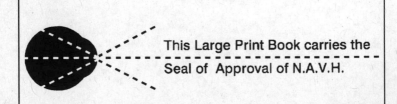

This Large Print Book carries the
Seal of Approval of N.A.V.H.

THE INTERESTINGS

MEG WOLITZER

WHEELER PUBLISHING
A part of Gale, Cengage Learning

GALE
CENGAGE Learning·

Detroit • New York • San Francisco • New Haven, Conn • Waterville, Maine • London

GALE
CENGAGE Learning·

LIBRARY OF CONGRESS CATALOGING-IN-PUBLICATION DATA

Wolitzer, Meg.
  The Interestings / by Meg Wolitzer. -- Large print edition.
    pages ; cm (wheeler publishing large print hardcover)
    ISBN 978-1-4104-6220-6 (hardcover) -- ISBN 1-4104-6220-X (hardcover)
  1. Gifted persons--Fiction. 2. Self-realization--Fiction. 3. Friendship--Fiction.
  4. Large type books. I. Title.
  PS3573.O564I58 2013b
  813'.54--dc23   2013019818

Published in 2013 by arrangement with Riverhead Books, a member of
Penguin Group (USA) Inc.

Printed in Mexico
5 6 7 17 16 15 14

For my parents, who sent me there

And for Martha Parker, whom I met there

While riding on a train goin' west
I fell asleep for to take my rest
I dreamed a dream that made me sad
Concerning myself and the first few
friends I had

— Bob Dylan, "Bob Dylan's Dream"

. . . to own only a little talent . . . was an awful, plaguing thing . . . being only a little special meant you expected too much, most of the time.

— Mary Robison, "Yours"

■ ■ ■ ■

PART ONE:
MOMENTS OF
STRANGENESS

■ ■ ■ ■

ONE

On a warm night in early July of that long-evaporated year, the Interestings gathered for the very first time. They were only fifteen, sixteen, and they began to call themselves the name with tentative irony. Julie Jacobson, an outsider and possibly even a freak, had been invited in for obscure reasons, and now she sat in a corner on the unswept floor and attempted to position herself so she would appear unobtrusive yet not pathetic, which was a difficult balance. The teepee, designed ingeniously though built cheaply, was airless on nights like this one, when there was no wind to push in through the screens. Julie Jacobson longed to unfold a leg or do the side-to-side motion with her jaw that sometimes set off a gratifying series of tiny percussive sounds inside her skull. But if she called attention to herself in any way now, someone might start to wonder why she was here; and really, she knew, she had no reason to be here at all. It had been miraculous when Ash Wolf had nodded to her earlier in the night at the row of sinks and asked if she wanted to come join her and some of the others later. *Some of the others.* Even that wording was thrilling.

Julie had looked at her with a dumb, dripping face, which she then quickly dried with a thin towel from home. *Jacobson,* her mother had written along the puckered edge in red laundry marker in a tentative hand that now seemed a little tragic. "Sure," she had said, out of instinct. What if she'd said *no?* she liked to wonder afterward in a kind of strangely pleasurable, baroque horror. What if she'd turned down the lightly flung invitation and went about her life, thudding obliviously along like a drunk person, a blind person, a moron, someone who thinks that the small packet of happiness she carries is enough. Yet having said "sure" at the sinks in the girls' bathroom, here she was now, planted in the corner of this unfamiliar, ironic world. Irony was new to her and tasted oddly good, like a previously unavailable summer fruit. Soon, she and the rest of them would be ironic much of the time, unable to answer an innocent question without giving their words a snide little adjustment. Fairly soon after that, the snideness would soften, the irony would be mixed in with seriousness, and the years would shorten and fly. Then it wouldn't be long before they all found themselves shocked and sad to be fully grown into their thicker, finalized adult selves, with almost no chance for reinvention.

That night, though, long before the shock and the sadness and the permanence, as they sat in Boys' Teepee 3, their clothes bakery sweet from the very last washer-dryer loads at home, Ash Wolf said, "Every summer we sit here like this. We should call ourselves something."

"Why?" said Goodman, her older brother. "So the world can know just how unbelievably *interesting* we are?"

"We could be called the Unbelievably Interesting Ones," said Ethan Figman. "How's that?"

"The Interestings," said Ash. "That works."

So it was decided. "From this day forward, because we are clearly the most interesting people who ever fucking *lived,*" said Ethan, "because we are just so fucking *compelling,* our brains swollen with intellectual thoughts, let us be known as the Interestings. And let everyone who meets us fall down dead in our path from just how fucking interesting we are." In a ludicrously ceremonial moment they lifted paper cups and joints. Julie risked raising her cup of vodka and Tang — "V&T," they'd called it — nodding gravely as she did this.

"Clink," Cathy Kiplinger said.

"Clink," said all the others.

The name was ironic, and the improvisational christening was jokily pretentious, but still, Julie Jacobson thought, they *were* interesting. These teenagers around her, all of them from New York City, were like royalty and French movie stars, with a touch of something papal. Everyone at this camp was supposedly artistic, but here, as far as she could tell, was the hot little nucleus of the place. She had never met anyone like these people; they were interesting compared not only with the residents of Underhill, the New York suburb where she'd lived since birth, but also compared with what was generally *out there,* which at the moment seemed baggy suited, nefarious, thoroughly repulsive.

Briefly, in that summer of 1974, when she or any of them looked up from the deep, stuporous concentration of their one-act plays and animation cels and dance sequences and acoustic guitars, they found themselves staring into a horrible doorway, and so they quickly turned away. Two boys at camp had copies of *All the President's Men* on the shelves above their beds, beside big aerosol cans of Off! and small bottles of benzoyl peroxide meant to dash flourishing, excitable acne. The book had come out not long before camp began, and at night when the teepee talk wound down into sleep or rhythmic, crickety masturbation, they would read by flashlight. *Can you believe those fuckers?* they thought.

14

This was the world they were meant to enter: a world of fuckers. Julie Jacobson and the others paused before the doorway to that world, and what were they supposed to do — just walk through it? Later in the summer Nixon would lurch away, leaving his damp slug trail, and the entire camp would watch on an old Panasonic that had been trundled into the dining hall by the owners, Manny and Edie Wunderlich, two aging Socialists who were legendary in the small, diminishing world of aging Socialists.

Now they were gathering because the world was unbearable, and they themselves were not. Julie allowed herself another slight degree of movement, crossing and recrossing her arms. But still no one turned and insisted on knowing who had invited this awkward, redheaded, blotchy girl in. Still no one asked her to leave. She looked around the dim room, where everyone was mostly inert on the bunks and on the wooden slats of the floor, like people in a sauna.

Ethan Figman, thick bodied, unusually ugly, his features appearing a little bit flattened, as if pressed against a mime's invisible glass wall, sat with his mouth slack and a record album in his lap. He was one of the first people she'd noticed after her mother and sister drove her up here days earlier. He had been wearing a floppy denim hat then, and he greeted everyone around him on the lawn, grabbing the ends of trunks, allowing himself to be smashed into platonic hugs with girls and soul handshakes with other boys. People cried out to him, "Ethan! Ethan!" and he was pulled toward each voice in turn.

"That boy looks ridiculous," Julie's sister, Ellen, said quietly as they stood on the lawn, fresh out of their green Dodge Dart and the four-hour drive from Underhill. He did look ridiculous, but Julie already felt the need to be protective of this boy she didn't know.

"No he doesn't," she said. "He looks fine."

They were sisters, only sixteen months apart, but Ellen, the older one, was dark-haired, closed-faced, and held surprisingly condemnatory opinions, which had often been dispensed in the small ranch house where they lived with their mother, Lois, and, until that winter, their father, Warren, who had died of pancreatic cancer. Julie would always remember what sharing close quarters with a dying person had been like; particularly what it had been like sharing the single, peach-colored bathroom that her poor father had apologetically monopolized. She had begun to get her period when she was fourteen and a half — much later than anyone else she knew — and she found herself in need of the bathroom at times when it wasn't available. Huddling in her bedroom with an enormous box of Kotex, she thought of the contrast between herself, "emerging into womanhood," according to the movie that the gym teacher had shown the girls much earlier, in sixth grade, and her father, emerging into something else that she didn't want to think about but which was upon her at all times.

In January he was dead, which was a grinding torment and also a relief, impossible to focus on or stop thinking about. Summer approached, still unfilled. Ellen didn't want to go anywhere, but Julie couldn't just sit at home all summer feeling like this and watching her mother and sister feel like this; it would lead to madness, she decided. At the last minute, her English teacher suggested this camp, which had an open spot and agreed to take Julie on scholarship. Nobody in Underhill went to camps like this one; not only wouldn't they have been able to afford it, it wouldn't have occurred to them to go. They all stayed home and went to the local bare-bones day camp, or spent long days oiled up at the town pool or got jobs at Carvel or loafed around their humid houses.

No one really had money, and no one ever seemed to think much about not having money. Warren Jacobson had worked in human resources at Clelland Aerospace; Julie had never understood exactly what his job entailed, but she knew that the pay wasn't enough to allow the family to build and maintain a pool in their small backyard. Yet when she was suddenly offered a chance to go away to this camp in the summer, her mother insisted she accept. "Someone should have a little fun in this family," said Lois Jacobson, a new, shaky widow at age forty-one. "It's been a while."

Tonight, in Boys' Teepee 3, Ethan Figman seemed as confident as he'd been on the lawn that first day. Confident, but also probably conscious of his own ugliness, which would never go away over the whole of his life. On the surface of the record album, Ethan began rolling joints with efficiency. It was his job, he'd said, and he clearly liked having something to do with his fingers when there was no pen or pencil held between them. He was an animator, and he spent hours drawing his short animated films and filling the pages of the little spiral notebooks that always bulged from his back pocket. Now he took tender care with the tiny shovelfuls of grain and twig and bud.

"Figman, increase the velocity; the natives are restless," said Jonah Bay. Julie knew almost nothing yet, but she did know that Jonah, a good-looking boy with blue-black hair that fell to his shoulders, and a leather string around his neck, was the son of the folksinger Susannah Bay. For a long time, his famous mother would be Jonah's primary identifying characteristic. He had taken to indiscriminately using the expression "the natives are restless," although this time it did make partial sense. Everyone here was restless, though none of them were native to this place.

That night in July, Nixon was still over a month away from being lifted off the White House lawn like a rotten piece of outdoor furniture. Across from Ethan, Jonah Bay sat with his steel-stringed guitar, wedged between Julie Jacobson and Cathy Kiplinger, a girl who moved and stretched all day in the dance studio. Cathy was big and blond and far more womanly than most girls could be comfortable with at age fifteen. Also she was "way too emotionally demanding," as someone bluntly later observed. She was the kind of girl who boys never left alone; they were relentless in their automatic pursuit of her. Sometimes the outline of her nipples would appear through the fabric of a leotard like buttons on a sofa cushion, and they would need to be ignored by everyone, the way nipples often needed to be ignored in their vicissitudes.

Up above them all, on a top bunk, sprawled Goodman Wolf, six feet tall, sun sensitive, big kneed, and hypermasculine in khaki shorts and buffalo sandals. If this group had a leader, he was it. Literally, now, they had to look up to him. Two other boys who actually lived in this teepee had been politely but emphatically asked to go get lost for the night. Goodman wanted to be an architect, Julie had heard, but he never spent time figuring out how buildings stayed up, how suspension bridges withstood the weight of cars. Physically he was not quite as spectacular as his sister, for his good looks were a little muddied by troubled, stubbled skin. But despite his imperfections and his general air of laziness, he was a huge and influential presence here. The previous summer, in the middle of *Waiting for Godot,* Goodman had climbed into the lighting booth and plunged the stage into darkness for a full three minutes just to see what would happen — who would scream, who would laugh, how much trouble he'd get into. Sitting in the dark, more than one girl secretly imagined Goodman lying on top of her. He would be so big, like a lumberjack trying to fuck a girl — or, no, more like a *tree* trying to fuck a girl.

Much later, people who'd been at camp with him agreed that it made sense that Goodman Wolf was the one whose life had such an alarming trajectory. Of course they were surprised, they said — though not, they made sure to qualify, all that surprised.

The Wolfs had been coming to Spirit-in-the-Woods since they were twelve and thirteen; they were central to this place. Goodman was big and blunt and unsettling; Ash was waifish, openhearted, a beauty with long, straight, pale brown hair and sad eyes. Some

20

afternoons in the middle of Improv, when the class was talking in a made-up language, or mooing and baaing, Ash Wolf would suddenly slip away from the theater. She would return to the empty girls' teepee and recline on her bed eating Junior Mints and writing in her journal.

I'm beginning to think I feel too much, Ash wrote. *The feelings flood into me like so much water, and I am helpless against the onslaught.*

Tonight the screen door had winced shut behind the departing, shooed-away boys, and then the three girls from the other side of the pines had arrived. There were six people altogether in this single-bulb-lit conical wooden structure. They would meet again whenever they could over the rest of the summer, and frequently in New York City over the next year and a half. There would be one more summer for all of them. After that, over the following thirty-odd years, only four of them would meet whenever they could, but of course it would be entirely different.

Julie Jacobson, at the start of that first night, had not yet transformed into the far better sounding Jules Jacobson, a change that would deftly happen a little while later. As Julie, she'd always felt *all wrong;* she was gangling, and her skin went pink and patchy at the least provocation: if she got embarrassed, if she ate hot soup, if she stepped into the sun for half a minute. Her deer-colored hair had been recently permed at the La Beauté salon in Underhill, giving her head a poodle bigness that mortified her. The stinking chemical perm had been her mother's idea. Over the year in which her father was dying, Julie had occupied herself by zealously splitting her split ends, and her hair had become frizzed and wild. Sometimes she discovered a single hair with an uncountable number of splits, and she would tug on the whole thing, listening to the crackle as the hair broke between her fingers like a branch, and experiencing a sensation that resembled a private sigh.

When she looked in the mirror one day, her hair appeared to her as bad as a pillaged nest. A haircut and a perm might help, her mother said. After the perm, when Julie saw herself in the salon mirror, she cried, "Oh crap," and ran out into the parking lot, her mother chasing her, saying it would die down, it wouldn't be so big tomorrow.

"Oh honey, it won't be so *dandeliony*!" Lois Jacobson called to her from across the blinding rows of cars.

Now, among these people who had been coming to this teenaged performing-arts and visual-arts summer camp in Belknap, Massachusetts, for two or three years, Julie, a dandeliony, poodly outsider, from an undistinguished town sixty miles east of New York City, was surprisingly compelling to them.

22

Just by being here in this teepee at the designated hour, they all seduced one another with greatness, or with the assumption of eventual greatness. Greatness-in-waiting.

Jonah Bay dragged a cassette tape deck across the floor, as heavy as a nuclear suitcase. "I've got some new tapes," he said. "Really good acoustic stuff. Just listen to this riff, it will amaze you." The others dutifully listened, because they trusted his taste, even if they didn't understand it. Jonah closed his eyes as the music played, and Julie watched him in his state of transfixion. The batteries were starting to die, and the music that emanated from the tape player seemed to come from a drowning musician. But Jonah, apparently a gifted guitarist, liked this, so Julie did too, and she nodded her head in an approximation of the beat of the music. More V&Ts were served by Cathy Kiplinger, who poured one for herself in a collapsible drinking cup, the kind you took on campouts and which never really got clean, and which, Jonah remarked, looked like a miniature model of the Guggenheim Museum. "That's not a compliment," Jonah added. "A cup isn't supposed to collapse and reconstruct. It's already a perfect object." Again, Julie found herself nodding in quiet agreement with everything that anyone here said.

During that first hour, books were discussed, mostly ones written by spiky and disaffected European writers. "Günter Grass is basically *God,*" said Goodman Wolf, and the two other boys agreed. Julie had never actually heard of Günter Grass, but she wasn't going to let on. If anyone asked, she would insist that *she too* loved Günter Grass, although, she would add as protection, "I haven't read as much of him as I would like."

"I think Anaïs Nin is God," Ash said.

"How can you say that?" said her brother. "She is so full of pretentious, girly shit. I have no idea why people read Anaïs Nin. She's the worst writer who ever lived."

"Anaïs Nin and Günter Grass both have *umlauts,*" remarked Ethan. "Maybe that's the key to their success. I'm going to get one for myself."

"What were you doing reading Anaïs Nin, Goodman?" asked Cathy.

"Ash made me," he said. "And I do everything my sister says."

"Maybe *Ash* is God," said Jonah with a beautiful smile.

A couple of them said that they had brought paperbacks with them to camp that they needed to read for school; their summer reading lists were all similar, featuring those sturdy, adolescent-friendly writers John Knowles and William Golding. "If you think about it," said Ethan, "*Lord of the Flies* is basically the opposite of Spirit-in-the-Woods.

One's a total nightmare, and the other's utopia."

"Yeah, they're diametrically opposed," said Jonah, for this was another phrase he liked to use. Although, Julie thought, if someone said "diametrically," could "opposed" be far behind?

Parents got discussed too, though mostly with tolerant disdain. "I just don't think that my mother and father's separation is any of my business," said Ethan Figman, taking a wet suck on his joint. "They are completely wrapped up in themselves, which means they basically pay no attention to me, and I couldn't be happier. Though it would be nice if my father kept some food in the refrigerator once in a while. Feeding your child — I hear it's the latest fad."

"Come to the Labyrinth," said Ash. "You'll be totally taken care of." Julie had no idea what the Labyrinth was — an exclusive private club in the city with a long, twisting entrance? She couldn't ask and risk showing her ignorance. Even though she didn't know how she had come to be included here, the inclusion of Ethan Figman was equally mysterious. He was so squat and homely, with eczema running along his forearms like a lit fuse. Ethan didn't take his shirt off, ever. He spent free-swim period each day under the boiling tin roof of the animation shed with his teacher, Old Mo Templeton, who had apparently once worked in Hollywood with Walt Disney himself. Old Mo, who looked eerily like Gepetto from Disney's *Pinocchio.*

As Julie felt the effects of Ethan Figman's wet-ended joint, she imagined all their saliva joining on a cellular level, and she was disgusted by the image, then she laughed to herself, thinking: we are all nothing more than a seething, collapsing ball of *cells.* Ethan, she saw, was looking at her intently.

"Hmm," he said.

"What?"

"Telltale private chuckling. Maybe you want to slow down a little over there."

"Yeah, maybe I should," Julie said.

"I'm keeping an eye on you."

"Thanks," she said. Ethan turned back to the others, but in her precarious, high state she felt that Ethan had made himself her *protector.* She kept thinking a high person's thoughts, focusing on the collage of human cells that filled this teepee, all of it making up the ugly, kind boy; and the ordinary nothing that was herself; and the beautiful, delicate girl sitting across from her; and the beautiful girl's uncommonly magnetic brother; and the soft-spoken, gentle son of a famous folksinger; and, finally, the sexually confident, slightly unwieldy dancer girl with a sheaf of blond hair. They were all just countless cells that had joined together to make this group in particular — this group that Julie Jacobson, who had no currency whatsoever, suddenly decided she loved. That she was *in love with,* and would stay in love with for the rest of her life.

Ethan said, "If my mother wants to abandon my father and screw my pediatrician, let's pray he's used soap and water after he's had his hand up some kid's ass."

"Wait, Figman, so we're supposed to assume that your pediatrician puts his hand up all his patients' asses, including yours?" Goodman said. "I hate to tell you this, man, but he's not supposed to do that. It's against the Hippocratic oath. You know, 'First, do no hand up the ass.' "

"No, he doesn't do that. I was just trying to be disgusting to get your attention," said Ethan. "It's my way."

"So, okay, we get it; you are *disgusted* by your parents' separation," said Cathy.

"Which is not something Ash and I can relate to," said Goodman, "because our parents are as happy as clams."

"Yup. Mom and Dad practically tongue kiss in front of us," said Ash, pretending to be appalled but sounding proud.

The Wolf parents, glimpsed briefly by Julie on the first day of camp, were vigorous and youthful. Gil was an investment banker at the new firm Drexel Burnham and Betsy his artistically interested, pretty wife who cooked ambitious meals.

"The way you act, Figman," Goodman continued, "is all 'I don't give a shit about my family,' but in fact a shit is *given*. In fact you suffer, I think."

"Not to move the conversation away from the tragedy of my broken home," said Ethan, "but there are far bigger tragedies we could discuss."

"Like what?" said Goodman. "Your weird name?"

"Or the My Lai massacre?" said Jonah.

"Oh, the folksinger's son brings up Vietnam whenever he can," said Ethan.

"Shut up," said Jonah, but he wasn't angry.

They were all quiet for a moment; it was perplexing to know what to do when atrocity suddenly came up against irony. Mostly, apparently, you were supposed to pause at that juncture. You paused and you waited it out, and then you went on to something else, even though it was awful. Ethan said, "I'd like to say for the record that Ethan Figman is not such a terrible name. Goodman Wolf is much worse. It's like a name for a Puritan. *'Goodman Humility Wolf, thy presence is requested at the silo.'* "

Julie, in her stoned state, had the idea that all this was *banter,* or the closest they could get to banter at their age. The level of actual wit here was low, but the apparatus of wit had been activated, readying itself for later on.

"There's a girl in our cousin's school in Pennsylvania," Ash said, "named Crema Seamans."

"You made that up," Cathy said.

"No, she didn't," Goodman said. "It's the truth." Ash and Goodman looked suddenly earnest and serious. If they were performing a synchronized, sibling mindfuck, they had worked out a convincing routine.

"Crema Seamans," Ethan repeated thoughtfully. "It's like a soup made from . . . various semens. A *medley* of semens. It's a flavor of Campbell's soup that got discontinued immediately."

"Stop it, Ethan, you're being totally graphic," said Cathy Kiplinger.

"Well, he *is* a graphic artist," said Goodman.

Everyone laughed, and then without warning Goodman jumped down from the upper bunk, shuddering the teepee. He planted himself on the bed at Cathy Kiplinger's feet, really *on* her feet, causing her to sit up in annoyance.

"What are you doing?" Cathy said. "You're crushing me. And you smell. God, what is that, Goodman, *cologne*?"

"Yes. It's Canoe."

"Well, I hate it." But she didn't push him off. He lingered, taking her hand.

29

"Now let's all observe a moment of silence for Crema Seamans," Julie heard herself say. She hadn't planned to say a word tonight; and as soon as she spoke, she feared she'd made a mistake inserting herself into this. *Into what?* she thought. Into *them.* But maybe she hadn't made a mistake. They were looking at her attentively, assessing her.

"The girl from Long Island speaks," said Goodman.

"Goodman, that comment makes you seem kind of horrible," said his sister.

"I am kind of horrible."

"Well, it makes you seem kind of *Nazi* horrible," said Ethan. "As if you're using some sort of code to remind everyone that Julie's Jewish."

"I'm Jewish too, Figman," said Goodman. "Just like you."

"No, you're not," said Ethan. "Because even though your father is Jewish, your mother isn't. You have to have a Jewish mother, or else they will basically throw you off a cliff."

"The Jews? They aren't a violent people. *They* didn't commit the My Lai massacre. I was just playing around," Goodman said. "Jacobson knows that, right? I was just goofing on her a little, right, Jacobson?"

Jacobson. She was excited to hear him call her that, though it was hardly what she'd imagined a boy might ever call her. Goodman looked at her and smiled, and she had to prevent herself from standing up and reaching out to touch the planes of his golden face; she'd never spent so much time this close to a boy who looked as magnificent as he did. Julie didn't even know what she was doing as she lifted her cup again, but he was still watching her, and so were the rest of them.

"O Crema Seamans, wherever thou art," she said loudly, "your life will be tragic. It will be cut short by an accident involving . . . animal desemenizing equipment." This was a suggestive, nonsensical remark that included a made-up word, but there were approval sounds from around the teepee.

"See, I knew there was a reason I invited her in," said Ash, turning to the others. " 'Desemenizing.' Go, Jules!"

Jules. There it was, right there: the effortless shift that made all the difference. Shy, suburban nonentity Julie Jacobson, who had provoked *howls* for the first time in her life, had suddenly, lightly changed into *Jules,* which was a far better name for an awkward-looking fifteen-year-old girl who'd become desperate for people to pay attention to her. These people had no idea of what she was usually called; they'd hardly noticed her in these first days of camp, though of course she'd noticed them. In a new environment, it was possible to transform. *Jules,* Ash had

31

called her, and instantly the others followed Ash's lead. She was Jules now, and would be Jules forever.

Jonah Bay pulled at the strings of his mother's old guitar. Susannah Bay had taught acoustic guitar at this camp in the late 1950s, before her son was born. Every summer since then, even after she became famous, she appeared at some point for an impromptu concert, and apparently this summer would be no exception. She would just show up one day, though no one knew when, not even her son. Now, Jonah began a few prefatory strums, followed by some fancy picking. He barely seemed to be paying attention to what he was doing; he was one of those people whose musical ability seems effortless, careless, ingrained.

"Wow," Jules said, or just mouthed — she wasn't sure if the word had come out — as she watched him play. She imagined that he would become famous in several years like his mother; Susannah Bay would draw Jonah into her world, call him up onto a stage; it was inevitable. Now, when it seemed as if he might break into one of his mother's songs, like "The Wind Will Carry Us," he instead played "Amazing Grace," in honor of that girl from Goodman and Ash Wolf's cousin's school in Pennsylvania, who either did or did not exist.

They had only a little over an hour together,

and then one of the counselors on coed patrol, a blunt-haired weaving instructor and lifeguard from Iceland named Gudrun Sigurdsdottir, came into the teepee with a bulky, indestructible flashlight that looked as if it were meant to be used during night ice fishing. She peered around and said, "All right, my young friends, I can tell that you have been smoking pot. That is not 'cool,' though you may think it is."

"You're wrong, Gudrun," said Goodman. "It's just the scent of my Canoe."

"Pardon?"

"My cologne."

"No, you are having a pot party in here, I think," she went on.

"Well," said Goodman, "it's true that there's been an herbal component. But now that you've made us see the error of our ways, it'll never happen again."

"That is all well and good. But also, you are consorting with mixed sexes," said Gudrun.

"We aren't consorting," said Cathy Kiplinger, who had rearranged herself on the bed right beside Goodman, neither of them appearing flustered to be seen so close together.

"Oh no? Then tell me what you are doing."

"We're having a meeting," said Goodman, lifting himself up on one elbow.

"I know when my leg is being pulled on," said Gudrun.

"No, no, it's true. We've formed this group, and it's going to be a lifelong thing," said Jonah.

"Well," said Gudrun, "I do not want to see you sent home. Please break this up now. And, all you girls, please go back through the pines at once."

So the three girls left, heading away from the teepee in a slow, easy herd with their flashlights leading them. Jules, walking down the path, heard someone say "Julie?" so she stopped and turned, training her light on the person, who was revealed to be Ethan Figman, who had followed her. "I mean, Jules?" he said. "I wasn't sure which name you preferred."

"Jules is fine."

"Okay. Well, Jules?" Ethan came closer and stood so near to her that she felt she could see right into him. The other girls kept walking ahead without her. "Are you a little less high now?" he asked.

"Yes, thanks."

"There ought to be a control. A knob on the side of your head that you could turn."

"That would be good," she said.

"Can I show you something?" he asked.

"Your head knob?"

"Ha-ha. No. Come with me. I'll be quick."

She let herself be led down the hill toward the animation shed. Ethan Figman opened the unlocked door; inside, the shed smelled

34

plasticky, slightly scorched, and he threw on the fluorescent lights, which stuttered the room into its full majesty. Drawings were tacked up everywhere, a testament to the work of this freakishly gifted fifteen-year-old boy, with some nominal attention given to the work of other animation students.

Ethan threaded a projector, then shut off the lights. "See," he said, "what I'm about to show you are the contents of my brain. Since I was a little kid, I've been lying in bed at night imagining an animated cartoon that plays in my head. Here's the premise: There's this shy, lonely little kid called Wally Figman. He lives with his parents, who are always fighting, who are basically horrible, and he hates his life. So every night, when he's finally alone in his room, he takes out a shoe box from under his bed, and inside it is this tiny little planet, this parallel world called Figland." He looked at her. "Should I go on?"

"Of course," she said.

"So one night Wally Figman actually finds that he's able to go *into* the shoe box; his body shrinks down and he enters that little world. And instead of being this nobody anymore, he's a grown man who *controls* all of Figland. There's a corrupt government in the Fig House — that's where the president lives — and Wally has to fix it. Oh, and did I say that the cartoon is funny? It's a comedy. Or it's supposed to be, anyway. You get the

35

idea, I think. Or maybe you don't." Jules started to reply, but Ethan kept talking nervously. "Anyway, that's what *Figland* is, and I don't even know why I want to show it to you, but I do, and here it is," he said. "It just occurred to me in the teepee tonight that there was a slight possibility that you and I had something in common. You know, a sensibility. And that maybe you might like this. But I'm warning you that you might also really, really hate it. Anyway, be honest. Sort of," he added with an anxious laugh.

A cartoon sprang up on a sheeted wall. "FIGLAND," read the credits, and antic characters began to prance and splat and jabber, speaking in voices that all sounded a little bit like Ethan. The characters on the planet Figland were alternately wormy, phallic, leering, and adorable, while in the excess light from the projector Ethan himself was touchingly ugly, with a raw sheath of arm skin etched with its own ugly dermatological cartoon. On Figland, characters rode trolleys, played the accordion on street corners, and a few of them broke into the Figmangate Hotel. The dialogue was sharp and silly at the same time. Ethan had even created a Figland version of Spirit-in-the-Woods — Figment-in-the-Woods — with younger versions of these same cartoon characters at summer camp. Jules watched as they built a bonfire, then paired off to make out and even, in one case, have sex. She was mortified by the humpy, jerking movements and the sweat that flew in the air, meant to signify *exertion,* but her mortification was immediately painted over by awe. No wonder Ethan was beloved here at camp. He was a genius, she saw now. His cartoon was mesmerizing — very clever, and very funny. It came to an end and the film flip-flapped on its reel.

"God, Ethan," Jules said to him. "It's amazing. It's totally original."

He turned to her, his expression bright and uncomplicated. This was an important moment for him, but she didn't even understand why. Incredibly, her opinion seemed to matter to him. "You really think it's good?" Ethan asked. "I mean, not just *technically* good, because a lot of people have that; you should see what Old Mo Templeton can do. He was sort of an honorary member of Disney's Nine Old Men. He was basically the Tenth Old Man."

"This is probably really stupid of me," said Jules, "but I don't know what that means."

"Oh, no one around here knows. There were nine animators who worked with Walt Disney on the classics — movies like *Snow White.* Mo came in late, but he was apparently in the room a lot too. Every summer since I've been coming here, he's taught me everything, and I mean everything."

"It shows," said Jules. "I love it."

"I did all the voices too," Ethan said.

"I can tell. It could be in a movie theater or on TV. The whole thing is wonderful."

"I'm so glad," Ethan said. He just stood before her smiling, and she smiled too. "What do you know," he said in a softer, husky voice. "You love it. *Jules Jacobson loves it.*" Just as she was enjoying hearing the strange name said aloud, and realizing that already it had become a far more comfortable name for her than dumb old *Julie Jacobson,* Ethan did the most astonishing thing: he thrust his big head toward hers, bringing his bulky body forward too, pressing himself upon her as if to line up all their parts. His mouth attached itself to hers; she'd already been aware that he smelled of pot, but up against her he smelled worse — mushroomy, feverish, overripe.

She yanked her head back, and said, "Wait, *what*?" He had probably reasoned that they were at the same level — he was popular here but still a little bit gross; she was unknown and frizzy-headed and plain, but had captured everyone's attention and approval. They could join together, they could *unite.* People would accept them as a couple; it made both logical and aesthetic sense. Though she'd gotten her head free, his body was still pressed against her, and that was when she felt the lump of him — "a lump of *coal,*" she could say to the other girls in her teepee, eliciting laughs. "It's like, what's that poem in school

38

— 'My Last Duchess'?" she would tell them, because at least this would demonstrate some knowledge of something. "This was 'My First Penis.' " Jules backed up several inches from Ethan so that no part of her was in contact with any part of him. "I'm really sorry," she said. Her face was hot; certainly it must have been turning red in various places.

"Oh, forget it," Ethan said in a hoarse voice, and then she saw his expression simply change, as if he'd made a decision to switch over into the self-protective mode of irony. "You have nothing to feel sorry about. I think I'll find a way to live. A way not to *commit suicide* because you didn't want to make out with me, Jules." She didn't say anything, but just looked downward at her feet in their yellow clogs on the dusty shed floor. For a second she thought he was going to turn away furiously and leave her here, and she would have to head back through the trees alone. Jules saw herself stumbling over exposed tree roots, and eventually Gudrun Sigurdsdottir's sturdy flashlight would be used to find her in the woods, where she would be sitting against a tree, shaking. But then Ethan said, "I don't want to be a dick about this. I mean, people have been rejected by other people since the dawn of time."

"I've never rejected anyone before in my life," Jules said fiercely. "Although," she added, "I've never accepted anyone before

39

either. What I mean is, it's never come up."

"Oh," he said. He stayed by her side as they trudged back up the hill together. When they reached the top, Ethan turned to her, and she expected to be met with something sarcastic, but instead he said, "Maybe the reason you don't want to do this with me isn't even because of *me.*"

"What do you mean?"

"You say you haven't rejected or accepted anyone before," he said. "You are one hundred percent inexperienced. So maybe you're just nervous. Your nervousness could be masking your real feelings."

"You think so?" she asked, doubtful.

"Could be. It happens to girls sometimes," he added, overstating his worldliness. "So I have a proposition for you." Jules waited. *"Reconsider,"* Ethan said. "Spend more time with me and let's see what happens."

It was such a reasonable request. She could spend more time with Ethan Figman, experimenting with the idea of being part of a couple. Ethan was special, and she did like being singled out by him. He was a genius, and that counted for a great deal with her, she understood. "All right," she finally told him.

"Thank you," said Ethan. "To be continued," he added cheerfully.

Only when he'd dropped her off at her own teepee did he leave her. Jules went inside and stood getting ready for bed, pulling off her T-shirt and unhooking her bra. Across the teepee Ash Wolf was already in bed, encased in her sleeping bag that was red flannel lined, with a repeating pattern of cowboys swinging lariats. Jules intuited that at one point it had probably belonged to her brother.

"So where were you?" Ash asked.

"Oh, Ethan Figman wanted to show me one of his films. And then we started talking, and it just got — it's hard to explain."

Ash said, "That sounds mysterious."

"No, it was nothing," said Jules. "I mean, it was something, but it was strange."

"I know what they're like," Ash said.

"What what are like?"

"Those moments of strangeness. Life is full of them," Ash said.

"What do you mean?"

"Well," said Ash, and she got out of her own bed and came to sit beside Jules. "I've always sort of felt that you prepare yourself over the course of your whole life for the big moments, you know? But when they happen, you sometimes feel totally unready for them, or even that they're not what you thought. And that's what makes them *strange.* The reality is really different from the fantasy."

"That's true," Jules said. "That's just what happened to me." She looked with surprise at the pretty girl sitting on her bed; it seemed that this girl understood her, even though

41

Jules had told her nothing. The whole evening was taking on various exquisite meanings.

A first kiss, Jules had thought, was supposed to magnetize you to the other person; the magnet and the metal were meant to fuse and melt on contact into a sizzling brew of silver and red. But this kiss had done nothing like that. Jules would have liked to tell Ash all about it now. She recognized that that is how friendships begin: one person reveals a moment of strangeness, and the other person decides just to listen and not exploit it. Their friendship did begin that night; they talked in this oblique way about themselves, and then Ash began struggling to scratch a mosquito bite on her shoulder blade, but she could hardly reach it, and she asked Jules if she could put some calamine lotion on it for her. Ash yanked down the collar of her nightgown in back, and Jules dotted on some of the bright pink fluid, which had the most recognizable odor imaginable, appetizing and overbearing at the same time.

"Why do you think calamine lotion smells like that?" Jules asked. "Is it the *real* smell, or did some chemists just come up with this random smell for it in the laboratory, and now everyone thinks it's what it actually has to smell like?"

"Huh," said Ash. "No idea."

"Maybe it's like pineapple Lifesavers," Jules said.

"What are you talking about?"

"Well, they don't taste like actual pineapple at all. But we've gotten so used to it that we've come to think that that's the *real* taste, you know? And actual pineapple has basically fallen by the wayside. Except maybe in Hawaii." She paused and said, "I would give anything to try poi. Ever since I learned the word in fourth grade. You eat it with your hands."

Ash just looked at her, and began to smile. "Those are kind of weird observations, Jules," she said. "But in a good way. You're funny," she added in a thoughtful voice, yawning. "Everyone thought so tonight." But it seemed as if *funny* was a distinct relief to Ash Wolf. Funny was the thing, other than calamine lotion, that she needed from Jules. Ash's family and her world were high-test, and here was this funny girl who was amusing and soothing and *touching,* really, in her awkwardness and her willingness. Nearby, the other girls in the teepee were having their own involved conversation, but Jules barely heard anything they said. They were just background noise, and the central drama was here between herself and Ash Wolf. "You definitely make me crack up," said Ash, "but promise you won't make me *crack up.*" Jules didn't know what she meant, and then she did: Ash had awkwardly tried to make a joke, a pun. "You know — don't ever make me go insane," Ash

43

explained, and Jules politely smiled and promised she wouldn't.

Distantly Jules thought of the girls she'd been friends with at home — their mildness, their loyalty. She saw all of them marching to their lockers at school, their corduroy jeans swishing, their hair fastened with barrettes or rubber bands or let loose in wild perms. All of them together, unnoticed, invisible. It was as though she was saying good-bye to those other girls now, here in the teepee with Ash Wolf sitting on her bed.

But the newly forming friendship was paused briefly by the presence of Cathy Kiplinger, who moved into the center of the teepee, taking off her own big, complicated bra and unharnessing her duo of woman-sized breasts, distracting Jules with the thought that these spheres inside this conical building were the equivalent of a square peg in a round hole. Jules wished Cathy weren't here at all, and that Jane Zell wasn't here either, or somber-faced Nancy Mangiari, who sometimes played the cello as if she were performing at the funeral of a child.

If it were just Jules and Ash, she would have told her everything. But the other girls were circling, and now Cathy Kiplinger, dressed only in a long pink T-shirt, was passing around a huckleberry crumble purchased at the bakery in town that afternoon, and a warped fork from the dining hall. Someone

— could it have been silent Nancy? Or maybe Cathy? — said, "God, it tastes like sex!" and everyone laughed, including Jules, who wondered if sex, when it was really good, actually offered the pleasures of a huckleberry crumble — all goo and give.

The subject of Ethan Figman was now lost for the night. The crumble went around a few times, and everyone's lips became tribally blue, and then the girls lay down in their separate beds and Jane Zell told them about her twin sister who had a shocking neurological disorder that sometimes caused her to slap herself in the face over and over.

"Oh my God," said Jules. "How awful."

"She'll be sitting there, just totally calm," said Jane, "and she suddenly starts to smack herself. Wherever we go, she makes a scene. People freak out when they see it. It's horrible, but I'm used to it by now."

"You get used to whatever you get," Cathy said, and they all agreed. "Like, I'm a dancer," Cathy continued, "but I have these enormous boobs. It's like carrying around sacks of mail. But what am I supposed to do? I still want to be a dancer."

"And you should try to do what you want," Jules said. "We should all try to do whatever we want in life," she added with sudden and unexpected conviction. "I mean, what is the point otherwise?"

"Nancy, why don't you take out your cello

and play us something," Ash said. "Something with atmosphere. Mood music."

Even though it was late, Nancy got her cello from the storage area and sat on the edge of her bed, her bare legs opened wide, intently playing the first movement of a cello suite by Benjamin Britten. As Nancy played, Cathy stood on someone's camp trunk, her head perilously near the slant of the ceiling, and she began to perform a slow, free-form routine like a go-go dancer in a cage. "This is what guys like," Cathy said confidently. "They want to see you move. They want your boobs to swing a little, as if you could hit them in the head with them and knock them unconscious. They want you to behave like you have *power,* but also like you know they'd win the battle if it ever came down to it. They are so predictable; all you have to do is move your hips in a kind of swivel, and get a kind of jiggle rhythm going, and they're completely under the influence. It's like they're cartoon characters with eyeballs popping out of their heads on springs. Like something Ethan would draw." Beneath the pink T-shirt her body moved in snake segments, and once in a while the shirt would ride up so that the vaguest hint of pubic darkness was revealed.

"We are the modern music and porn teepee!" Nancy cried with glee. "A full-service teepee, to meet every male's artistic and perverted needs!"

46

All the girls felt fired up, overstimulated. The stark music and the laughter, drifting from the teepee and scribbling among the trees, headed toward the boys, a message in the darkness before lockdown. Jules thought of how she was nothing like Ethan Figman. But she was nothing like Ash Wolf either. She existed somewhere on the axis *between* Ethan and Ash, slightly disgusting, slightly desirable — not yet claimed by one side or the other. It was right not to have agreed to go over to Ethan's side just because he had wanted her to. As he'd said, she had nothing to feel sorry about.

Over the following few weeks of the eight-week season, Jules and Ethan spent a great deal of time alone together. When she wasn't with Ash, she was with him. Once, sitting with him by the swimming pool at dusk, with a couple of bats soaring around the chimney of the Wunderlichs' big gray house across the road, she told him about her father's death. "Wow, he was only forty-two?" Ethan said, shaking his head. "Jesus, Jules, that's so young. And it's just so sad that you'll never see him again. He was your *dad.* He probably used to sing you all these little songs, am I right?"

"No," said Jules. She let her fingers drape through the cold water. But then suddenly she remembered that her father had sung her one song, once. "Yes," she said, surprised. "One. It was a folk song."

"Which one?"

She began to sing in an unsteady voice:

"Just a little rain falling all around,
The grass lifts its head to the heavenly
    sound,
Just a little rain, just a little rain,
What have they done to the rain?"

She stopped abruptly. "Go on," Ethan said, and so, embarrassed, Jules continued:

"Just a little boy standing in the rain,
The gentle rain that falls for years.
And the grass is gone,
The boy disappears,
And rain keeps falling like helpless tears,
And what have they done to the rain?"

When she was finished, Ethan just kept looking at her. "That killed me," he said. "Your voice, the lyrics, the whole thing. You know what that song's about, right?"

"Acid rain, I think?" she said.

He shook his head. "Nuclear testing."

"Do you know *everything*?"

He shrugged, pleased. "See," he told her, "I heard that back when it was written, when Kennedy was president, the government had been doing all this aboveground nuclear testing, which put strontium ninety into the air. And the rain washed it down into the ground, and it got into the grass, where all the cows ate it and then gave milk, which children drank. Little radioactive children. So this was a protest song. Your dad was political? A lefty?" he said. "That's very cool. My dad is a bitter slug ever since my mom left. You know the fighting that Wally Figman's parents do in my cartoons? The shrieking and wailing? I think you can guess where I get my ideas."

"My father wasn't political," said Jules. "And he definitely wasn't a lefty, at least not in a big way. I mean, he was a Democrat, but he certainly wasn't radical," she said, with a laugh at the absurdity of this idea. But she clipped off her own laugh as she thought of how she hadn't known her father all that well. He had been Warren Jacobson, a quiet man, a ten-year employee of Clelland Aerospace. He'd once told his daughters, without their having asked, "My job does not define me." But Jules hadn't asked him what did define him. She had almost never asked him anything about himself. He was thin, fair-haired, burdened, and now he was dead at forty-two. So she began to get stirred up thinking of how she would never know him very well. And then she and Ethan were crying together, which led to inevitable kissing, which wasn't nearly as bad this time, because they both tasted identically of mucus, and it didn't matter to Jules that she didn't feel excited. Instead, she felt mostly desperate thinking about her father being dead. Ethan intuited that this was the exact kind of foreplay Jules Jacobson required.

They went along like this, and she came to expect that they would sometimes go off together and have such moments. In this and other ways, Jules's life was changing rapidly here, advancing like a flip-book. She'd been *no one,* and now she was right in the middle of this group of friends, admired for her previously unknown sly humor. Jules was a source of interest to all of them, and she was Ash's great friend and Ethan's object of worship. Also, since she'd been here, she'd instantly become an *actress,* trying out for plays and getting parts. She hadn't even wanted to audition at first. "I'm not nearly as good as you," she'd said to Ash, but Ash had advised, "You know the way you are when you're with all of us? How great it is? Just be that way onstage. Come out of yourself. You have nothing to lose, Jules. I mean, if not now, when?"

The theater department would be putting on Edward Albee's *The Sandbox,* and Jules was given the part of Grandma. She played the role as an ancient but lively crone, talking in a voice that she didn't know she had. Ethan had given her voice lessons, telling her how he came up with voices for *Figland.*

"What you want to do," he'd said, "is speak it exactly the way you hear it in your head." She played a woman older than anyone she'd ever known; at the performance, two actors carried her onstage and set her down gently. Even before Jules started speaking, but just made vague cud-chewing facial movements, the audience began to laugh, and the laughter fed upon itself in the way it sometimes did, so that by the time she spoke her first line, a couple of people in the audience were snorting in laughter, and one excitable counselor almost seemed to be shrieking. Jules *killed,* everyone said when it was over. She absolutely killed.

The laughter seduced her that time and every time afterward. It made her stronger, more serious, poker-faced, determined. Later, Jules would think that the rolling, appreciative laughter of the audience at Spirit-in-the-Woods had cured her of the sad year she'd just gotten through. But it wasn't the only element that had cured her; the whole place had done that, as though it was one of those nineteenth-century European mineral spas.

One night, the entire camp was instructed to gather on the lawn; no other information was given. "I bet the Wunderlichs are going to announce that there's been an outbreak of syphilis," someone said.

"Or maybe it's a tribute to Mama Cass," someone else said. The singer Cass Elliot of

51

the Mamas and the Papas had died a few days earlier, supposedly having choked to death on a ham sandwich. The ham sandwich would turn out to be a rumor, but the death was real.

"When is it going to start? The natives are restless," said Jonah as they all waited.

Ethan and Jules sat together on a blanket on the hill and waited. He leaned his head against her shoulder, wanting to see what she would do; at first, she did nothing. Then he moved his head down into her lap, settling himself in and looking up at the darkening sky and the jumpy Japanese lanterns strung on wires between trees. As if cued to do so, Jules began to stroke his head of curls, and each time she did, his eyes closed in happiness.

Manny Wunderlich appeared before everyone and said, "Hello, hello! I know you're all wondering what's going on, and so without further ado I'd like to introduce our very special surprise guest."

"Look," said Ash from down the row, and Jules craned between the people in front of her to see a woman in a sunset-colored poncho carrying a guitar by its neck, picking her way across the grass to take her place on a platform. It was Jonah's famous folksinger mother, Susannah Bay! In person she was beautiful in the way of very few mothers, her hair long and black and straight — the opposite of Jules's mother with her acorn-cap hairdo and Dacron pantsuits. The crowd cheered her.

"Good evening, Spirit-in-the-Woods," said the folksinger into a microphone when everyone was quiet. "Are you having a great summer?" A series of affirmative calls rose up. "Believe me, I know this is the best place on earth. I spent a couple of summers here too. Nothing is as close to heaven as this little patch of land." Then she strummed hard on her guitar and began to sing. In person her voice was as strong as it sounded on her albums. She sang several songs that everyone knew, and some folk standards to which the audience was invited to sing along. Before her last song, she said, "I've brought an old friend with me tonight who happened to be in the neighborhood, and I'd like to invite him to join me now. Barry, would you come on up? Barry Claimes, everybody!"

To applause, the terrier-bearded folksinger Barry Claimes, formerly of the sixties trio the Whistlers, and, as it happened, briefly Susannah Bay's boyfriend back in the summer of '66, came up beside her with a banjo strapped around him. "Hello, my lads and ladies!" he called out to the crowd. Though the Whistlers had all worn peaked caps and turtlenecks in concert and on their album covers, Barry had abandoned both when he struck out on his own in 1971. These days, he tucked his wavy brown hair behind his ears and wore soft, checkered shirts that made him look like a mild mountaineer. He waved modestly to the campers and then began to play his banjo while Susannah played her guitar. The two instruments came together and then backed off shyly, then came together again, finally forming the preamble to Susannah's signature song. Quietly at first, then more forcefully, she began to sing:

"I've been walkin' through the valley, and
    I've been walkin' through the weeds
And I've been tryin' to understand just why
    I could not meet your needs.
Did you want me to be like she was?
Is that all that was in your heart?
A prayer that the wind would carry us . . .
Carry us . . . apart . . ."

After the performance, which was full of feeling and warmly received, everyone stood around and ladled up pink punch from a big metal bowl. Tiny fruit flies twittered on the surface of the punch, but mostly no one could see the rest of the bugs in the descending dark. The number of them ingested that summer was formidable: bugs in punch bowls, in salads, even scarfed down on the inhale in openmouthed sleep at night. Susannah Bay and Barry Claimes mingled with the campers. The two old friends and ex-lovers,

54

moving among the crowd of teenagers, looked happy, flushed, natural — elder-statesman countercultural figures who were treated with appreciation.

"Where's Jonah?" someone asked. A girl said she'd heard he'd slipped out during his mother's concert and gone to his teepee, complaining of nausea; several people said it was a shame he didn't feel well on this night of all nights. Looking at Susannah, it was easy to see the origins of Jonah's beauty, though it was more tentative and unassuming in its boy form.

Jules felt excited and stiff standing not too far from Jonah's mother. "I've never been near someone *famous,*" she whispered to Ethan, knowing that she sounded like a hick but not minding. She was relaxed around Ethan by now, and she was also relaxed around Ash. It still shocked Jules that the lovely, delicate, sophisticated girl in her teepee chose to spend so much time with her, but their friendship was indisputably easy, open, and real. At night Ash sat at the foot of Jules's bed before they went to sleep; Jules cracked her up often but listened well to her too; Ash was observant and offered guidance about a range of subjects, though never bossily. They sometimes whispered for so long after lights-out that the other girls had to shush them.

Now, after the concert, Ethan sipped his

punch like it was brandy from a snifter, and when he was done he tossed his paper cup into a bin, and dropped his arm upon Jules's shoulder. "The way Susannah sings 'The Wind Will Carry Us' is so sad," he murmured.

"Yeah, it really is."

"It makes me think of the way people devote their lives to each other, and then one of them just leaves, or even dies."

"I hadn't thought of it that way," said Jules, who had never understood those lyrics, in particular how a single wind could carry two people apart. "I know this sounds picky, but wouldn't the wind carry them *together*?" she asked. "It's *one* breeze. It just blows one way, not two."

"Huh. Let me think about it." He thought briefly. "You're right. It doesn't make sense. But still, it's very melancholy."

He was somber, watching her, seeing if the melancholy mood could make her respond to him again. When he kissed her moments later as they stood slightly away from everyone else, she didn't stop him. He was ready, like a doctor who's given his patient a little bit of an allergen in the hopes of triggering a reaction. He wrapped his arms around her, and Jules willed herself to want him as her boyfriend, for he was brilliant and funny and would always be kind to her and would always be ardent. But all she could feel was

56

that he was her *friend,* her wonderful and gifted friend. She had tried so hard to respond to him, but she knew now that it probably wouldn't ever happen. "I can't keep trying," she said all in a flood, unplanned. "It's too hard. It's not what I want to do."

"You don't know what you want," said Ethan. "You're confused, Jules. You've had a major loss this year. You're still feeling it in stages — Elisabeth Kübler-Ross and all that. Hey," he added, "she's got an umlaut too."

"This isn't about my father, okay, Ethan?" Jules said, a little too loud, and a few people looked over at them in curiosity.

"Okay," Ethan said. "I hear what you're saying."

Galloping into the lantern light at that moment came Goodman Wolf, along with a pouting ceramicist from Girls' Teepee 4 who always had clay under her fingernails. They stopped on the edge of the circle and the girl tipped her head up toward his, and Goodman leaned down and then they kissed, their faces both dramatically lit. Jules watched as Goodman's mouth pulled away with what she could swear, even from a distance, was a smear of the girl's colorless lip gloss on his lips, like butter, like a prize. Jules imagined exchanging Ethan's face and body parts with those of Goodman. She even imagined debasing herself with Goodman in some crude, Figland-type way. She pictured cartoon drops of sweat flying out from their joined and suddenly naked selves. Thinking about this, she was suffused with a blast of sensation like the light from Ethan's projector. Feelings could come over you in a sudden wild sweep; this was something she was learning at Spirit-in-the-Woods. She could never be Ethan Figman's girlfriend, and she was right to have told him she would no longer try. It would have been exciting to be Goodman Wolf's girlfriend, of course, but that wasn't going to happen either, ever. There would be no pairing off this summer, no passionate subsets formed, and though in some ways this was sad, in other ways it was such a relief, for now they could return to the boys' teepee, the six of them, and take their places in that perfect, unbroken, lifelong circle. The whole teepee would quake, as though their kind of irony, and their kind of conversation and friendship, was so strong it could actually make a small wooden building chug and sway in preparation for liftoff.

TWO

Talent, that slippery thing, had been the frequent subject of dinner conversation between Edie and Manny Wunderlich for over half a century. They never tired of it, and if someone studied word frequency in the dialogue of this now elderly couple, they might note that *talent* kept appearing; though really, Manny Wunderlich thought as he sat in the underheated dining room of the big gray house off-season, occasionally when they said it, they meant "success."

"She became a great talent," his wife was saying as she served him a spoonful of potato, banging the spoon against his plate to release it, though it apparently did not want to be released. When they first met in Greenwich Village at a party in 1946, she was a modern dancer, and she leapt around her bedroom on Perry Street wearing just a bedsheet, with ivy twined in her hair. In bed, the callused bottoms of her feet were sharp against his legs. Edie was a gorgeous, avant-garde girl back in the day when that could be a full-time occupation, but in marriage she slowly became less wild. To Manny's great disappointment, though, her domestic skills didn't rise to the fore as her sexual and artistic ones receded. Edie proved to be a dreadful cook, and throughout their life together the food she prepared was often like poison. When they opened Spirit-in-the-Woods in 1952, they both knew that finding an excellent cook would be essential to the enterprise. If the food wasn't good, then no one would want to come. Edie's shy second cousin Ida Steinberg, a survivor of "that other kind of camp," as someone had tastelessly said, was hired; and in the summertime the Wunderlichs ate like royalty, but in the off-season, when Ida only worked occasionally, for special events, they generally ate like two people in a gulag. Glutinous stews, potatoes in various iterations. The food was bad but the conversation was vigorous as they sat and talked about many of the campers who had come through these stone gates and slept in these teepees.

Lately, as the year 2009 came to a close, they could no longer remember all of them, or even most of them, but the coin-bright ones shone through the murk of the Wunderlichs' memory.

Manny had unconsciously begun grouping the campers over the decades into categories. All he needed was a name, and then the thought process and classification could begin. "*Who* became a great talent?" he asked.

"Mona Vandersteen. You remember her. She came for three summers."

Mona Vandersteen? *Dance,* he suddenly thought. "Dance?" he said tentatively.

His wife looked at him, frowning. Her hair was as white as his hair and his out-of-control eyebrows, and he could not believe that this thick, tough old pigeon was the same girl who'd loved him the way she had done back on Perry Street just after the Second World War. The girl who'd sat on a bed with a white iron headboard and parted her labia in front of him; he had never before *seen* such a sight, and his knees had almost given out. She had sat there, opening herself like little curtains and smiling at him as though this was the most natural behavior in the world. He'd just stared at her, and she'd said, "Well? Come on!" without any indication of shyness.

Like a giant Manny had crossed the room in one big step, throwing himself upon her, his hands trying to part her further, to split her and yet own her at the same time — conflicting goals that somehow got worked out over the next hour in that bed. She grasped the rails of the headboard; she opened and closed her legs upon him. He thought she might kill him accidentally or on purpose. She was wild that day and for a long time afterward, but then eventually the wildness faded.

The only part that now remained of that slight, flexible girl was the cheese-grater texture of the heels of her feet. Her body had been stocky since the early 1960s, and it wasn't childbirth that had done this; the Wunderlichs had been unable to conceive, and though there was pain in this fact, it had been blunted over time by all the teenagers who came through Spirit-in-the-Woods. Edie, back in late middle age, seemed to have been physically rebuilt in the image of a pyramid; no, she was built, Manny realized one day, like one of the teepees they could see out their window across the road — one of the teepees that had lasted all this time and never needed repair, never needed *anything,* because they were so primitive and basic and self-contained.

"Mona Vandersteen was not a dancer," Edie said now. "Think again."

Manny closed his eyes and thought. Various girls from camp obediently appeared before him like the Muses: dancers, actresses, musicians, weavers, glassblowers, printmakers. He pictured one particular girl with her arms thrust into a bucket of purple dye. Now he felt an old twitch and stir in his hiked-up trousers, though this was only phantom-limb arousal, since he was on hormones for prostate cancer and had budding breasts like a

62

girl and hot flashes of the kind that his fairly stupid mother used to complain about as she fanned herself with a copy of *Silver Screen* magazine in their Brooklyn apartment. Manny was a physical disaster now, chemically *castrated* — his young doctor had actually, cheerfully used that word — and almost nothing got him going anymore. He thought of the name Mona Vandersteen, and a new image rushed to meet him.

"Yes, she had wavy blond hair," he said to his wife with false certainty. "Back in the 1950s, she was one of the earliest group of campers. Played flute and went on to join . . . the Boston Symphony Orchestra."

"It was the sixties," Edie said, seeming a little annoyed. "And oboe."

"What?"

"She played the oboe, not the flute. I remember this, because she had reed breath."

"What is reed breath?"

"Didn't you ever notice that the woodwind players who use reeds always have a certain kind of bad breath? You never noticed this, Manny? Really?"

"No, Edie, I did not. I never noticed her breath, or anyone else's," he said piously. "I just remember that she was so talented." Also he remembered that she'd had narrow hips and a big, pleasing ass, but this he did not add.

"Yes," Edie said, "she was very talented."

Together they ate their potatoes under a shimmer of brown sauce and individually thought of Mona Vandersteen, who had been so talented and who had gone on to greatness for a while. Though if she'd been in the Boston Symphony Orchestra all the way back in the 1960s, then who knew what she did now, or if what she did was lie in her grave.

The Wunderlichs were older than everyone; they hovered like God and God's wife, white-headed, still living in the house across the road from the camp. The collapsing economy was terrible for all summer camps — who had seven thousand dollars to spend now so their kids could throw pots? A couple of years earlier they had hired a young, energetic man to do planning and run the day-to-day operations, but the sessions remained pitifully undersubscribed. They didn't know what they were going to do now, but they knew the situation wasn't good and that eventually it would reach a crisis.

Whatever happened, they would not sell the camp. They loved it too much for that; it was a little utopia, and the kids who came to it were self-selecting, always the same type — utopians themselves, in a way. The camp needed to remain intact, serving its valuable purpose of bringing art into the world, generation after generation.

Each Christmas, former campers crammed the Wunderlichs' mailbox with letters from their lives, and Edie or Manny walked slowly to the end of the driveway, opened the stiff door of the silver box, then brought the mail back inside the house, where Edie read the letters aloud to her husband. Sometimes she skipped lines or whole paragraphs when they grew too boring. Neither of them was particularly interested in the family lives of these former campers: where their children had been accepted to college; who had had a coronary bypass — *oh boo hoo,* everyone's life was hard, and if you'd survived the hardship, why write about it? Survival itself was enough. Sometimes Manny thought that the campers should have sent the Wunderlichs a pared-down, expurgated version of a Christmas letter, and all it would contain would be evidence of the great talent of that person. Slides, audio samples, manuscripts. Examples of what he or she had gone on to accomplish in the years and decades after leaving Spirit-in-the-Woods.

But here was where the question of talent became slippery, for who could say whether Spirit-in-the-Woods had ever pulled incipient talent out of a kid and activated it, or whether the talent had been there all along and would have come out even without this place. Most of the time Manny Wunderlich took the former view, though lately, as his head and eyebrows gathered even more white hairs, giving him a snowy and deceptively mellow appearance, he thought that he and his wife had merely been like railroad conductors on a talent train, collecting the tickets of many brilliantly able kids as they passed through Belknap, Massachusetts, on their way to somewhere even better. He thought dispiritedly that the main thing Spirit-in-the-Woods had created in anyone was nostalgia. At the bottom of a card, a camper would write lines like:

Dear Manny and Edie,
I wanted you to know that I think about my summers at camp every day of my life. Though I have performed in Paris, Berlin, you name it, and though the Barranti Fellowship last year gave me the freedom to really concentrate on my libretto and not have to teach at the conservatory anymore, nothing has been as wonderful as Spirit-in-the-Woods. Nothing! I send you my love.

Whenever Manny Wunderlich became despondent, he sank into himself and felt his heart working hard, and he looked across the road and out over the winter lawn, where the tips of the teepees poked up. He felt himself falling, and only his wife's voice could pull him back, as though she were yanking him by his suspenders, or as though an earlier, sexually devilish version of her were bringing him back into vitality. "Manny," she said from across time. "Manny."

He looked up from behind the glaze of his failing eyes, into her eyes that were hard and blue. "What?" he said.

"I saw you disappear," she said. "Let's talk about someone else. We received a very interesting card today. With one of those Christmas letters inside."

"All right," he said, waiting. Which former camper would he have to try and remember now? Would it be a flutist, a dancer, a singer, a designer of surreal theater sets? All of them had passed through here at some point or another.

"You'll like this one," said his wife. Then she smiled, her mouth appearing soft in a way it rarely did anymore. "It's from Ethan and Ash."

"Oh!" he said, and he was silent, appropriately reverent.

"I will read it to you," she said.

THREE

The envelope, made of a vellum so thick and smooth that it seemed to have been massaged with lanolin and special oils, remained unopened on the little mail and keys table in the front hallway of the Jacobson-Boyds' apartment for a day or two before they decided to open it. For many years this had been a way of tolerating the inadequacy of their own lives in relation to whatever was described in the annual letter. Whenever they opened one of these envelopes, Jules felt as if a wall of flames might roar up and fry the air above it. With enough time and age her envy of her friends' lives had diminished and become manageable; but still, even now, when the Christmas letter arrived Jules allowed herself to experience a new, small surge of a very old feeling. It wasn't as if Ash and Ethan's Christmas letter had ever been bloated with self-regard, even back when their lives had first become so extreme. Instead, the writers of the letter always deliberately seemed to hold back, as if not wanting to assail their friends with the minutiae of their good fortune.

Ash and Ethan's letter went into the mail each year in the protective sheath of a thick, square, fat envelope that included on the back only a return address, though not one they ever lived at for more than a few weeks in a given year: "Bending Spring Ranch, Cole Valley, Colorado."

"What kind of a ranch is it anyway?" Dennis had asked Jules originally when the property had been purchased. "Cattle? Dude? I wasn't really sure."

"No, it's a *tax* ranch," she'd said. "See, they raise little tax brackets there. It's the only one of its kind in the world."

"You're bad news," he'd said, mostly joking, but they both knew, back then, that her envy had no power of its own; it was a sickly and spreading thing that enclosed her, and all she could do was make lightly sarcastic jokes in order to expel a little hostility and remain friends with Ash and Ethan. Without the jokes, the sarcasm, the muttered comments, she wouldn't have been able to cope too well with how much Ash and Ethan had in comparison with her and Dennis. So she talked on and on about life on the tax ranch, telling Dennis about the ranch hands who'd been hired to lasso the little tax brackets that tried to get away; she also described how the ranch owners, Ash and Ethan, sat on their porch swing, contentedly watching the laborers in action. "Not a single child laborer can be found on that ranch," Jules said to Dennis. "The ranch owners are very proud."

But her scenario suggested that somehow in reality Ash and Ethan were lazy and casually cruel taskmasters, when both of them were actually known to be respectful and generous to the people who worked for them, and not in a knee-jerk fashion but in a real way. Also, as everyone knew, Ash and Ethan worked constantly, going from project to project, both artistic and philanthropic. Even Ethan, in possession of a series of successes that, by the time the Christmas letter of 2009 had arrived, spanned more than two decades, never stopped and never wanted to. "When you stop, you die," he'd said once at dinner, and everyone at the table had somberly agreed. Stopping was *death.* Stopping meant you'd given up and turned the keys of the world over to other people. The only option for a creative person was constant motion — a lifetime of busy whirligigging in a generally forward direction, until you couldn't do it any longer.

Ethan Figman's ideas were so much more valuable now than they had been in 1984, when, only three years after graduating from the School of Visual Arts in New York City, he'd made a deal for an animated adult TV show called *Figland.* After the pilot was finished and had tested well, the network ordered a whole season. Ethan had insisted on doing the voice of Wally Figman's amusingly infuriated father, Herb Figman, and that of a lesser character who lived in the parallel universe of Figland, Vice President Sturm. He'd also insisted that he had to stay in New York, not move to LA, and after a lot of tense discussion, the network, astonishingly, agreed, opening a studio for the show in an office building in midtown Manhattan. In its first year, *Figland* became a startling hit. Very few people had any idea that Ethan's technique had been learned in an animation shed on the grounds of a summer camp under the tutelage of Old Mo Templeton — who had probably never, Jules realized, been referred to in his lifetime as Young Mo Templeton. Ethan, though, stayed youngish over the years of all his accomplishments. At fifty he was as deeply homely as he'd been at fifteen, but his curls had thinned out and turned a kind of burned goldish silver, and his homeliness gave him cachet. Once in a while, someone recognized him on the street and said, "Hello, Ethan," as though he or she knew him personally. Though he often still wore T-shirts with kitschy silk-screened animation figures on them, some of his collared shirts were made of expensive textured materials that resembled the skins of Japanese lanterns. At the beginning of his success, Ash had encouraged him to shop in better places — real stores, not tables on street corners, she'd said — and after a while he'd even seemed to enjoy some of the clothes he owned, though he would not admit it.

Ethan had so many ideas that they were like Tourette's syllables that needed to be spat out in chaotic yips and explosions. But many of them, even most of them, paid off in some way. After his success with the show was well established, he'd become an anti-child-labor activist in the mid-1990s and founded a school in Indonesia for children who'd been saved from labor. Alongside him Ash had become involved in this mission too, and their benevolence was genuine, not just a brief phase that soon bored them. Now Ethan was heading into the second year of the Mastery Seminars, a week-long summer event he'd created at a resort in Napa, California, where politicians, scientists, Silicon Valley visionaries, and artists gave presentations about ideas in front of a privileged audience. The first year had been a success. Still several steps below other, similar conferences, the Mastery Seminars had gotten attention quickly. Even though it was only December now, the next season was already selling out.

Jules and Dennis Jacobson-Boyd read the 2009 Figman and Wolf Christmas letter one evening right before Christmas. New York

City was in its annual crisis. Traffic didn't move. Families from out of town, carrying blooms of shopping bags, meandered along sidewalks. Despite the decimated economy, people still came here for the holidays; they just couldn't stay away. Canned music rang out in the streets, including those terrible 1950s Christmas novelty songs that made you "want to die," as one of Jules's clients had said to her that day. Everyone who lived in New York was weary, annoyed at the temporary occupation of their city, and forced into a state of imposed celebration. Jules had just gotten home from seeing her last client of the day and of the whole week. Years earlier, many therapists, including herself, had stopped using the word *patients.* Having *clients* still seemed a little unnatural, though; it made Jules feel that she was a businessperson, someone in, say, consulting, that vague field that she'd never really understood, though over the years through Ethan and Ash, she and Dennis had met people who made their livings this way. No one wanted to be a patient anymore; everyone wanted to be a client. More to the point, everyone wanted to be a consultant.

The last client on her schedule was Janice Kling; her name was a little amusing, considering that Janice did not want to leave therapy, ever. She clung marsupially, and her attachment was moving and sometimes unsettling. She had started seeing Jules many years earlier when she was in law school at NYU and had become frightened of the Socratic method, clobbered into silence when called upon by an intimidating professor. Now Janice, who'd initially imagined becoming an academic, had become an overstressed and underpaid lawyer for an environmental group. She worked long hours, trying to save the world from deregulation, but in Jules's office she sank into the chair with slumped posture and a hopeless expression.

"I can't stand living without intimacy," Janice had said recently. "Going to meetings, fighting mean-spirited GOP legislation, then falling into bed alone and wolfing down leftover pad thai at midnight. Even, you know, using a vibrator in my apartment, where I haven't had a chance to put anything on the walls and it echoes. Is that pathetic to admit? Particularly the echoing vibrator part? Does it sound just, you know, sad?"

"Of course not," Jules had said. "They should hand out vibrators if they're going to demand so much of you that you can't find time for a private life. And even if you *can* find time," she quickly added. The two women had laughed together over the image of overworked professional women and their vibrators. Some therapists were motherly types, caftanned and big-lapped. Others seemed to make a point of being frosty and clinical and detached, as though coldness itself possessed curative properties. Jules felt neither particularly maternal nor remote as a therapist. She was herself, in concentrate, and clients had sometimes told her that she was funny and encouraging, which they meant as a compliment, but which she uneasily knew was not, entirely.

Today, in Janice Kling's session, Janice was talking about a familiar theme, loneliness, and perhaps because it was Christmas season the conversation had a desperate charge. Janice said that she had no idea how people went on year after year, not being touched or spoken to intimately. "How do they do it, Jules?" she asked. "How do *I* do it? I should go to an intimacy prostitute." She paused, and then looked up with a sharply smiling face. "Maybe I do go to one," she said, pointing.

"Well, if I'm an intimacy prostitute," Jules said lightly, "then I should charge you much, much more." Her fees were low as a rule. Managed care had changed everything, and most health plans now paid for only a handful of sessions. And, of course, drugs had replaced therapy for a lot of people. Jules and a few other clinical social worker friends met once in a while to discuss how much worse the climate was this year than it had been last year. But still they kept their practices, sharing offices to keep their costs down; still they

75

hung on. All of Jules's clients were struggling, and, though they did not know it, so was their therapist.

Now she had come home from a session of mild laughter and mild crying. She and Dennis had been living in their modern, modest apartment in the west Nineties for over a decade. On their street were brownstones and prewar buildings and small, anonymous elevator buildings like theirs, and a nursing home where, when the sun shone, a lineup of old people in wheelchairs were stationed out front, their eyes closed, their pink and white heads tilted up toward the light. The apartment belonged to Jules and Dennis; there was a narrow-aisled, sagging supermarket two avenues away; Central Park was close by; and they were settled here for good. They had raised their daughter, Rory, here; sent her to the local public school and taken her to the park so she could run and kick balls.

When Jules opened the front door, the apartment was bright with cooking; apparently Dennis was making steamed five-spice chicken. She stood and looked at the mail that had accrued today, a small, dull pile of bills and cards. Beside the fresh pile was the square card that had been lying on the front hall table for a couple of days already, unopened.

The Christmas letter.

Jules brought it into the kitchen, where Dennis stood over the stove in his Rutgers sweatshirt. He always looked too big for their small New York kitchen, his body solid and indelicate, his movements broad. He couldn't seem to keep his face free of hair growth. "My Chia Pet," she'd called him in bed back in the beginning, twenty-eight years earlier. He was big, black-haired, male, artless, at least in the sense that he had no *art,* no personal need for refined aesthetics. He liked to play touch football on the weekend with his friends who sometimes came to the apartment afterward for beer and pizza, high-fiving one another without evident irony. Like several of these friends, Dennis was an ultrasound technician, a field he'd chosen not because he'd grown up with a desire to know what lay beneath surfaces but because after a rough emotional time in college and then a shaky recovery, he'd seen a convincing ad on the subway for ultrasound school. Now, decades later, he worked at a busy clinic in Chinatown. Sometimes on the way to the subway home, walking past the row of Chinese vendors on the street, he would pick up some star anise or long beans or a twisted root that looked like an old wizard's hand. His proximity to these vendors kept him somehow a little exotic himself.

Dennis turned away from the stove and walked toward her with a dripping spoon.

"Hello," he said, kissing her; their lips suctioned, springy, and they held the kiss.

"Hello," Jules finally said. "It smells good in here. When did you get home?"

"An hour ago. I went right from a pelvic ultrasound to this. Oh, there are two messages on the machine. Your mother and Rory. Your mother said it's not necessary to call her back, she was just checking in, and wondered if you'd heard from Rory yet. And Rory said that she'd arrived safely at Chloe's house in New Hampshire and that the roads weren't bad."

"They shouldn't let college students drive," said Jules. "They get in these crappy cars that their parents no longer want, and hit the road. It's sickening."

"It's sickening that they have to ever move out," said Dennis. But this wasn't really true in their case. Though they'd been struck hard when Rory went off to college, and had been dumbly bewildered that she no longer lived there, she'd always been self-contained, eager to go outside; and so sending her to college all the way upstate was a little like returning an animal into the wild.

"Well, she's fine," said Dennis. "They're going to cross-country ski. She'll have a great time." Then he noticed what Jules held. "Hey, the letter," he said.

"Yes," she said. "The letter from our friends, the ranchers."

"You still want to do the thing this year? Where I read it aloud? You're still not past that?"

"Oh, I'm past it," she said. "I just like doing it. One of our only rituals — you the lapsed Catholic and me the short-sedered Jew."

"The what? Oh, *short-sedered*," said Dennis, amused. "Yes, that's exactly how I describe you to everyone."

"And still in need of a read-aloud Christmas letter," said Jules.

"Okay. But wait, I have wine," he said.

"Oh, good. Thank you, honey."

He went to the cabinet and poured glasses of red, then sat with her at the table in their barely eat-in kitchen, while snow pinged the narrow window that overlooked the alley. There was a silent moment as Dennis pushed his finger inside the envelope, revealing an oxblood lining. Suddenly Jules remembered Ash's sleeping bag from camp with its own suggestive red lining. The illustration on the card was, as always, a new Ethan Figman drawing, seasonally relevant. This time he had drawn the Three Wise Men, each one plump and eccentric in a robe and tall hat; each one crankier than the last. Jules and Dennis studied and admired the drawing together. The corners contained tiny asides — throwaway jokes about the trashed economy and illustrations of anthropomorphic piles of resin

79

with dialogue bubbles above them: "Hello there, I'm Frankincense. Well, technically I'm Frankincense's *monster,* but everyone gets that wrong."

One year the Christmas letter had included an advent calendar with windows that hid wonderful little cartoon scenes. Another year, when you opened the card, the theme song from *Figland* played, though the technology was not advanced yet, and the sound was like miniature children trapped inside the card, singing *"Ee-ee-ee."* In 2003, memorably, a burst of pink powder had flown out, though some recipients had apparently been frightened, thinking it was a letter bomb, which horrified Ethan and Ash, who had just imagined it would be a cool effect. So the Christmas card became tame again, but it always contained a classic Ethan Figman illustration as well as a detailed accounting of the previous year.

The earliest letters had had an arch and jokey tone, but fairly soon they turned into a more earnest project. Jules and Dennis had never sent their own letter; other than the fact that even the term "Christmas letter" seemed corny, for a long time the years had been mixed. Some years had been catastrophic, though that hadn't been true for a while. Mostly, the years were just ordinary or mildly disappointing. What would she and Dennis even write about themselves? *"In* recent months, Jules lost two clients, whose insurance plans no longer offer mental health benefits." Or, "Dennis continues his job at the clinic in Chinatown, though the office is so understaffed that this week one patient waited seven hours to be seen." Or, perhaps, "Our daughter, Rory, a student at the state university in Oneonta, has no idea what to major in, and has a roommate who was prom queen in high school."

But the years had been very different for Ethan Figman and Ash Wolf, and every Christmas they obviously enjoyed the task of writing to all their friends. Jules wondered if, in the beginning, they had perched together writing — Ash used to own a powder-blue Smith Corona typewriter at Yale and then, a few years later, a gum-colored early-model Mac — their voices overlapping as they each contributed to the letter. Now, when Ash and Ethan's life together was so massive, Jules could only picture the two of them sitting in a vast room together, at either side of a desk that had once been a redwood tree or a giant geode, getting up and pacing once in a while, saying, "If we bring up the trip to Bangalore, will it seem self-serving? Even obnoxious?"

But perhaps the Christmas letter was no longer much of a shared project. Maybe Ash read it aloud to Ethan while he poked along on a treadmill in front of a wall of windows, and he nodded his approval, which in both their minds made him cowriter. Or maybe Ethan read it aloud to his assistant, Caitlin Dodge, who made editorial suggestions and then sent it out to everyone on the list. Jules realized she could no longer even take a rough guess at the number of people who received the Figman and Wolf Christmas letter. She'd lost a grasp of what the number might possibly be, the way she'd lost track, some years ago, of the current population of the earth.

The extensiveness of the friendship pool of Ash and Ethan was not something you could look up online. How many people did they consider their friends? What did it take to *be* their friend? Jules was securely among their closest friends. She'd seen everything that had gone on between them over three decades in New York City and also during the decade before, in the teepees and theater and dining hall of Spirit-in-the-Woods. Jules was in it forever, in a way that very few people were who had come later. Probably anyone who received this letter felt gratified. Everyone wanted to receive a Christmas letter from Ethan Figman and, by association, from Ash Wolf. Hundreds, maybe a couple thousand of them, did:

Dear friends,
Even those words give us pause, because

throughout the year we receive so many letters that also begin "Dear friends," asking for a donation to some cause or other. And for the most part, we aren't the actual friends of those askers. But you are the genuine article and we love you, so please forgive us as we once again foist a play-by-play of the previous twelve months upon you. You may foist one upon us as well, if you like, and in fact we hope you do.

We're writing this from the ranch in Colorado, where we've been holed up with both kids and a bunch of great performers. Ash, who's working on a production of *The Trojan Women* that she'll direct at Open Hand, invited the whole cast out here, and amazingly they agreed to leave their busy lives and come.

So all the bedrooms are full of Trojan Women, or at least Trojan Women with Equity cards. We are thrilled, because when we first bought the ranch we fantasized that someday it could sort of be an arts center (or an arts *centre,* Ash confesses she pretentiously imagined), and now it has materialized (aka *materialised*).

We've been lighting big fires in the hearth at night, and the actors are up with the roosters. Greek tragedy! Unnecessary violent deaths! Hayrides! What's not to like? As for Ethan, he's taking a long-planned break over the holidays, and hopes to read the books that have been following him from city to city, country to country, plane ride to plane ride, but which he's so far barely cracked. On his e-reader there's a history of minor-league baseball parks and a concise explanation of string theory (whatever that is. Ask Ethan — but not until January). Perhaps he'll really get through them this time, though he's infuriated that his e-reader allows him to only know the *percentage* of a book he's read, not the number of pages. This, he thinks, is 92 percent stupid.

In far more important developments, the Anti-Child-Labor Initiative has had another year of expansion, thanks to the kindness and compassion of the people to whom we have also written "Dear friends." (But we don't feel for them a fraction of what we feel for you. *Honest.*) This isn't the place to go on about the essential work the initiative accomplishes. (Please link to a-cli.net for more about that.) But let's just say here that we have a staff of extraordinarily dedicated people in the New York office who give of themselves in ways that continually amaze us. We wish we could spend more time onsite, but this year has been a fertile one for *Figland.* Barreling toward a quarter-century on the air (oy!), the ancient TV show amazingly thrives.

We've worked constantly this year, and we've traveled to India, China, and Indonesia, along with our staff and a few helpful folks from UNICEF, overseeing the expansion of the Keberhasilan ("Success") School that we proudly helped found. And we've also carved out a little time to travel just for our own pleasure. The sobering tragedy of underage labor could of course not be countered by the pleasures we experienced. But the first and foremost way to address the situation is to educate people about it. And that's what we continue to try and do.

With waves of insufferable pride we'd like to tell you about our daughter, Larkin Figman, who's managed to survive nineteen years with a name that hovers in the region between a misanthropic twentieth-century English poet and a certain familiar cartoon character. Friends, she is the most incredible young woman! She came with us on the Indonesian leg of our trip, as she has done before, and worked as an aide at Keberhasilan, but had to return immediately afterward for college. As many of you know, she's a student at her mother's alma mater, Yale, living in Davenport and studying theater and art history. We would have loved her even if she were a math geek, which she certainly is not. However, as many of you also know, her younger brother Mo is, and we love him no less for it. A boarding student at the Corbell School in New Hampshire, Mo believes his dad's TV show could be A LOT better, and that the plays his mom directs are boring, but he tolerates us anyway.

On a more serious note, we want to add here that we'll soon be revealing some important news about the Foundation for Poverty, because some of you have asked how you can help.

The letter went on for another dense page of type. All the information in it Jules already knew, since she spoke to Ash several times a week much of the time, and she and Ethan sent each other frequent brief e-mails. The two couples had dinner when they could, which wasn't that often anymore, but it didn't matter; they were close, they were sealed. Their lives were much too different now for Jules to have kept up a sustained level of envy. Mostly, she had given up her envy, had let it recede or dissipate so that she wasn't chronically plagued by it. But still, whenever the Christmas letter came each year, cataloging the specifics of the enormous life of Ethan and Ash beat by beat, Jules indulged in a few dark thoughts.

By the time Dennis was done reading aloud now, Jules saw that somehow the bottle of wine had emptied. It wasn't even anything good — they never bought good wine but grabbed whatever cost around nine dollars, a figure they'd arbitrarily settled on — but Jules had been drinking the whole time he'd been reading to her, her hand lifting and lowering, though she'd barely noticed what she was doing. Now she felt as if she were dully humming with an unpleasant, low-grade drunkenness. She made a variation on the same dumb, unkind joke she'd occasionally made over the years: "Why would they call it the Foundation *for* Poverty? Doesn't that imply that they approve?"

"Yes, someone should have done something about that by now," Dennis murmured agreeably.

"You know what, Dennis? I have gotten over most of my stupid thing about them, but it does rear its head very predictably when we do this. Remember last year? We read the letter, and we were drinking, and we went out walking in the snow on Riverside Drive. I joked about falling down in a snowbank and dying of a combination of hypothermia and envy. That was what we said it would say in the coroner's report."

"Oh right," Dennis said, smiling again. "Well, you didn't die. You got through it, and you'll get through it again." Throughout their marriage, he often smiled at her with a kind of sympathetic affection. "Anyway," he said, "everything gets bad around Christmas. There's also seasonal affective disorder, right? I always worry about that."

"That's not going to happen. You're fine," she said.

"And so are you," said Dennis, clearing away the glasses.

Her tongue felt unmoored, and her whole mouth felt in danger of coming apart as she spoke. "This is just my usual relapse," she said. "I'm sure it will pass."

"It's not like you didn't already know everything they wrote in the letter," said Dennis. "You know all the details already."

"But just hearing it aloud or seeing it on the page reminds me of everything. I can't help it. Despite my wisdom by now, I am small-minded and predictable." She paused and said, "You know that I love them, right? I need to make sure you know this."

"God, of course. You don't have to say that."

"Do you remember how much worse I used to be?"

"I certainly do," he said.

She ate his five-spice chicken, and it was cooked perfectly, the flesh as tender as a change purse, she told him — "not that I've eaten a change purse, though I bet it would be exactly this tender if I did" — but Jules felt herself drop even lower. Ash and Ethan had a personal chef who knew all their likes and dislikes. Here, in this little kitchen, Dennis used the Chinese ingredients he found on Canal Street as he headed to the subway after a day at the clinic spent plowing a transducer through the warm gel spread across sections of people's bodies. He had worked hard on his chicken, and she had worked hard on Janice Kling and the other clients who preceded her; while off in Cole Valley, Colorado, on the Figman and Wolf ranch, the whole place fibrillated with good work and industry. Ash and Ethan were never idle, never still. The work they did invariably became something wonderful. If they cooked a chicken, it would feed a subcontinent.

Jules ran a socked foot against the kitchen tiles that never entirely got clean. They were inexpensive tiles, and you could scrub and scrub them, but still they appeared the milky yellow that implied there wasn't enough money in this household or enough attention being paid to detail. There wasn't some woman with a curved back kneeling on the floor cleaning these tiles each week. This concentrated and renewed burst of ancient Ash-and-Ethan envy had turned Jules into someone shameful. And it wasn't as if Ash and Ethan didn't have problems too. First of all, they had a son with an autism-spectrum disorder. Though the Christmas letter did not refer to this, probably most of the people who received it already knew.

Jules had been with Ash during Mo's two-day evaluation and diagnosis long ago when he was three; they'd driven up together to New Haven to the Yale Child Study Center because Ethan had said he had to go to LA and couldn't get out of the trip. The driver took the two women and Mo in the black Range Rover, and during the ride Ash said, "So this is my big return to New Haven. And not to have lunch with an old professor, or give a talk, but to learn what's wrong with my uncommunicative and unhappy little boy." The nut of what she was saying was: this is awful. Mo couldn't hear her; he was listening with headphones to a CD of a picture book about a runaway truck, the same CD he listened to often. The two women regarded him for a few seconds, then Ash unbuckled her seat belt and reached over, pressing her face into his soft white neck. He twisted around to get away but saw he was trapped by the seat belt and soon stopped protesting.

Jules knew, during the drive, that Mo would be given a diagnosis the next day, and it seemed clear finally what it might be. But until not long before Ash had made the appointment it hadn't occurred to them that Mo was "on the spectrum," as everyone casually put it lately, just the way people also casually said "chemo," all of it seen as part of the perils of the modern age. Instead, before then, Mo had seemed mostly anxious and disconnected, shrieking and crying for reasons that he was unable to explain. An elderly, famous child psychiatrist had spent hours with him asking what he was afraid of when he lay in bed at night.

At the end of the following day, during the trip home from New Haven, Ash cried on her cell phone in the car to Ethan. Jules sat there awkwardly, looking out the window and wishing she didn't have to hear them talk. Ash said to Ethan, "No, I know you love me, that's *not* what I'm saying," and then, "I know you love him too. Your love is not in question, Ethan. Sometimes I just need to cry. No, he's listening to a CD. He's got headphones on. He's completely oblivious. I wish I was too." Then she listened to Ethan for a few moments, and suddenly said, "All right," and handed the phone to Jules, who was startled.

"What?" whispered Jules. "Why does he want to talk to me? You're in the middle of a whole thing together."

"I don't know. Just talk to him."

"Listen, hi, Jules," Ethan said on the phone, his voice tight. "Will you stay at the house tonight with Ash? Is that at all possible? I feel so bad I couldn't go with her, and I realize I'm asking for a lot, but I don't want her to have to be alone. I mean, I know the kids will be there, and Rose and Emanuel, but I would really love it if you were there too. Because you can" — here his voice broke a little — "you can remind her that, you know, we've always gotten through everything. That's what we've always done, since the beginning, with her parents and Goodman. Remind her of this, will you, because she feels so *down*. Maybe you can reassure her, like I was trying to do, that Mo will have a good life. There's no way he won't. We've got the resources, and it'll be okay. We'll make it be okay. Please tell her that. But say it later, when Mo's not around to possibly hear any of it, okay?"

Jules stayed the night at Ethan and Ash's house on Charles Street with the staff and the delicately wonderful meals appearing as if they'd been summoned up merely through wishing. She sat with Ash in the basement level of the house by the side of the compact lap pool, while Ash swam her short, dull laps for a long time, her head above water, once in a while stopping and peering up to say, "Will it be okay, do you think?"

"Yes," Jules had said, reaching down to take Ash's wet hand. "It will be. I know it will."

She meant it, too. Things were always set right in Ash's life. The family could at last move forward with what had seemed like a generically emotionally fragile son, but instead was a son with a specific diagnosis: pervasive developmental disorder, not otherwise specified, or PDD-NOS. He was on the autism spectrum, the doctors had explained, and now he could finally get some real help. Always, the Figman and Wolf family rallied; just as, long in the past, the Wolf family had rallied too. But the loss of possibilities was always undeniably painful. This had been true when Ash's brother, Goodman, essentially ruined his life in one night and thundered impulsively ahead from there, as if trying to ruin the lives of everyone around him as well.

By 2009, Jules had been with Ash at most of the significant moments in her family story, and she knew how much Ash had suffered. Still now, on the night that Jules and Dennis read the latest Christmas letter, Jules had her series of mildly envious thoughts that could not be quieted as quickly as she would have liked, and she and Dennis went to bed early, with Ethan's card of the Three Wise Men propped on the radiator. All winter the heat in this apartment was either too voluminous or stingy. Tonight was one of the stingy times, and they lay together, her husband's thick arms around her, keeping her not exactly warm enough; and her arms around him, probably doing the same incomplete job. Elsewhere, in a hearth on a Colorado ranch, a fire glowed and gathered.

FOUR

Dennis Boyd was one and a half years past his first serious depressive episode when he and Jules Jacobson met at a dinner party in the late fall of 1981. She had moved to the city that September after college to try to be an actress — or, actually, an *actor,* Ash said they should now call it — the comedic, "character part" type, which was helped along by her reddish hair; though she knew that attempting to channel Lucille Ball could take you only so far. Depression wasn't anything that she and her friends ever thought about. Instead they thought about their temp jobs; auditions; graduate school; finding a rent-stabilized apartment; and whether, if you'd slept with someone twice, it meant you were involved. They were trying to figure out the world through a series of experiments, and mental illness was not one of them. Jules was too naive about mental illness to know much about it unless it appeared before her in its churning, street-aggressive male form or its despairing, Plathian female form. Anything other than that, and she missed it entirely.

Isadora Topfeldt, the hostess of the dinner party, had given a few details about Dennis Boyd in advance of the evening, though she'd left out his depressive episode. When naming the different people who would be at her dinner, she'd said to Jules, "Oh, and also my downstairs neighbor Dennis Boyd. You remember, I've told you about him."

"No."

"Sure you do. *Dennis.* Big old Dennis." Isadora jutted her jaw a little and thrust her arms outward in illustration. "He's this bearish guy with thick black hair. He's *regular,* you know?"

"Regular? What does that mean?"

"Oh, just the way you and I and most of the people we know are *ir*regular, Dennis isn't. Even his name: Dennis Boyd. Like blocks of wood side by side: Dennis. Boyd. It could be the name of anyone on earth. He's like . . . this *guy.* He's not in the arts whatsoever, which makes him different from a lot of people we know. He's working as a temp at a clinic, answering phones. Has no idea of what he wants to do with his life. He's from Dunellen, New Jersey, working class, 'very hardware store' were I believe his exact words, and he went to Rutgers. He doesn't say all that much. You have to sort of drag things out of him. He plays touch football in the park with his friends," Isadora added, as though this was an exotic detail.

"Why did you invite him?"

Isadora shrugged. "I like him," she said. "You know what he really looks like? A young cop."

The building in which Isadora Topfeldt and Dennis Boyd both lived was a narrow tenement walk-up on West 85th Street just off Amsterdam Avenue, still a dubious stretch of street back at the start of the 1980s. Everyone who lived on the Upper West Side then told stories of having been mugged or nearly mugged at least once; a mugging was a rite of passage. Isadora, a loud, broad-shouldered woman who favored vintage dresses, had talked to her neighbor Dennis at the mailboxes, and they'd hung out a couple of times in her apartment. On one recent evening, after a few long silences, Dennis had stiffly told Isadora what had happened to him in college; and though Isadora was usually a gossip, she hadn't repeated the story of his depressive episode and hospitalization to Jules or either of the other guests in advance, because, as she later explained, it wouldn't have been fair to him.

Jules had graduated from the State University of New York at Buffalo, and after a summer spent living with her mother in Underhill, where everything was the same as always but slightly different — the family-style Italian restaurant was now a nail salon; the Dress Cottage was also a nail salon; the Wanczyks next door were both dead of back-to-back heart attacks, and their house had been sold to an Iranian family — she had found an extremely cheap studio apartment in the West Village. The building seemed to be a firetrap, but it was in the *city.* Finally she could say she lived here, in the place where all her friends from Spirit-in-the-Woods had lived when she'd first met them. Now she was no different from them.

Ash and Ethan lived directly across town from her in the East Village, and their own studio apartment — the first apartment they'd ever lived in together — wasn't any better than hers. It had a working fireplace, but the single room was minuscule, with a loft bed and a drawing table beneath it. All of them lived their lives in tiny apartments; it was what you did as soon as you got out of school. The near-squalor of Jules's one room on Horatio Street wasn't a source of shame to her. She had a night job as a waitress at La Bella Lanterna, a café where kids from the suburbs who'd recently moved to the city came in and blithely ordered that orangeade called Aranciata, trilling the tongue on the *r* like native speakers of Italian. During the day when she could, Jules went to open-call theater auditions, and only once received a callback, but still she kept going to them.

Her friends were too nice to suggest that she might think about an alternative field. Parents were the ones who handed you law school admission test study guides unprompted, and when you responded with revulsion or rage, they defensively said, "But I just wanted you to have something to fall back on." The world of law was filled with the fallen, but theater wasn't. No one ever "fell back" onto theater. You had to really, really want it.

Jules had thought, at the beginning of her time in New York City, that she had really, really wanted it. Her three summers at Spirit-in-the-Woods had given her the desire, which had stayed with her. She'd become more confident as an actor and even occasionally bold. Her social awkwardness had turned into what seemed to other people like a deliberate affect. She sometimes wore strange, elfish outfits now, including little John Lennon eyeglasses for reading, and a short, flared skirt that could technically be described as a dirndl. "You just like saying *dirndl,*" Ethan accused her, correctly. Jules often made idiosyncratic remarks — not even actual jokes — and she was surprised to find that most other actors weren't funny, as a rule, so in fact they were a very easy audience. All she had to do was throw out a phrase that was vaguely ethnic or funny *seeming* — "My kishkas, my kishkas," she'd said when she got hit in the stomach with a Frisbee, and all the actors around her had laughed, even though Jules knew she was cheating by not actually being funny but instead being in the *neighborhood* of funny.

Ethan understood the distinction when she told him. "Yeah, it was kind of cheating," he'd agreed, "using your Jewishness in this sort of low-rent way."

"But, you know," she said, "I was sure to invoke the Fanny Brice Act, which was passed by Congress in 1937."

She and Ash were now taking an acting class together at the private studio of a legendary teacher, Yvonne Urbaniak, a woman in her late seventies who wore a turban — a look that, unless you had impeccable bone structure, wasn't flattering to a woman and usually suggested chemotherapy. "She's Isak Dinesen's stunt double," Jules kept saying. Yvonne was extremely charismatic, if suddenly capable of cruelty. "No, no, no!" Yvonne had said to Jules more than once. Ash was one of the stars of the class; Jules was one of the worst. "Definitely in the bottom two," Jules had said once. Ash had murmured something in contradiction, but not forcefully.

On Thursday nights during that first year after college, Jules and Ash met for class in the barely furnished living room of a brownstone along with ten other people. They read scenes, they did exercises, and fairly often someone in the class cried. Occasionally it was Ash. Jules never cried there; sometimes, seeing one of the other actors become overwhelmed during an exercise, she felt a spike of nervous tension and a sudden inexplicable desire to laugh. She didn't have a strong emotional connection to the work, and she attempted to convince herself that a comedic actor didn't need to find an emotional connection. That all she had to be was a comic colt, galumphing around the stage winningly. But Jules wasn't good enough at that either.

After class she and Ash ate a late dinner at an East Village restaurant where varenyky, the Ukrainian version of fat pierogi, slid around on buttered oval china plates. These dinners were a destination and a relief. After the tension of the class, Jules welcomed the starch and the oily sheen you could lick from your fork, and also the pleasure of sitting across from Ash with no one else around.

"I should quit," Jules said.

"No, you shouldn't. You're too good."

"No, I'm not."

Ash always encouraged Jules, despite the truth. Maybe she'd been pretty good at fifteen, but that was a brief and unusual flare. Her first night onstage at camp in *The Sandbox* had been her best night of all, followed up over the subsequent two summers by slightly weaker imitations. Then in college, though she was cast in several plays, Jules could see her place in all this. Some actors had resolve but no talent; others were all talent but breakable, and the world had to discover them before they shrank back and disappeared. Then there were people like Jules, who tried so hard, the effort showing clearly. "Keep going," Ash said. "That's all there is, right?" So Jules kept going, without any reward or encouragement from anyone outside her friends.

Still, between Yvonne's tough class and all the pointless open-call auditions, Jules Jacobson could still be described as an "actor," and so at Isadora Topfeldt's dinner party she was introduced to Dennis Boyd this way. Dennis, in turn, was introduced by Isadora as "my neighbor, the very nice temp at a clinic." Both of them shyly said hello. When you were twenty-two in 1981 and met someone of the opposite sex, your thoughts did not go to couplehood. Ash and Ethan were the only couple their age that Jules knew, and they didn't count, for they weren't like anyone else. The somewhat freakish childhood-sweetheart phenomenon of Ash and Ethan could not entirely be explained.

The dinner party at which Dennis appeared took place on one of those evenings that came in a spasm in the early eighties, when everyone was first learning to cook and dinners

featured elaborate food within limited parameters, since they all owned the same two ap-
proachable cookbooks. Chicken marbella was
ubiquitous. Prunes, those unloved things,
beetle-backed and shiny, with guts like meat,
finally found their context. Cilantro was
briefly everywhere, creating miniflurries of
conversation about whether you did or did
not like cilantro, which invariably included
someone in the room saying, "I can't stand
cilantro. It tastes like soap." That night,
candles released tongues of red wax onto Isadora's tablecloth and windowsill, where it
would leave an eternal crust, but it was no
matter; Isadora's crappy furnishings, and
even the apartment itself, would be abandoned when all the life practicing had exhausted itself and new desires replaced old
ones. They all hated Ronald Reagan with a
uniform loathing, and it astonished Jules Jacobson that other people in America — a
majority, apparently — actually liked him.
Nixon had been an outright grotesque, and
as far as she could see Reagan was one too,
with his oiled hair and padded shoulders like
some dunderheaded uncle.

"Have you ever noticed," Jules had once
said to her friends, "that Reagan's head is
kind of *slanted*? It's shaped like the rubber
top of a bottle of that brown kind of glue.
What's that glue called . . . oh, mucilage."
Everyone had laughed. "Our president is

Mucilage Head!" she'd said. "And semi-relatedly," she'd continued, bringing out something she'd once said to Ethan back at camp, "have you ever noticed the way pencils look like collie dogs? You know, like Lassie?" No, no one had noticed. Someone brought out a pencil and Jules showed them how, if looked at from the side, a pencil had a shaggy orange fringe like a collie's fur, and a black tip that resembled a collie's snout. Yes, yes, they all saw it, but they were still thinking about Mucilage Head, and how, to their despair, they lived in his America now.

The house on Cindy Drive, which had always been small and a little dowdy, seemed tragic post-college. Since her father had died in 1974, her mother hadn't been able to keep the place in good enough shape; the mailbox hung at a slant, and there was an old ceramic pumpkin on the porch filled to the top with crisping, yellowed copies of the *Underhill Clarion.* Lois was all over Jules the minute she came in the front door, and during meals she seemed to sit and keenly observe the way Jules ate. This was unnerving. When Jules moved to the city, it was so good to mostly go unwatched and therefore unjudged. Even at the cheap haircut place in the Village, your skinny androgyne of a haircutter hardly even looked at you as he or she cut your hair, but mostly looked into the mirror and across the big industrial basement room at another skinny androgyne haircutter. A song by the Ramones rattled the barbers' chairs, and you could close your eyes and listen to it along with the strangely satisfying sounds of your own wet hair being severed from your head.

Now almost everyone at this party had the spiked hair of dogs fresh from a dogfight in the rain. Dennis Boyd, who sat across from Jules Jacobson, separated from her by a thick candle like a Doric column, did not. He had a head of conventional wavy black hair, a darkly shadowed, slightly unshaven face, and deep-set, dark eyes that almost appeared to have light bruises beneath them. It wasn't clear, really, what he was or who he was. He lived in this building and worked at a job that he would outgrow. This was a time of life, she understood, in which you might not know what you were, but that was all right. You judged people not on their success — almost no one they knew was successful at age twenty-two, and no one had a nice apartment, owned anything of value, dressed in expensive clothes, or had any interest in making money — but on their appeal. The time period between the ages of, roughly, twenty to thirty was often amazingly fertile. Great work might get done during this ten-year slice of time. Just out of college, they were gearing up, ambitious not in a calculating way, but simply eager, not yet tired.

Isadora's big neighbor Dennis was a little

different. He was still in his work clothes, his creased white button-down shirt invoking a set of clean cotton sheets. He did appear solid, as Isadora had said, and, yes, it was true that with his short, traditional haircut and thick arms and New Jersey accent he also resembled her idea of a young cop. It wasn't too much of a stretch to imagine him in uniform. But he was also shyer than anyone else in the room, which included Isadora, a girl named Janine Banks whom Isadora knew from her hometown, and a guy named Robert Takahashi from the copy place where Isadora worked. Robert was small and handsome with spiky black baby-chick hair, and built like a compact action figure. He was gay, Isadora had said, and from a traditional Japanese-American family that had been ashamed when he'd come out to them, then never referred to his gayness again. Whenever he went home to Pittsburgh for a visit, though, he took his current boyfriend with him if he had one, and his mother boiled udon noodles and cooked eel in sauce for the two men and treated them well.

For a moment Jules thought that maybe Robert should meet her friend Jonah Bay, but she didn't think Jonah was quite ready to meet anyone yet, after his summer living in Vermont on a farm along with other members of the Unification Church — the Moonies. He'd been drawn into the church when he was still living in Cambridge after having graduated from MIT. For reasons no one understood, Jonah had been vulnerable to indoctrination, and had moved to that farm and been part of the Moonies until his friends managed to bring him back to New York a month earlier, in order to have him de-programmed. Now, he was only barely social, like someone resting after a seizure.

At the table, Robert Takahashi began to talk about how one of his friends from the copy place, Trey Speidell, was very sick. It was extremely disturbing the way it had all come about, Robert said. After work one night the two men had gone out to the Saint, and under the club's perforated planetarium dome they'd begun to dance. Shirts had been removed and poppers had been cracked even though it was a weeknight — because, really, why not? It was 1981, and they were two young men with new haircuts, getting up each day to go to jobs that didn't require much brainpower. They could stay up late and dance, jumping up and down. Fast numbers were followed by slow ones, and they ground themselves together, and ended up back at Trey's little shared apartment.

"We began fooling around," Robert explained now. "It was thrilling." Everyone listened intently, as though he was telling a sea yarn. "Trey is extremely cute; take my word for it."

"He really is," echoed Isadora.

"And afterward it was sort of dark in the room, and I was just tracing my finger along his shoulder, and I said something like, 'Follow the dots.' And he said, 'What?' And I said, 'Your birthmarks.' He insisted he didn't have any, and he was kind of insulted. He went into the bathroom to prove he was right, and I followed him in, and he turned on the light and there were these big purple dots on him like someone had taken a Magic Marker and just drawn them on. The next day he went to a dermatologist at lunch hour, and afterward he didn't come back to work. And now he's in the hospital, and they say it's cancer. A really rare kind. They brought in doctors from other hospitals to consult. Even one from France."

One minute Trey Speidell was fine, Robert told them, in great shape, twenty-six years old, and now he was in St. Vincent's, in a special unit for puzzling cases. Robert feared that there was a toxin in the ventilation system at Copies Plus that had poisoned Trey and would soon poison the rest of the employees, the way Legionnaires' disease had killed those conventioneers. He worried that he and Isadora would come down with it next. "I think we should quit Copies Plus Monday morning," he said. "Just get out of there. It's a horrible place anyway."

"You're being really neurotic about this,"

said Isadora. "One of our co-workers has cancer, Robert. People get cancer, even young people."

"The nurse at St. Vincent's said that only old people get cancer like this."

"My sister, Ellen, had shingles last year," Jules put in. "That's supposed to be only for old people too."

"Exactly," said Isadora. "Thank you, Jules. Trey Speidell getting some geriatric cancer does not mean there's going to be a Copies Plus epidemic of it."

"My plan of attack, when I get worried about something?" said Dennis suddenly, and his voice in the conversation surprised Jules, because she realized he had spoken less than anyone else at this dinner. Everyone looked toward Dennis with expectation, and he seemed to back down a little, unsurely. "Well," he said, "what I do is, I try to do behavior mod on myself."

"Behavior *mod*?" said Isadora. "What is that? It sounds so swingin' sixties."

"It's just a thing where you try to think about what's realistic in your reaction and what's not," said Dennis. He licked his lips, nervous from the attention.

"I know about behavior mod," said Jules. "I wrote a paper about it for a psych class."

"Oh. Nice," said Dennis. The two of them looked at each other and smiled at the same time.

"Jules and Dennis sitting in a tree, k-i-s-s-i-n-g," chanted Isadora with wild inappropriateness, and Robert and Janine groaned and insulted her, but Jules and Dennis said nothing, just looked down at their plates in the odd moment. Then Isadora turned back to Robert and said, "I think you need to relax, Robert. We all need to. That's why I brought us a nice fat spliff for dessert."

No one looked all that interested in the spliff; Jules wasn't even certain what it was. Isadora sometimes larded her conversation with unnatural colloquialisms. Robert Takahashi was moodily distracted for the rest of the evening, which made Isadora become more talkative, as if she was afraid the silence in the room would ruin one of the first dinner parties she'd ever given in her life. Regular-looking Dennis Boyd looked too big for his flimsy little dining table chair that Isadora had bought cheaply at the Third Avenue Bazaar. Jules worried that Dennis would actually break the chair, taking a spill that would embarrass him. She didn't want him to be embarrassed; he already looked so uneasy here in the room.

After Robert's sudden emotional, frightened story about Trey Speidell, and the ensuing gloom at the table, Isadora dominated the night, and her friend Janine joined in, the two of them telling stories from the job they'd had in high school flipping burgers. Finally it was just so boring, all of them trapped at the table on unstable chairs listening to these two girls, that Jules offered her own story from the job she'd had during her sophomore year at Buffalo. "I was a theater major, but I minored in psych," she told the table, "acting in plays and also working for a psych professor performing experiments on other students, who were paid twenty dollars each. I performed one experiment in which I had to ask the subject to describe the most emotionally painful experience he or she had ever had. 'This will all be confidential,' I said to them."

She told the people at the dinner party how these students she'd never known before, but had perhaps seen on campus, had freely told her about their breakups with their beloved high school boyfriends or girlfriends or the deaths of their mothers or even, once, the diving-accident death of a little brother. But the words they spoke were immaterial; they didn't know that the only aspect she was studying for the experiment was body language. Jules watched their hands and their head movements, taking notes. After a while, the raw and emotional material just started sounding to her like ordinary revelations. The pain of others became like an actual substance, one which Jules did not underestimate or take lightly. She even imagined herself as one of these people, sitting and talking about the long-ago death of her own father, her voice as fragile and tremulous as theirs. They were *relieved* telling her about their pain, even though it didn't actually matter how well she listened.

In the middle of dinner Dennis Boyd's leg jumped a few times against the table, and he was so big that he actually lifted it slightly off the floor. Isadora said, "Dennis, stop that, it's like a séance," and she hit him on the arm. She often hit men, supposedly out of affection.

Jules asked, "What was Dennis doing?"

"Jiggling," said Isadora. "His leg. Like a boy."

"I am a boy," said Dennis. "Or anyway, I was."

"Not all boys jiggle their legs," Jules said, her version of flirting, though why was it that *archness* supposedly indicated flirting and sexual interest? Why didn't earnestness indicate this? Or melancholy?

"This boy does," said Isadora. "Constantly, believe me."

A year or so later, Isadora would leave New York, traveling the country and sleeping on the sofas of friends of friends — couch-surfing decades before it became an established activity — sending Jules and Dennis antic postcards from roadside attractions like the Hamburger Museum, or the "actual" house of the old woman who lived in a shoe.

"Actual?" Jules had said to Dennis when that card came in the mail. "How could the old woman in the shoe have an actual house? *She doesn't exist.* It's a nursery rhyme." Together they had laughed at Isadora. Then, no one heard a word from her after 1984. And then, much later, in 1998, when the Internet existed fully and Jules thought to search her name on Yahoo, she found only a single mention of an "I. Topfeldt," proprietor of a dog-grooming salon in Pompano, Florida. Could *that* be Isadora? She never remembered Isadora once discussing a love of dogs. Almost no one she'd known in his or her twenties in New York City had a dog. But clearly life took people and shook them around until finally they were unrecognizable even to those who had once known them well. Still, there was power in once having known someone.

Jules did look Isadora up on the Internet one more time, in 2006, expecting to find the same dog-grooming information, which would have been oddly comforting. When you located someone from the past online, it was like finding that person trapped behind glass in the permanent collection of a museum. You knew they were still there, and it seemed to you as if they would stay there forever. But this time, when Jules typed in Isadora's name, the top hit was a paid death notice from four years earlier in 2002, which told the story of a traffic accident on a highway outside

Pompano. Accidents always seemed to take place "outside" of places you'd heard of, never directly in them. It was definitely the right Isadora Topfeldt, described as age forty-three, a graduate of the State University of New York at Buffalo, survived only by her mother. "Dennis," Jules called in a tight, loud voice as she sat at the computer with the death notice before her, not quite knowing what to do with it or how to feel. She wanted to cry, but she wasn't even sure why. "Look."

He came and stood behind her. "Oh no," he said. "Isadora."

"Yes. Who introduced us."

"Oh, I feel so bad."

"Me too." Jules and Dennis wondered at their own mutual fog of sadness, which was poignantly so much sharper than the affection they'd ever felt for Isadora Topfeldt back when they actually were friends with her.

At that first dinner party, Dennis Boyd had sat across from Jules Jacobson with slightly wet-looking dark eyes, and each time his gaze moved toward her, she received a new, pleasing little bang of his interest. It had been a long time since she had truly liked a boy, or a man, as people were now starting to call them. Up at college in Buffalo, everyone had worn bundled clothes outdoors, rendering their bodies identically asexual; indoors, the men were in hearty flannel, throwing back beers. Foosball was played, that perplexingly popular game with all those knobs; and the Ms. Pac-Man machine was a regular destination in the back of Crumley's, the bar where everyone spent Friday and Saturday nights. Jules had had vaguely vomit-flavored sex with two different, uninteresting guys — the theater department guys were all gay, or else only interested in the very beautiful theater department girls — and had taken long showers afterward in a stall in her dorm, wearing flip-flops so she would not get a foot fungus.

Her suite mates were a group of girls as mean as you could ever find, not to mention slatternly, unacademic. It was just a piece of bad luck that she had been put with them. The suite smelled of hot comb. The girls screamed at one another with abandon and contempt, as though this place were some kind of halfway house for the deranged. "EAT MY PUSSY, AMANDA, YOU ARE SUCH A LYING SACK OF SHIT!" one girl shouted across the common room with its leaking beanbag furniture and splayed-open pizza boxes and Sony Trinitron TV and, of course, its hot combs lying around like the swords of knights during their day off.

In the first snow of freshman year, Jules Jacobson walked to the phone booth across the street from the dorm, and there she plied the phone with coins, calling Ash Wolf at Yale. As soon as Ash answered, Jules could detect seriousness of purpose. "Hello," said Ash in the distracted, aloof voice of someone writing a Molière paper.

"Ash, I hate it here," Jules said. "This place is so enormous. Do you know how many students there are? *Twenty thousand.* It's like an entire city where I don't know anyone. I'm like an immigrant who's come alone to America. My name is Anna Babushka. Please come get me." Ash laughed, as always. Her laughter on the phone now became for Jules the highlight of the call; the fact that she could elicit this response in Ash caused her to preen a little bit. Even in her unhappiness, she became aware of feeling a small strand of power.

"Oh, Jules," said Ash. "I'm sorry you're upset."

"I'm not upset. I'm unhappy. I mean it."

"Give it a chance, okay? You've only been there two and a half months."

"Which is a decade in dog years."

"You could go to student counseling."

"I did. But I need more than that." Jules had had five sessions with a disheveled social worker named Melinda, who was as kind as the kindest mother, nodding in sympathy while Jules railed against the stupidity of college life. Later, she would barely remember what Melinda had said to her, but at the time her presence had been soothing and necessary, and certainly Jules unconsciously imitated some of Melinda's style later on when

115

she herself started a therapy practice.

"College takes some getting used to," said Ash. "I felt the same way too in the beginning, but it got better recently."

"You go to Yale, Ash; it's completely different. Everyone is always shit-faced here."

"Lots of people get drunk here too," said Ash. "Believe me. If you listen hard now, you can hear the sound of people puking in Davenport." All Jules heard was the sound of a match being lit. With a cigarette in hand, Ash often looked like a fairy smoking or a delinquent angel.

"Well, *here,* people put their mouths directly under a keg nozzle," Jules said. "And there's supposed to be thirty inches of snow next week. Please come visit me this weekend, before I am buried alive."

Ash thought about it. "This weekend? God, it would be so great to see you. I hate that we still don't live in the same place."

"I know."

"All right. We'll drive up on Friday," Ash said.

We. Ash Wolf and Ethan Figman had become "we" and "us" the summer before senior year of high school, to everyone's shock, and the *we* hadn't ended, even with the two of them heading off to different colleges in the fall.

On Friday, as promised, Ash and Ethan appeared at Jules's dorm in Buffalo, Ash small, beautiful, and bright-faced; Ethan oily and rumpled from the long drive. They had brought along some emergency New York City supplies that were meant to cure Jules's upstate loneliness. The bagels were almost uncuttable, and the scallion cream cheese was slightly liquefied from sitting on the floor of the front seat beneath the heater of Ethan's father's old car, but the three of them sat eating in Jules's tiny cinder-block dorm room with the door closed upon the voices of her terrible suite mates.

"All right, I see what you mean. You've got to get away from these girls," Ash said quietly. "Just taking one look at them out there, I see that you haven't been exaggerating."

"Look, figure out who the smartest people in your classes are," Ethan said. "Listen to the comments they make. Then follow them around after class and force yourself on them."

"*Force herself* on them?" said Ash.

"Shit, I didn't mean it that way," said Ethan. "God, I'm sorry. I'm such an idiot."

In the days after the weekend, Jules began to take their advice, and escaped her suite mates often. She found that there was serious intelligence in clusters all around her; in her unhappiness she had been unable to recognize it. She made eye contact with a couple of students from her Intro to Psych section, and then formed a study group with them. In

117

the psych lab, and then afterward in the student union, she and Isadora Topfeldt and some other slightly alternative types sat on modular furniture and talked about how much they all hated their suite mates. Then they went to a bar on the other side of campus called the Barrel, and everyone drank as much as they did at Crumley's. This was upstate New York, where the snow layered upon itself, rising like one of those out-of-control lemon meringue pies in the glass case at the Underhill Diner. They drank and drank, and were comfortable, tribal, if not particularly close.

Now, in November 1981, a full twenty-one years before Isadora Topfeldt's death, and while the friendship still held, Jules sat at her dinner party in the West 85th Street apartment.

Isadora scraped around at the bottom of the serving dish and held up a scrap of food on a fork and said, "Is there anything sadder than the scrawniest little piece of uneaten chicken at a dinner party?"

"Hmm," said Jules. "Yes. The Holocaust."

There was a pause, then some ambivalent laughter. "You still slay me," said Isadora. To the table she said, "Jules was very funny in college."

"I had to be," said Jules. "I lived with the meanest girls. I had to keep my sense of humor."

"So," Dennis Boyd asked her, "what was Isadora like in college?"

"Dennis, college was only last spring," Isadora said. "I was the same as I am now. Watch your leg," she warned, as the table seemed on the verge of being lifted once again by Dennis's knee.

"Yes," Jules said. "She was the same." But of course she liked Isadora less now, because she needed her less and saw her more clearly. Ash and Ethan and, since he'd been returned to them recently, Jonah, were the friends she saw and spoke to all the time. "What's she like *now*?" Jules asked. "You're her neighbor."

"Oh, she scares the shit out of me," Dennis said. There was a moment of silence, and then they both laughed at the same time, as if to cover the accidental moment of truth-telling.

Dennis left the party early, saying he had a touch football game in Central Park at the crack of dawn. None of the others could imagine getting up so early on a weekend, and especially not for something athletic. "A bunch of guys get together in the Sheep Meadow," he'd explained. He turned to Robert Takahashi and said, "I hope your friend feels better soon." Then, with a quick smile that was either general or, possibly, directed especially at Jules, he retreated downstairs to his own apartment.

As soon as he exited, Isadora began to talk

119

about him. " 'A bunch of guys,' isn't that great?" she said. "I know he seems like he's built out of simple parts — I don't mean dumb parts, I just mean less fucked-up parts than we're built out of. But the truth is more complicated. Yes, he's totally regular, he plays touch football, he isn't so needy all the time like we are."

"Speak for yourself," said Robert Takahashi.

"But actually he's a depressive. He told me he fell into a real depression in the middle of his junior year at Rutgers, and basically had a breakdown. He stopped going to class and didn't hand in any of his papers. By the time he got to Health Services he'd barely been to the dining hall in weeks — I mean, his card had gone unscanned — and he only ate ramen, without cooking it."

"How can you eat ramen without cooking it?" asked Janine. "Do you even use water?"

"I have no idea, Janine," Isadora said impatiently. "Health Services saw what shape he was in, and they called his parents. And then they arranged for him to take a medical leave and be put into a hospital."

"A mental hospital?" Robert Takahashi asked. "Jesus." A reverent, worried silence moved across the table, wavy like the air above the candles.

"Yes," said Isadora. "It's that same one where those poets used to go. Not that

Dennis Boyd is a poet. Hardly," she added, a little unnecessarily, Jules thought. "But they sent him all the way up there to New England because the Rutgers psychiatrist told his family that it had an unusually good adolescent unit. Plus, insurance covered it. After he recovered he went back to college and finished up, going to summer school and also taking extra classes. He didn't do that well, but they let him graduate."

"What hospital where those poets used to go?" Jules asked.

"You know. That famous one in the Berkshires," said Isadora.

"Langton Hull?" Jules said with surprise. Dennis had actually lived at the Langton Hull Psychiatric Hospital, in Belknap, the same small town where Spirit-in-the-Woods was located.

Near the end of the evening, Isadora served espresso from a machine her parents had bought her, and which she had not figured out how to use very well. Finally she brandished the promised spliff, saying, "Here you go, *mon,*" in a so-called Jamaican accent, thrusting her head forward in chicken bobs as if to some inaudible reggae, and the thing was passed around the room. "Picture me in one of those weird knit Rasta hats with all my hair tucked inside," Isadora said. "Picture me black."

Jules had done most of her pot smoking as

a teenager, a lifetime's worth. All that pot smoking in the 1970s had exhausted her, and the idea of getting high was unappealing now. She imagined herself talking too much, being loud and outgoing and almost a little obnoxious, and it all made her feel unclean and unhappy, so she barely breathed the smoke in, suspecting that neither did Robert Takahashi, who seemed to like the idea of staying lucid too. Only Janine and Isadora sucked at the big joint like it was a teat, laughing and making incomprehensible in-jokes about their shared burger-flipping past.

As she left the apartment, Jules ran into Dennis Boyd on the stairs, on his way to take his garbage out, but she couldn't say to him, "We were all talking about you, and I found out you were in Langton Hull. Did you ever hear of Spirit-in-the-Woods?"

What she said was, "Hello. You missed cookies."

"Too bad. I like cookies," he said. "But I try not to eat them. Getting a bit of a gut. Don't want to look like my dad yet. Or ever." In illustration, with the hand that wasn't holding a twist-tied garbage bag that looked wet through the translucent white plastic, he patted his stomach. He was now wearing a green sweatshirt and jeans — post-party clothes. It would turn out that he was a little soft-middled because of the medication he took for his depression. Antidepressants were crude then, slapping at depression with a big, clumsy paw.

"And you missed Isadora's spliff," Jules said with a smile that she hoped appeared sardonic. She wouldn't say anything against Isadora Topfeldt unless Dennis said it first, but she supposed, and hoped, that he felt as she did.

"I don't think I know that word. *Spliff.* But it's pot you mean, right?"

"Yeah."

"You want a drink or something?" Dennis Boyd asked, and Jules said no thanks, she was tired and full from dinner, and couldn't bear to drink anything more tonight. It was true that she was trying to watch herself after the four-year kegger that had gone on all around her in Buffalo. But all he had meant was did she want to come over, and she hadn't known the correct, adult way to answer. The invitation had surprised her, and so she'd said no, even though almost immediately she realized that she would have liked to come over to his apartment. She wanted to see the way he lived, see his modest collection of belongings. She bet he was neat, thoughtful, touching.

"Okay," he said. "Well. Have fun then. See you around."

"See you," she said. If she had looked at him longer, taking in the sight of him so young and burly and unfinished, a bag of garbage tied in his hand, the sleeve of his sweatshirt too short on his thick hairy wrist, then maybe they would have started something that night. Instead, it took nearly two more months, a period during which they each performed their separate life tasks in seeming preparation for nothing, but which turned out to be preparation for so much.

Jules Jacobson saw Dennis Boyd next on the street in winter. Once again he held a plastic bag. She was on her way to Copies Plus to have a scene from a play xeroxed for an audition. Jules saw the top of a brown bottle poking out of Dennis's grocery bag, and was touched to realize that it was Bosco, the chocolate syrup that hadn't made an appearance in her life since childhood. He had purchased Bosco and tortilla chips. Jules remembered Isadora's indiscreet story about Dennis having been in a mental hospital, and she thought that he still didn't know how to take care of himself very well. Though really, who did? Jules had never sent in the form and the check to Prudential to purchase health insurance, though her mother had made her swear she would. Jules was uninsured, and not only that, she had never used the stove in her disgusting little kitchen, except to heat up a sock full of uncooked rice once when she had a stiff neck. But the idea of big, dark, unshaven Dennis Boyd not taking good care of himself upset her.

"I'll come with you," Dennis said, and Jules said okay, and he accompanied her to the copy place. The doorbell jingled, and they entered and stood together in the bright white store, inhaling the astringent smell of toner. There was Isadora Topfeldt in her red employee polo shirt, her hair up in little-girl pigtails, looking more eccentric and marginal than the last time Jules had seen her. Isadora seemed to have been lulled into a zombie-employee state by the *slush-slush* sound the machines made while their lights flowed back and forth across plates of glass. Behind her, her friend Robert Takahashi was straightening the edges of somebody's documents. Jules said hello and reminded him that they'd met at Isadora's.

"Hey, hi," he said, and smiled.

"How are things here?" she asked him. "Your coworker was sick?"

"Trey. He died recently."

"Oh my God."

In an unsteady voice Robert said, "I accept that it wasn't the ventilation system here that caused his cancer. But it was all very strange and very fast, and I just can't stop thinking about it."

"I'm really sorry," she and Dennis echoed together, and in front of them Robert began to cry. Everyone was a little awkward and no one knew what to say, so they just said nothing. Finally Dennis put his groceries down on the counter and reached across it to give Robert Takahashi a standard bear hug, encircling him the way he might encircle a football as he ran with it across the meadow in Central Park. It was a sight, the big indelicate guy in the thick winter jacket and the small, handsome Asian one in the red shirt, and though the gesture was deeply self-conscious, it was also genuine, and Robert seemed grateful. Big Dennis let him go, and then Jules patted Robert's arm, and finally Robert turned away in tears and went back to the stacks of paper all around him, because despite his sorrow it was still a workday.

Jules felt she had to leave this place immediately, where someone very young had fallen ill and then actually died; also, this place where someone overbearing and unappealing worked; and someone else who was congested with grief. It was a place that could make you understand that your own life would be limited in scope — everyone's was. When Jules turned and left the store with Dennis, going with him toward his apartment, where it was understood they would now go to bed together, she really imagined they were casting off limited possibilities and unpleasantness and even *death* — death by a rare, old-person's cancer, or any other cause — and were heading somewhere wide open and unexplored. He slung the grocery bag over one arm and grabbed her hand, and they broke into a run.

Sex at twenty-two was idyllic. Sex at twenty-two wasn't college sex at eighteen, which carried with it a freight of insecurities, nerve endings, and shame. Sex at twenty-two also wasn't self-sex at twelve, which was just about being quiet and discreet in your narrow bed and thinking how strange it was that you could feel this way just by doing *this.* Sex at twenty-two wasn't, either, sex at fifty-two, which, when it took place all those decades later in the middle of the Jacobson-Boyds' lengthy marriage, could be a sudden, pleasing surprise that awakened one of them from sleep.

But sex at twenty-two, well, that was really something, Jules thought, and Dennis apparently thought so too. Both of their bodies were still perfect, or perfect enough; they would come to see this later on, though they couldn't see it at the time. Self-conscious, dying with embarrassment, but *so excited,* they stripped to their skin for each other for the first time standing beside the loft bed in his apartment that day, and she made him go up the ladder first so he wouldn't be able to watch her from behind — knowing that if he did, as she lifted a leg to reach the next rung the most private section of herself would have been briefly cleaved and displayed. The hair, the shadow, the pinch of lip, the stingy little anus — how could she let him watch *that* particular show?

"After you, kind sir," she said — oh God, had she really said that? And *why*? Was she pretending to be a Victorian prostitute? — sweeping out her arm. Dark, woolly Dennis swung up the ladder naked. She watched as his parts did the male version of what hers would have done, his balls moving, if not swinging, and his downy ass separating into two as he bent his knee and climbed the vertical ladder into the bed near the ceiling. Dennis Boyd's loft bed was so high up that they could not sit upright in it, but could only half-slouch, or else lie flat, or lie with their bodies on top of each other like a two-car pileup.

The bed encouraged intimacy of a kind that Jules was not used to, and which now alarmed her. Dennis said, "I want to look at you," his face so close that he could really, completely see her.

"Oh God, do you have to?" she said.

"I do," said Dennis solemnly.

She hoped her chin was not broken out, and she tried to remember what she'd thought of herself that morning when she'd looked in the mirror. Dennis, she saw now, was already in need of a shave. He was sturdy-looking, thick-chested, big-cocked, his pubic hair like a small black loincloth, but for all of that she also knew he was inwardly shaky. In their run from the copy store they had felt like two people who'd escaped a hellish, dead-end future.

This man would climb a ladder first and let her see his balls and the thick dark twine of hair that wrapped them in some kind of atavistic protection. The slipperiness of those balls in their thin sack made even a large, strong, athletic man seem fragile. But this was an illusion; he wasn't that vulnerable, but instead he was *forceful* with her, and following that he was smiling, happy that he had given her a solid, no-faking orgasm. She'd said "Oh oh oh," and then he'd said, "You are wonderful!" She was wonderful because her responsiveness had made him feel good and successful. He was pleased with the size of his penis; he didn't have to say this, but she knew it.

An hour later, drinking milk lightly tinted with Bosco in tall Rutgers Scarlet Knights glasses in bed, the milk dripping down their necks a bit as they lounged half-slanted like two people lying in traction in some ski-chalet hospital, they told each other the roughest outlines of their personal autobiographies. She heard about his family in Dunellen, his mother and father and three brothers. The family business was a hardware store called B & L, and two of Dennis's brothers were planning on running the store soon. Dennis could go in with them if he wanted, but he told

Jules that the idea of doing that with his life was like "the death of the soul." She was relieved when he said this. A man who used the phrase "the death of the soul" was complicated. He drank out of college football glasses, and he was figuring out a rudimentary way of taking care of himself. His family had never had any money, but every Christmas they traded expensive gifts and decorated the front of the house with rococo lights and a crèche and piped-in sound. There were big holiday occasions at which everyone sat around the living room and the den for hours, but these weren't happy experiences, just boring and "itchy," Dennis said. There was always friction, he told her, because nobody really liked anyone else all that much. "My brothers and I beat each other up all the time," he told her.

"When? Now?"

"Then. I mean, *beat up* in the past."

"Sorry," she said. "Obviously, *beat up* can mean either the past or the present. I thought maybe you were still doing it."

"No," said Dennis. "Because then we would be assholes. And I try not to be. I grew up with a lot of assholes." Then, worriedly, he added, "Do I look like one?"

"No, not at all," said Jules, but she knew why he was asking. He had that standard young male look, which she'd seen in packs at the mall throughout her childhood, and then everywhere out in the world, including in college. She had never been attracted to it before, not when it was associated with generic maleness, but she liked it in him. He'd been troubled, but he was solid, big, reliable. Her father came to mind; cancer had made Warren Jacobson into a leaf, insubstantial, his slight self turning slighter as he became sick. But still, when Jules was a little girl, she had thought of him as big. She recalled the way he'd entered the house after work, wanting to hear about his daughters' days at school.

"Tell me about the new math," he would say, for that was what they called it back then, unaware that by designating something new, you are already hastening its oldness. He had been very present, and then he was gone; and as the years added up since then, it became harder to think of him as someone who'd ever been present at all. Her father was past tense now; the present could never be held, it did not allow it. But here was Dennis Boyd, present tense personified, and with him in the bed, an ancient, daughterly part of Jules's brain was stimulated with jumper cables. Imagine: a man who would not leave! A substantial, reliable, ultra-present man. She'd lost her father at age fifteen, and then a little later Ethan Figman had tried to bring her toward him, and though it was sweet, it was physically all wrong.

131

Now Dennis, a burly man with no obvious exceptional talents and no desperate desire in any one direction, somehow could do what Ethan could not. She was absorbed in Dennis, already devoted. He was caring and good and not ironic, which to her surprise was an element she was attracted to, after all those years of relentless adolescent irony. Lying beside him, Jules wondered when she could see him again. There was nothing aesthetically astute in Dennis, nothing all that subtle except for his bashfulness, which was lovely. He crashed quietly through the world. If he sat on a flimsy chair, he might break it. If he entered a woman with his big, thick penis, he would have to make sure to angle himself correctly, or she might cry out in pain. He had to be careful; he had to modulate. The boys in his house growing up had all yelled at their mother, "*Ma!* Make us some Kraft macaroni and cheese!" They never yelled at their father, who sat glowering in front of the TV, watching football and documentaries about the Third Reich. They'd been scared of him, and still were.

When Dennis got to the part of his life story about his stay at Langton Hull, his voice became tentative and questioning, and he looked to Jules to see if this information would be a deal-breaker. Was he too unbalanced for her, and would she now forever see him as an inpatient in a bathrobe, eating an institutional dinner at five p.m.? A woman at the beginning of a romance with a man might not be able to recover from such an image. Actually, she was preoccupied not with an image of him but with whether she should reveal that she already knew about his depression and hospitalization from Isadora. In which case, she would have to tell Dennis that they had all been talking about him at that dinner party back in the fall, after he left Isadora's apartment.

"Oh," was what she said, and looked concerned, touching his arm the same inadequate way she had touched Robert Takahashi's arm in the copy place.

That night, after they'd finally parted, Jules called Ash, and as soon as she answered, Jules said to her, "Well, I slept with someone." She and Ash spoke nearly every day, and saw each other once a week at their acting class, and sometimes more often. Ash was working part-time in her father's office, doing filing, the worst job in the world, she said, and was also going for auditions. She'd recently been cast as a mermaid in an experimental play that would be performed for one week in front of the New York Aquarium in Coney Island; apparently, the producers were interested in hiring her for their next production too. It was a start, and though it paid very little, Gil and Betsy Wolf were covering the rent on the apartment she and Ethan shared. He was working as an animator on industrials, but the pay was spotty. One of these days he would get a real job in an animation studio, he said. Until then, he did lots of small jobs, and was always drawing in those little spiral notebooks that thickened his back pocket.

"Who?" Ash asked in a suspicious voice. "Who was it?"

"Why do you sound so shocked? Some people have been known to *want to see* my naked form." The connection crackled and faded; Ash and Ethan had recently received one of those new cordless phones as a gift from Ash's parents, but the big, clunky thing hardly seemed worth it, for the connection almost always went from strong to weak before the conversation had really gone any-where.

"See your what?" said Ash. "I couldn't hear."

"My naked form."

"Oh, that. Well, sure, of course. It's just that you haven't slept with anyone since we've both been living in the same city," said Ash. "In the past, when you told me about them, they were always invisible lovers."

"Don't say *lovers.*"

"I always say *lovers.*"

"I know you do. You and Ethan — *lovers.* I've never liked it, but I didn't tell you."

"What else didn't you like?" Ash said.

"Nothing. I like everything else about you."

This was actually true. Ash still had so little about her that was objectionable. The fact that she used the word *lover* could not be held against her. Talking to Ash now, telling her about Dennis, was in its own way almost as pleasurable as going to bed with Dennis had been. "He is just so *present,*" she wanted to say, but Ash would have asked her to explain further, and Jules wouldn't have been able to. Maybe his *present-tense* nature indicated a lack of *future tense;* maybe, because he had no plans for himself yet, no anything except what was right here, she couldn't count on him. But she already knew that wasn't true.

Soon enough, Jules suspected, there would be a group dinner. Probably it would be at one of the cheap Indian restaurants on East 6th Street. Everyone would be very attentive and talkative, and Ethan and Ash would love-bomb Dennis over spitting iron plates of tandoori. But even so, everyone would see how different Dennis was, and despite Jules having warned them, they would be a little surprised. Someone might mention David Hockney's swimming pools. "What are those?" Dennis would ask ingenuously, unashamed, and Ash would explain that David Hockney was an artist who often painted beautiful turquoise swimming pools, and that they should all go see his show. "Sounds good," Dennis would say. When the evening was over he would tell Jules, "Your friends are so nice! Let's go with them to see that David Hackney show." She'd have to quietly say, "Hockney." And *they* would say, when they called her up the next day, "He's obviously crazy about you. And that's the main thing."

He wasn't in the arts, wasn't dying to be an actor or a cartoonist or a dancer or an oboist. He wasn't Jewish, or even half. Almost no one in his life was like Jules or her friends; Isadora Topfeldt came the closest, but she was more eccentric than artistic. In the city, ever since college, Jules would occasionally run into someone from Spirit-in-the-Woods; whenever this happened, or whenever Ash ran into someone from the camp, they would call the other one up and say in a dramatic voice, "I had a *sighting.*" People who had gone to Spirit-in-the-Woods, even people who hadn't been their close friends there, represented the world of art and artistic possibilities. But this post-college world felt different from everything that had come before it; art was still central, but now everyone had to think about making a living too, and they did so with a kind of scorn for money except as it allowed them to live the way they wanted to live. Nothing was as concentrated as it had been up at Spirit-in-the-Woods. They were all spreading out, stretching, staying close as friends but getting the lay of land that looked very different when you were on your own. Dennis, not arty, was very smart and very willing. He wasn't an *asshole.* She wanted to be around him, wanted to touch him, liked his smell, liked his bed near the ceiling, and the idea of how much he enjoyed her company. Dennis liked learning; he was interested in finding out about things. "I watched a documentary on channel thirteen about the Stanislavski method last night," he said. "Did you ever try that method when you were acting?" Or, "I spent twenty minutes talking to this guy on the street who was protesting apartheid, and he gave me all this literature, which I stayed up reading, and it was extremely shocking and sad." There was no life Dennis burned to live except, it seemed, a life that wasn't depressed.

Then there would probably be more group dinners, and Ash and Ethan and Jonah would welcome Dennis completely into their world. Jonah would perhaps appear less often, because it was always slightly *off* when everyone was in a couple except for one person. The entire group tended to single that person out, as if to try and make him feel better in his aloneness, as though it were an unnatural state. Jules imagined having her own dinner party in her little apartment with its cheap plates and silverware. They could sit on Jules's approximation of adult furniture and form a foursome or a fivesome. She fantasized that much later they would think back on this time in their lives, remembering it as if through a clear, highly polished lens. All the conversations they'd had. All the hummus they'd eaten. All the cheap foods and utensils and undemanding decorations of their early to mid-twenties.

"Is it serious?" Ash asked on the phone after Jules had slept with Dennis. After all, Ash had known it was serious the moment she slept with Ethan, or possibly even before then.

"Yes," said Jules, picturing Dennis Boyd's dark face above her, the ceiling only inches beyond. "Careful," she'd said to him, cupping his skull. "I don't want you to crack your head."

"No, I would be of no use to you with a cracked head," he'd said, and she worried then that he was thinking that his head had already been cracked once, in a way, in college, and the fissure had repaired, and that Jules knew nothing about it, though of course she did know.

"He had a nervous breakdown, Ash, and he told me all about it, but he doesn't know I already knew before he told me," Jules suddenly said in a rush. "So what do you think: do I tell him I already knew, or is this a meaningless lie of omission, and I should forget about it?"

"You tell him," said Ash without qualification. "You have to. He has to know what you know. You can't start off with a secret."

"*You're* saying that?" said Jules, light but sharp.

A long silence ensued. "Yes," Ash said finally.

Strange, Jules thought later, that she didn't press Ash on this, or try to make her admit that it was hypocritical of her to take such a position. But stranger, maybe, that Ash seemed so comfortable taking that position. From time to time over the years Jules would wonder if Ash remembered this conversation, or whether she'd found a way to inure herself to contradictions and then forget them immediately. But on the phone Jules said nothing more about it, because this conversation wasn't supposed to have been about Ash at all. It was supposed to have been about Jules and Dennis, and so she turned it back in that direction, realizing that she did agree with Ash's advice: she had to tell Dennis what she knew about him.

"I sort of lied the other day," she said to him the next time they saw each other. They had agreed to meet in Central Park, and were going to go to the zoo. "I already knew about your thing — your breakdown — when you brought it up," she said right away as they paid and entered. "I shouldn't have acted surprised the way I did. Isadora told everybody after you left."

"She did? You're kidding. Oh, this is bad," he said. "It's basically my fear about what happens when you leave a room. Everyone says the thing about you that you really can't bear." They walked down the path of the worn-looking zoo and through the curved entryway of the penguin house, and he said, "But I actually *can* bear it now. It doesn't seem to matter so much to me anymore."

"Really?"

Dennis nodded and shrugged. The person who had collapsed at Rutgers in the middle of his junior year was not exactly the same person who lay bare bodied in bed with her. That earlier person had recovered. This person could take care of another person and also let himself be taken care of when needed.

Dennis was very appealing to Jules in ways that would be hard to explain to Ash, but then she remembered the night she had first seen Ash and Ethan together; that night, she had dumbly thought *What? What?* Part of the beauty of love was that you didn't need to explain it to anyone else. You could *refuse* to explain. With love, apparently you didn't necessarily feel the need to explain anything at all.

"I knew I had a family history of gloom," Dennis said as they entered the dank gray penguins' sanctuary. Those muscular, determined little animals whipped through the cloudy water like speedboats, while schoolchildren stood in the fish stink watching, hands and noses and slack mouths against the glass wall. It felt illegal not to be in school anymore herself, to have freedom in the daytime to go with a man to the zoo, or to bed. Dennis and Jules hung back. He stood with his hands in his pockets, and said, "My grandma Louise, my dad's mother, never left the house, and apparently *her* dad barely did, either. Whenever we went over there it was like being in a horrible dark room where nobody really talked. My grandmother never had any food for us. Only those cookies called Vienna Fingers."

"I remember those cookies. We had them."

"Yeah, but yours probably weren't all broken, like hers were. We would sit with a plate of broken Vienna Fingers in front of us, and the name always creeped me out, as though they were human fingers. Jews' fingers. My grandmother always had a low-level anti-Semitism going on. 'The Jews this,' 'the Jews that.' Don't worry, though, you won't have to meet her, she's dead. When the sun went down, someone would turn on the tiniest table lamp. I couldn't wait to leave. But I never connected any of that with myself. Or even with my dad, who's really uncommunicative. I just thought he didn't like me, but it wasn't that. He's basically an untreated depressive, that's what the psychiatrist at the hospital said. But no one in my family admits to any of it. They're 'against' therapy. It was embarrassing to them what happened to me. I think they basically believe college made me fall apart, and that I would've been fine if I'd stayed at home and worked at the store with my brothers."

Jules lightly mentioned then that she knew of the Langton Hull Psychiatric Hospital from her summers at camp; she'd seen the sign downtown that pointed toward the road where the hospital was situated. He in turn said he knew of Spirit-in-the-Woods too, had seen the sign pointing toward it on the road outside Belknap. He said he had imagined what it would have been like if he had gone there instead of the hospital. Yes, it turned out that he too had eaten the huckleberry crumble, during a group outing into town with one of the nurses.

Dennis had been depressed but he wasn't depressed any longer; the antidepressant he took was one of the so-called MAO inhibitors. "Like Chairman Mao," he explained to her that night after the zoo, as they sat in her fold-out bed in her apartment, which was just a little better than his.

"So what would a Mao inhibitor be?" she asked. "The threat of capitalism?" Dennis smiled politely, but he seemed serious, distracted. He had brought over dinner for them, some things he'd cooked, "nothing fancy," he warned her, not understanding yet that the gesture itself was winning. He explained to her, as he laid out the meal on a towel across her bed, that each food was an item he'd either seen her eat before or that she'd mentioned that she liked. "At Isadora's dinner party, you were one of the ones who said they liked cilantro," he said. "I remembered that. I had to go to two places to find it. The guy at the Korean place tried to sell me parsley, but I stood my ground." Dennis and Jules ate carrot and celery sticks with a cilantro yogurt dipping sauce he'd made, and then the still-warm spaghetti he'd brought over in a plastic container. "Do you ever cook?" he asked her.

"No," Jules said, embarrassed. "I don't really do anything like that. I haven't even paid my health insurance premiums."

"I don't see the connection, but okay," he said. "That's fine. I like to cook." The unsaid thing was that it was fine if he ended up doing the cooking *in their couple.* They were going to be a couple, they really were. Then he said, "About food, there are some issues. Me and my MAO inhibitor — well, there are a lot of things I can't eat."

"Really?" she said, curious. "Like what?"

He told her the list of contraindications, which included smoked, pickled, or preserved meats; aged cheeses; liver; pâté; Chinese pea pods; soy sauce; anchovies; avocados. And also, he said, some beers and wines, as well as cocaine. "I definitely can't ever have cocaine," Dennis warned. "So please don't give it to me."

"Too bad," said Jules, "because though as I said I generally don't cook, tomorrow I was going to make you a three-year-old Gouda and cocaine sandwich. And force it up your nose," she added. Actually, looking at the sweetly eclectic little meal he'd brought, she was so touched that she wanted to buy a cookbook and cook for him sometime. Try out her oven, see if the pilot light was lit. Her desire to do this was a little embarrassing to her, as if it were a housewife throwback; she couldn't explain how this had come about, but they had entered love and mutual care-taking, which unexpectedly involved feeding and food.

"Ah, what a shame," said Dennis. "I would've really liked that sandwich."

"Out of curiosity, seriously, what would happen if you ate one of those foods?" she asked. "You'd get depressed again?"

"No," he said. "Much worse than that. My blood pressure could skyrocket. They gave me a whole pamphlet about it. Foods with tyramine in them are potentially deadly to me."

"I never even heard of tyramine," Jules said.

"It's a compound in a lot of foods. And seriously," he said, "I could die."

"Don't do that," she said. "Please don't do that."

"Okay. For you I won't."

To fall in love with a man who was emotionally precarious meant not only helping pay attention to what he ate but also knowing that there was a potential for him to fall disastrously. He was really well now, he had assured her, fixed at a reasonable mood state by the mysterious MAO inhibitor that made alterations to his brain, that got in there like the gloved fingers of a surgeon and moved various parts around. He was really well, he repeated. In fact, he felt pretty great. And he was hers, if she wanted him.

FIVE

After that first summer at Spirit-in-the-Woods, returning home was a calamity. Lois and Ellen Jacobson seemed exceedingly slow to Jules; did they possess no curiosity about anything? They were both passive for long stretches of time, and then suddenly they became opinionated about the most boring subjects imaginable: hem length this season according to *Glamour* magazine. Whether the new Charles Bronson movie was too violent for teenagers. Lois: "Yes." Ellen: "No." And, most disturbing, they didn't even recognize the pain that being forced to live with them was now causing Jules. The summer had turned her superior and quietly angry, though she hadn't known this about herself until her mother and sister appeared on the last day of camp in their Dodge Dart, which looked greener and boxier than ever. From the window of her teepee she saw the car make its way along the narrow, bumpy road. Jules had felt like an interloper when she'd first been invited to join Ash and the others in Boys' Teepee 3, but here were the real interlopers, driving toward her and having the nerve to stop on the road behind Girls' Teepee 2 and try to claim her for their tribe.

"Do I have to go with them?" Jules said to Ash. "It isn't fair."

"Yes, you have to. I have to go with mine too, whenever they show up. They're always late. My mother likes to go antiquing."

"It's fine for you to go back to your family," said Jules. "You belong there. And you've got Goodman to live with, and all the other people from here living *near* you, and you've got the whole city, in fact. I mean, it isn't comparable, Ash. I am in Siberia. I'm going to slash my wrists and leave a bloody trail along my suburban street, which happens to be called Cindy Drive. Can you believe it? Cindy? What street do you live on again?"

"Central Park West. But look, we'll see each other all the time," Ash said. "This summer isn't going to just go away like it never happened."

Ash put her arms around her, and from her peripheral vision Jules saw Cathy Kiplinger turn away in mild annoyance. Jules didn't blame her; girls hugged on a dime, taking any opportunity when emotion gathered in their throats. Like babies or kittens, girls wanted to be held. But maybe Cathy Kiplinger was annoyed because she was jealous.

Everyone wanted to be held by Ash, not even to evoke a sensual feeling but just to have been singled out. Cathy was sexy, but Ash was beloved.

That final morning of the 1974 camp season, Jules had flipped through Ash's copy of the Spirit-in-the-Woods spiral-bound yearbook that they'd each been given a day earlier. Like Jules's yearbook, Ash's was filled with intensely scrawled, sentimental comments from other campers. But while the comments in Jules's book were mostly along the lines of, "Jules, you were hilarious in that Albee play. And you turned out to be a HILARIOUS person in real life, which I would never have guessed! I hope you go on to do great things. Let's stay in touch! —Your friend and teepee mate, Jane Zell," Ash's were different. Several handsome boys admitted in Ash's yearbook that they had been quietly and desperately in love with Ash all summer. Though Ethan Figman knew very well that while he longed to be Jules Jacobson's boyfriend, he could accept just being her close friend. But several boys, unable to say anything to Ash directly, finally said it in her yearbook. The sentiment went along certain lines:

Dear Ash,
I know that you and I have barely spoken. You probably won't remember this, but

once when I was practicing my bassoon in the meadow, you walked by and called to me, "That sounds great, Jeff!" And I swear to God, it was as if my role in life was to be in that meadow in order for you to walk by. I know that we orchestra types aren't fast and witty like you theater types. Though here is a pretty good bassoon joke:

How are bassoons similar to lawsuits?

Everyone cheers when the case is closed.

Well, that's it. Before I leave this place I want you to know that I was totally in love with you all summer, even if it was only from across a meadow.

Fondly,
Jeff Kemp
(Jeff with the bassoon, not the other Jeff, the douche who plays trumpet)

Jeff Kemp would go back to his life and his school orchestra and his metal folding chairs on a concert stage, and endure the whole year without the love of Ash Wolf, and she would come to symbolize all that he loved about girls. Girls as advanced, superior beings. Girls as delicate as squab, but also so thoughtful and kind that you had to have one around you. Even Jules experienced a little of that with Ash. "I promise you," Ash said on that last day of camp, August 24, 1974, "I won't let you slip away."

It wasn't only Ash, her closest friend, who Jules needed; it was all of them, and the feeling she had when she was with them. But the actual sensation of being at camp was already being pried up and loosened. It had been a strange and remarkable summer for her, but the whole country would remember it too: a sitting president had *resigned,* and then vacated the White House while everyone watched. He'd waved to them as though he was departing after his own special summer. She couldn't stand leaving here now, and she felt herself begin to cry. In the distance, other cars arrived. Above all the voices, Jules could hear Ethan's; once again, just like on the day of arrival, he was at the center of everyone, helping other campers and parents, using his thick body to lift trunks and duffels and push them into the open backs of waiting cars. Jules wasn't the only one in tears. The shoulder of Ethan's Felix the Cat T-shirt stayed wet the entire day.

"I don't want to leave; I don't even want to go out there," Jules told Ash, but at that moment her mother and sister came inside the teepee; they hadn't knocked but had just boldly entered like a police raid, trailed by the counselor Gudrun Sigurdsdottir, who said, "Look who is here!" Gudrun's eyes were frankly sad.

Jules let herself be embraced by her mother, who seemed genuinely emotional and pleased to see her, though perhaps some of that was just spillover from the long, hard year of her husband's illness and death. Lois Jacobson had no idea that she was taking home a different person from the perm-haired, tentative, grieving goofball she'd dropped off here at the end of June.

"Make sure you have your toiletries," Lois said, and Jules was appalled by the word and pretended not to have heard her.

"I think Jules has everything," said Ash. "We all cleaned out the cubbies."

"Jules?" said Ellen, looking at her sister. "Why is she calling you that?"

"Everyone calls me that."

"No they don't. No one does. God, you're totally bitten up," Ellen said, taking Jules's arm and turning it over for examination. "How did you stand it?"

"I didn't even notice," said Jules, who had noticed but hadn't minded. The mosquitoes had come in and out through an accidentally swastika-shaped hole in her screen while she slept.

Now Jules and her mother and sister began to carry her belongings out to the car, but Ethan appeared before them suddenly and grabbed one end of her trunk. "I'm Ethan Figman. I'm your daughter's animation go-to guy, Mrs. Jacobson," he babbled absurdly.

"Is that so?" said Lois Jacobson.

"Indeed it is. Any pressing animation question that Jules has had over the summer, I've answered it. Like, for instance, she might ask me, 'Wasn't *Steamboat Willie* the first cartoon with sound, Ethan?' And I'd say, 'No, Jules, but it was one of the first cartoons with *synchronized* sound. Also, it was the first time the world ever got a glimpse of Mickey Mouse.' Anyway, my point is that I've been there for her. You raised a great girl."

"Shut *up,*" Jules whispered to him as they stood at the car. "You're just talking out of your ass, Ethan. Why are you doing this? You sound like a deranged person."

"What do you want me to say?" he whispered back. " 'I kissed your daughter repeatedly and tried to feel her up a little, Mrs. Jacobson, except she didn't like it, even though she's crazy about me too? So we tried and tried but it got us *nowhere*?' "

"You don't have to talk to my mother at all," she said harshly. "It's not important that she like you."

He looked at her intently. "Yes, it is."

Ethan's face was congested and expressive; all around them people called to him as they had done the first day of camp, when he wore the floppy denim hat that he no longer wore. "You look like Paddington Bear," Jules had said to him once about the hat.

"And that's bad?" he asked.

"Well, no, not *bad,*" she said, hesitating.

"You don't like the hat."

"I don't love it," she qualified. Always, she would be the one to tell him the truth, even when other people didn't. The hat made him look worse than usual, and she wanted him to have some dignity.

"If you don't love it, then I won't ever wear it again," he said. "It is already *gone.* It is dead to me."

"No, no, *wear* it," said Jules plaintively. "It's not my decision to tell you what you should or shouldn't wear."

But the hat never made another appearance, even though he'd been very fond of it before he'd met her. Criticizing how he dressed seemed inappropriate, and she was sorry she'd said anything, because offering an opinion suggested she had a claim over him, and it wasn't fair to determine his wardrobe when she didn't want him physically. He would continue on through life as a thick, slightly distorted, doggish-looking boy; and maybe one day, she thought, an equivalent girl would love him, and they would join forces as two homely, wild brains, sitting in bed with pens and pencils and chunky notebooks and gamy breaths. But she was not that girl.

Jules had already also said good-bye to Ash and Cathy and sweet, beautiful Jonah Bay with his guitar. "Jules," he'd said, taking her hands, "it is so great that you came here. See you soon, okay?" He hugged her, this enigmatic boy who she loved to look at but who she'd never once daydreamed about.

"Keep playing your guitar," she said inadequately. "You're so good."

"I don't know, we'll see," Jonah said, and he shrugged. Their friendship was even-tempered and not deep.

"See you, Jules," said Cathy when they said good-bye. "You did well here," she added, and then she looked past Jules to where two tall, blond, Valkyrian parents were getting out of a long black car. "I've got to go," Cathy Kiplinger said, hugging Jules quickly; Jules could feel Cathy's breasts push against her and then retreat as she went to greet her mother and father.

Goodman Wolf, to whom Jules had remained silently and stoically attracted all summer, had not sought Jules out even to say a quick good-bye, so she hadn't sought him out either. But now she wanted to see him one more time, and she strained to find him among all the campers who were on the lawn or lugging bags to cars in the parking lot. Everywhere she looked she saw a mass of crying and embracing people; they seemed to have all experienced a shared trauma. The Wunderlichs wandered among the crowd, telling everyone to work hard and have a good year, and reminding them that they would be together again next summer.

Jules stood looking all around. She picked

Goodman Wolf out from behind a screened window in the dining hall, in the now dark, shut-down room. Why was he in there, when everyone else was out here? "I'll just be a minute," Jules said to her sister.

"I'm not going to keep loading the car without you, *Julie,*" said Ellen. "I'm not your frigging maid."

"I know that, *Ellen.* I have to go see someone. I'll be back soon."

"I didn't even want to come today," Ellen added quietly, as if to herself. "Mom made me. She thought it would be *nice.*"

Jules turned around and went into the dining hall. The smells from breakfast had mostly faded, and would not return for a full year. Still now she could make out a trace of egg and some kind of natural cleaning fluid; but it was all muted and sad, dissipating quickly like skywriting, and the saddest part was the sight of Goodman Wolf sitting at a table by a window, his arms folded, his head half-leaning against the screen, as if in deep, moody thought. When Jules walked in, he looked up.

"Jacobson," he said. "What are you doing?"

"Everyone's leaving. I saw you and I wondered why you were in here."

"Oh," he said. "You know."

"No," she said. "I really don't."

Ash's brother lifted his head. "I go through this every summer," he said. "Today is the bad part."

"I somehow thought you'd be above it."

"It's obvious that what you *think* and what's *true* are different," Goodman said.

"I guess so," Jules said, not sure of what she was agreeing with.

Goodman's body was narrower and longer than at the beginning of the summer, his feet already too big for his very big sandals. He spilled out of every environment he was in. If he had gotten up and walked over to her then, taking her by her shoulders and bluntly laying her down on a tabletop beside the little metal rack with the tamari bottle and the salt shaker studded with rice grains, she would have done anything with him; she would have done it in daylight, with campers everywhere outside, some of them even looking in. As soon as Goodman lay with her on that tabletop, she would have gone into action, moving like one of the occasional sexualized figures in Figland, knowing exactly what to do because Ethan Figman, ironically, had been the one to teach her, both in his animated movies and in the sessions of kiss and stroke that they'd enacted in real life without any success, as far as she was concerned.

"Life is a harsh place," Goodman said. "At least, my life is. My parents think of me as this fuckup extraordinaire. I want to be an architect — a contemporary Frank Lloyd Wright, you know? But my dad tells me I

156

don't give it my *all*. What all? I'm sixteen. And just because I was asked to leave my last school. And because I'm not like Ash."

"That's not fair. No one's like Ash."

"You tell him that. I am constantly getting shit from him," said Goodman. "And my mom, she's a lot nicer about it, but she sort of goes along with him."

No one here criticized Goodman, as far as Jules knew. He strode freely around the grounds like some indulged, precious wildlife. Summers were apparently the best time for him. Here he could work on his little models of buildings and bridges; here he could get high and make out with girls and slide through a perfect, easy summer. Camp meant everything to him, and of course it meant everything to her too. For both of them, being here was better than being anywhere else. In this way they were oddly similar, though of course she wouldn't point it out, for he would have insisted it wasn't true. One day, eventually, Goodman would get serious and things would come together for him, not just here but out there too, she thought. "They shouldn't do that to you," Jules said. "You have so much to offer."

"You think so?" he said. "I suck as a student. I have no 'follow-through,' they tell me." He looked at her again. "You're a funny little person," he said after a moment. "A

157

funny little person who got inside the inner circle."

"What inner circle? Don't flatter yourself," she said, because it was a phrase girls sometimes said to boys who got obnoxious and needed to be put on warning.

Goodman just shrugged. "Shouldn't you be getting ready to leave or something?" he asked, seeming suddenly very sleepy, starting to retreat from her.

"Shouldn't *you*?" Jules said, and she came forward without waiting for an answer. She was aware now that the lit corridor behind her was probably illuminating the corona of what remained of her frizzled and rusty perm. Goodman was arrogant, and she allowed him the full display of his arrogance; it was a flaw in him, just as her own physical imperfections and gawkiness made up a flaw in her. But he was also full of possibility like his sister. His idyll was ending today, and she felt sorry for him, and sorry for herself, for her own idyll was ending too.

Jules reached out to give him a good-bye hug, the same way she'd hugged Jonah Bay, the same measured *level* of hug, but behind her she heard footsteps, and then her sister's voice said, "We've just been standing there while other people are driving away, Julie. Are you going to finish loading the car or not?"

Jules turned hard and saw Ellen and her

mother, both of them grossly backlit. Enraged, Jules said, "I *told* you, Ellen, I'll be right there."

"It *is* a big trip, Julie," her mother added, though her voice was gentle.

Goodman didn't even introduce himself. He just said, "See you, Jacobson," then clomped away in his buffalo sandals and went out the banging screen door. Immediately Jules heard cries of "There he is!" And, "Goodman, Robin has her stepmom's Polaroid and we want to get some pictures with you!" Jules never got to hug him. She never got to feel the press of the bony plate of his chest against herself. He wouldn't be around her and the others for too much longer, not that they could have known this — only, maybe, sensed it. Goodman was hard and arrogant but also, she now knew, vulnerable. He was the kind of boy who fell out of a tree or dove off a rock cliff and died at seventeen. He was the kind of boy to whom something would happen; it was unavoidable. She would never have the experience of feeling his chest against hers — what a meager desire, a *girl's* desire, the desire of "a funny little person" — though of course she would still be able to sense what it would have been like, for her imagination had been lit this summer, and now she could sense anything. She was clairvoyant. But her mother and sister, appearing doltishly in the doorway of the din-

ing hall at an exquisitely unfortunate moment, had kept her from having this actual
experience.

"Is that boy someone special to you?" her
mother carefully asked.

"Oh sure, *that's* likely," said Ellen.

Jules Jacobson cried so furiously in the moments before leaving camp that when she
finally got into the backseat of the car, she
could barely see. She had thought, in recent
days, that the summer had made her bigger
hearted — for now she was open to music of
the kind she would never have listened to
before, and difficult novels (Günter Grass —
or at least she was planning to read Günter
Grass) that she would never have read before,
and people of the sort she would otherwise
never have gotten to know. But in the back of
the green Dodge, slowly going over the barely
navigable dirt road that led to the main road
in Belknap, Jules wondered whether the summer had made her bigger hearted or just
meaner. She saw, as if for the first time, the
slight hump of fat on the back of her mother's
neck, as though it had been added there with
a putty knife. In the passenger mirror, when
Ellen pulled it down to look at herself, as she
did within seconds after getting into the car,
Jules noted the too-thin, surprised curve of
her sister's eyebrows, which created an
aesthetic that labeled Ellen Jacobson as

someone who would never have fit in at this camp.

Jules was neither bigger hearted now, nor meaner, she decided. She had gone away as Julie and was returning as Jules, a person who was *discerning*. And as a result she could not look at her mother and sister without understanding the truth of who they were. They had taken her away from the people she would dream about forever. They had taken her away from *this*. The car reached the main road and paused there, then her mother made a left and hit the gas. Gravel shot out from under the wheels as Jules was sped away from Spirit-in-the-Woods, like the victim of a silent but violent kidnapping.

The house on Cindy Drive was worse than when she'd left, but it was hard to say exactly why. She would leave her hot bedroom and go into the kitchen for a cold drink, passing the den where her sister and mother cracked pistachio nuts with their teeth like gunshots, and watched brain-dead TV shows. Jules grabbed a can of Tab from a fleet of them that her sister kept in the fridge, then closed herself in her bedroom again and called Ash in New York City.

You never knew who was going to answer the phone at the Wolfs' apartment. It might be Ash or Goodman or their mother, Betsy — never their father, Gil — or else it might be a family friend who was staying in the Labyrinth for an indefinite period of time. There, then, was the answer to a puzzle that had been laid before Jules when the name "the Labyrinth" had been casually mentioned at camp. Jules had thought maybe it referred to a private club. Instead, it was the building on Central Park West and 91st Street where the Wolf family lived. "Cerberus is our doorman," Ash had said, and it wasn't until Jules went to the Underhill Public Library to look up "Cerberus" in the encyclopedia that she even got the reference.

"Come into the city," Ash said.

"I will, I will." She could not admit her fear — that in the hard, school-year light of New York, the others would realize they'd made a mistake with her, and they would send her back to where she had come from, gently telling her they would call her soon.

"We're just hanging around the apartment all day," Ash said. "Our dad is hysterical about it; he says Goodman is undisciplined and will one day be unemployable. He says he wishes we'd both gone to banking camp. He told me I have to write a big play and make a fortune. My version of *A Raisin in the Sun.* The white version. He expects nothing less of me."

"We're all going to be unemployable," Jules said.

"So when are you coming?"

"Soon."

Sometimes at night Jules composed letters to Ash and Ethan and Jonah and Cathy and even to Goodman. The letters to Goodman, she realized, were highly flirtatious. When you wrote flirtatiously, you did not say what you felt; you did not write, *"Oh, Goodman, I know you're not entirely nice, and in fact you're sort of a dick, but despite everything, you are my heart's desire."* Instead, you wrote, *"Hey, it's Jacobson here. Your sister says I should come to the city, but I hear it's a SLUM."* How different this was, she thought, from the way Ethan had been with her. Ethan had said exactly what he felt; he hadn't tried to hide any of it. He had presented himself before her, letting her know that he was offering himself up, and did she want him? And when she'd said no, he hadn't pretended that this wasn't what he'd meant at all; he'd simply said, let's try again. So they had tried. And though at the end of the failed experiment there were no hard feelings, he'd finally admitted he would always be a little wounded by her rejection. "Just a tiny amount," he'd said. "It'll be like when you see someone who's had a war injury and now it's a million years later, but their foot still drags a little. Except in my case, you have to *know* about the injury in the first place in order to see it. But it will last my whole life."

163

"That isn't true," she said uncertainly.

She wrote Ethan a dutiful letter describing the awfulness of her days in Underhill, and he wrote back at once. His letter was covered with Figland figures. They danced, fished, jumped off buildings, and landed with stars over their heads but otherwise unhurt. They did everything but kiss and have sex. He would not draw those images in a letter to Jules, and because his cartoons often included a depiction of sexual activity, its absence here was notable. But, again, as with a very slight war injury, you had to know about it to see it, or in this case to see that it wasn't there.

"Dear Jules," Ethan Figman began, his handwriting thin and tiny and delicate, so different from the thick hand that held the pen.

I am sitting in my room overlooking Washington Square now, and it's 3 a.m. I'm going to describe my room for you so that you can experience the ambience for yourself. First, imagine the scent of Old Spice in the air, creating an atmosphere both mysterious and nautical. (Should I wear Canoe, like a certain person we know? Would that drive you wild?) Then imagine a room with bars on the window, because my dad and I live on the first floor of this crappy building (no, not ALL people from Spirit-in-the-Woods are rich!), and junkies like to wander around outside. My room is absurdly cluttered, and though I would like to tell you it's cluttered with the stuff of an *artiste,* it's actually filled with Ring Ding wrappers and *TV Guide*s and gym shorts: the kind of room that would make you want to run from me forever. *Oh wait, you've already done that.* (A JOKE!) I know you haven't run, exactly, though if I were drawing a cartoon of you, I'd certainly make your hair fly up, as if the wind was carrying you . . .

Carrying you "apart."

(By the way, you are so fucking right about "carrying you apart" making no sense as lyrics in "The Wind Will Carry You.")

All right, I am very very tired. My hand has been working all day (cue the jerking-off jokes) and it needs sleep, and so do I. Ash and Goodman want to get everyone together at their place for a reunion very soon. I miss you, Jules, and hope you're surviving the start of autumn in Underhill, which I hear is known for its fall foliage, and for you.

Love,
Ethan

P.S. A weird thing happened this week: I

was chosen for this dumb article in *Parade* magazine called "Teens to Watch Out For." The principal at Stuyvesant, my high school, told them about me. An interviewer and a photographer are coming to see me. I will have to commit ritual suicide when the article comes out.

They all met up in the city on the Saturday after the school year began; Jules took the Long Island Railroad train in, emerging from low-ceilinged Penn Station with a backpack strapped onto her as if she were going hiking. There they were, waiting for her on the wide steps of the main post office across the street — Ash, Goodman, Ethan, Jonah, and Cathy. Already there was a difference between her and them. She had her big bag with her, and a sweater tied around her waist, which suddenly struck her as a bad, senior-citizens-on-holiday type of choice. Her friends were in thin Indian cotton shirts and Levi's, carrying nothing because they lived here and didn't need to take their belongings with them like nomads wherever they went.

"You see?" said Ash. "You survived. And now we're all together again. We are *complete.*"

She said it so earnestly; she was a serious and faithful friend, never anything other than that. She wasn't funny, Jules thought then, God no. Over Ash's whole life, no one would

166

ever describe her as funny. They'd call her lovely, graceful, appealing, sensitive. Cathy Kiplinger wasn't funny either, but she was hard-edged, brassy, emotionally demanding. Jules had the funny-girl role all to herself in their group, and she felt relieved as she re-inhabited it again. Someone asked her how school was going, and Jules said her history class was studying the Russian Revolution. "Did you know that Trotsky was liquidated in Mexico?" she said, a little manic. "That's why you can't drink the water."

Ash slipped her arm through Jules's, and said, "Yes, you are definitely still you."

Ethan stood rocking a little bit, slightly nervous. His *Parade* magazine piece had just come out, and though it was really just a box on the bottom of a page, and featured a not too horrible photograph of Ethan with his curls falling into his eyes as he worked, his friends were merciless about the interview, in which he'd apparently said, in response to a question about why he had chosen animation over making comic strips, "If it doesn't move, it doesn't groove."

"Did you actually *say* that?" Jonah Bay wanted to know as they all had lunch at the Autopub in the GM Building, everyone sitting two by two in the chassis of actual cars, eating meals that were brought around by carhop waitresses. Distantly, an episode of *The Three Stooges* was projected on a wall, in an attempt to create a drive-in movie atmosphere. "No girl has ever liked the Three Stooges," Jules said to no one in particular.

"Yes, yes, I said it," Ethan said to Jonah miserably in the darkness.

"Why?" Jonah asked. "Didn't you know how it would sound? My mother always says that no matter how much control you think you have with a journalist, you really have none. She did that big interview with Ben Fong-Torres in *Rolling Stone* in 1970, and people still ask her about that one line about 'self-love.' She has to tell them again and again, 'It was taken completely out of context.' She was definitely not talking about masturbation but about, you know, self-esteem. It's not that journalists are necessarily trying to *get you.* It's just that they have their own agenda, which may not be in your best interest."

"*You* try being interviewed," said Ethan.

"No one will ever interview me," said Jonah, and it was true that unless he became a famous musician, which could easily happen if he wanted it to, his mildness made it easy to overlook him. His face, however, was unusually beautiful; someone could interview him about his face.

"I would love to be interviewed," said Goodman.

"What would they interview *you* about?" Cathy asked. "Your little Golden Gate Bridge made of popsicle sticks?"

"Just anything," he said.

"My guidance counselor came in the other day with pamphlets about careers," said Jules. "Now we have to think about becoming experts. We have to have a *field*." She thought for a second. "Do you think most people," she asked, "who do have a field, sort of stumbled into it? Or were they being shrewd when they decided to learn everything about butterflies or the Japanese parliament, because they knew it would make them stand out?"

"Most people aren't shrewd," Jonah said. "They don't think that way at all." But right then Jules ached for her own field too. No field had come to find her; theater didn't exactly count, for she wasn't brilliant at it. Still, she had loved being in the theater at camp, loved the moment when the cast of a play gathered around the director for notes. Each production resembled a floating island, and nothing at the time seemed more important than perfecting that island.

Ethan Figman was silent and respectful as they all rambled on about the fields they might or might not find or be found by. Ash, they agreed, could go the distance in her field, "but I have to know that I really want it," Ash said. Ethan had definitely found his own field, or it had found him, when he was younger and caught in the middle of his parents' bad marriage and lay in bed at night dreaming up an animated planet that existed in a shoe box under a little kid's bed. Though he'd said something inane to a reporter from *Parade* magazine, Jules thought that maybe Ethan was on his way to somewhere great, and none of them would be able to go there with him.

"Jonah has the curse of the famous person's son," said Goodman. Then he said, "I wish I had a famous mother too. I have to become famous on my own, and that's so much harder." They laughed, but Goodman's laziness was consistent, authentic. He wanted things done for him; he even wanted someone else to create his reputation. Ethan was the only one of them who was actually getting a reputation, and already it seemed to the others that he might ruin it.

On this day, they went from lunch straight down to the Village. Because this was during the golden age of weak, mellow marijuana, the fading days of thinking you could do what you wanted out in the open in the city, they shared a joint as they walked along 8th Street. They wandered in and out of bead stores and poster stores, and then they went uptown on the subway, emerging in a loose, noodling mass. Six abreast and taking up the width of the sidewalk, they headed along Central Park West to 91st Street, which was slightly too high up back in those days, though eventually all of Manhattan would unimaginably be colonized by the rich, and there would remain very few areas where you felt you could not walk. Together, now, they walked into the Labyrinth.

SIX

When he was eleven years old in 1970 and sitting backstage at the Newport Folk Festival, where his mother was one of the headliners, Jonah Bay happened to catch the eye of folksinger Barry Claimes, of the Whistlers. Barry Claimes had remained friends with Susannah since their affair in 1966, and they ran into each other frequently on the folk circuit. Susannah said she genuinely liked Barry; they hadn't ever really broken up, but had simply been involved and then not been involved. Barry had been to the Bays' loft on Watts Street frequently over the several months of their relationship, but he'd never shown all that much interest in Jonah, who at the time was a very quiet, dark-haired little boy, a miniature version of his mother, somber, always building with Lego, which could catch under your bare foot and leave deep marks in it.

But here in Newport, Jonah looked and behaved differently. Instead of just playing with Lego, he was becoming a musician, and he wandered around backstage at all the folk shows, playing whatever guitar happened to be available. "The kid's good," one of the roadies had observed to Barry, nodding toward Jonah, who was sitting and sweetly singing a weird little song he'd made up on the spot. In his high, preteen voice, Jonah sang:

"Because I am a piece of toast
You can bite me,
you can break me,
you can butter me,
you can take me . . ."

Then the lyrics and music ran out, and Jonah lost interest and put down the guitar. But Barry Claimes recognized that Susannah's son and his song fragment were delightful. Barry's own songwriting had always been forced. He was never going to be a good lyricist like Pete, one of the other Whistlers, who got all the credit for everything. Barry came over near Jonah and busied himself with a fancy, elaborate banjo riff, which naturally captured Jonah's attention. Over the next hour, the boy and the man sat together in the Whistlers' dressing room while the other members of the trio were elsewhere, and Barry gave Jonah a long, patient lesson on his banjo with the rainbow painted on the

173

surface, and offered him cubes of cheese and sliced fruit and brownies from catering. They became friends quickly. When Barry asked Susannah if he could borrow Jonah for a day, take him to the house that the Whistlers had rented in Newport and let him explore the bluffs, Susannah agreed. Barry was a decent guy, a "softie," people said. Jonah needed male companionship; he couldn't spend all his time around his mother.

The next morning, Barry Claimes picked Jonah up at the hotel and brought him to the estate that the Whistlers' manager had rented for the group. It looked out on the harbor, its minimal furniture was white wicker, and a housekeeper walked around putting lemon water in pitchers. They sat together in the solarium, and Barry said, "So why don't you mess around with the guitar and see what you come up with?"

"Mess around?"

"Yeah, you know. Play some stuff, like you were doing the other day. You came up with some really neat beginnings of songs."

Jonah said, in a formal voice, "I don't think I can do that again."

"Well, you'll never know if you don't try," said Barry.

Jonah sat for an hour with the guitar, while Barry sat in the corner observing him, but the scene was so peculiar that Jonah felt nervous and unable to come up with much of anything. "Not a problem," Barry kept saying. "You'll come back again tomorrow."

For some reason, Jonah did want to come back; no one other than his mother had ever paid this much attention to him before. Sitting in that living room again on the second day, Barry Claimes asked him, "You like gum?"

"Everybody likes gum."

"That's true. It sounds like a song you'd write. 'Everybody Likes Gum.' But there's a new kind. It's wild. You should try it."

He pulled a pack of ordinary-looking Clark's Teaberry gum from his pocket, and Jonah said, "Oh, I've had that kind before."

"This is a limited edition," said Barry. He handed a stick to Jonah, who unwrapped it and folded it into his mouth.

"It's bitter," said Jonah.

"Only at first."

"I don't think it's going to be very popular."

But the bitterness went away, and the gum was like all gum everywhere, putting you more in touch with your own saliva than you'd ever wanted to be. Barry said, "So. Guitar or banjo? Choose your poison."

"Guitar," said Jonah. "And you play banjo."

"I'll follow your lead, my lad," said Barry. He leaned back against the couch, watching Jonah as he painstakingly picked his way through the few new chords that his mother had taught him. Barry took his banjo and played along. This went on for half an hour, an hour, and at a certain point Jonah noticed that the walls of the room appeared to be going convex and concave, buckling but not collapsing. It was like a slow-motion earthquake, except there was no vibration attached to it. "Barry," he finally managed to say. "The walls."

Barry leaned forward eagerly. "What about them?"

"They're breathing."

Barry smiled in calm appreciation of Jonah's words. "They do that sometimes," he said. "Just enjoy it. You're a creative guy, Jonah. Tell me what you see, okay? Describe it for me. See, I've never been particularly good at describing my surroundings. It's one of my many failings. But you have clearly been born with the powers of description. You're very, very lucky."

Jonah, when he moved his hand, saw a dozen hands following it. He was going crazy, he knew. He was a little young to go crazy, but it happened to people. He had a cousin Thomas who had become a schizophrenic in high school. "Barry," said Jonah in a tortured voice. "I'm a schizophrenic."

"Schizophrenic, that's what you think? No, no, you're just a really visual and creative person, Jonah, that's all."

"But things look different to me. I wasn't feeling this way before and now I am."

"I'll take care of you," said Barry Claimes magnanimously, and he reached his large hand out to Jonah, who could do nothing but take it. Jonah was very afraid, but he also wanted to laugh and stare at the trails his fingers left in the air. When he felt the need to curl into a fetal position and rock for a while, Barry sat with him, smoking and patiently watching over him. "Look," said Barry at some point as the afternoon wore on in its bending way, "why don't you fiddle with the guitar again, maybe sing some more funny lyrics. That'll take your creative energy and put it to some use, my lad."

So Jonah began to play, and Barry encouraged him to sing. The words fell out of Jonah, and Barry thought they were great, and he went into another room and got a tape deck, put in a cassette, and let it roll. Jonah sang words, though most of them made no sense, but being called "my lad" was amusing, and so he began to sing in the voice of Barry Claimes.

"Go make me a peanut butter sandwich, my lad," he sang in an imitative melancholy brogue, and Barry said it was priceless.

This went on for nearly an hour, and Barry flipped the cassette tape to the other side. "Sing me something about Vietnam," said Barry.

"I don't know anything about Vietnam."

"Oh, sure you do. You know all about our

country's dirty war. Your mom has taken you to peace marches; I went with the two of you once, remember? You're like a mystic. A child mystic. Unspoiled."

Jonah closed his eyes and began to sing:

"Tell them you won't go, my lad
to the land of the worms and the dirty dirt
Tell them you won't go, my lad
'Cause you've got life to live right here on
    earth . . ."

Barry stared at him. "Where's this land you're singing about?"

"*You* know," said Jonah.

"You mean death? Jesus, you can do dark too. Not sure about 'dirty dirt,' though, but beggars can't be choosers. It's a strong concept, and even the melody's good. It could really become something." He reached out and lightly pinched Jonah's cheek. "Nice going, kid," he said, and he shut off the tape recorder with a snap.

But Jonah, though he was done playing guitar and writing words, continued to hallucinate for the rest of the day. If he stared at the butcher-block counter in the massive kitchen, the wood grain swam as if it were a whole colony of living things being looked at under a microscope. Wood grain swam and walls pulsed and a hand in motion left residue. It was exhausting being a schizophrenic, which he was still convinced he was. Jonah sat on the floor in the living room of the house with his head in his hands and began to cry.

Barry stood and stared at him, not sure of what to do. "Oh, *shit,*" muttered Barry.

Eventually the two other Whistlers wandered in, accompanied by a few groupies. "Who's the little guy?" asked a beautiful girl. She didn't appear to be older than sixteen, Jonah noticed, much closer to his own age than to the men's, but she was as unreachable as the rest of them. He was entirely alone. "He looks like he's zonked," she said.

"I'm a schizophrenic like my cousin!" Jonah confessed to her.

"Wow," said the girl. "Really? Oh, you poor little boy. Do you have a split personality?"

"What? No," said Barry. "That's something else. And he's not schizophrenic; he's just being dramatic. His mother is Susannah Bay," he added for emphasis, and the girl's eyes went wide. Barry came over to Jonah and sat beside him. "You'll be fine," the Whistler whispered. "I promise."

It was true that by the time Barry drove Jonah back, the hallucinations had quieted. All that remained was the occasional pale pink and green speckling on a white surface. Still, though, the hallucinations hovered, reminding Jonah that they might return at any time. "Barry, am I crazy?" he asked.

"No," said his mother's ex-boyfriend. "You're just very creative and full of wise ideas. We have a term for people like you: an old soul." He asked Jonah not to say anything to his mother about how he'd felt today. "You know the way mothers get," Barry said.

Jonah wouldn't tell her what had happened. He couldn't talk to her that way; she wasn't that kind of mother, and he wasn't that kind of son. She loved him and had always taken care of him, but her work made her happiest; he accepted this about her. It didn't even seem unnatural or wrong. Why shouldn't her work make her happier than a boy with needs? Her work *bent* to her needs. She had been born with an extraordinary voice, and her guitar playing was excellent too. Her songwriting was fine — not great, but the instrumentality of her voice lifted it up and made it seem great. When she sang, everyone listened with deep pleasure. The world Jonah had grown up in so far was one of early calls and vans filled with equipment and the occasional march on the National Mall in Washington, which by the time they arrived wasn't usually a march at all but simply just another enormous concert, held in the street. Someone was always leading Jonah up a freestanding metal stairway onto an airplane; he might accidentally leave his phonics workbook in a hotel suite, and another one would be sent to him in the next city. He

180

spent a great deal of time by himself, constructing little machines out of Lego and describing for himself what those machines could do.

Susannah Bay wrote a song about her son that became, if not exactly anthemic at the level of "The Wind Will Carry Us," then at least a generator of impressive royalties for the next couple of decades. "Boy Wandering" ended up putting Jonah through MIT. "I mean it *literally* is doing that," Jonah explained to his friends when they all went off to college. "There's a fund in my name at Merrill Lynch that we call 'Boy Wandering Money Market Fund,' and that's all I'll ever need for tuition and expenses."

If hallucinating with Barry Claimes had been a one-off in 1970, Jonah Bay supposed the experience might have been folded into a whole life of experiences. He might even have been proud of it in an odd way. But it seemed that for the following year, wherever Susannah was, the Whistlers were there too. They performed at the same folk festivals, and they shared stage after stage, and Barry sought out Jonah as if they were close friends. According to this legend, Jonah was desperate to learn the banjo; he said nothing to contradict it. He did learn the banjo, and his guitar technique improved too over that year, but between lessons he went to whatever house Barry and the Whistlers were staying in, and

181

each time he was there he soon found himself hallucinating, and sitting around writing fragments of little songs, which Barry dutifully taped. Once Jonah came up with an entire song about a character called the Selfish Shellfish, and Barry found this particularly hilarious. Off the top of his head, Jonah sang:

". . . And the ocean belongs to me, just me
I really don't want to share this sea
Maybe I'm really, really selfish
But selfishness is something that happens
    to shellfish . . ."

"The last two lines are a little artless," Barry said. "Selfishness doesn't 'happen' to someone. It's how they behave. Plus, you're squeezing too many words in there. And 'really, really' isn't a good idea in a song. But never mind, the concept is solid. A selfish shellfish who wants the whole ocean to himself! Oh, man, you're a genius, lad."

Barry never took Jonah back to his mother's hotel suite until he was himself again. "By which I mean," said Barry, "your regular-world self. Not your creatively inspired old-soul self, which I somehow seem to bring out in you." Never once did Jonah tell anyone about how he felt when he and Barry were alone for hours, and never once did anyone suspect anything unusual. Susannah herself said she was grateful that Jonah had a father

182

figure; his biological father, she'd told him when he was young, had been a one-night stand, a folk archivist from Boston named Arthur Widdicombe, whom she'd introduced to Jonah when he was six. Arthur was a solemn young man with a shabby jacket and a patrician face, as well as the same long-lashed eyes as his son. He gripped a bursting old briefcase stuffed with papers about the history of American folk music and political activism from Joe Hill on upward. Arthur had come to the Watts Street loft to visit them exactly once, smoking heavily and anxiously, and then when a reasonable amount of time had passed he charged out as if sprung from a taxing labor. "I think you must have spooked him," Susannah remarked after he suddenly left.

"What did I do?" Jonah had sat very quietly and respectfully throughout his biological father's visit. At his mother's urging he had offered Arthur Widdicombe a cup of haw-thorn tea.

"You existed," said his mother.

Sometimes after that day Arthur's name would come up, but not very often, and it wasn't as if Jonah pined for him. To say that Barry Claimes became a father figure was a wild overstatement — God knows it hadn't happened at all back when Barry was sleeping with Susannah — though maybe his relationship with Barry was more father-son than Jonah imagined, for he felt greatly ambivalent about Barry, which was the way most sons seemed to feel about their fathers. Only when those fathers were not on the premises could they be elevated and deified. Barry Claimes was kind of a pain in the ass. He was pushy, he was demanding, and when Jonah didn't feel like playing music into Barry's tape recorder, Barry sometimes got annoyed, or became cold, and then Jonah had to apologize and try to get Barry to pay attention to him again. "Look, look, I'm singing another song for you," Jonah would say, and he would grab the guitar or the banjo and make up something on the spot.

Somewhere around age twelve, it was as if Jonah Bay finally understood that what had been happening for a year whenever he saw Barry had been happening to *him*. He thought back on all those long days he'd spent with this member of the Whistlers in rented houses and hotel suites, "going creatively insane," as they had ended up calling it, and then sitting around for hours with Barry, writing dumb lyrics, becoming afraid, being soothed, pacing, feeling his jaw tighten, swimming in pools and in the ocean, and once eating a hamburger at a drive-through and feeling the burger pulse in his hands as though the chopped-up cow still somehow managed to have a heartbeat in its chopped-up heart. (This would be the last

184

time Jonah ever ate meat in his life.) All those sensations and behaviors weren't those of a schizophrenic, or a "creatively insane" person, or an old soul. They were, Jonah finally, *finally* knew — and it had taken him almost a full year to know this — the sensations and behaviors of a person under the influence.

Back home in New York City for a few unbroken weeks, Jonah walked to a bookstore on the Lower East Side. Grown men and women stood around looking at novels and art books and the *Partisan Review* and the *Evergreen Review.* Jonah went to the counter and nervously whispered to a sales clerk, "Do you have books about drugs?"

The clerk looked him over, smirking. "What are you, ten?"

"No."

"Drugs. You mean, like, psychotropics?" asked the clerk, whatever that meant, and Jonah took a gamble and said yes. The clerk walked him toward a section against the wall and pulled a book out from a tightly packed shelf, then pushed it against Jonah's chest. "Here's the bible, little buddy," he said.

That night, Jonah sat in bed reading *The Doors of Perception* by Aldous Huxley, and by the time he was only a quarter of the way through, he knew that he, like the author, had been experiencing the effects of hallucinogens, though in Jonah's case it was involuntary. He thought back to some of the different times he'd been to Barry Claimes's place, and he took out his math notebook and on a clean page made a list of the foods he could remember that he'd eaten when they were together — not during the creative insanity but in the period of time at the start of each visit, before the insanity began. He wrote:

1) a piece of Clark's Teaberry gum
2) a slice of pound cake
3) a bowl of Team cereal
4) NOTHING (?)
5) Another piece of Clark's Teaberry gum
6) Lipton's onion dip and potato chips
7) two Yodels
8) beef chili
9) C.T.G.* again

* C.T.G. = Clark's Teaberry gum

It all made sense, except for that fourth time. He was positive he'd had nothing to eat or drink that time, because he'd just gotten over a stomach flu. But what *had* happened that day? Jonah generally had a heightened ability to remember events that had taken place even months earlier, and he thought back to that afternoon of sitting around the house that the Whistlers had rented in Minneapolis. Barry had asked him to go mail a

186

letter. He'd handed it to Jonah and said, "Would you take this to the mailbox on the corner for me?"

But Jonah pointed out that there was no stamp, and so Barry said, "Oh, you've got a good eye," and went and handed Jonah a stamp. And what had happened then?

Jonah had licked it. This counted as eating something, didn't it? The stamp-licking had been *planned.* At age twelve Jonah looked back on the previous year of his life with the dreadful comprehension that over all that time he had been slowly fed drugs by a folksinger — *psychotropics* — and his mind had been stretched and distorted, his thoughts pushed into the mesh of a perceptual net whose shape had been changed by the hallucinogens Barry Claimes had been giving him for his own purposes. There were residual effects: moments when Jonah still woke up in the night thinking he was hallucinating. When he waved his hand across his field of vision, he could occasionally still see trails. He was on the edge of thinking his mind had been shattered for good, even though he wasn't schizophrenic, just fragile. Fragile and prone to seeing images that weren't quite there. Also, he had increasingly confused ideas about reality, which now seemed to him a not fully graspable thing.

So not long after that, when Jonah's mother wanted to take him to California, where she was to perform in the Golden Gate folk fest, he declined, saying he'd outgrown being a folksinger's kid walking around backstage with an all-access pass around his neck. He had thought this would be the end, but it was not. Barry Claimes called Jonah from the folk fest, because he still had Susannah's home number. "I was so disappointed not to give you another banjo lesson," said Barry on the long-distance call. Deep in the background came the sound of applause; Barry was phoning from backstage, and Jonah could imagine him taking off his aviator glasses and rubbing his watering blue eyes, then putting them on again, doing this half a dozen times.

"I have to go," Jonah told him.

"Who's on the phone?" asked Jonah's babysitter, coming into the room.

"Come on, don't do this, Jonah," Barry said. Jonah didn't say anything. "You are an extremely creative person, and I love being around your energy," Barry went on. "I thought you had an interesting time with me, too."

But Jonah just repeated that he had to go, then quickly hung up. Barry Claimes called him back a dozen times, and Jonah didn't realize that he could simply not answer. Each time the phone rang, Jonah answered. And each time, Barry Claimes said he cared about him, he missed him, he wanted to see him, Jonah was his favorite person, even including all the folksingers he had known — even including Susannah and Joan Baez and Pete Seeger and Richie Havens and Leonard Cohen. Jonah reminded him again that he had to go, and got off the phone, suddenly producing one of those horrible vomit burps that seem in danger of turning into actual vomiting but don't. The next day, Barry called three times, and the day after that he called twice, and the day after that, only once. Then Susannah returned from the road and Barry no longer called at all.

A few months later, Barry Claimes abruptly left the Whistlers and then struck out on his own with an album of political songs. The chorus of his one hit from that album was an antiwar ballad that was spoken more than sung:

"Tell them you won't go, my lad
to the land of the worms and the spaded
    dirt
Tell them you won't go, my lad
for you've got a life to live right here on
    earth."

The first time Jonah heard the song on the radio he said, "What?" but no one was in the room to hear him. "What?" he'd said again. "Dirty dirt" had been traded up for the superior term, "spaded dirt." Jonah didn't even know what "spaded" meant, but the

189

central ideas and the unusual melody of the song had been his, and then Barry Claimes had worked on it and structured it and made it into something of his own. There was no one Jonah could tell, no one he could complain to about the injustice. Certainly not his mother. His music had been stolen and his brain had been manipulated, and he was in skittish shape for a very long time, though he tried very hard to hide it. Sometimes at night he would see remnants of etchings in the ceiling, and he would lie awake and wait them out, relieved when the morning came and the room was again bland and normal. "Tell Them You Won't Go (My Lad)" had a bit of staying power near the middle and then the bottom of the charts; and whenever the song came on the radio, Jonah felt as if he were going to explode, but he kept himself carefully contained, riding it out. Finally the song disappeared, only to return many years later on every "best of the oldies" compilation album ever sold or given away during fund drives for public television; and eventually the acid flashbacks faded in frequency and intensity. One day Jonah was alarmed to see a pattern of menacing leaves and vines on a white wall, but then he realized that it was only wallpaper.

By the time they all entered Goodman and Ash Wolf's apartment building, the Labyrinth, in the fall of 1974, what was left of

Jonah's flashbacks had been tamped down to very, very occasional frequency, and his obsessive thoughts about Barry stealing ideas from him and almost liquefying his brain had also lessened. He had other things to think about now. He was in high school, he was in the world. Jonah had known, roughly since first grade, that he liked boys — liked thinking about them, liked "accidentally" touching them during games — but it wasn't until puberty that he allowed himself to recognize the meaning of that thinking and that touching. Still, he hadn't done anything yet with any boy, and he couldn't imagine how it would ever happen. He wasn't about to tell anyone his desires, not even his great friends from Spirit-in-the-Woods, and he thought he might well end up living a monkish life. His life also probably wouldn't involve music, even though he had been told repeatedly that he had the talent for a big career. His music had been taken from him, siphoned off by Barry Claimes's greed.

At Spirit-in-the-Woods Jonah often got high with his friends, but he did it defiantly, knowing that *he* was drugging himself, and no one else was doing it. And he didn't ever use hallucinogens. Until this summer, Jonah hadn't come upon Barry Claimes in a couple of years, and in that time Jonah had changed and lengthened. He'd let his dark hair grow very long, and since camp ended he'd begun to cultivate the vaguest start of a beard that he didn't quite know what to do with: Shave it? Ignore it? Shape it into a Fu Manchu? He gave himself a perfunctory glance in the mirror on the morning of the first casual Spirit-in-the-Woods reunion, and with a razor he scraped the skimpy thing off, like a cartographer erasing a land mass from a nascent map.

"Good," said his mother when he appeared in the kitchen area of the loft. "I wasn't going to say anything, but this is much better."

She was at home more frequently lately, sitting at the table with a cigarette and a newspaper and a sheaf of contracts. Susannah could still fill concert halls, though smaller ones. She was now sometimes booked in the auditorium upstairs, as opposed to the main stage. Lately she'd been playing the occasional suburban venue with expensive pots of fondue and two-drink minimums. Her audiences were aging more dramatically as the seventies ground on, becoming consumers of soothing foods and increasingly sophisticated wines; but of course Susannah was aging too. Jonah sometimes looked at his mother and saw that while she was still beautiful, with a physical appearance like no one else's mother, she no longer resembled the winsome hippie girl in the poncho he recalled from his early childhood. Jonah held a particular memory of sitting beside her on a tour bus during an overnight ride, his head leaning against her shoulder, the filaments of poncho wool brushing against his eyelids in the dim, sleeping bus. Like many female folksingers, Susannah Bay's power, which was sensual, gentle, intermittently political, had always seemed at least partially to reside in her hair. But now her long hair made her look a little old, and he was afraid she was going to get that middle-aged coven-member look cultivated by some older women with long hair.

Jonah was protective of her, even as she had never been particularly protective of him. He hadn't allowed her to protect him, hadn't told her what had happened with Barry Claimes, so what was she supposed to have done? Amazingly and horribly she remained friendly with Barry, and they occasionally appeared in folk shows together or went out to dinner in the city or on the road. Jonah couldn't believe he had to hear stories about Barry even now, after having been drugged and terrorized and robbed of his music by him for a full year in his childhood.

Since Jonah had begun spending those relieving summers at Spirit-in-the-Woods, he was determined to place his friends at the center of his thoughts, not that man. Summers in Belknap were extraordinary, as his mother had assured him they would be, but this year Susannah had shown up with *Barry,* for God's sake, and Jonah had been so furious he hadn't known what to do. He'd stormed off from the hill and headed back to his teepee, where he lay in the suffocating dark; luckily no one followed him there, though he supposed he hoped someone would — a boy, a comforting boy.

Now, Jonah and the others stood in a gold elevator car in the Labyrinth, rising. The Wolf parents' design taste was handsome, Jonah had always thought since the first time he'd gone over to Ash and Goodman's apartment two years earlier, though also heavy and effortful. The walls were painted deep and brooding colors, and there were various hassocks scattered around. The Wolfs' dog, a loping golden retriever called Noodge, nosed his way into the group, excited and needing attention, but was finally ignored by everyone. Ash and Goodman's parents were gone for the day to visit friends out at the beach, so Jonah and his friends spread out, commandeering different rooms. The Wolfs had a fine stereo system with enormous speakers, but Jonah wasn't impressed. In his mother's loft downtown, with the spare white walls and plain wood floors, the stereo system was sleek and Danish and far better than this one. If there was one thing Susannah Bay cared about, it was quality of sound. The Wolfs' stereo was just one among many high-end appliances. Jonah thought about how Ash and Goodman had been raised among a riot of objects. If either of them fell, they would be cushioned; everything they needed over the whole of their lives was here for them in the Labyrinth.

After eating snacks together in the living room now, they tacitly divided up into groups of two. By design, by default, the beautiful Jonah Bay found himself with the beautiful Ash Wolf, and because this was her home, she asked him if he wanted to see her room. He'd been in there many times before, but he felt that he would be seeing it in a different way now.

They sank down onto the swamp of her bed with all its slaughtered stuffed animals that were loosely and unevenly filled from all those years of having been loved by a young girl, then having been thrown around by a thoughtless adolescent and her friends. Jonah would have liked to sleep there with Ash and the animals, just sleep and sleep. But she was beside him on the bed, her heavy door closed, and honestly, though he felt no sexual pull toward her, Ash Wolf was like a strange and beautiful object. He had always liked looking at her, but it had never occurred to him to touch her. Now, though, he considered that touching her might not be a bad idea. They'd always been the pretty ones in the group; Goodman was incredible looking, of course, *Jesus,* but could not be described as pretty or fine-lined. Cathy, too, was so strongly female, so full; physically she was much more than pretty. Though Ash was a girl, Jonah thought it was possible that touching her might feel pleasant in the way that touching himself was.

"You have such amazing eyes, Jonah. Why didn't we do this in the summer?" Ash asked as he tentatively ran his hand along her arm. "We wasted valuable time."

"Yeah, it was a big mistake," he said, though it wasn't true. Touching her arm felt good, certainly, but there was no urgency attached to the swishing motion. They lay against each other, both of them hesitant.

"I like this so much," said Ash.

"Me too."

Did people in bed usually say things like "I like this so much?" and "Me too"? Or weren't they more likely to be utterly quiet and entranced, or else loud and chugging and apelike? Girls at camp and at parties at the Dalton School had kissed Jonah before, and he'd obligingly kissed them back, though in recent years he'd tried to picture boys when this happened, transforming a pretty girl's face into the face of a laughing, flexing boy. Girls tended to love him, and the previous summer at Spirit-in-the-Woods, he'd walked around holding hands with a blond pianist named Gabby. Jonah was good-natured about these pretty girls who developed crushes on him. Ash was simply the most extreme example of such a girl.

Love, he thought, should be as powerful as a drug. It should be like chewing a stick of laced Clark's Teaberry gum and then feeling your neurons blasting all around you. He remembered the specific moment each time when he'd felt as if he was going mad. He could pinpoint the exact fraction of a second when the drug had dropped over him. Jonah wanted a tiny bit of that feeling now — not too much, just a little — but instead he felt understimulated, a little bored, and safe.

In Ash Wolf's bed, the two friends kissed for a very long time. It was a marathon of kissing, not thrilling but certainly not bad, because Ash was like some kind of overgrown meadow. She seemed to be a walking version of her own bedroom, replete with hidden corners, surprises, and delights. Her saliva was thin and inoffensive. The sun dimmed over Central Park, and the afternoon fell away, and the kissing never revved up into anything beyond itself, which was actually fine with him.

Walking out of Ash's bedroom, still holding her hand, Jonah sensed that all of them had coupled up today in significant ways. Goodman and Cathy were off in Goodman's room, probably going very far together, perhaps going all the way. Goodman's door was closed, Ash announced now, having quickly gone down the hall to check. Jonah pictured the mess that was Goodman's room, the perennially unmade bed, the little half-finished and abandoned architectural models, the clothes he threw everywhere just because he could. The housekeeper Fernanda would be in first thing Monday morning, and she'd stand in the teen stink of Goodman's room, folding, smoothing, and disinfecting. Jonah suddenly pictured Goodman positioning himself between Cathy Kiplinger's sturdy legs, and the image disturbed him.

As for Jules and Ethan: where were *they*? By default the two homeliest of the group were probably off doing something lovelike too. He knew that they'd tried to be a couple over the course of the summer, though Ethan had finally said there was really nothing between them. "She's just my friend," he'd confided. "We're leaving it at that." "I hear you," Jonah had replied. As Jonah followed Ash down the hall into the living room, heading toward the kitchen to get something to drink after all that kissing, he heard a sound and turned. On the floor behind the couch, in an alcove of the large, overdressed living room, were Jules and Ethan. What were they doing? Not sex, not even kissing. They were playing the board game Trouble, which they'd dug up from the chest in the window seat that contained all the treasures of the Wolf family's game nights over the years: Trouble, Life, Monopoly, Scrabble, Battleship, and a couple of off-brand board games called Symbolgrams and Kaplooey!, which no one outside the Wolf family had ever heard of.

Ethan and Jules were deep into their game, their palms beating down on the plastic dome, which made that strangely satisfying *pock* sound. The game of Trouble was predicated on the idea that people liked the novelty of this sound. People wanted *novelty*. Sex was a novelty too; if Cathy Kiplinger gave a blow job to Goodman Wolf, at the end of it his dick might pop out of her mouth with a *pock* sound like the dome in Trouble being pushed. Jonah only made that connection now as he heard the sound and saw Ethan and Jules, this *non*-couple, sitting and playing the game with the contentment of two people who don't need to do anything physical and extreme. Song lyrics came into his head, unbidden:

"Now his dick popped out of the bubble
making a sound like the game of
    Trouble . . ."

Jonah imagined himself sitting with Barry Claimes and writing these stupid lyrics; he saw Barry listening intently, the wheels of his cassette tape turning. The image was sickening, and he tried to return to thoughts of Ash. He wondered if he'd graduated to being Ash Wolf's boyfriend now, and if so, what that would entail. He almost thought of being a boyfriend as like being a duke or an earl; it was as if he had *land* to oversee now, and ribbons to cut. Ash took his hand and led him past the board-game-playing couple, then into the kitchen where they drank glasses of New York City tap water, then down the hall past the probably-going-very-far couple, Goodman and Cathy, and finally into the den, a room filled with reeds jutting from ceramic urns, and low, cracked-leather couches.

"Let's lie down," Ash said.

"We've been lying down," said Jonah.

"I know, but we haven't been lying down in here. I want to try every couch and every bed with you."

"In the world?" he asked.

"Well, eventually. But we can start with this one."

He couldn't tell her that what he wanted now, more than anything, was to fall asleep beside her. No touching, no kissing, no stimulation. No sensation, no consciousness. Just the act of sleeping beside someone you liked to be with. Maybe that was love.

SEVEN

Of the many people who came to the apartment on the sixth floor of the Labyrinth and stayed a day or two or even longer, most were so pleased to feel wanted that they forgot to ask themselves if there was anywhere else they ought to be. Over the years, various people considered themselves honorary members of the Wolf family, believing briefly that being allowed to stay here as long as you liked was the same thing as being one of them. But no matter how many times Jules Jacobson walked into the foyer, greeted with wild enthusiasm by Noodge the dog, and then headed down the long hallway that was crowded with photographs of the Wolfs doing various Wolfish things, she never felt that she entirely belonged here, just as she had not belonged in that teepee on that first night. But no longer did she feel like an interloper.

Gil and Betsy Wolf didn't seem overly curious about their daughter's sudden closest friend, Jules, and when she stayed for dinner their questions to her were friendly if perfunctory ("Jules, have you ever tasted chicken saltimbocca before? No? Well, that's a crime"), but still Ash said she was always welcome. The place was a constant hub for Spirit-in-the-Woodsians. Jonah, who'd become Ash's first serious boyfriend since that day in September, was often here during the week and on weekends. Cathy, who had now officially become Goodman's girlfriend — also since that same day — kept a leotard in Goodman's bureau drawer, which seemed to Jules and Ash a spectacularly mature gesture. Cathy and Goodman fought a lot, and the words that came through the walls sounded like the argument of adults, not teenagers. "STOP TREATING ME LIKE GARBAGE, IT ISN'T FAIR!" Cathy would yell, but her rage would immediately be engulfed by tears.

"If you don't stop crying, then we are *through,*" Goodman would say in a tight, furious voice. Sometimes he suddenly told her to leave. Days would go by during which Cathy wouldn't hear from him at all, and she would call the Labyrinth, demanding to know where he'd been. Several times he told Ash to tell Cathy he wasn't home. "I just can't deal with her," he said to his sister.

Ethan came over to the Wolfs' whenever he could, though he was often at home making one of his cartoon shorts. His public-defender father, with whom he shared the cramped apartment in the Village since his mother had run off with the pediatrician, had allowed him to turn the dining room into an animation workspace, and so the table was covered with Ethan's work, and the plastic smell of cel paint was in the air. Ethan's family had very little money, he'd told Jules. Stuyvesant, the very good public high school he attended, was of course free. "Thank God for Stuy," Ethan said. Though the school was known as a powerhouse for math and science, the teachers respected Ethan's big talent and let him work on independent-study projects. He made funny cartoons that he sometimes screened to great reception at assembly. Ethan's life was busy and chaotic; his father's apartment was filthy, and he told Jules that he never wanted her to see it, which was fine with her, since she'd told him she never wanted any of them to see the house in Underhill — not because it was filthy, which it wasn't, but just because it was ordinary.

Since Jules had first gone to the Wolfs', all she had wanted was to find ways and excuses to get back there. But there were times when, for no good reason, her mother wouldn't allow her to go. It was as if Lois Jacobson knew she was in the process of gradually losing her younger daughter — had maybe already lost her. Jules expressed increasingly open contempt for her mother and sister. The Wolfs, however, were cosmopolitans, a cultured, lively family that celebrated everything. Ash and Goodman teased their pretty peahen of a mother about her pronunciation of the word *latke* around Chanukah.

"I can't help it," Betsy Wolf said. "I didn't grow up with the word. Your grandfather would have been quite upset to see me frying up a pan of these."

"Of these *what,* Mom?" Goodman goaded her.

"Lat-kees," she said, and the Wolfs all laughed. In honor of their mother's non-Jewishness they put up a "latke mistletoe" over the door at their Chanukah party: a single potato pancake dangling from a string, under which all guests might receive a kiss. Just the idea of a latke mistletoe, something jokey and indigenous to one particular family, was alien to Jules. She fell into a funk thinking of her own childhood, which in comparison withered like a latke on the vine.

The Wolfs could do no wrong; they were stylish in separate, distinct ways. Betsy, a Smith College graduate, was the aging New England glamorous type, strands of hair waving from her loose bun; Gil was the Drexel Burnham banker, though full of yearning. Ash was the tiny one who would go very far as an actress or playwright, and with whom everyone took great care. Goodman was the disturbingly charismatic boy who had no "follow-through" and who enraged his father and entertained other people with his seductive, erratic nature. He'd been kicked out of his traditional all-boys' school back in seventh grade, for cheating. "For cheating *openly*," Ash had clarified to Jules. The other boys had been so much more surreptitious than Goodman. Everything he did was big and blustery, performed with ill-advised flourish. "The pressure's always been on me to be the one who *doesn't* screw up," Ash explained to Jules. "The perfect, creative one. It's sort of a full-time job." But of course it seemed like a good job to Jules, to whom that whole family was so vivid and desirable.

"What is it you get from them?" her sister, Ellen, once asked when Jules was preparing to go into the city for the weekend.

"Everything," was the only answer.

Freshman year in college a few years later, living in a suite with that group of nasty girls and escaping one night to the dorm room of a boy named Seth Manzetti, of interest to her mostly for his satyr's head and slightly mossy body smell, Jules Jacobson had lain very still on his bed that was covered with velour sheets, and considered how, as of five minutes earlier, she was no longer a virgin. She quickly assessed that she didn't feel *at home* in this state, yet still wanted to be in it. Her thighs felt a little banged-up, and her nipples raged from the satyr's zealous attentions. But here in this state was where she would stay and where she would want to return and maybe sometimes live. Not with Seth Manzetti, to be sure, but in the beds and corridors of sex and love, adult love. Jules Jacobson wished that somehow she'd been able to *trick* Goodman Wolf into touching her in some sensual way that first summer, or even over the course of the following year and a half they all still had with him. A modestly homely girl should be allowed one such moment, just to know what she was missing, and then be able to move on. Not to have to long for it forever, wondering what it would have felt like.

The Wolf parents were party givers. Once in a while, Jules would enter the apartment on a weekend only to find Gil or Betsy standing in the foyer with a couple of party-rental people. "Jules, we were having a scintillating conversation about chairs," Gil once said. "Cousin Michelle on my wife's side is getting married here next month."

"Goodman can DJ!" called Ash from the living room, where she'd been sitting on the window seat with a notebook, curled up against Noodge's side, writing a play.

So Goodman was hired, and at the wedding he proved adept at spinning 45s and making suggestive patter. "This next song is for Michelle and Dan," he said, leaning in close to the microphone so that his voice was distorted. "Because tonight *is* going to be one of those nights spent in white satin. Until Dan . . . takes her satin . . . *off.*"

"Maybe you should go into radio," his mother said later, and the comment was meant to be helpful, but it also reflected his parents' anxiety that Goodman had no "real" talent yet. Yes, he wanted to be an architect, but you couldn't have an architect who carelessly forgets to include a girder. There was pressure for him to "get his act together," as his father often said. But why did he need to have a workable skill already? Jules wondered. Goodman at sixteen was an indifferent, restless student at his alternative high school. Standing behind the turntable at cousin Michelle's wedding allowed him to reclaim the power he had every summer at Spirit-in-the-Woods.

There was a New Year's Eve party held at the Labyrinth every year too, and the friends from camp attended. They snagged puff pastry canapés as they made their way around the room in the final hours of 1974, and Ash snatched up a cocktail shaker of martinis and brought it into Goodman's dark, slovenly bedroom. In a beanbag chair, Ash sat in her boyfriend Jonah's lap. Jules watched from a corner as Cathy Kiplinger leaned against Goodman on the bed with the pineapple-shaped finials, her mouth on his ear. *On his ear!* He, unperturbed, openly pleased, put his hand deep into Cathy's blond hair. Jules thought of how her own hair lacked the high silk content that boys like Goodman and all the men in the world apparently wanted. But Ethan hadn't seemed to want to put his hand in hair like that this summer. He'd only wanted Jules's hair, had only wanted Jules.

The two of them, Ethan and Jules, now sat together by default as midnight approached, and when the New Year officially arrived, Ethan Figman's lips were upon Jules's, and he could not resist seeing how much of a kiss he'd be allowed. Because it was New Year's Eve she didn't immediately draw back from him. The sensation wasn't too terrible this time, but she couldn't forget that this was Ethan, her friend. Ethan, who did not attract her. Finally, after a couple of seconds, she ducked away and said, "Ethan, what are we doing?"

"Nothing. That was a nostalgia kiss," he said. "It's sepia colored. People in that kiss are . . . wearing stovepipe hats . . . and children are rolling hoops down the street, and eating penny candy."

"Yeah, right," was all she could say, smiling.

Jules noticed that on the bed, Goodman seemed as if he wanted to *eat* Cathy, to absorb her into himself. But there was no similarly intense activity taking place between Ash and Jonah, who continued to kiss like two matching birds on a branch cooperatively passing a worm back and forth, beak to beak.

"Happy New Year, Jules the Great," Ethan Figman said, looking into her eyes.

"I'm not great," she said.

"I think you are."

"Why?" she couldn't help but ask. She wasn't trying to fish for compliments; she just wanted to understand.

"You're just so much yourself," he said with a shrug. "You're not all neurotic like some girls — watching what they eat all the time, or pretending to be a little less smart than a boy. You're ambitious, you're quick, you're really funny, and you're a good friend. And, of course, you're adorable." His arms went around her once again; and even though he understood that there might be a moment like this one every now and then, still nothing sexual or even romantic was ever going to happen between them. They were friends, just friends, though friendship counted for so much.

"I'm really not great," she persisted. "I have no greatness in me."

"Oh I think you do. It's just not show-offy. I like that. But you should let other people see it too," Ethan said, "not just me. Although," he added after a second, hoarsely, then clearing his throat, "once they see it, they'll snap you up, and I'll be sad."

Why was he so faithful to her, and to the idea of her? His fidelity made her want to be better than she really was: smarter, funnier, with broader range. *Be better,* she told herself sternly. *Be as good as he is.*

A little while later, Jules and Ethan got ready for sleep, lying side by side in the Wolfs' den on the white rug that appeared made of sheepdog. The fish tank threw carbonated light onto the books that lined all four walls, the names of the authors confirming that here was a home where thoughtful, intelligent, up-to-date people resided, people who read Mailer, Updike, Styron, Didion. Jules might have whispered to Ethan, "I'm very happy right now," but it would have sounded like a tease. She lay beside him, smiling, and he had to say, "What's so funny? Are you making fun of me?"

"No, of course not. I just feel content," she said carefully.

"That's an old person's word," said Ethan. "Maybe you used it because you're settling in to old age."

"I might be."

"Nineteen seventy-five. Doesn't that sound extremely old? Nineteen seventy-four was already pushing it. I liked nineteen seventy-two; that's the one for me," he said. "In answer to the question 'What year is it?' I feel like the answer should always be 'Nineteen seventy-two.' George McGovern, remember him?" Ethan said, sighing. "Good old George?"

"Do I remember him? I'm not brain damaged, Ethan."

"He just came and went. We put him up like idiots, and we got beaten down, and then time passed. Everything," he said with passion, "is going to move farther and farther away from what feels familiar. I read somewhere that most of the really intense feelings you'll ever feel take place right around our age. And everything that comes afterward is going to feel more and more diluted and disappointing."

"Oh, don't say that. It can't be true," Jules said. "We haven't even done anything yet. Not really."

"I know." They were both quiet and somber, considering this.

"But at least you're starting to," Jules said. "*Parade* magazine thinks so."

"I mean I haven't done anything, as in have *experience,*" he said. "Life experience."

"Oh, experience like Goodman has?" Jules asked, trying to make her voice sound dismissive, as though what she and Ethan had in their platonic friendship was far superior to the physical pleasures Goodman regularly received from and gave to Cathy Kiplinger. Her mouth on his ear. Her dancerly legs opening so his penis could find its rightful notch.

"Yes, all right, sex and other things. Emotional things," Ethan said. "Dark, dark moods."

"You are the least dark person I know," said Jules. Ethan was deep, and a worrier, but somehow he cheerfully adapted to all situations.

"But why do girls always want someone dark and moody?" Ethan asked. "I see a moody person in your future."

"Oh, you do?"

"Yes. While I sit at home with no food in my fridge, and my little cartoons, weeping over how the Democrats were crushed in seventy-two. Please send me postcards from out there in the world," Ethan said. "Mail them to the place where I will spend the rest of my solitary life."

"And where will that be?"

"Just address the postcards to 'Ethan Figman, Hollow Tree number six, Belknap, Massachusetts, 01263.' "

"That sounds nice," Jules said, and she pictured Ethan inside his hollow tree, making tea for himself in a kettle over a fire, wearing a quilted maroon satin robe. In this image he was transformed into some kind of C. S. Lewis furred woodland animal character who still bore Ethan's distinctive facial features.

"But what if things *don't* go well?" Ethan said. "At Spirit-in-the-Woods I've always been, you know, the weird-looking animation guy, the roly-poly joint roller, while everyone else understood that things essentially suck. *I* knew they sucked too. Watching the nightly news, sitting there with my dad with the TV on, eating Beefaroni. But you and I and everyone we know, we were just a little too young to actually see it up close. My Lai, all that horrible tragedy. We sort of fell between the cracks."

"Yes." It had hardly occurred to Jules to think about what it might be like not to have fallen between the cracks in the way he described. She hadn't known what it might feel like to be inside real drama. To do something important. To be *brave.* What an imponderable thought: bravery.

"I can't decide if that's good or bad," he said. "It's definitely good, in that we're not *dead.* I didn't die some pointless death in Hanoi, probably accidentally shooting myself with my own M16. On the other hand, it's bad that we missed out on experience. You know what I want?" Ethan said, suddenly sitting up in the dark den. Fluff clung to his hair from the rug, like a dusting of snow that had landed there when he'd briefly poked his head out from Hollow Tree number 6.

"Experience?" Jules said.

"Yeah, that too, but something else. This will sound pretentious," said Ethan, "but I want to not think about myself so much." He looked at her for a reaction.

"I'm not sure what you're saying."

"I want to not think so much about what *I*

213

want, and what *I* missed out on. I want to think about *other* things — other people, in other places even. I am so tired of all the little ironic in-jokes, and reciting lines from TV shows and movies and books. Everything from the . . . circumscribed world. I want an uncircumscribed world."

"And an uncircumcised world," Jules said, for no reason other than that it was the kind of thing they said to each other, calling it wit. It was exactly the kind of talk Ethan was saying he no longer wanted. "You can have that," she quickly said. "I'm sure you can have all of that."

"It'll be my New Year's resolution," he said. "So what's yours?"

"I have no idea."

"Well, let me know when you come up with one," said Ethan, and he yawned, his mouth so wide that she could see his many fillings.

Jules suspected that her resolution wouldn't be noble like his. She would want something that concerned herself and her own gratification. And then she suddenly knew what it was: she wanted to be loved by someone who was not Ethan Figman. The cruelty in this realization could knock her over, but she knew she wanted to be loved by someone and to *respond to* him, even if he was not worthy. Goodman would have been so perfect. She thought of his hand in Cathy Kiplinger's hair, and his mouth smeared with that other girl's colorless lip gloss. But Goodman Wolf was already taken, and in so many ways he was a horrible choice, not to mention the critical fact that he did not desire Jules, and would never desire her — and that was the most important element here: He needed to desire her too. She wished she could make Goodman do that this year, which would be the last full year that all of them would be together. Even not knowing that yet, she felt an intuitive urgency. What she wanted — and wanted now — was to be loved by someone who excited her. There was nothing wrong with that. But still it felt unkind to Ethan, and unfair.

In other rooms, the revelers were winding down. "I'm sorry to say that though I am really enjoying this conversation, I have to go to sleep," said Ethan, and he turned away from Jules, unaware of her secret resolution, giving her the curved wall of his back, which rose and fell into the morning and the true start of 1975.

Over that next year, the changes among them all were subtle instead of striking. Their faces became longer, their handwriting altered slightly, and their sleeping arrangements shifted. Jules's New Year's resolution did not come true, and she stayed absorbed in the relationship dramas of her friends, all of whom went to different schools in the city. In

Underhill, Jules sat in the classrooms of her enormous high school, looking out the window in what seemed to be the general direction of New York City. Ash and Jonah were no longer a couple, having broken up in late February, for reasons that were only vaguely explained to the others.

"I'm glad we had a relationship," Ash would say to Jules on the phone, "but now it's over. Of course it's sad, but I'm really busy, so it's probably just as well." Ash had written a one-woman play called *Both Ends,* which was about the life of Edna St. Vincent Millay. It had been performed at Talent Night at Brearley, her all-girls' school, and her friends had gone to see it. The auditorium went silent and attentive as Ash stood onstage in a nightgown, holding a single candle, and began to speak so deliberately quietly that everyone instinctively leaned forward so as not to miss a word. " 'My candle burns at both ends,' " she recited. " 'It will not last the night . . .' "

Jonah, since the breakup, had also been reticent about it, but this was more in keeping with his usual way of being. He'd gotten involved in the robotics club at Dalton, and though the other boys who stayed late in the science room with their mechanized creations were nothing like Jonah — none of them had had a girlfriend yet, and none of them would ever have a girlfriend like Ash unless they created her out of robot parts — he didn't mind, and actually felt serene among cogs and motors and batteries. In Jonah's reserve, his friends sensed great feeling; to them, Jonah and Ash had experienced a potent but fragile love.

A month later, Goodman and Cathy's breakup was as loud and difficult as Ash and Jonah's had been mild. The Wolf family had gone on vacation in March 1975 to Tortola in the British Virgin Islands, and on the soft white beach Goodman met a British girl who was staying at the hotel with her family. Jemma was pretty and sly, and at night Goodman went off with her after both sets of parents were asleep. He came back to the hotel suite once at two a.m. bearing a fresh hickey like a badge, and his father was furious. "We had no idea where you were," Gil Wolf said. "We thought you'd been *kidnapped.*" But they hadn't thought that at all.

Upon the Wolfs' departure from Tortola, Goodman sensed he wouldn't ever again see Jemma, the girl who spoke and looked like a sexier and more experienced Hayley Mills, but now he didn't want to go back to being the boyfriend of Cathy Kiplinger, who made so many demands on him. He bluntly broke up with Cathy the morning after his family returned home, and she cried and called him a lot to try and make him change his mind, and she required long phone calls and hasty meetings with Ash, Jules, Jonah, and Ethan, but still none of them were seriously worried about her.

Then there were a few weeks of social discomfort, and when they all got together on a weekend, either Cathy or Goodman would not appear. They tag-teamed each other in this manner for a while, until finally it seemed that they had both moved on and could bear being in each other's presence again. But unlike Jonah and Ash, who had simply returned to their previous friendship incarnation, Cathy and Goodman were now strained and strange when together.

Three months later in late June, back at Spirit-in-the-Woods again, the six of them resumed their summer formation full force, though Cathy Kiplinger showed up for their gatherings in Boys' Teepee 3 less and less frequently. "Where is she?" Goodman asked the other girls, and the answer was always, "Dancing." Cathy, finally recovered from Goodman, had returned to the dance studio, and despite her too-big breasts and too-wide hips, she still danced with great relief and strength. Her talent wasn't overlooked here, but was instead celebrated.

"Go get Cathy," Goodman told Ash one night as they all sat around Boys' Teepee 3. "Tell her that her presence is requested in this teepee."

"God, Goodman, why do you *care* if she's

218

here?" his sister asked.

"I just want everyone together again like we used to be," he said. "Come on, go get Cathy. Jacobson, see that she goes, okay?"

So Ash went off with Jules beside her, the mission feeling important and exciting. Already from down the path, music could be heard: Scott Joplin's saddest rag, "Solace." Through the unscreened window of the dance studio, the big blond girl was dancing with a tall black boy while a record spun. His name was Troy Mason; he was seventeen, and this was his first summer at Spirit-in-the-Woods. He was from the Bronx, here on scholarship like Jules, a quiet, strongly built dancer with a wide Afro, one of only five nonwhite kids at the camp. ("We must do more outreach," Manny Wunderlich said.) At lunch earlier that week Troy had mentioned that not only had he never eaten mung bean sprouts before, he had never heard of them. In response, Cathy had piled them on Troy's plate from the salad bar, and he'd loved them and wanted seconds. Now he was dancing with her to this mournful rag in a dreamy but disciplined way.

Jules and Ash stood at the window like orphans looking in on a feast. *Love.* That was what they were seeing. Neither of them had had it yet — not the beautiful Ash or the un-beautiful Jules. They were outside love, and Cathy was in. Her breasts would sink the possibility of her dancing professionally, but right now she didn't have to think about that at all. She had gotten over Goodman Wolf, that exciting but unmanageable figure, that disaster of a boyfriend, and had turned toward someone else. They couldn't bring her back to Boys' Teepee 3 tonight, and maybe not any other night either.

From their place in the blackberry bush in the dark, Ash whispered, "What am I supposed to tell my brother?"

In the late afternoon of the last full day of that second summer, Manny and Edie Wunderlich gathered everyone on the lawn. Some people assumed Susannah Bay was about to appear — she hadn't yet shown up at all — but Jonah told his friends that his mother wasn't coming this year. She was finishing a few tracks of an album, having signed with a new label after being rudely dropped by Elektra. This album wasn't even folk, really, but actually it had "a disco quality," Jonah said, keeping his voice as unjudgmental as possible. "Disco folk."

"Dolk," corrected Ethan.

The Wunderlichs had gathered everyone not to listen to Susannah Bay, and not to watch another president resign, but to have an aerial photograph taken with all the campers lying on the grass head to toe. "Your counselors will be walking around to help you get into position," Manny boomed to them through a megaphone. He looked ecstatic whenever he got a chance to address the entire camp. Beside him, Edie stood beaming. The Wunderlichs seemed like dinosaurs of the arts, and how could you not respect that? They had known people like Bob Dylan, who, in the early 1960s when he was a lamb-faced, milk-complexioned boy, had sat in their Greenwich Village apartment, sent there by Susannah Bay, a friend of his from the emerging folk scene. "Crash at Manny and Edie's," Susannah had apparently told him. "I used to teach guitar at their summer camp. They won't give you any grief." The young boy folksinger had shown up on the Wunderlichs' doorstep in a thin coat with the collar turned up and a hat that looked Cossack, and of course they'd had the generosity and foresight to let him in.

Now Manny Wunderlich stood with his wife on the lawn, explaining how all the campers were going to form letters of the alphabet with their bodies for the aerial photograph, spelling out *Spirit-in-the-Woods 1975.* The hyphens would be formed by the three youngest and shortest campers. It took more than an hour to get everyone curving the right way, and Manny and Edie walked around and made adjustments like the choreographers of a massive avant-garde performance.

Jules lay with the top of her head against

the bottoms of Ethan's cold bare feet; her own feet touched the big head of Goodman, and she felt with certainty that this was the closest she would ever in her life come to touching him. How pathetic it was that because she was a girl who looked the way she did, she would have to use her *feet,* and her feet only. For good measure she bent her toes, pressing down against the hard, masculine nut of Goodman's skull. And as she did, she could feel Ethan's feet pressing against her own head, for he too was getting in a surreptitious little foot feel, the only kind now permitted him.

As they all lay still, the sounds of an airplane churned in the sky, and then the twin engine came into view. The cook, Ida Steinberg, was up there with Dave, the groundskeeper, who had a pilot's license. Ida lifted the Nikon F2 and recorded the moment.

That night, at the farewell party in the rec hall, Cathy Kiplinger and Troy Mason held each other and danced to every number, slow or fast. The Rolling Stones played and Cream and the Kinks, with Goodman serving as DJ for the first hour. But the sight of Cathy being held by her dancer boyfriend was too much for Goodman, and he abruptly headed back to Boys' Teepee 3, where a hasty round of V&Ts were mixed, and Goodman knocked back a few drinks, with everyone else becoming respectfully silent, until he suddenly announced, as if bewildered by this realization, "I am totally plastered."

From outside the teepee came a particularly strong round beam of light, and behind it appeared the weaving teacher and lifeguard Gudrun Sigurdsdottir, with her hardy Icelandic flashlight, whose chunk of a battery would probably outlive them all. She came into the teepee, saying, "Relax, this is a friendly visit," and uncharacteristically sat down on one of the boys' beds, where, even more surprisingly, she lit up a cigarette. "Do not ever do what I'm doing," Gudrun told them after she took a drag. "First of all, the result of smoking — cancer — is proven. Then there is the safety issue. What is the expression: 'This place can be engulfed like a tinder-chamber'?"

"That's not an expression," Ethan said. "At least," he added politely, "not one that I've heard." They sat for a while, but after Gudrun put out her cigarette in a collapsible cup and said she should leave, they begged her to stay a little longer. She was twenty-eight years old, dark-blond-haired, slightly worn looking but subtly exotic. Jules wondered what it was like to be a bohemian in Reykjavik, and whether Gudrun felt alone there. No one had ever thought to ask the counselor anything about herself. She taught weaving and watched over the swimming pool here at a place where most people didn't exactly *swim*. In the mornings she gave diving lessons to a

223

motivated few, though the pool didn't have the most pristine surface. Leaves would collect, and in the unfurling mist right before the wake-up recording of Haydn's *Surprise* Symphony that was played at seven a.m. each day, Gudrun Sigurdsdottir could be seen at poolside with a net, skimming the surface for all the dropped bits of nature and the dead or doomed frogs that had haplessly seaplaned there overnight.

"Gudrun, tell me something," the very drunk Goodman said. "Why do you think women act the way they do? Being all needy and then getting you completely drawn in, then screwing things up. Doing this little back and forth with you. Why are relationships so fucked up? Does it ever change? Is it different in Denmark?"

"I am not from Denmark, Goodman."

"Of course you're not. I knew that. I was just wondering if you knew how it was in Denmark."

"Nice save, Wolf," said Ethan.

"What are you asking me exactly?" Gudrun said. "Why do I think the problems between the men and women of the world are the way they are today? You want to know whether the problems that you teenagers feel — will they follow you over the rest of your lives? Will your hearts always be aching? Is that what you are asking me?"

Goodman shifted in discomfort. "Something like that," he said.

"Yes," said the counselor in a suddenly plangent voice. "Always they will be aching. I wish I could tell you something else, but I wouldn't be telling the truth. My wise and gentle friends, this is the way it will be from now on."

No one could say anything. "We are so, so fucked," Jules finally said, wanting to assert herself and make sure she remained essential to these people. Already, she couldn't ever imagine being without them.

The last night of camp grew cold, and when the rain began to batter the slanted wood of the boys' teepee, the girls inside made a run for it, heads down. They wanted beds and warmth; they wanted the summer not to be over, but it was.

Back in the city, Goodman remained bitter and never entirely sobered up. When the school year began, he drank on weekday afternoons, alarming his parents, who sent him to see a highly recommended psychoanalyst. "Goodman said that Dr. Spilka wants him to tell him everything," Ash said to Jules. "He wants him to tell him what, quote, 'sexual intercourse' with Cathy was like. My parents are paying sixty dollars an hour for this; have you ever heard of anyone paying that much for a shrink?"

Over the school year, during constant,

urgent visits to the city, Jules tracked Goodman's increase in surliness. One weekend in November they all returned to the Autopub, and this time Cathy brought her boyfriend, Troy, with her. They sat together in an antique Ford, making out while the Marx Brothers played. Goodman sat in his own car beside his sister, slouched down as he watched Cathy and Troy from behind.

"Goodman is being very difficult, even for Goodman," Ash said quietly to Jules as they all stood on the subway platform afterward; they stayed slightly apart from the others so they could talk. "It's been, what, eight months since he and Cathy broke up. That's enough already. You know, he keeps vodka in his work boot in his closet."

"Just poured into it?"

"I mean in a flask in his boot. Not sloshing around loose, Jules."

"Why should he be so upset?" Jules asked. "He's the one who broke up with *her.*"

"No idea."

"I like Cathy."

"I like her too," Ash said. "I just don't like what it's all done to my brother."

"She really seems in love with Troy," said Jules. "Imagine getting to see a male dancer naked every night. That would really be something. Seeing his . . . *loins.*" The two girls laughed like conspirators.

"And then you could go to your psychoanalyst the next day," Jules said, "and lie down on the couch and tell him all about what *sexual intercourse* was like. He probably wants to hear about it because he's never tried it himself."

"Jonah and I almost did it, you know," Ash suddenly said. "The deed." She raised her chin toward Jonah, who was up ahead on the platform talking to Goodman.

"Really? You never told me this." Jules was shocked at not having known; usually, she knew so much about Ash.

"I didn't feel I could talk about it at the time. He brought along a Trojan; I'd asked him to, I was curious — but he wanted me to do everything, and of course *I* didn't know what I was doing. We needed guidance, and we didn't have it. Neither of us was willing to take the lead." Then she added, "So we went to see an X-rated movie for inspiration."

"You did? Which one?"

"*Behind the Green Door.* A revival was playing at this really creepy theater, and I can't even believe they let us in. Guess how many lines Marilyn Chambers has in that movie."

"Twelve."

"*Zero.* She never speaks. She just has all kinds of sex, and she lets people do things to her, insert things into her. It's disgusting and sexist. I swear, I'm going to devote my life to being a feminist. Jonah and I watched it together, and it was like a nightmare, but the thing I couldn't get away from is that even though it was a movie, and it was all so fake, and these actors were being paid to be in it, and probably in real life they were all heroin addicts or something — they actually seemed *into* it. I think Jonah and I both had the same thought, which was that what was happening in *Behind the Green Door* was much more intense than what *we'd* ever done. It was really nice, Jonah and me, I'm not saying it wasn't. But we didn't exactly go together. We weren't Cathy and Troy. Jonah's so hard to read; it's like he's standing behind a screen door all the time. Get it? A *screen* door, not a *green* door."

"I'm sorry, Ash," Jules said. "It's sort of like me and Ethan. Not meant to be."

Back at the Labyrinth, Goodman went into the closet in his bedroom, reached into his work boot, pulled out the Smirnoff, and soon he became hot-faced, sloppy, and unpleasant. At the end of the afternoon the Wolf parents came home from a concert in the Brooklyn Botanic Garden. Betsy's hair had been gathering a slight frosting of silver lately; she was now forty-five years old. "The music was terrific," said Gil. "All Brahms. It made me think how talented some people are. True talent is extraordinary. Ash has it, and I can't wait to see what she does with it."

"Don't hold your breath, Dad," Ash said.

"Oh, I won't need to, my girl," said her

father. "You're on your way with your plays and all that. *Both Ends* was wonderful. You're going to be very big one day."

"As opposed to your *boy,*" Goodman muttered, "who is on his way to nowhere."

Glowering, inebriated, Goodman regarded them from one of the flowing-upholstered sofas in the middle of the room where everyone always collected. Ash went to her room; Gil walked down the hall. Betsy drifted off to the kitchen to start a Bolognese sauce, and Ethan followed.

"Ethan," Betsy said, "be my *sous-chef.* You can do the onion, and tell me what's new in that cartoon world of yours. Hanna-Barbera," she added vaguely.

"Pardon?"

"Isn't that those cartoon people? That's the extent of my knowledge," she explained.

"Oh, I see," he said. He turned to Jules on his way into the kitchen and said, "Join us."

As Jules followed, walking past Goodman who was still sprawled on the couch, he suddenly reached up and grabbed her wrist. Startled, she looked down, and Goodman said to her, "You know what? You're all right, Jacobson." He continued to hold her wrist, so she didn't move. Ethan was already banging around in the kitchen with Betsy; Jules and Goodman were alone here. The only other time they had been alone was the summer before last, in the dining hall on the final day of camp, and they'd been interrupted by her mother and sister. Here was a chance to make up for that interruption.

Goodman stood and brought his enormous rock of a face close to hers, creating in Jules a deep sense of panic. But it wasn't *disgust* panic, as she'd felt with Ethan originally in the animation shed. It was *arousal;* yes, this was the real thing, as distinctive as a giraffe or a flamingo. Even though Goodman was drunk, even though he'd never shown her any interest before, she was aroused by him, nearly to the point of twitching. She couldn't even try to imagine what it might be like to see Goodman Wolf in full flower, behind the green door.

Because no one else was here, and his head was right in front of hers, Jules instinctively closed her eyes and let her mouth open. Then Goodman's unfamiliar mouth was against hers, opening too. The tip of Jules's tongue came forth like a little plant shoot against Goodman's tongue, and both tongues engaged in that silent, strange mime that apparently everyone's tongues knew how to do. Jules heard herself groan; she couldn't believe she hadn't stopped herself from making a sound. The delirium of the kiss continued for another moment until, suddenly, Goodman's mouth closed and he backed away from her, the way she had backed away from Ethan. When she looked at him she saw that he was already thinking about something or someone else. He'd gotten *bored* in the middle of this kiss that had been so exciting to her.

"All right, you had your kicks," Goodman said. "Go help with dinner."

"Don't be an asshole," she said, to which he reached out and messed up her hair.

Then, soon, everything, the six of them, was over. Or if not over, then changed into something so different from what it had originally been as to be unrecognizable. Jules never got a chance to pause and watch this exquisite part of her life recede, then grieve for it. On her second New Year's Eve with them, the New Year's Eve that was to begin the endlessly promoted bicentennial year, taxis pulled up in front of the Labyrinth all evening, and the doormen sent everyone to the correct elevators. Many of the buttons in the south elevator were lit up to signal for the various floors, and the door slid open upon party after party. Nineteen seventy-five was ending, one more year in a sequence of shameful years. In his cartoons, Ethan had inserted the U.S. failure and military retreat from Vietnam. His animated figures literally limped home, whimpering and saying *"owwww"* in Ethan's distinctive voice.

On 3, the Veech party was dominated by the family's college-aged children and their friends; a sirocco of pot smoke swept toward

231

the elevator when the doors opened. Up on 6, Jules Jacobson and Ethan Figman walked together into the Wolfs' apartment, which had been dotted with red, white, and blue touches, and where loose-limbed Herbie Hancock music was playing — the finger-snapping music of aging dads. Deep in the living room, dressed in a long, lavender fairy dress, Ash was politely listening to her mother's oldest friend. "Of course, you girls don't need to go to single-sex colleges anymore, like we did," said Celeste Peddy, already more talkative than usual from two glasses of champagne. "Your mom and I lived in the same house at Smith, but I imagine that when it's time for you to go to college, a girl like you, complete catnip, will want boys around as distractions, especially after having put in all this time in the absolute nunnery of Brearley."

Ash smiled politely. "Yes, I'll definitely want a coed school," she said.

"And no more M.R.S. degrees, thank God," said Celeste Peddy with a battering little laugh. "That was what we all got, and we lived to regret it. But now everything's different. Gloria Steinem — a Smithie too, I might add."

"I know," said Ash. "She's amazing. I plan on getting involved in the women's movement in college. It's a cause I really believe in."

"Good for you," said Celeste, looking her over. "We need women who look like you and Gloria Steinem. We can't just have those dumpy bull dykes representing the cause. Oh," she said, "listen to me, talking like this. What's wrong with me?" She put a hand to her mouth and laughed. "I guess I'm a little drunk."

When Ash saw Jules and Ethan approach, she popped up and made excuses to her mother's friend. "Come on, let's go," Ash whispered to Jules. "Celeste Peddy is starting to reveal her true self." They all slipped from the living room and made their way down the hall to Ash's room, which had lately become overgrown with prisms, stuffed animals, theater posters, and a generalized spray of dog hair. By ten-thirty, Goodman was already drunk.

"Where's your boyfriend?" Goodman asked Cathy when she showed up alone. Though they all knew it was strange having her there, it would've been stranger not having her there. Cathy explained that Troy was off dancing that night at a black-tie benefit his dance program was putting on to raise money for arts in the public schools. Here was Cathy, self-consciously alone on New Year's Eve but trying to appear casual, dressed in a black Indian-print blouse with tiny mirrors speckling the front. Tonight Jules wore a peasant blouse and a peasant skirt — "appropriate, in this crowd, in which I'm the peasant," she'd said to Ethan.

Jonah came wearing an old tuxedo shirt that he'd found at a vintage clothing store, and Jules had the thought again that he was unavailable, inscrutable, and she wished she could say to him, "What's the *deal* with you, Jonah?" Tonight he had brought a water pipe he'd found in the corner of his mother's loft; one of her musician friends had left it behind. "This is my contribution to the evening," Jonah said, showing off the long violet glass pipe and the small lump of hash that he'd found inside the bowl. They all smoked and sucked and burbled, and Jules became so high that it took her a while to realize that eventually Jonah, Cathy, and Goodman were gone from the room.

"Where'd they go?" she asked, but Ethan and Ash were also too high to really hear her or pay attention. She sank back against the pile of stuffed animals, then picked one up, an ancient, pale purple unicorn, and held it to her face, noticing that it smelled distinctly like Ash.

Jonah reappeared a little later, and Jules asked him where he'd been. "I helped our friends get a cab," he said with a smile.

"What do you mean?"

"Goodman and Cathy. They said they had a secret adventure planned. They were really stoned, and afraid they'd have trouble getting a cab on their own. I have no idea of what a 'secret adventure' meant, and I don't want to know." He fell onto the bed, that place where he used to lie with Ash, and closed his eyes with their startlingly long lashes, and within seconds he appeared to be asleep.

When midnight was about to arrive, Dick Clark, still nearly as boyish and box-headed as ever, began his New Year's countdown with Average White Band on the bandstand in Times Square. Ash, Ethan, Jonah, and Jules sat watching it on TV, and as the ball fell, the boys chastely kissed the girls in turn. The kisses made Jules wonder where Goodman and Cathy were right now and what their adventure was. She felt a low-level jealousy about it and hoped, somehow, that it was a disappointment to them both.

"God, I'm high," said Ash. "I don't like the way I feel." It took almost nothing for Ash to get too high; she weighed so little, and she felt everything strongly and immediately.

When Ash's pink Princess phone ("My *ironic* Princess phone," she'd insisted, "bought when I was twelve, okay?") rang just before one a.m., Ethan reached over and grabbed it. "Wolf house," he said. "The wolves are being fed right now. We give them little bits of Red Riding Hood, lightly seasoned. May I take a message?" But then Ethan said, "Goodman? What? *Jesus.*" He motioned for everyone to be quiet, and when

235

they wouldn't, he called out for them to shut up. Jonah turned off the record player, the needle skidding to a warping stop, and they all watched Ethan, who looked stricken as he listened into the phone. "You're not fucking with me, right?" he finally said. "I mean, is she okay? *What?* All right, hang on, I'll get them." Ethan pressed the receiver to his chest and said to Ash, "Go tell your parents to pick up the phone. Your brother's been arrested."

"What?" Ash said.

"Ash, just go *tell* them."

"But what did he do?" Her voice rose, and her hands flapped in the air.

"Cathy said he raped her."

"That's insane."

"Go! Get your parents on the phone!" Ethan said. "This is that one phone call they give you."

Ash ran from the room and down the hall, tearing through the mess of adults. Soon the Wolfs were on the line, and Ethan quietly hung up Ash's extension. "From what I could tell, they asked the cab to take them to Tavern on the Green," Ethan explained to everyone.

"That was the adventure?" said Jonah, agitated. "Tavern on the Green?"

"Yeah," said Ethan. "Apparently they wanted to see if they could sneak in to the New Year's Eve party there and score some hors d'oeuvres and champagne. I think Cathy said it would be impossible, they'd get thrown

236

out, and Goodman said no they wouldn't. And I guess it was so hectic at the hostess's station that they actually got in unnoticed. So they grabbed a couple of glasses of champagne off a tray and slipped down a hall and into a storage room. They started, you know, fooling around, Goodman said, and then something happened. He says it was a total misunderstanding. But I guess people heard Cathy screaming, and the police were there in about a second, and Cathy told them he raped her, so they arrested him. They took her to the hospital for an exam and everything."

"Oh my God," said Jonah, his hands to his head. "I got them the cab."

"So? That's irrelevant. It's not your fault," Jules said. "You didn't know what would happen."

"But it is my fault," he insisted. "And I brought the hash too. It's way stronger than our usual shit." He looked searchingly at his friends. "I *drugged* them both," he said. "It's completely my fault."

"Jonah," said Ethan, "quit it right now. I don't know why you're being so weird. So you got them a cab. Big deal. So you brought the hash. We've all been getting high together since the minute we met each other. You didn't *drug* anyone; what an odd way to put it. And Goodman has basically been fucked up all year. This isn't about you or anything you did, okay?"

"Okay," Jonah said quietly, but he looked shaken and ill.

"The thing is," said Jules, and then she let her voice trail off. "Oh, nothing."

"You can say it," said Ethan.

They were each thinking as hard and fast as they could, even Jonah, who seemed to be struggling to climb out of his guilt; so Jules carefully asked, "Is there any chance? I hate to ask it, but, you know, it's there, right?"

Neither boy said anything, then Ethan said, "Goodman says he didn't do anything wrong. But is he capable of it? Am *I*?" he added.

They were all quiet again, stewing. "He does get into these little rages," Jonah said. "But I always thought they were just bad moods."

"His hostile side is only one part of him," said Jules. "Boy," she added, "Ash would not like this conversation at all." They looked toward the door nervously.

"But what about Cathy?" Ethan said. "If it isn't true, why would she say it? Is she really still that pissed off because he broke up with her?"

"She did lose her shit when they broke up," said Jonah. "But she's the kind of girl who loses her shit a lot."

They all nodded. Cathy Kiplinger was the first needy girl any of them had known well. What was it about needy girls? Jules wondered. They felt that they had the *right* to be needy, because they knew that other people would be interested in — although annoyed at — their needs. Jules had never felt entitled to take nearly as much as those girls did. They got all the attention. Boys turned their focus toward them, and messy situations resulted.

I will never be in a profoundly messy situation with a boy, Jules Jacobson thought with an unaccountable little burst of despair. I will never get that kind of attention. No matter what I do, the only attention I will receive will be from faithful, dogged Ethan Figman, who will love me until the day I die, and then even afterward.

She saw herself as a pile of underground bones laced and encircled with worms, while aboveground Ethan knelt in the grass and cried. The next image that appeared, of Cathy lying on the floor of a storage room in a restaurant that glittered like a disco ball, was somehow irritating now too. Why do girls like that always *get* things? Maybe Cathy was lying. Maybe she had to lie to keep everyone interested. It wasn't enough that she had breasts like Marilyn Chambers and the face of a woman of experience. Everyone would continue to give Cathy Kiplinger all the attention she could ever want. Even right this minute she was probably getting attention from doctors and nurses and police officers and from her parents. All of them would be huddled behind a curtain in the ER, talking to Cathy in gentle but inquisitive voices.

Jules realized that it had grown quiet out in the living room. The party was breaking up; the Wolfs were sending their guests home. The bedroom door opened then and Ash stood with her father right behind her. "We're going down to the precinct," Ash said. "I personally think it's fine if you all wait here, but my parents say you have to leave."

"We'll come with you," Ethan said.

"No," said Gil. "Absolutely not."

"Some of us can go see Cathy," Ethan said. "We can split up."

"We don't even know where Cathy is," said Ash.

"You didn't ask what hospital?"

"No, I didn't think of it."

"Then we'll find out later," Jonah said. "But we'll all go to the police station now. We want to come," he said with emphasis and anxiety. "We really, really do."

"No, kids, it's just not a good idea," said Gil Wolf.

"Dad, I need them there, okay?" said Ash. "They're my *friends.*" She looked at her father with a tortured expression. "Please, Dad," she said. *"Please."*

Her father paused; Ash held her expression and would not budge. "All right," he said. "But hurry up, all of you."

They got themselves together quickly. In the chaos no one gave much thought to how they would appear to the police when they showed up smelling of pot and alcohol. They filed out grimly, but animated by fear and excitement too, and found their coats on the rack in the hall. The other coats were all gone, except for one lonely London Fog raincoat, which belonged to a junior colleague of Gil's from Drexel Burnham, who was passed out in the guest room.

"I really hope Cathy's all right," Ethan said to Ash as they waited for the elevator. "Do you know if anyone talked to her?"

"No idea," Ash said. "Why would she say Goodman did this? It's clearly bullshit."

No one said anything to support or contradict this; out of nervousness Jules reached out and ran her hand along the gift-wrap-striped wallpaper that lined the hall. "We'll get it all sorted out," Gil said to his wife. "I'm calling Dick Peddy to step in as counsel. He was just here ten minutes ago; I should have grabbed him then." He paused and shook his head. "Goodman couldn't stay *in,* could he? Had to go off somewhere. Just like on Tortola."

Jonah turned to Jules and mouthed something. "What?" she said, and he mouthed the words again: *"I drugged them."*

"Stop it, Jonah," she hissed at him.

Outside the building, the Wolfs climbed into

a taxi that was already waiting. Jules, Ethan, and Jonah stood in front of the Labyrinth in the same spot where, a couple of hours earlier, a fleet of partygoers had arrived in long coats, cradling bottles in gold or silver foil. Now the three of them were empty-handed, and there wasn't another taxi in sight.

EIGHT

Goodman wolf, the Prep-School Park Perp, a clumsy and unmemorable name, spent the earliest hours of the bicentennial year alternately sobbing and sleeping in a holding cell in the detectives' area at the local precinct, a windowless room he shared with two drunk men who had no memory of what they'd been told they'd done. One crime apparently involved public urination, the other assault. After Dick Peddy arrived and spent a long time inside, he came out to the waiting area and told the Wolfs and Ash's friends that there was no way that Goodman would be arraigned today. He would have to spend what was left of the night here, and then probably the next day too. Then he would be brought down to 100 Centre Street and be put in another cell to wait for his arraignment. There was no point in everyone waiting here any longer, the lawyer told them, and he promised that he would take care of everything and stay in close touch with Gil and Betsy. As for Cathy, no one would give out any information about where she'd been taken.

"Happy bicentennial year, everyone," Ash said under her breath as they walked out onto the street. She looked so small in her lavender party dress and incongruous ski parka.

A few photographers and reporters were waiting, and a couple of them stepped forward and said, "Did your son rape that girl in Tavern on the Green?" "Is he innocent?" "Is Goodman actually a 'good man'?" They seemed rude at the time, but in retrospect they were astonishingly respectful, and when Betsy Wolf, short, graceful, and patrician, said, "All right, that's enough now," they obeyed her and backed off.

On the street, Ethan was the one to pull Ash close. Jonah hung back, uncertain in his role as Ash's ex-boyfriend. It was as if he didn't think he should presume she'd want to take comfort from him; over his entire life, he never wanted to presume. Both Wolf parents were too upset to talk anymore to their daughter and her friends, and they walked up ahead unsteadily, holding on to each other. Jules might have come and stood beside Ash, her closest friend, and looped her arm through hers, but Ash's problems seemed suddenly overwhelming and far outside Jules's understanding. So instead Jules walked alone, a few paces behind her. Ethan, though,

244

immediately knew that Ash needed someone to help her right then. Without asking, he put an arm around Ash and brought her against him; her head promptly fell against his rounded shoulder as they walked down the street in the blue morning.

Taxis were procured, and good-byes said. In the last minutes, Ethan Figman kept holding on to Ash Wolf in a way that he'd never held on to her before. Jules saw this and didn't comment, for it was clearly only an aberration. Ethan told Ash now that he thought she should go home and try to sleep. "I want you to get a few hours in, okay?" Jules heard him say. "Just shut everything out. Lie down in your bed with all those stupid stuffed animals —"

"They're not stupid." Ash was smiling a little; Ethan could cheer her up even now.

"Well, in my view they actually are a little stupid," he said. "Eeyore. And Raggedy Ann with her bizarre head of *yarn* hair. You know, you could tie that yarn into knots, put her in a brown uniform, and call her *Knottsy*. With a K. Like Nazi."

"You are insane," Ash said, but she was still smiling.

"And there's also that creepy Poppin' Fresh Pillsbury Doughboy stuffed animal of yours, who's all gray looking and, what, supposed to look like he's made of raw dough? How unappealing is *that*? Some kids have teddy bears;

245

you have a raw dough doll."

"Give me a break, I sent away for him when I was *eight,*" said Ash, "with Pillsbury crescent roll proofs of purchase."

"He's not technically even an animal at all," Ethan said. "But go lie down with all of them and get some sleep. I'll take care of you." The words were said lightly but with feeling; he was signing on, this was the moment it happened, and Jules saw it but didn't know it.

Goodman's story would have to be gone over carefully, again and again, and Cathy's too. Jules shaped the narrative for herself to try to get it to make sense. In the floating sentimentality of New Year's Eve, she thought, Goodman and Cathy had taken up where they'd left off when they'd broken up. In her version of the scene, Goodman and Cathy had been making out in that storage room, then it went further, and at some point . Cathy probably remembered Troy, and tried to pull away. But Goodman couldn't exactly stop. He was too close, he had to keep going, and Cathy's protests sounded to him like ardor.

Why would she accuse him? Because, Dick Peddy later said, she was embarrassed. She worried that Troy would break up with her if he found out about this little adventure. No one was allowed to talk to Cathy, Dick Peddy had warned, for she was now the accuser, the opposition. But Cathy was also their friend, and even though she occupied a slightly odd role in the group — the sexual, moody dancer, the emotionally overwhelming girl — she was one of them, and she wouldn't do such a vindictive thing to Goodman, and yet for some reason she had.

From then on, whenever Jules went to the Labyrinth, Gil and Betsy talked about the case, and also, often, about money. The legal bills were enormous — "grotesque," said Gil Wolf. There was very little further conversation about the Democratic primaries, or the upcoming presidential election. No one cared about any of that anymore. And there were no more last mutterings about Watergate or the retreat from Vietnam or that movie *Taxi Driver* that was opening soon and was supposed to be so intense.

"Dick Peddy's fees are disgraceful, and our wives have known each other since Smith," Gil said one night at dinner, cutting into Betsy's stuffed pork loin. "We're all going to be in the poorhouse."

"That's not exactly true," Betsy said.

"Would you like to have a look at our bills? Because I'm happy to turn them over to you, dear. Then you'll see what kind of shape this has put our finances in."

"You don't have to be sarcastic to Mom," said Goodman.

"Fine, I'll be sarcastic to you, then. I'll talk rapturously to you about how one day you'll pay me back, no doubt, with all your earnings from your architectural career. Until your first building collapses because you didn't pay attention during Structural Soundness 101."

"Gil, *stop* it," said Betsy, placing her hand on his arm. "Stop it right now."

"What am I doing?"

"Creating tension," she said, and her eyes filled and her mouth trembled and turned downward.

"I'm not creating it. It was already here."

"I just want everything to be okay," Betsy said. "I want to get past this bad part of our lives, and then Goodman can go off to college and study whatever he likes. Architecture . . . or . . . Zulu tribes. I just want it all to be okay. I want our family to be happy again. I want this to be *over.*"

Goodman was supposed to be going to Bennington College in Vermont in the fall, having been accepted there early decision (strings had had to be pulled, even for admission to such an alternative institution, given Goodman's unstellar school record), but now the dean of student affairs had written a formal, chilly letter saying that Goodman couldn't matriculate until his legal situation had been "resolved favorably." In order for him to go to college in September, there would have to be a trial first; but the trial, Dick Peddy had warned, might not take place for a long time. The courts in New York were packed; city crime was remarkably high, and waiting for a trial lately was like waiting on line at the gas pump.

January stamped forward, with Goodman going to school each morning and seeing Dr. Spilka three times a week in the afternoon, and coming home only to disappear into his bedroom to drink work-boot vodka or smoke a joint, trying to both exist and not exist. Ash called Jules one weeknight and said, "My brother is really in trouble."

"I know that."

"I don't just mean legally, I mean emotionally."

From the next room Jules could hear her sister Ellen's roaring blow-dryer, and the same Neil Young album that seemed to be on autoplay, with the singer's thin voice now singing, *"There were children crying / and colors flying / all around the chosen ones."* She tugged on the yellow cord of the phone until its coils unwound themselves, and the connection thinned out and disappeared for a moment, then was restored. Jules sat in her closet on a few pairs of different-colored clogs, settling in to the conversation. "Don't forget that this happens with him," Jules said. "He gets really screwed up, and then he's okay again."

"I don't think he'll be okay this time," said Ash. "Dad is so furious. And Dick Peddy tried to reason with Cathy's lawyer, but no, no, Cathy and her parents insist on going ahead with it. There's really going to be a trial, Jules, can you believe it? My brother could actually go to jail for *twenty-five* years; it happens to innocent people all the time. He would be totally destroyed. Instead of doing whatever he's meant to do with his life, he would become this grizzled *con.* Can you imagine that? This is just so surreal, and none of us can stand it. But Dick Peddy says that no one in my family is allowed to call Cathy; it might look like we were putting pressure on her."

"That makes sense to me," said Jules, who knew nothing.

"I guess."

There was silence, and Jules thought the connection had died again. "Hello?" she said.

"I'm still here." Ash paused, then said, "Maybe you could call her. Or even go see her."

"Me?"

"Dick Peddy didn't tell you not to, did he?"

"No," said Jules after a long, considered moment.

"Then will you go?" Ash asked. "Will you go for me?"

Jules Jacobson arranged to meet Cathy Kiplinger at the fountain at Lincoln Center on a Saturday in February 1976 at noon, after

Cathy's dance class ten blocks south at Alvin Ailey. Snow was falling heavily on the plaza that day, and the pavement was iced over to the extent that the girls could have skated toward each other. There was Cathy in a long, eggplant-colored down coat, her face flushed red from the extreme heat of dancing and the extreme cold of the day. They warily nodded hello — it was the first time they'd seen each other since New Year's Eve — and then they walked across Broadway and sat in a booth at a coffee shop. Cathy quickly drank down the first of several Tabs, "with extra ice," she instructed the waitress, as though the ice might dilute this diet drink down to something so thin that not only wouldn't it add a fraction of fat to a body on the precipice, it would also reverse the fat-gathering process. It was too late, though; Cathy had been right about her physical self that first summer; her breasts were too big for a professional dancer's. "Sacks of mail," she'd called them, and now they looked even bigger, and so did her hips. She did what she could to forestall bursting womanhood, drinking Tabs with extra ice and eating very little, but her body was taking its own form. Troy had a perfect dancer's physique, thick and powerful. It was different for men. His arms could lift ballerinas into the air, and would do so for a long time with the Alvin Ailey American Dance Theater, causing a need for cortisone shots and shoulder surgeries. But along the way he would dance constantly, and would get to do what he'd always wanted to do, never feeling he was settling or selling out or giving in to commercial forces. Cathy would have a very different life.

Now, at the start of it, she sat with her Tab, picking at her nails; Jules saw that those formerly perfect ovals were now like little slices embedded in her fingers. Each nail had been relentlessly chewed on since New Year's Eve and was surrounded by shredded, inflamed, slightly puffed-out skin. If sex was like trying to eat the other person, this was like trying to eat yourself. Cathy lifted her hand and tore at her thumb skin; Jules almost expected to see blood on her mouth, as if Cathy were an animal that had been caught in a moment of predation and bliss. A cat with a bird in its mouth, staring defiantly at a human being and saying, *So? What are* you *looking at?*

Cathy was casual in her mutilation, and then she took another swig of Tab — a fingernail and finger-skin chaser. Jules remembered how, the year her father was dying, she had savaged her own hair. She hadn't wanted her hair to look like that, and now Cathy certainly wouldn't want her hands to look like this. But she drank her Tab and she ate her fingers, busy at the table, whether listening to Jules or, more of the time, talking. She didn't even seem to find it strange or embarrassing to be doing this in front of someone else. But the gratification was so important, the relief so necessary, that she seemed like someone masturbating in a coffee shop. Jules wanted to say, "Cathy, are you all right? You're frightening the shit out of me," but what a stupid question that would have been, for Cathy had already told them all the answer.

Jules recalled the sexy go-go dance Cathy had done for the girls in their teepee, the *wow* of it all as she moved her snaky body freely, mostly unembarrassed by its encumbrances and also proud of its special powers. But now, Jules thought, that was over. No more freedom. No more pride. No more unselfconscious teepee dancing for Cathy Kiplinger ever again.

In college in Buffalo freshman year, Jules would attend a Take Back the Night march, walking through dark streets among hundreds upon hundreds of somber women carrying candles. Many marches like that one sprang up around the country, so different from the raucous SlutWalks that would come thirty years later, when young women would wear whatever the hell they wanted — baby doll pajamas, see-through blouses, leopard costumes — taking pictures of one another and posting them online seconds later. In the old days of Take Back the Night, you could march with other women and feel that all the rapists of the world were small and powerless. You with your candles had the power. *Sisters!* The men, those dead-eyed, furious losers who grabbed you in parking garages, had nothing at all.

"It didn't happen the way he says," Cathy said now, jamming the straw into the ice of her Tab like a little pickax. "It happened the way I said. I wouldn't make it up." She took a bite of her fingernail, and a string of skin became separated, unpeeled.

"I believe you, of course. But I guess I don't think he would make it up either," said Jules.

Cathy Kiplinger looked across the table. Cathy was mature, and Jules was a child, the best friend of the beautiful and anguished girl, sent here to do her bidding. "Why do you think that?" Cathy said. "He cheated in school, you know. He looked at another boy's paper. Just ask him. That's why he had to switch schools. They made him leave."

"I know all about it," said Jules.

Cathy had a distinctly cartilaginous nose; though she wasn't crying now, her eyes were red rimmed because she'd been crying a great deal since New Year's. "Honest, Jules," said Cathy, "it's like you just don't know anything. You're just so *goony* about him, and about Ash, and about good old Betsy and Gil. You think they all saved you from a boring life. But unlike you, I don't despise my family. I actually love them."

"I don't despise my family," Jules said meekly, shocked to have been *discovered,* her voice miserably disappearing into her throat as she spoke.

"My parents have been wonderful to me," said Cathy. "And so has Troy, though I doubt he's going to stick around much longer. I'm a mess, and he knows it. I can't concentrate. I cry a lot. I'm not exactly the greatest girlfriend. The teachers at Nightingale are all being really nice about it, but this thing changed me, and now I'm different." She leaned forward and said, "Goodman pushed himself into me. Jules, are you hearing me? I wasn't ready; I was *dry.* Do you even know what I'm talking about — *dry*?" Jules nodded, though she also thought: Wait, do I really know what that means? She sort of did and sort of didn't. Sex and secretions still existed only in half-consciousness for her. They lurked like light under a door, or more like water flooding under a door. Soon the whole floor would be covered, but not just yet. "I was dry and it hurt, it really hurt," said Cathy, "and I yelled at him to stop, but you know what he did?" Her mouth went wavy. "He just smiled down at me like he thought it was funny, and he kept doing his thing. It was like he was turning a *crank.* Can you feel it now, when I say it?"

Yes, Jules felt it, and her jaw went stiff and

her thighs automatically tensed; she and Cathy were on the rack together, and no one could help them. She wanted to eat her own fingers now. She looked at Cathy in desperation. Jules blinked, attempting to loosen herself. The crank turned the other way, releasing her. She regained herself and said the only sentence she could think to say. It would disappoint and disgust Cathy Kiplinger forever, but she lamely said it anyway: "You'll probably start to feel a little better at some point, you know."

Cathy took a moment, then said, "And what is this opinion based on? Some special research you did?"

"No," said Jules, and she felt herself go warm-faced. "I guess I just meant that I want you to feel better."

"Of course you do. You just want it to go away. But none of you knows what it felt like when he was fucking me and I got abrasions, okay? That's what the doctor said when he examined me. *Labial abrasions.* How's that going to sound in court?"

Cathy was sitting across from Jules in the booth with her inflamed face and tiny, hard eyes and ten maimed fingers. Somehow Jules had really believed that Cathy would "come around" and that the force field of sentimentality that surrounded the six of them would be the catalyst. Jules would be able to go to the Wolfs' apartment tonight knowing that

Cathy was bagged and passive. Jules would be the heroine of this story, and all the Wolfs would admire her, including Goodman, who would rise out of his extended dark mood and give Jules a crushing hug. She pictured his long face and big strong teeth.

"Couldn't you have misinterpreted what happened?" Jules said. "Isn't there a way that that's possible, even slightly?"

"You mean, isn't there another view? Like *Rashomon*?"

"Yes, something like that," said Jules. Ethan had taken her to see that film recently at the Waverly Theater in the Village; it was one of his favorites, and she'd wanted to love it too. "I loved it *theoretically,*" she'd said to him afterward as they walked out; this was the way she'd learned to speak.

"This is nothing like *Rashomon,*" said Cathy, and she stood up. "God, Jules, you are so incredibly weak."

"I know," said Jules. Cathy's remark seemed to be the truest thing that anyone had ever said about her. In times of self-laceration she'd thought herself to be ignorant, awkward, unschooled, clumsy. But weak was what she really was. Even more miserably now, speaking out of that weakness, Jules asked, "But do you really need to take him to court? He could be sent to jail for twenty-five years. His life could go one way, or it could go another. All because of something that was maybe a misunderstanding. We all only get one life," she added.

"I'm fully aware of how many lives we get. My one life has already been fucked up," Cathy said. "And do I *need* to take him to court? Yes, I do. If it was a stranger who had jumped out at me in a stairwell, you'd be saying, 'Oh, Cathy, you *have* to take him to court, and we'll all be there to provide moral support.' But you're not saying that, because it's Goodman. And because you're so completely captivated by him, and by those supposedly magical summers at camp, and by some idea about the end of childhood, and being accepted for the first time in your life. Troy can't even *believe* that I hung around with all of you for so long. Your totally privileged group. You know, he was on scholarship at Spirit-in-the-Woods. He always felt completely different from everyone else there. That camp was extremely white, have you ever noticed that? I mean, my parents wanted me to go to a traditional all-girls camp in Maine where you wear uniforms and play sports all day and salute the flag, but I told them no thank you, I already go to an all-girls school. I wanted something different. I wanted to dance; I wanted to get outside my little insular life. But just look at Spirit-in-the-Woods. When Troy first got there, he said he felt like a freak."

"So did I!" said Jules. "It's not just him.

And by the way, I was on scholarship too, just so you know."

Cathy was unimpressed. "The point is that you got caught up in some fantasy, and now you can't see anything at all. But I can." Cathy's mouth took on a feral shape. "The only one of you who's tried to find out how I am is Ethan," she said.

"Ethan?" Jules was really surprised.

"On that first night, after it happened, he left a long, tortured, Ethan-y message on my parents' answering machine."

"I didn't know that."

"Yes. And he still calls me. Mostly I rant, and he listens. He never tells me to *buck up,* or whatever the rest of you think I should do. Sometimes," she admitted, "I even call *him.*"

"You call Ethan? I had absolutely no idea." Dick Peddy had expressly said they were not to talk to Cathy; Ethan had apparently just ignored this order, without clearing it with Ash or anyone.

"But the rest of you, *Jesus,*" said Cathy. "You were all my closest friends — not that you and I ever had that much to say, let's be honest."

Jules couldn't fully explain herself. She had said all the wrong things here from the start. In Improv class at camp Jules had once acted out a scene based on "The Love Song of J. Alfred Prufrock," and she'd had to recite a line to the boy facing her across a tea table,

259

the way Cathy faced Jules now. She'd looked into that boy's eyes and said, " 'That is not what I meant at all. That is not it, at all.' "

It wasn't supposed to go like this with Cathy. "We should have tried to talk to you," Jules said. "You're right, we really should have. But it was complicated. That lawyer was so insistent. It scared me. I'd never been in a situation like this before."

"Truly, you make me want to puke," Cathy said, winding her crocheted scarf around her neck. "When are you going to learn to think for yourself, Jules? You're going to have to eventually. You might as well start now."

Then the teenaged version of Cathy Kiplinger was gone from the coffee shop and summarily gone from *them.* In twenty-five years she would return through a time portal in a changed, late-middle-aged-woman form. Her hair would be artificially made the same yellow color it had once naturally been, her breasts would be surgically reduced after two decades of chronic back problems, and her tense face would shine from low-concentration Retin-A cream and the occasional oxygen facial, but the tension itself would never be unlocked and released.

"Here you go," said the waitress, lightly slapping down the check. Cathy had drunk six Tabs. Jules paid for them, then in a sick fog took the subway up to the Wolfs' apartment, where Ash was waiting.

"Well?" said Ash. "What did she say?"

Jules threw herself facedown onto the cluttered bed and said, "She's a total mess."

"So?"

"What do you mean, *so*? Isn't the question *why* is she a total mess? If she was making it all up, would she really be such a mess? Wouldn't she be more of a *fake* mess? More, you know, photogenic? More studied?"

After a few seconds of silence Jules craned her head around from where she lay on the bed, in order to see Ash in the swivel chair at her desk. Even from this angle, she could see that her mood state had changed. Ash stood and said, "I think you should go home now, Jules."

Jules scrambled to stand too. "What? Why?"

"Because I can't believe you're saying this."

"We can't even discuss it as a possibility?" Jules said. "Cathy's our friend too. She's never made things up before. She seemed genuinely fucked up, Ash. You should see her fingernails."

"What do her fingernails have to do with anything?"

"They're all chewed up, like a cannibal ate them."

"And because of her *fingernails,* my brother's guilty?"

"No. But I just think we owe it to her to —"

"Please go," said Ash Wolf, and she actually

261

went to the door and held out her arm. Hot-faced, shocked, Jules walked out of the room and down the hall, passing the gaggle of family photos. In the distance, she saw Goodman in the living room with headphones on, nodding dully to a private, thudding beat.

Nearly two weeks of an unbearable freeze-out passed. Jules cowered and hulked in Underhill, walking through the school halls blankly, paying no attention in class. If she couldn't be at the Labyrinth with Ash and Goodman and their parents, then what was the point? Jonah stayed in touch sometimes, and Ethan tried to cheer her up on the phone every night. "Ash will come around," Ethan said.

"I don't know. How do you manage to walk this tightrope?" Jules asked him. "Having everyone like you and respect you no matter what you do."

There was silence on the line except for Ethan's mouth breathing. Finally he said, "Let me see. I guess, maybe, I don't rush to conclusions. By the way," he said after another pause, lightly, as if trying not to make her feel too bad about what he was about to say. "Jonah and I had dinner at the Labyrinth last night."

"Oh."

"Yeah. It felt very weird not having you there. But even if you were there, it would've been weird because it's very tense. In case you're interested, Betsy made sea bass and orzo."

"What's orzo?"

"It's this new kind of pasta, shaped like rice but bigger. You'd like it. The food was good, but the mood over there is getting even worse. They're all scared to death of the trial, but no one says it. Goodman's used to having everything work out for him. Even after getting kicked out of Collegiate, they got him into Walden, right? And he's a powerful guy. He can't believe things aren't working out this time; that none of the fail-safes are in place. He thinks he might really be in danger now. He pulled me aside after dinner and told me that he needed me to know he didn't do anything wrong. I told Ash it's not my place to figure out what happened that night at Tavern on the Green, or what should happen now. I said that's what a trial is for — like I even know what I'm talking about. My credentials are basically that my dad and I used to sit around and watch *Owen Marshall: Counselor at Law.*"

Jules said, "Did Ash say anything about me?"

"She said she misses you."

"Well, she's very angry with me."

"No, not really," said Ethan. "Not anymore. I've been smoothing that out. She's embarrassed that she made you leave the apartment. She wishes she could take it back, but she doesn't think you'd let her."

"I'd let her."

So Ethan brokered the peace between them. He refused to attempt to broker an end to the legal fight between Goodman and Cathy — it was corrupt to try and interfere with the legal process, he said — but he was happy to help Ash and Jules become friends again. Later that night, Ash called Jules and said, "I'm so sorry I acted like that. I don't know if you can forgive me, but I hope you can." Jules told her yes, of course she already forgave her. Jules didn't need to say that she knew Goodman hadn't done anything wrong; instead, she only had to agree that the situation was horrible, and that the trial would correct the wrongness of the accusation; and she had to agree to return on Saturday to the Labyrinth.

Over the next weeks, Ethan was the only one of them who really spoke at all about Cathy Kiplinger. "I talked to her last night," he announced one day when they were all sitting together on a bench in Central Park in cold sunlight.

"Who?" said Jonah.

"Cathy."

Goodman and Ash gave him a sharp side-long look. "Cathy?" Goodman asked.

"Cathy?" Ash echoed.

"Hope you two had a very nice chat," said Goodman.

"I know it's hard for you to understand," Ethan said. "I get that."

"I just can't believe you're speaking to her," Ash said, lighting a cigarette and holding the match out to her brother, lighting his cigarette as well.

"I see why you feel that way," said Ethan. "But I just wanted her to know I was thinking about her. I felt that this was important to convey." He sat up straighter on the bench and said, "I have to make my own decisions about what's right."

" 'Thinking about her,' " said Ash. "Well, I guess that's true enough." Then she said, "My feeling is that Cathy's probably gone a little insane — remember how Jules described her when they went to the coffee shop? — and now she actually believes her own story. That's what Dr. Spilka told Goodman. Isn't that what he said, Goodman?"

"I don't know," said Goodman.

The trial was expected to be in the fall, and it was all that any of them could talk about over the rest of the school year. The outside world and its political chatter remained remote and of only intermittent interest, while Goodman's upcoming trial and, well before that, the "adjourned date" in late April, when certain motions would be filed, the lawyer had explained, were far more compelling. Goodman prepped with his lawyer and his lawyer's two associates; they wore him out with all their prepping. But no one saw the extent to which Goodman had just had enough of all this and could not take much more. The extent to which he was frightened, or to which maybe he felt guilty. Cathy had been strong and believable in the coffee shop, but Jules couldn't hold on to her words. If she held on to them, if she remembered them and completely absorbed them, then she might not have still been lingering around the Labyrinth.

His family believed Goodman to be entirely innocent — though actually, Ash had confessed to Jules, she'd had an odd moment late one night with her mother, when Betsy had come into Ash's room. "Sometimes I think the male of our species is unknowable," Betsy Wolf had said, despairingly, in response to nothing. And Ash had tried to find out what she meant, but then her father appeared in the doorway, looking for her mother, and it became clear to Ash that her parents had been having an argument. Then they said good night to her; and weeks later, when Ash told the story to Jules, she said that she hadn't known if her mother had been trying to find a way to talk about Goodman and who he was. Or whether, instead, she'd only been making a comment about Gil, after a marital argument that, one way or another, must surely have been about Goodman. Maybe Betsy, who'd always protected and loved her difficult son, even as she pushed him in certain ways, had briefly wavered. But there was no way to know, because she never again said anything to suggest it. In fact, she even seemed to become more righteous about his innocence, disgusted by what Goodman had to endure.

None of the Wolfs had spoken to Cathy, as Ethan and Jules had. But even having spoken to her, Ethan and Jules were only sixteen years old, and much later it would be clear that they couldn't have been expected to know what to do, or exactly what to feel. Cathy's words had been disturbing, even shocking, but the firm, unified belief of the Wolf family carried its own, more significant weight.

At the Wolfs' apartment, everyone nervously watched Goodman, and they saw him become almost a non-person, and they said to one another, "At least he's still going to Dr. Spilka," as though this psychoanalyst they'd never met could keep him intact. Even when Ash heard Dr. Spilka's halting voice on the Wolfs' answering machine on a Thursday afternoon in early April, she wasn't made anxious. "Hel-lo, this is Dr. Spilka," he said in a formal voice. "Goodman did not show up for our appointment today. I would like to remind you of my twenty-four-hour cancellation policy. That is all. Good day."

Ash, home after school and sitting in the

kitchen with two classmates eating raw cookie dough and rehearsing for the upcoming Brearley play, Paul Zindel's *The Effect of Gamma Rays on Man-in-the-Moon Marigolds,* had been the one to play back the message on the machine, but she didn't particularly worry when she heard it. So Goodman hadn't been to his shrink today; big deal. He wasn't a reliable person. She imagined he was lying on his bed down the hall right now listening to music or perhaps getting high, but she didn't feel like interrupting her rehearsal to go in and visit her brother in his lair.

Ash Wolf had a great tolerance for the ways of boys; she forgave them their primitive traits, and she sympathized with Goodman almost entirely. When something happened to him, she'd once explained to Jules, it seemed as if it were happening to her too. She and her school friends rehearsed their lines from the sad and wonderful play about an emotionally disturbed mother and her daughters, and then after the other girls left, her own relievedly undisturbed mother came home from an afternoon of stuffing envelopes for a muscular dystrophy charity run by a friend whose son had the disease, and Ash helped her make dinner.

Even in the midst of Goodman's tremendous problems, Betsy Wolf continued to prepare excellent meals. Ash was handed a rubber-banded bunch of leeks, and at the sink she unbound them, then soaked the individual thick-bulbed stalks to remove the sand and dirt, and chopped and sautéed them, and by the time her father walked into the apartment right before seven, already muttering about the latest legal bills, Ash remembered the phone call from Dr. Spilka, and that Goodman hadn't yet left his foul cave. She felt uneasy suddenly, and went to his door, banged once, then entered. The place was much cleaner than usual. Sometime between last night and this morning when he was supposed to have left for school, her brother had actually cleaned his room. He had lined up his little architectural models on the desk, and he had made his bed. It was as disturbing in there as a crime scene, and Ash turned and ran back down the hall to get her parents.

Goodman was really gone; gone with the passbook from a special account his maternal grandfather had set up for him at Manufacturer's Hanover Trust. His parents had arranged for a cap on all withdrawals, making sure Goodman never dipped in too deeply to buy drugs or do something stupid. Today, they learned, he had made the maximum withdrawal. He was also gone with his passport, as well as every other relevant official document that he'd been able to find, including his birth certificate and his social security card, which had been kept in a catchall drawer in his parents' bedroom bureau. He'd just dug around in there when no one was in the room and grabbed whatever had his name printed on it. Maybe he was planning on leaving the country, maybe not. If you thought of Goodman Wolf, there wasn't any one place that you imagined he might go.

Except, said Ash, for Spirit-in-the-Woods. He loved it there so much; he was a powerful figure there, he had currency, he was seen as big and important and erotically charged and free of his father's criticism, and, of course, he was happy there. It was a long shot, but Gil Wolf called the Wunderlichs and asked if by any chance their "wayward son" had turned up today. Gil tried to keep his voice light. The Wunderlichs, who already knew something about the legal situation, said no, they'd been away in Pittsfield for the day, but to their knowledge Goodman had not been there.

Next the Wolfs called Dick Peddy, who instructed them on what and what not to do. "We don't have to jump to conclusions," Dick said.

"Jesus, I've already done that, Dick. The kid is gone."

"You don't know that. Consider his absence a kind of reflective vacation."

"Reflective? Goodman doesn't reflect; he just *does*."

"As long as he shows up on the adjourned

date," said the lawyer, "then all will be well."

The Wolfs knew that Goodman was not likely to show up then; why would he have left home, only to appear in court on the appointed day? Their best hope was that he was with some pot-smoking friend in the city who they didn't know about — and that he would crash at this friend's place in the interim and eventually would come home, or would even just show up at the court in a couple of weeks in wrinkled, unwashed clothes.

At nine a.m. on the adjourned date, Betsy and Gil Wolf sat very still in the paneled courtroom on the fourth floor of a courthouse downtown, and waited with their lawyer. The assistant DA coughed repeatedly, and the judge offered him a lozenge. "Fisherman's Friend; works wonders," said the judge, taking out a little rattling tin box from a drawer and handing it to the bailiff, who handed it to the assistant DA. Minutes passed; Goodman did not show. A bench warrant was issued, and Detectives Manfredo and Spivack took the Wolfs aside and instructed them that as soon as they heard from Goodman, they needed to report it, as well as urge Goodman to turn himself in.

When the city tabloids found out that the boy who'd been arrested on New Year's Eve at Tavern on the Green had not shown up for a court appearance, they sent photographers to hang around outside the Labyrinth, and

Ash was discreetly approached as she headed for the crosstown bus to school. "Prep-School Park Perp Flight Shocker" was not a story with much traction, though, because in the last days of April, two men were apprehended after they'd robbed and shot a fifty-year-old woman in Central Park, near the Boat Basin. Now, whenever Goodman was occasionally mentioned in the *Post* and the *Daily News,* it was in the context of the dangers of Central Park, particularly for women. Unrelatedly, a hundred-pound tree branch broke off and killed a teenaged girl in the park near 92nd Street, but still all these stories were unsettling. The whole city had begun to seem even more unsavory, and not just the park. Muggings were constant. The squeegee men stood at the mouths of tunnels with their tools and buckets of dark water, aggressively approaching cars. Goodman Wolf, Prep-School Park Perp, became just a small part of a big, seething story, mild in comparison with what would come.

It would be ten years before the notorious case in which another prep-school boy attacked a girl in Central Park, but that boy also killed that girl. And it would be thirteen years before a young female investment banker out for a jog in the park at night was raped and beaten into a coma, thought to be the victim of a gang of boys out "wilding," as people called it, though much later the convictions would be overtturned when someone else confessed. Who ever knew what really happened? The park was a dark, beautiful, and now intimidating stretch of green that seduced and divided the city.

Decades earlier, Manny and Edie Wunderlich had traveled through New York on elevated trains. They went to Socialist meetings and avant-garde operas, and then, eventually, to folk club after folk club, and every single activity apparently cost "a nickel," at least the way they told it. The Hudson River shone on one side of Manhattan, the East River on the other. Between the two rivers, young bohemians owned this place. Now they no longer did, and because of that it was all much worse. But Goodman wasn't lumped in with the worst; he was given a tiny mention in the catalog of the great city's decline; and with a little time, he faded away.

But here he was now, still — vivid, fresh, the locus of a pain that didn't lessen. Ash was on the phone constantly to Jules, crying and smoking and talking, or else just being silent; she missed Goodman so much, she said. She knew he was a fuckup, but until now all his fuckups had been redeemable. This had been his role since they were kids; and it had been almost funny back then, because he was also charming and bad and always made family life so much livelier. He used to dress their dog, Noodge, in Ash's training bra. He used to wake Ash up in the middle of the night and take her up onto the forbidden roof of the Labyrinth, where they would sit sharing a bag of mini-marshmallows while looking out over the paused, exhaling city. Her parents' sadness at their loss was intolerable now, and so was her own.

One Saturday morning in May, Ash took the Long Island Railroad out to Underhill to spend the weekend at the Jacobsons'. There was a time when Jules would have dissuaded her from coming, but not now. None of her friends had seen her small house or her dull, unfancy suburb; they had all expressed an interest in visiting her before, but Jules had deflected it, saying something meaningless like, "All in good time, my pretty." But now Ash needed to get away from her parents and the city. Before she arrived, Jules went around the house, glaring at everything, trying to find clever ways to make the place look better. She stalked through the rooms, her eyes narrowed in assessment, snatching up an ugly ashtray and spiriting it into a drawer, removing a pillow that her mother's sister, Aunt Joan, had embroidered from a kit with the words *Home Is the Place Where When You Have to Go There They Have to Take You In — Robert Frost.* Jules couldn't bear the image of Aunt Joan, who had never read a poem in her *life,* stitching the name *Robert Frost* in

274

green yarn, as if that somehow made her "literary." The pillow went into the drawer beside the ashtray, and as Jules closed the drawer her mother saw her and said, "What are you doing?"

"Just straightening up."

Lois glanced around the room, noticing the way the rug had been vacuumed within an inch of its life, items on surfaces had been regrouped, and a shawl had been thrown across the couch, not to hide any stain or imperfection but to hide the couch itself. Seeing her mother see the house from Jules's perspective made her ashamed of herself. Suddenly Lois Jacobson, who had been given no credit for anything, seemed to know everything. She'd lived through the death of her young husband, and now she was a single mother with two daughters, one in college at nearby Hofstra but living at home for financial reasons; and one who had made it clear that she preferred a richer, more sophisticated and engaging family over her own. Lois had recently started working again for the first time since getting married. "Women's lib had something to do with it," she'd said. "But also I need the income now." She had gotten a job as an assistant to the principal at the Alicia F. Derwood Elementary School, where Jules and Ellen had once been students, and she liked being out of the house and in the jumping, unpredictable environment of the school.

"Well, it looks very nice," Lois finally decided to say as she took in all that Jules had done to the living room. "Thank you."

The bigger surprise that weekend was that Ash liked her mother, and that her mother liked Ash. The only uneasy person here was Jules, who found it hard to manage the overlap of these two worlds. When the train arrived, Ash stepped off onto the platform looking like a child who has been sent to the countryside to escape the London blitz. Jules, in the parking lot with her mother, leapt out of the car and strode up the metal steps to greet Ash, as if her city friend wouldn't be able to descend these stairs without assistance.

"Welcome to Underhill," Lois said when Ash climbed into the backseat.

"Yes, welcome to beautiful Underhill," said Jules in the sort of voice that might be used to accompany a corny old educational film-strip. "A bustling metropolis that is home to three art museums and six orchestras. In addition, the next summer Olympics will be held in our fair city."

Ash pretended not to hear her. "Thank you, Mrs. Jacobson. I am really glad to be here. I had to get away. You don't know it, but you're kind of saving my life."

"First stop, the extremely glamorous and

elegantly named Cindy Drive!" said Jules as they pulled into the development of identical ranch houses that sat shoulder to shoulder along the straight street. When you took a shower at the Jacobsons', you could see right into the shower at the Wanczyks'. Once, Jules and Mrs. Wanczyk had stared straight at each other with a neck-up view, while water simultaneously beat down on their heads. "Did you know that Zsa Zsa Gabor lives across the street?" Jules said to Ash. "No, really, right over there! Nine Cindy Drive. There she is, putting on a boa! She is such a sweet person. Hallooo, Ms. Gabor!"

"Please ignore my daughter, Ash," said Lois. "She seems to have gone mad."

The weekend was spent partaking of all the suburban activities that Jules generally hated. Ash Wolf was actually grateful for the Walt Whitman Mall, whose name Jules had mocked mercilessly with her friends in the summer. Decades later, archly describing her childhood at a dinner party, she would say, "Could there be a bigger oxymoron than the *Walt Whitman Mall*? Maybe only . . . the *Emily Dickinson Waterpark.*" Now Jules and Ash walked together around the enormous space, laughing at almost anything, going in and out of stores. They also went to the movie theater to see *All the President's Men,* and while it played, Jules thought again about Nixon's departure from the White House lawn, which the entire camp had watched. But really, before that day all the campers had been like industrious cobblers at work in a forest, only partly aware of the outside world — the move toward impeachment, the noise — and willing themselves a way to stay in that indefensible state of half-consciousness as long as they could. Now, out in the world and much more conscious, Ethan had begun devoting his energy to drawing sketches of Jimmy Carter as a figure in Figland, and perfecting that drowsy Southern accent. "I wish we had someone a lot more liberal, but I think he's pretty ethical, which is rare," said Ethan. "I'll take what I can get."

At night during that weekend in Underhill, Jules and Ash lay together in her bed, with Ash's head against the footboard. Many years later, they would lie across other beds with their children playing all around them, and it was a relief to know that even in getting older and splitting off into couples and starting families, you could still always come together in this way that you'd learned to do when you were young, and which you would have a taste for over your entire life. Ash, up close in Jules's bed in Underhill, having performed a series of elaborate nighttime ablutions in the house's single, peach-colored bathroom, now smelled milky and peppery at once. Maybe the soap she'd brought with her from the city was called Pepper Milk, Jules thought as she grew sleepy. Whatever it was, anyone would want to be around that smell, to drink it in from a girl if they couldn't drink it in from a bottle.

"So what do you think will happen to Goodman?" Ash asked.

"I don't know."

"Because he's a boy it's probably easier for him out in the world," said Ash. "But because he's Goodman it's harder. It's always been harder. He just sort of blunders through. He doesn't even try to play the games you need to play. Like, I always knew, since I was little, how to please teachers. I would write these really elaborate short stories and turn them in for extra credit. You want to know the secret? The stories were *long*. They weren't all that good, but they showed purpose. That's my strength: purpose. I'm sure they wore my teachers out. 'The Secret of the Gold-Leaf Mantelpiece.' 'The Carson Triplets on Wandering Bluff.' They were exhausting! I also made birthday cards for my parents every year — I mean, I spent hours on them. Once I even *tie-dyed* a card — and Goodman would completely forget about their birthdays, and I'd remind him, and at the last minute he'd ask me to let him sign the card I'd made. But they never thought he'd spent a second on it. I know we live in a very sexist world, and a lot of boys do nothing except get in trouble, until one day they grow up and dominate every aspect of society," Ash said. "But girls, at least while they're still girls and perform well, seem to do everything better for a while. Seem to get the attention. I always did."

"I never did," said Jules. "Not until I met all of you."

"Do you think we're horrible narcissists — those of us who swept you up into our clutches?"

"Yes."

"You do? Thanks a lot." Ash tossed a pillow at her in a halfhearted attempt at female playfulness. But that was not what their friendship was. They didn't sit around polishing their nails and talking dreamily; their roles were different from that. Ash still fascinated Jules and showed her how to be in the world; Jules still profoundly amused and comforted Ash. She still cracked her up without cracking her up.

"I'm kidding," Jules quickly said. "Of course you're not narcissists. And by the way, you smell really good right now."

"Thank you." Ash yawned. "Maybe, if I don't make it in the theater, they can write that on my gravestone: 'She smelled really good.' "

" 'She had olfactory brilliance.' "

They were quiet. "I wonder exactly when we'll die," Ash said. They both thought of their own eventual deaths and felt sorry for themselves, but that passed quickly, like a shiver. Then Ash said, "I wonder when Goodman will die. And if he'll do anything with his life first. If only he'd had someone like Old Mo Templeton to guide him along and be his mentor. Help him with his architecture, or whatever else he decided to do. If only he'd had a talent that was brought out and *worked on.* That would have helped. Talent gets you through life."

At the end of the weekend in Underhill Ash seemed stronger. "I can't thank you enough, Mrs. Jacobson," she said as she stood in the kitchen, clutching her weekend bag. "It's just been so stressful at home, and I didn't know what to do —" Here her voice collapsed, and Jules's mother impetuously hugged her.

"I'm so glad you came," Lois said. "I see why Jules is so fond of you. And you're beautiful too," she added. Jules knew that mentioning Ash's beauty was an indirect comment on Jules's lack of it, but somehow it was okay, even pleasurable, to hear her mother say this. Jules took pride in Ash's beauty, as if she'd had something to do with it. "You are welcome anytime," Lois went on. "Just say the word."

"Yes, there's always a place for you on exclusive Cindy Drive," Jules said. "Only three blocks away from the Dress Cottage."

Ash said, "Oh, shush," smiling, and waved her off.

That afternoon, after they'd driven Ash back to the train and then returned home, Jules went into the drawer of the hutch cabinet and took out the ashtray and the embroidered pillow, returning them to their rightful places in the living room. Within half an hour, though, she saw that her mother had removed them again. From then on, Lois Jacobson didn't seem to feel as threatened when Jules went into the city weekend after weekend.

Life at the Wolf household remained in trauma mode. Still no one knew where Goodman was; he might be anywhere at all. Whenever he was found, or whenever he returned home, he would immediately be arrested; the lawyer had made this clear to them. They waited for Goodman to call or write so they could find out if he was okay and urge him to come home, telling him they knew he'd gotten frightened, but this wasn't the way to handle it. They knew he was innocent, they would remind him, and soon everyone else would know it too. Come home, they would say. But he didn't contact any of them, and the school year ended like a regular school year, except Goodman didn't graduate from high school, didn't advance in life as he was meant to do. He hadn't had a chance to mature into something other than what he was. His story paused there.

This was to be the last summer the rest of

them would spend at Spirit-in-the-Woods, except now Ash didn't even know if she could bear to go. Cathy wouldn't be coming back, of course; she still wasn't speaking to any of them. Troy was too old now even if he'd wanted to come back, which of course he didn't. The absence of Goodman — who also would've been too old to come back, since he was supposed to have gone off to college in the fall — made the idea of a summer there seem wrong. But the following year they would all be too old, so Ash, Jules, Ethan, and Jonah decided they would go back one more time.

Not long after Jules arrived again in Belknap at the end of June, she knew it was a mistake. Most of the other campers seemed so much younger now. There were plenty of new ones, and some were a little different from campers of the past. On the path to the lake, Jules overheard a very basic, crude *fart* joke. Did these kids not know that if you were going to make a fart joke, the punch line would have to have something to do with, perhaps, *Brecht*? In Girls' Teepee 2 for this final summer lived Jules, Ash, Nancy Mangiari, and Jane Zell. Sleeping in Cathy Kiplinger's old bed was a new girl, Jenny Mazur, an introverted glassblower with a habit of talking in her sleep, the only time she let loose. "Mother! I did not betray you!" she cried as the others listened with prurient fascination.

Ash's sadness and preoccupation with Goodman were known throughout the camp. Sometimes at night, when the trees scratched the roof of their teepee, or a flashlight popped on through the pines and then the beam dashed away, Ash briefly held the fantasy that Goodman had come back. "It's not impossible, Jules. He knows where to find us," Ash once whispered. "He'll tell us he's been hiding out somewhere around here, maybe living in some shitty apartment in Pittsfield. There was this Grimms' fairy tale that our mother used to read us," she said. "A brother and sister run off into the woods to get away from their evil stepmother. It's always a stepmother, never a stepfather; even fairy tales are sexist. Anyway, the brother gets really thirsty, but the stepmother has enchanted all the springs. And there's this one spring that, if he drinks from it, he'll turn into a deer. And the sister says, 'Please don't drink from it, because if you turn into a deer you'll run away from me.' And he says, 'No, no, I promise I won't,' and he drinks from it and of course he turns into a deer."

"And runs away from her like she predicted, right?" said Jules. "To join a hunt? I remember this fairy tale."

"Yes, right. And she's devastated. But he keeps coming back to visit her in his deer form, and with his hoof he knocks on the door of the house where she's staying, and he says, 'My little sister, let me in.' He keeps doing this, night after night, and he goes back and forth into the woods. And one night he comes to her and says, 'My little sister, let me in.' And she lets him in and sees that he's been wounded. That's what I keep thinking," said Ash in an agitated voice. "That Goodman's going to show up one night, and he'll be wounded in a way. Something will have happened to him out there. And I'll let him in, and take care of him, and make him stay with me." She looked somewhat childishly at Jules. "Don't you think it could happen?" she asked.

"In real life?" Jules said, and Ash nodded. "Maybe," was all she could bring herself to say.

But Goodman didn't come. The scratching heard on the roof was an overhanging claw of a branch, and the footsteps outside the teepee were wandering counselors, whose flashlights threw yellow scattershot beams among the pines. Everything was different this summer. Even Gudrun Sigurdsdottir, the Icelandic weaver and lifeguard, had not returned. Someone said she'd gotten married over there. The Wunderlichs, too, seemed exponentially older. Ida Steinberg, the cook, looked especially tired. Those three had been there since the founding of Spirit-in-the-Woods — the Wunderlichs *were* Spirit-in-the-Woods — and they always said that the camp kept them young, but perhaps you could not drink from that particular spring forever.

Ethan did the best work he'd ever done, working side by side with Old Mo Templeton, who was now, Jules remarked once to Ethan — then immediately regretted it — Decrepit Mo Templeton. One day Jules saw Ethan helping Mo walk to the animation shed, carefully holding the arm of his mentor to make sure he didn't trip and fall. Sometimes, Ethan would mention to Old Mo a detail from the early days of animation and ask him a complicated question about it, and in the past Old Mo had always replied expansively. But now, when Ethan referred to the short *Skedaddle,* from the Slowpoke Malone series of 1915, Mo smiled and just said, "Yes, that was good work they did back then." Yet when Ethan wanted to hear more about it, Mo touched his hand and murmured, "All your questions, Ethan, all your questions." And that was that. It was as if Mo Templeton was conserving his energy for waking up in the morning when the day started, and walking down the hill, and sitting among these teenagers and their ideas, and looking at their drawings of figures who seemed suddenly and exhaustingly in motion.

It was time for the old to step aside and the young to take a big step up. It was unequivocally time. Over the summer, Jules and Ash walked everywhere together around the grounds, going deep into the pine forest where they'd never wanted to go before. Two girls less interested in nature and natural phenomena could hardly be found anywhere on earth. But now nature walks seemed to be called for, and the Dr. Scholl's sandals that Jules and Ash both wore pressed down on the bed of red and brown pine needles. Occasional groups of mushrooms popped up after a rainstorm like carbuncles. Both girls jerked away when they saw an embryonic bird that had been munched upon by a carpet of flying and walking creatures. When you looked closely at anything, you could almost faint, Jules thought, although you had to look closely if you wanted to have any knowledge at all in life.

One afternoon Ash wasn't around to take a walk. Jane Zell said she'd seen her leave the teepee looking upset, the way she often looked this summer, but Jane had no idea of where Ash had gone. That night, in bed, in a humidity of a particularly savage degree, the five girls tossed and flopped. They talked a little, each of them telling stories from their home lives, except for Jenny Mazur, who only began to talk after the other talking ended. In her sleep she said, "The man had a face! He had a face!"

"Don't they all," said Nancy Mangiari.

Someone yawned. "It's crazy late," said Ash. "See you in the morning, ladies."

The others hushed; the sleep talker stilled. Even through the heat, their bodies had circadian rhythms, and they managed to fall under. But later, close to two in the morning, after the counselors had ceased their half-hearted patrol, Jules awakened to the sound of the teepee door opening and footfall on the wooden floorboards. It was a male step, and in her half-conscious state she thought she actually might hear Goodman Wolf say the words, "My little sister, let me in." Jules traveled up the flume of sleep in hopes of being fully awake at the moment when Goodman was reunited with his sister, and then with all of them. Tired, worn-out, maybe even injured Goodman, back from his misguided, panicked journeys. He would be a deer or he would be a boy, but it wouldn't matter. Whatever had happened to him, he could be restored. His legal problems would slowly be worked out, Jules thought. The lawyer would get on the phone to the DA's office and cut a deal that most likely would involve probation but no jail time. The trial would take place eventually, as it was supposed to have done, and in the end Goodman would no doubt be acquitted. Cathy, in time, would admit that she'd been immature back then — really fucked up and overly dramatic — and now she'd seen that maybe she'd distorted what had actually happened. What mattered was that Goodman was here now. Jules, still lying in bed, felt a bolt of dopey hope that awakened her further.

But once awake, she heard only, *"Shh,"* and then a chuckle, and then the sound of Ash fiercely whispering to someone, "No, over *here.* That's Jenny Mazur. She'll start to shout about the man with a face."

"What?" he said.

"Come here. It's okay. They're asleep."

Ethan Figman climbed into the bed of the most beautiful girl he'd probably ever seen, and if happiness made its own light, it might have pulsed from the bed across the hexagonal interior surface area of that teepee, radiating outward into the dark. Surely he was vibrating with happiness — but so, possibly, was Ash. Ethan and Ash. Ethan and Ash?

It made no sense. A pulse jumped in Jules's eye as she tried to understand this. How was it possible that Ethan was the one Ash wanted? Jules hadn't wanted him. But of course people were different, she remembered; they were *allowed* to be different. Everyone's neurologies and tastes were singular. She forced herself to think about this as she turned her own body sharply away from their bodies, facing the window and the hot night, which expelled a small quantity of bad air through the screen. The voices across the teepee became low and unified, and then became *coos,* as if two doves were huddling together in bed. Sad, lovely, delicate Ash Wolf, and wonderful, ugly, brilliant Ethan Figman, improbably together, improbably pressed together on this extremely hot night, for privacy's sake inside the sleeping bag with the red lining and the repeating pattern of cowboys and lariats, began to murmur and babble. Ash whispered to him, "Take off your shirt," and he whispered, "My shirt? I don't think so." "You *have* to." "Well, okay. Wait, it won't come off. Look, look, it's stuck." And Ash whispered, "You are insane," and in response, agreeable Ethan laughed insanely, followed by the soft, almost imperceptible sound of him most likely taking off his shirt in front of a girl for the first time ever. "There you go. That's nice," Ash whispered. "See?"

Then there were slurping, excruciatingly human sounds, and the doves returned again, and there was rotisserie-style turning inside overheated flannel. Love could not be explained. Jules Jacobson-Boyd would eventually know this when she became a therapist, but now Jules Jacobson knew it anecdotally, and she felt suddenly snide and defensive in response to it. Furious, actually. She felt as if she'd done everything wrong, *as always.* She had a wild need to say something to Jonah tomorrow about what she'd witnessed tonight. She imagined coming upon him as he sat curled over his guitar, and telling him,

"Guess what? Apparently opposites really do attract, freakish though that is in this case."

In the morning, the air returned to a reasonable temperature, and only the five girls remained in the teepee. They sat up in their beds to the opening strains of Haydn's *Surprise* Symphony, which the Wunderlichs still played each day on a turntable and blasted across all of Spirit-in-the-Woods, waking everyone from their slumber.

Nine

It wasn't easy to understand how the love between two other people could diminish you. If those two people were still accessible to you, if they called you all the time, if they asked you to come into the city for the weekend as you'd always done, then why should you feel, suddenly, intensely lonely? Jules Jacobson was lonely for the entire first year after Ash Wolf and Ethan Figman became lovers. *Lovers* was their word, not hers. No one she knew had ever used that word before, but Ash spoke it without any awareness that it was unusual for a teenager to say. Ash and Ethan had taken up with each other that summer in a state of deep, almost telepathic mutuality. It had not occurred to them before to be lovers, they explained to everyone. But after knowing each other well for several years, spending summers on the same piece of land in the Berkshire Mountains, they had been thunderstruck, and now they never wanted to be apart.

It was April 1977, and they had been a couple for eight months. Ethan had been by Ash's side when the Wolf family's dog developed an inoperable tumor and needed to be put down. Ash could not bring herself to actually go into the room with Noodge to have it done, so Ethan went instead. He accompanied Ash's mother, and the two of them stroked the frantic, heaving side of that lovely golden dog — the dog of Ash and Goodman's childhood — as the vet injected him with a drug that stopped his heart. Ethan comforted his girlfriend's mother — his future mother-in-law, as it would turn out — and then he went back out into the waiting room and let Ash fall into his arms and cry. It seemed that Ethan Figman had become the repository of all female weeping. "Goodman wasn't even here," Ash said as she stood with her head against him. "Noodge was *our* dog, his and mine, and we both loved him so much, and Goodman missed his death, Ethan. He *owed* it to Noodge to be here today. We both did." But Ethan hadn't missed the death of this dog; Ethan was there for it, and for all other important occasions.

This week everyone had gotten their letters from colleges. Ash had been accepted to Yale, where her maternal uncles and grandfather had gone; Ethan had been accepted into the animation program at the School of Visual Arts in the city. They would be living two

293

hours apart, but would commute frequently to see each other. Jonah, who'd said he had no interest in pursuing music in college, was going to MIT to study mechanical engineering, hoping to focus on robotics. And Jules, whose family had limited funds and who had been an indifferent student in high school since her attention had been on everything and everyone from Spirit-in-the-Woods, was going to the State University of New York at Buffalo. She thought about Ash and Ethan's trips to see each other, picturing Ethan behind the wheel of his father's old car, gripping it hard as he merged onto I-95. Jules could also picture Ash on the Amtrak train, her head in a Penguin classic. Everyone else was either bewildered or impressed by what Ash and Ethan had found in each other, but Jules felt that she and Jonah were the only ones who could perceive the intense degree of their friends' commitment. Goodman, missing now for an entire year, had caused this relationship to take hold. Ash and Ethan would *never* have fallen in love if he hadn't run off and become a fugitive.

"If *encoupled* is a word," Jules said to Jonah one evening that spring before college, "then that is what they are."

"Yeah," he said, nodding. "I think it is a word. And that's definitely what they are."

*Un*encoupled, if that too was a word, was what Jonah and Jules were. They sat in Jonah

Bay's mother's loft, a large, not entirely finished space on Watts Street. Jules didn't understand the feeling of loneliness she had all the time now. It didn't make sense that the phenomenon of Ash and Ethan's couplehood should have caused it. Jonah didn't have the same feeling, exactly, but he admitted that he felt inadequate — embarrassed and even *appalled* when he thought back to the several months he'd been Ash's boyfriend the year before, and what a bad job he'd done.

"It isn't supposed to be a job," Jules said.

"No, I guess not." Jonah shrugged, but he didn't elaborate. Neither of them yet knew how to be a boyfriend or girlfriend. This was not a skill set that could be taught; you just had to do it, and you had to want to do it, and somehow through doing it you became better at it. Surely at MIT there would be plenty of other people who didn't know how to be boyfriends or girlfriends. Maybe, in that environment, tentative and virginal Jonah Bay could flourish.

"Kids!" called his mother. "Come listen to this. I need your opinion." Susannah Bay and two other musicians sat in the alcove off the main part of the loft. They played a song with a *wah-wah* underbeat that made it sound a little like the soundtrack to a cop show. His mother was trying hard to stay relevant, Jonah had said. Her voice was still strong; it hadn't been trashed like the voices of some of the women she'd come up with in the early days of the folk scene — women who'd started out as angelic sopranos and ended up sounding like someone's uncle with emphysema.

Susannah Bay could still sing anything, but the question was whether people wanted to hear her anymore. When she gave a concert at one of the very few remaining folk clubs in the city, or in other cities, places with an increasingly heavy cover charge, there was always a nostalgic demand for "The Wind Will Carry Us" and "Boy Wandering" and some of the other old songs that reminded the audience of where they had been the first time they'd heard them — and how much their lives had changed since then, and how shockingly old they were now. Those beloved songs had to be interspersed generously throughout the set at a concert; you could sense restlessness and even hostility when you went on too long without singing something familiar.

"The tide is turning," Susannah frequently said. But the tide always turned. When it was your tide, you took notice. Folk was over as a *scene,* and that was tremendously sad for all the people who'd been there in those early years, when an acoustic guitar and a single voice had seemed capable of hastening the end of a war; but now there was exciting music of all kinds — folk and not folk —

everywhere. It was just that Susannah Bay's new songs hadn't made the graceful leap into the closing years of the 1970s. When her impromptu set in the loft was finished, Susannah anxiously asked Jonah and Jules if they thought that this was the sort of music that they and their friends might want to listen to. She asked, "Could you imagine a bunch of you sitting around and putting on my new album?"

"Oh, definitely," Jules said, to be kind, and Jonah echoed her. Susannah seemed cheered by this, but the musicians knew it wasn't true, and they headed out somewhat mutely, then eventually Jules left too.

"See you," said Jonah at the door. They squeezed each other lightly, then patted each other on the back, making small physical gestures that affirmed their long-standing connection. They were the only two who were left now, the two who were still alone. Jonah was so good-looking that Jules marveled about it each time they had a moment of physical contact. His dark hair had recently been trimmed so that it now ended above his shoulders. He still sometimes wore a leather string around his neck, and a pocket T-shirt. He seemed almost embarrassed by his own beauty, and wanted to pretend that it was an optical illusion. Jules could also not understand why he'd always deflected talk about his musical talent, and why he'd abandoned it. She knew how good he was at guitar and singing and songwriting. Elektra, the label that had rejected his mother, might have wanted him now instead. But he didn't want any of that; instead, he would be at MIT in a lab, doing things that Jules would never be able to understand. "Is it that performing makes you anxious?" she'd once tried to ask him, but he'd only regarded her with an uncharacteristically cold expression, and shook his head as if to say she had no idea what she was talking about. Jules decided that Jonah was just too modest to be a musician or to possibly become famous; he didn't have the temperament, and she supposed this was honorable, and it made her own cravings for a big life, maybe even as a funny stage actress, seem a little crass.

Jules came to the loft often because she felt she needed to limit her time at the Labyrinth, where Ash and Ethan had essentially begun to live together. "You can set up shop in Goodman's room," Betsy Wolf had offered Ethan that spring. "Oh no, I can't do that," Ethan said. "But I really want you to," Betsy said. Her desire to have Ethan "set up shop" had to have come out of her longing for her son, and though it was probably hard to see another boy in that room — the wrong boy — it helped her too. Goodman had an enormous desk below curling posters of Pink Floyd and Led Zeppelin and *A Clockwork*

Orange. Gently, nervously, Ethan moved some of Goodman's surface objects to the side. On that desk, under the strong light of a green gooseneck lamp, Ethan Figman went to work, drawing frames for *Figland* cartoons.

Soon he was spending weekends at the Wolfs', and then, more and more frequently, weeknights. As high school seniors, he and Ash were a facsimile of an adult couple, and the Wolfs were progressive about sex and said their daughter's private life was none of their business. Ash had recently gone to Planned Parenthood and gotten fitted for a diaphragm; Jules had of course gone with her, sitting in the waiting room and pretending that she too was there to get a diaphragm. *Oh yes,* she thought as she sat in her chair, *that's me, Diaphragm Girl.* She looked around at all the other women, and imagined that they thought she wasn't a virgin, just like them. It was a surprisingly pleasurable thought. Afterward, when Ash came out carrying a plastic clamshell case, she and Jules went across the street from the clinic, sitting together on a low brick wall, and Ash took the object out of the case and they both examined it closely.

"What's this dust on it, this powder?" Jules asked.

"Cornstarch; they gave me a sample. It's to keep the silicon from eroding," Ash said.

"Well aren't you the scientist. You get your degree from Heidelberg?"

The thing was yellow-beige, the color of raw chicken skin, and Jules regarded it as Ash held it up and demonstrated its springiness and resilience. Jules uncomfortably thought of a stirred-up froth of gel and cornstarch and *fluids,* that awful word that had to do with the end result of a person's, or two people's, physical excitement. Ethan's presence in the Wolfs' apartment cheered the family up and distracted them from their feelings of dread about Goodman and what had become of him. Jules knew they feared they'd never see him again: that he would die, or that he was already dead. Who knew how he was supporting himself? The hopeful presence of young love in the household was just what was required to keep terrible conclusions away.

Anyone could tell that Ash Wolf and Ethan Figman loved each other, improbable or not. The love and the sex made sense to the two lovers, who felt it was almost *insane,* as Ash said, that it had taken them this long to figure it out. These days, the diaphragm was rarely in its case. Ash had confided to Jules recently that Ethan was a surprisingly good lover. "I know he's not much to look at," she'd said shyly, "but honestly, he knows how to connect with me in a physical way. He isn't afraid, and he isn't squeamish. He finds sex fascinating. He said he thinks it's very creative. Like finger painting, he told me. He wants to talk about everything. I've never had conversations like that with anyone; I mean, you and I are unbelievably close, but we know what we're talking about without having to explain. Because he's male and I'm female, it's as though we're coming from different planets."

"Yes. He's on the planet Figland," said Jules.

"Right! And I'm on earth. He wants to know all about so-called 'female' feelings — whether, for instance, girls actually find penises attractive, even though objectively they're so bizarre looking; and whether, get this, my father and I are a little bit 'in love' with each other. The Electra complex. And then, kind of a side question, whether I think about death constantly, the way he does. 'If you don't obsess over the idea that one day you won't exist,' Ethan said to me, 'then you aren't the girl for me.' I reassured him that I was extremely morbid and extremely existential, and he was very relieved to hear it. I think it even made him horny."

Jules listened to this soliloquy in grim silence; she hardly knew what to say. Ash was describing an enclosed world that Jules too had been given a chance to enter, but hadn't wanted to. She still didn't want to, but the descriptions of the closeness and intensity of

301

that world only increased her loneliness. "Go on," was all she said.

"At first I didn't think it would take," said Ash. "I didn't think I could find a way to be attracted to him, because, well, objectively, *you* know. But once we really started doing serious things in bed, it was as if he was made for it. Made for me. And I wanted to be looser finally; I wanted to not have to be so *good* all the time, so held in and perfect, Little Ms. A student at the Brearley School. I never would have thought this could happen between Ethan and me. But it did, and what can I say?"

There was nothing else to say. Jules left Jonah's mother's loft and clattered down into the subway to head up to Penn Station, where she would catch a train home, alone. She reminded herself that she herself had not wanted Ethan as her boyfriend, her "lover," and still did not want him. She recalled Ethan's strong breath and his eczema, even. She remembered the fatal lump that had pressed against her as they stood in the animation shed. Love transcended all of this, apparently. Love transcended breath, eczema, fear of sex, and an imbalance in physical appearance. If love was real, then these bodily, human details could seem insignificant.

But obviously the physical imperfections of Ethan Figman hadn't risen in importance to Ash the same way that they had for Jules.

Ethan's hygiene was better now than it had been at fifteen, but beyond that, he was also changing, growing into himself. The Ash and Ethan experience was private and specific to *them.* What complicated it a little was that Jules loved Ethan too, in her own private and enduring way. He was so talented and smart and worried and unusual and generous toward her. He believed in her, he nodded thoughtfully at many of her remarks, appreciated her wit, encouraged her to think that she could have a big life one day, living in the city and maybe becoming a funny actress and doing what she wanted. He remained loving toward her, and would do anything for her. Clearly she'd undervalued him, she thought now darkly, as she stood on the nighttime subway platform without a piece of silicon snapped deeply and securely inside her, covering the cervix and waiting to be put to use.

Then Jules thought, no, she hadn't undervalued Ethan. She'd valued him highly, but she just hadn't *wanted* him. And in a pivotal moment of strangeness, Ash *had.* Ash Wolf choosing Ethan Figman elevated Ash to some higher plane of being. The mystery of desire was way beyond the conceptual abilities of Jules Jacobson. It was like . . . robotics. Just another subject that she couldn't understand at all.

The train came, and Jules Jacobson stepped

on and thought: *I am the loneliest person in this subway car.* Everything here looked ugly: the aqua subway seats; the ads for Goya products, as if a faded color illustration of now-gray guavas in gray syrup could make you want to eat them; the metal rails that had been grasped by thousands of hands that very day; the stations as they flowed past the window. *I am having a crisis,* she thought. *I suddenly feel a new, fragile sense of myself in the world, and it is unbearable.*

The year remained intensely lonely, and sometimes at night in bed Jules thought of how she and her mother and sister were all lying separately in their beds, each of them almost throbbing with aloneness. She suddenly couldn't imagine how her mother had survived widowhood at age forty-one. Jules realized that she had almost never wondered about this before. She'd mostly thought: *I am a girl whose father is dead,* and this had had a certain tragic cachet to it. Other people had said to her, "I'm very sorry for your loss," and after she'd heard this said often enough, she'd almost felt that the loss was hers alone. Jules wanted to apologize to her mother, to let her know that she'd been so self-absorbed until this moment, but the truth was that she was still extraordinarily self-absorbed.

After a certain age, you felt a need not to be alone. It grew stronger, like a radio frequency, until finally it was so powerful that you were forced to do something about it. While Jules lay alone in the bedroom on Cindy Drive, her two good friends lay without clothes in Ash's bed on the sixth floor of the Labyrinth. Ethan Figman in his vulnerable nakedness was somehow maybe even beautiful. He was no different from anyone in the world. He wanted what he wanted, and he'd found it, and now he and Ash were dumbly happy in their shared bed.

Goodman was rapidly disappearing from daily conversation since Ethan and Ash became a couple. The family remained troubled and sad about him, but you could tell that they were actually recovering. A summer trip to Iceland was in the planning stages; Ash said her father had business to conduct there. More than that, though, the trip would be a way for the three remaining Wolfs to be quietly together one more time before Ash went off to Yale in the fall. They would ride horses in Iceland and go swimming in a geothermal pool.

One day at the end of May, when Jules and Ash were standing in a bead store on Eighth Street, their hands roaming and sifting through bins of shining, buffed glass, Ash said, "So, what are you going to do this summer?"

"Getting a job at Carvel," said Jules. "Not very thrilling, but it'll give me some spending money for Buffalo. My sister used to work there. They said they'd hire me."

"When do you start?"

"It has yet to be determined. I'll have to check with Personnel." She paused, then added, "That was a joke."

Ash was smiling with deep secrecy. "Tell them you can't start until the end of July," she said.

"Why?"

"You're coming to Iceland."

"You know I can't pay for that."

"My parents invited you, Jules. They'll take care of everything."

"They invited me? Are you serious? It's not like inviting me to *dinner.*"

"They really want you to come."

"Did they invite Ethan too?"

"Of course," said Ash, a little flustered. "But he can't, because of Old Mo Templeton. You know, he even turned down that amazing internship because of Old Mo." Ethan's animation teacher was dying of emphysema in the Bronx, and Ethan had taken it upon himself to care for him instead of going to LA to work at Warner Bros.' Looney Tunes. "He can't come," said Ash. "But you can."

"She'll never let me go," Jules said, "she" being her mother. Then she remembered that Gudrun Sigurdsdottir, the former counselor from Spirit-in-the-Woods, lived in Iceland.

"Oh, you know what?" Jules said. "If I did get to go with you, we could look up Gudrun. That would be so weird, seeing her on her own turf."

"Oh, right, Gudrun the weaver," said Ash.

"And she could tell us more about a tinder chamber being engulfed with flames."

"God, Jules, you remember everything."

Lois Jacobson was predictably uncomfortable with the Wolfs' extravagant invitation. "It just makes me feel that Ash's parents must think of us as poor people or something," she said. "And that isn't true. But there isn't money for a trip like this. And I just hate the idea of someone else's parents paying for you."

"Mom, it isn't just someone else's parents. It's Ash's."

"I know that, honey."

Ellen, puttering around the kitchen during the conversation, looked at Jules and said, "Why are they being so nice to you?"

"What do you mean?"

"I don't know," said Ellen. "I just never heard of a family doing that."

"Maybe they like me."

"Maybe they do," said Ellen, who couldn't seem to imagine why a glamorous family she'd never met would be so interested in her sister.

Jules and the Wolfs left for Iceland on July 18, on a night flight from Kennedy Airport to Luxembourg, where they would change planes for Reykjavik. The first-class cabin was as comfortable as the Wolfs' living room, and after dinner Jules made her wide seat recline, and she and Ash lay under soft blankets. Later, over the Atlantic, Jules awoke in a fully formed and inexplicable state of fear and dread. But when she looked around her, she was reassured by the calm, purring golden cabin with a few pin lights that cast beams downward on their seats' occupants. Ash and her mother both slept, but Gil Wolf was awake, looking through papers in his briefcase and occasionally glancing out the little window into the blackness with what seemed to Jules, from her place across the aisle, like his own state of fear and dread.

The city of Reykjavik was notably clean and small, the buildings low and the sky wide. On the first day, trying to adjust to the time difference, the family stayed awake as long as they could, walking around the city, which felt like an appealing college town, and drinking coffee and Cokes and eating hot dogs from a street vendor. The music scene that later exploded in Reykjavik was not in place yet; Björk, the singer, was at the moment only eleven years old. Walking along a modest, well-kept little street, Jules felt unsteady. "Garden-variety jet lag," Betsy Wolf said. But soon Jules's mouth became wet with excess saliva, and then her stomach began to emit strange and unnatural noises. Jules could barely make it back into the Hotel Borg. The strangeness of strange places was now unbearable. Her mouth kept filling with saliva, and her legs shook, and once inside the hotel suite, Jules ran ahead and let loose a straight shot of vomit into the toilet. She actively vomited for so long that the Wolfs had the hotel's on-call doctor brought in, and he gave her a large, gelatinous-looking pill that she was about to put into her mouth before he stopped her and said in a kind but awkward voice, "No, miss, please. The *anal* opening," for it was a suppository.

Jules slept through much of the first evening in Iceland. When she could finally open her eyes, she had a dull headache but was also urgently hungry and thirsty. "Hello?" she said, trying out her voice. "Ash?" The hotel room was empty, and so was the adjoining one where Ash's parents were staying, and she had no idea what time of day or night it was. Jules pulled back the edge of the drape on the window and saw that the sky was still bright. She went into the bathroom and there was a note propped up on the sink, where she couldn't miss it, written in Ash's rounded, girlish hand on hotel stationery:

Jules!!!!
I hope you are better, poor you. We are at the Café Benedikt, which is VERY nearby.

Ask the concierge how to get here. Please come as soon as you can, SERIOUSLY.

Love you,
Ash

With a bar of green soap, Jules stood at the sink and washed her face, then managed to locate her toothbrush and toothpaste from the piece of red Samsonite luggage her mother had bought her as a going-away present. She cleaned her mouth, ran a brush through her hopeless hair, and went downstairs. The lobby was stately, with classical music playing softly. It was far dimmer in here than it was outside. Jules got directions from the concierge — everyone spoke English — and pushed through the door, heading into the sunlit Reykjavik night. This was a place that, in its puzzling continual daylight, appeared totally alien to her, a place where she had almost eaten a suppository. As she walked the two blocks to the café she sensed that she was walking toward something unusual. But maybe in life, she thought later, there are not only moments of strangeness but moments of knowledge, which don't appear at the time as knowledge at all. Jules walked down the street with her hair frizzing, a small splash of yellow vomit on the collar of her Huk-a-Poo blouse, though she hadn't noticed it yet. She wore the turquoise clogs she had brought with her — "Finally we will be wearing clogs in the right part of the world," she'd said to Ash before the trip — and they clacked loudly over stones, each step making her feel self-conscious and alone but purposeful. Many people here were wearing clogs, but none of them seemed to walk as percussively as she did.

Jules walked past men who were obviously drunk; she walked past a cluster of backpackers — latter-day hippies who were doing a tour of Iceland on almost nothing a day. A boy called out to her in a language she didn't understand, maybe Greek, but Jules kept walking. Because of the broken blood vessels in her eyes, she knew she must look like a zombie out on a death mission. She easily found the right street with its row of cafés, all of them crowded, and with the strong smell of cigarettes rolling out. When she located the Café Benedikt and looked in the window, the first face she recognized didn't belong to one of the Wolfs. Instead, it was a face completely out of context, and she had to take a second to recall the beam of the heavy, industrial-type flashlight that the weaver and lifeguard Gudrun Sigurdsdottir had first shone into the teepee in the summer of 1974. Gudrun was here again now, smiling, and from behind her, deeper in the packed restaurant, the Wolf family strained forward to make themselves seen by Jules too, and they were all smiling out at her with expressions that

311

were uniform in their intensity and peculiarity. Ash was looking right at Jules, her eyes wet and happy. Beside her at the table, only half-viewable from this angle, his face partly hidden by a wooden post, was Goodman. He raised his glass of beer, and then they all motioned for Jules to come inside.

"His voice on the phone just stopped me dead in my tracks," Betsy Wolf explained. " 'Mom.' "

"Mom," Goodman said now, for emphasis, and the name seemed to pierce Betsy Wolf all over again; she put down her glass of wine and took her son's hands in her own and kissed them. Everyone at the table had an emotional face on, even Gudrun. Jules too had been pulled in, and her shock had changed quickly, liquefying, going loose and responsive.

"We were going to tell you everything as soon as we got to the hotel, Jules," said Ash. "Goodman was working today and couldn't see us until tonight. We had a plan to sit down and talk to you first and explain everything. But then you got food poisoning, and it would have been too weird to suddenly spring this on you when you were throwing up. You probably would've thought you hallucinated it."

"I still think that."

"I'm real," said Goodman. "But you look

like an impostor, Jacobson. What's the deal with your eyes?"

"I broke my blood vessels throwing up," she said. "It looks a lot worse than it is."

"Yeah, you look like the girl in *The Exorcist,*" Goodman said. "But in a good way." This was the kind of amusing, insulting remark he would have made back when they all gathered in the teepee. But he'd long outgrown teepee life, and had entered someplace well beyond the rest of them. He now had the appearance of a sophisticated, bohemian European student who was perhaps at university on scholarship. He was not actually in school, he told Jules, because he would have needed too much legitimate documentation for that. He still longed to become an architect someday, but he knew he could never get licensed here or anywhere. Jules wondered whether that was entirely the case; could he possibly have found a way, if it was what he really wanted, and worked toward it? For the time being, he was working construction with Gudrun's husband, Falkor, which was what he'd been doing today, and why he couldn't see his family until evening. The two men gutted houses, and at the end of the workday they took hot saunas, and then, if it was warm enough outside, jumped into a cold lake.

Goodman, Jules found out as everyone at the table told her pieces of the story, had originally taken a Peter Pan bus from Port Authority up to Belknap, Massachusetts, on the morning he ran away. He'd banged on the door of the big gray house across the road from the camp, where Manny and Edie Wunderlich lived, but no one answered. He'd worked himself into a panic in the days building up to his sudden flight, afraid that the jury wouldn't believe him and he would lose his court case and be sent to jail until he was a middle-aged man. So after he decided to flee, and collected a large sum of money from his bank account, placing it in the duffel bag he used to take to camp with him, Spirit-in-the-Woods was the only place he'd thought to go. Goodman walked around and around the property of the camp, which was empty and still and appeared so melancholy off-season. Outside the dining hall he saw the cook, Ida Steinberg, taking out the garbage, and he went over and said hello. She'd had no idea of his arrest, but when he said he needed to get away, she understood that he meant he needed to get away and not be found.

The cook took Goodman inside the camp kitchen, sat him down, and ladled some lentil soup into a bowl. It was a lucky coincidence that she happened to be here today, she explained; she only worked for the Wunderlichs very infrequently in the off-season, but some workers were here doing intensive repairs to the grounds in anticipation of a facility inspection, and so her cooking services were needed. The Wunderlichs were in Pittsfield for the day, buying supplies. Goodman instinctively asked Ida not to tell them he'd been here. He knew that they liked his parents, but they also liked the Kiplingers.

"Go find a nice person to take you in," Ida Steinberg suggested to him. "Far away."

Goodman immediately thought of Gudrun Sigurdsdottir, who had come into the boys' teepee once and lounged on a bed, smoking and talking openly about the pain of life. As if Spirit-in-the-Woods had its own underground resistance, Goodman asked Ida if she could give him Gudrun's address and phone number. The cook dutifully retrieved it from the Rolodex in the front office. Goodman had money; he would fly to some city in Europe, then make his way to Iceland to find Gudrun and ask her to help him. His thinking was cockeyed — what if he traveled all that distance and she'd said no? What then? — but to him it was reasonable. First he took a bus to Boston and asked around about securing a fake passport. Three days later, after having moved into an SRO, Goodman purchased a shockingly expensive passport that actually worked, though before his flight took off for Paris out of Terminal E at Logan he sat shaking in seat 14D, his eyes fixed on a book he'd picked up in desperation in the airport, the kind of popular novel that he, who loved Günter Grass, would never have read in his life: *Curtain,* by Agatha Christie.

Under an assumed name, Goodman had been living here in Reykjavik with Gudrun and Falkor, sleeping on the futon in their tiny spare room. "But why did you pick Iceland?" Jules asked.

"I told you. Because of Gudrun," Goodman said.

"It just seems so random."

"She was the only one far enough away not to know about the whole thing with Cathy, and not to judge me. She never judged any of us, remember? She was kind."

Gudrun, listening, wiped her eyes a little. "Goodman showed up and said he needed help. I always liked him. He was in your nice group of friends."

Gudrun and her husband, who was also a weaver when he wasn't working construction, had very little money, and they lived plainly. Often the only food on hand was a kind of dark brown wood-pulp type of cracker and some skyr, the tartest, most monastic yogurt in the world. At night Goodman slept on the bare futon under one of Gudrun and Falkor's hand-woven blankets. But he longed for his parents and his sister; he felt desperate to reestablish contact with them. As the anniversary of the day he'd fled approached, Goodman experienced unbearable homesickness, thinking of his family in the apartment in New York, and the smells of his mother's cooking, and the comfort of being in a wonderful family, having a key that opened a door to a place where you lived. He knew it had been a fatal mistake to bolt. It had torn his family up, just as it had torn him up.

Day after day in his narrow new Icelandic life, Goodman had trudged past pay phones in Reykjavik, and had to keep himself from stopping and calling home. One day in March, he went to Gudrun and Falkor's place and gathered a large scoop of krónur and put it all in a satchel, and the next afternoon, on a break from a construction job in Breidholt, Goodman walked to a small store on the side of a road. Shaking, he peppered the phone slot with coin after coin until the line rang, and across the ocean his sad mother said hello in her pretty, motherly voice, and he said simply, *"Mom."*

Betsy Wolf breathed in a gasp, an inverted sigh, and then she said, "Oh my God."

He knew it was a big risk to call home, but so much time had passed since he'd run off, and perhaps no one was lying in wait for him anymore. Perhaps they had even forgotten. The lead detectives, Manfredo and Spivack, had called the Wolfs frequently in the beginning to ask if they knew anything, but then they called less often. "Frankly, we're overburdened," Manfredo had admitted to Betsy.

317

"In fact, we're kind of dying here. The department just laid off two people, and more cuts are coming. The city doesn't have the money." Many years later a teenaged boy from suburban Connecticut would be accused of two separate, vicious rapes, and would escape to Switzerland to live as a ski bum, his idle life bankrolled by his wealthy parents. But that boy was a predator, having assaulted more than one victim, and the case would not die; his arrest was seen as a triumph. Goodman's case had been less sensationalistic and less interesting from the start. When he fled, the Kiplingers had no desire to speak to the press, and after a while the case appeared to have gotten lost under other priorities. Goodman, nervily calling home from abroad, worried for a moment that somehow his parents and sister had forgotten him too, that they'd managed to move on with their lives. He said a few tentative words to his mother, and Betsy began to cry and begged him to tell her where he was.

"I can't. What if your phone is bugged?" he said.

"It isn't," Betsy Wolf said. "Just tell me. You're my child and I need to know where you are. It's been torture." He told his mother where he was, and then she said, "All right, fine, you're very young and you made a snap decision and it was a bad one; now we have to fix it."

"What does that mean?"

"You'll come home," said his mother. "You'll get on a plane and fly here, and we will meet you at the airport and you can voluntarily surrender."

"Surrender?" said Goodman. "You make it sound like I did something, Mom."

"Well," said Betsy, "you did do something: you fled. That's not nothing, honey, but we'll work it out, we'll smooth it over."

Goodman told her she was being naive, that life didn't always work out, and that he couldn't possibly come home. They went back and forth like this, his mother begging, and Goodman insisting that no, he wasn't coming back, he'd made a break and that was the way it was going to be; if he came back he might be sent to jail for a very long time, and if he stayed here at least he could have a life of some kind. Finally she saw that he was not going to change his mind. Though he was dreadfully homesick, he'd gotten used to the idea that this was where he now lived. Other than turn him in herself, she didn't see what she could do to get him to come back.

And so, acting parentally, brazenly, but telling no one — not even Ash — Betsy and Gil Wolf sent money to Iceland through elaborate banking channels. He was their son and they knew he was innocent, and if they could not convince him to come home, then this was what they felt they needed to do. After the money arrived without incident, they waited tensely, and finally they decided it was fair to assume that by some stroke of luck no one else was thinking about Goodman anymore, and that maybe they could conceivably even go see him. It was time to tell Ash, they decided.

"I came home from school one day," Ash explained to Jules at the café, "and my parents both sat me down in the living room. Their expressions were incredibly weird. I thought they were going to tell me that Goodman had been found, and that he was *dead.* I just couldn't bear it. But then they told me he was fine, he was in *Iceland,* and that they'd been sending him money, and that finally we were going to get to see him. I almost died. We all began to scream and hug each other. I thought I would *explode,* keeping that secret from you, Jules. But my parents said, 'Tell no one!' They were like the Mafia. And it was all I could do not to tell Ethan too. I mean, I tell him everything, now that we're together. I talk to him about extremely personal subjects, as you know."

"You and Ethan," said Goodman. "I still can't get over that. Mom wrote me. Damn, Ash, can't you do better than that? You're a catch, and he's . . . Ethan. I love the guy, but I would never have put my money on that horse."

"No one wants to hear your opinion of my

love life," said Ash, smiling but still crying too. Then she turned to Jules and said, "But I couldn't tell Ethan, of course, because who knows what he'd think. Or do."

"What?" said Jules. "Ethan still doesn't know?"

"No."

"Are you kidding? He's your boyfriend, and you have such a close relationship." She just stared at Ash.

"I know, but I can't tell him. My dad would kill me."

"That's for damn sure," said Gil Wolf, and everyone laughed politely, uncomfortably.

"Ethan has all these views of life that no one can control," said Ash. "All these ideas about what's ethical and what's not. That whole code of the road that he lives by. Did you ever see that cartoon he made where the president of Figland is impeached, and the vice president pardons him? And in the middle of signing the pardon, the vice president turns into a weasel? And then there was Ethan's insistence on cutting school to work for the Carter campaign."

"Well, that one worked out," said Jules.

"Or taking care of Old Mo instead of doing Looney Tunes. And remember how he just *had* to be in touch with Cathy when Dick Peddy said we weren't supposed to? If I told Ethan about Goodman, he might think he had to report it or something, out of respect for Cathy. Report all of us. Have us taken away and put on a chain gang."

"When in fact," said Goodman, "I didn't do anything to Cathy Kiplinger. She totally distorted it."

"Oh, we know that," said his mother. She looked longingly at him and said, "You really won't consider coming home and hoping for the best?"

"Mom," said Goodman sharply. "Stop it. I told you."

"God knows what a jury would think, Betsy," said Gil. Everyone was quiet for a moment, looking at Goodman, who, it was true, did not appear boyish or defenseless. Construction work had built up his long muscles. Jules dragged up the word *sinew* from somewhere in her vocabulary. Goodman — in this new, slightly older, Icelandic version — looked strong and handsome and more worldly. God knew what a jury would think of him. "Leave it alone," said Gil quietly, and then finally Betsy sighed and nodded, squeezing her son's hand.

Jules could not let go of the question of Ash telling Ethan, and she said to Ash, "But how could you not tell the person you're in love with?"

"You are the only one I can trust about this," Ash said. Which was maybe just another version of what Cathy Kiplinger had said to Jules: you are weak.

"But you'll have to tell him eventually, right?" Jules asked.

Ash didn't say anything, so her father spoke up. "No, she won't," he said. "That's the point I've been trying to make."

The moment was so stiff that Jules didn't know who to look at or what to say. Goodman stood up from the table then and said, "Good time to go take a leak." He loped away, more enormous than he'd been when Jules had seen him last. Construction work, the Icelandic sun, cup upon cup of skyr, sexual deprivation, an occasional gambling habit, the guzzling of Brennivin, aka Black Death, a kind of hardcore schnapps made from fermented potato and caraway seeds: all of it had contributed to making him into some kind of hulking young expat whose first name was now, someone had mentioned tonight, John.

While he was gone from the table the other three Wolfs drew closer, and Gudrun took this opportunity to go out and buy cigarettes. "Now look," Gil said, taking a drink of beer and then gazing directly at Jules, "I cannot emphasize enough that this is a heavy, heavy situation. You understand that, right?"

"Yes," she said in a whisper.

"And you can be absolutely trusted?" he asked. They were all looking right at her, gravely.

"Yes," she said. "Of course I can."

"Okay, good," Gil said. "Because the thing is, we did not want Ash telling anyone. *Anyone.* Not you. Not Ethan. The consequences could be so awful that I don't even want to think about it. But Ash insisted she had to talk to someone other than us, or else she would have a nervous breakdown. That may sound a little melodramatic —"

"I *wasn't* being melodramatic, Dad," Ash broke in, and her father turned to her.

"All right, you weren't. But we all know you react very sensitively to everything, and we took that into account." He seemed to struggle to contain himself, then he turned back to Jules, his face stern, fatherly, or, more than that, headmasterly. "When she goes off to Yale in the fall, she has to be able to focus," Gil said. "She can't be thrown off-balance by all of this. None of us can. We have to act as though nothing is new. Everything is the same."

Jules imagined returning to Underhill, and her mother innocently asking, "So was it the exciting trip you'd hoped it would be? Tell me all the highlights." Lois would be unaware that Jules had been initiated into this, and she wouldn't know how frightening it had felt, how independent. Jules wished that she could tell Ethan; he would guide her. "I have a moral puzzle for you," she'd tell him. "Go ahead," he'd say, and she would begin. "There was a family, uncommonly seductive

324

and alluring . . ."

"To tell you the truth, Jules," said Betsy Wolf, "in an ideal world only our immediate family would know that we've had contact with Goodman, and that we're trying to see to it that he has a decent life. We know he's innocent of those outrageous charges made by that very troubled girl, and when the time is right we will help ease his way back home. We'll speak to the DA's office and do what needs to be done. Goodman will make amends for leaving. But that time is not now. I don't want to insult you by saying the kind of thing people sometimes say: 'We think of you as family.' I once heard Celeste Peddy actually say that to the poor Peruvian — or is it Indian — woman who comes in once a week to basically stand in a closet and do her ironing. Only family is family, and it's an unjust fact of life. You have your own family. I've only spoken to your mother a couple of times, and I just met her the other day at the airport, but she seems like a very nice person. You aren't in our family, though it would be so nice if you were. I'm not your mother, and Gil's not your father, and we can't force you to do what we've decided to do. I think Ash manipulated us just a tiny bit to get us to include you on this trip —"

"Not true," Ash piped up.

"Well, we'll have to go into mother-daughter therapy one day to find out," said

Betsy with a small smile toward her daughter. "I'm sure it exists. We've paid for other kinds of therapy, so why not that? But the thing is, Jules, Ash loves you. You are the best friend she's ever had, and I guess she wouldn't mind my saying right now that she needs you too." Betsy's voice became unbound again, and Ash leaned across the table, putting her arms around her mother. They looked so much alike, the fine-featured, salt-and-pepper-headed mother and the shimmering daughter, whose looks would also one day turn in this same direction, still pleasing and fine, just no longer young and untouched.

Nearby, a gaggle of smoking, drinking students glanced over at the Americans and their open display of emotion, but no one at this table even tried to temper themselves tonight. "I love you so much, Mom," Ash said, her face collapsing.

"And I love you too, darling girl."

Goodman returned then, followed shortly by Gudrun, who immediately opened her pack of King's Original, tapped one out, and lit it. The counselor seemed chic here in Iceland. Her hair was well cut, and Jules thought for a moment of the poor living conditions that Goodman had described in Gudrun and Falkor's home. But then she remembered that for months now, money had steadily been coming into that household. Probably the living conditions had improved.

Gudrun looked like a smartly dressed artist or designer.

"What's going on?" Goodman said. "I go take a leak and all hell breaks loose."

"Don't worry," said Jules. "There's no relationship between your family's emotional outpouring and your *bladder* outpouring."

"It's just very, very intense around here," Ash said. She walked around the table and stood beside her brother, putting an arm around his shoulder; he had sat down again, but even sitting, he was almost as tall as she was.

"We were telling Jules how essential it is that we keep this to ourselves," said Gil. "More than essential."

"I know," Jules said. "I really do know."

"Thank you," Ash said from across the table.

"Tomorrow," said Gil Wolf, looking around at his family, "we'll all go swimming in a geothermal pool, and then we'll have a wonderful Icelandic meal. We'll have a great day," he said. "We deserve it. We need it."

Then the Wolf family began to talk to one another all at once. They discussed the death of their dog, and Ash said, "I can't believe you weren't there, Goodman," and Goodman said, "I know, I know, it *killed* me, I'm so sorry, I loved him too." And they talked about how strange it was that Jonah was going to MIT of all places, and how Cousin

Michelle was pregnant with twins, and about American politics, which Goodman usually only heard about through the filter of the Icelandic news. They talked and talked, bringing up anything that occurred to them. The family relaxed together in the close brown and gold quarters of the Café Benedikt. Jules drank another glass of water, and then she was suddenly weary again, but the Wolf family was still going strong, and might still be going strong for hours. Iceland, so far away from everywhere, stayed up late, as if to soothe itself in its isolation. Only Jules Jacobson and Gudrun Sigurdsdottir were left on the outer edges of this conversation, sitting in slightly formal silence, the teenaged girl and the grown woman. Jules looked at the former camp counselor, who looked at her, and they both smiled shyly, having nothing at all to say.

"So," Jules said finally. "Do you still have that flashlight?"

■ ■ ■ ■ ■

PART TWO
FIGLAND

■ ■ ■ ■ ■

TEN

On September 1984, at a small Japanese restaurant in New York City so expensive it had no name on the door and no prices on its calligraphic menu, Ethan Figman and Ash Wolf sat on pressed straw mats across from network executives Gary Roman and Hallie Sakin, both sleek and tailored and veneer-toothed, though it was clear that Gary had the power, and that Hallie's power came from its complementarity. He spoke first; she seemed to repeat a milder and less engaging version of what had just been said. "This has been a wonderful sequence of developments," Gary Roman said.

"So terrific," said Hallie Sakin.

A pilot had been made, a deal going forward had been finalized, and a full season of *Figland* had been ordered, to be produced out of the studio in midtown Manhattan that the network was opening expressly for this purpose. Because of Ethan's insistence on doing the voices of two recurring characters, he'd rendered himself permanently indispensable in this way as well as others. A few days earlier the executives had come in from LA for meetings with Ethan and his agent and his lawyers, and now, at last, for a celebration dinner.

A waiter took their orders, and then a waitress in a pale green kimono slid open the rice-paper doors and brought in wooden tray after wooden tray of food, while the waiter hovered and oversaw, the two of them like a Japanese version of Gary Roman and Hallie Sakin. Power structures were always fairly easy to figure out if you took a moment to observe the people involved. Ethan would mention this to Ash later, when they were back in their apartment and had a chance to deconstruct the evening, during which Ethan felt deeply and uncomfortably formal and not himself. First of all, the weirdness of sushi itself had put him off. At age twenty-five, Ethan Figman had only ever eaten a California roll, which was not remotely raw. But now a selection of sushi, and varied rhombuses of sashimi, were carried in accompanied by smears of something sinus-opening called wasabi. There were glistening little globes, the harvest of mysterious underwater ovulation, and amputated tentacles served with a dipping sauce that tasted like smoked caramel. Ethan was scared of the parasites that sometimes swarmed in raw fish, but he was intrigued by the food too, and tried to overcome his fears. Japanese food was, in its way, like an edible cartoon.

Ash, beside him, had eaten sushi and sashimi many times; she even said, later that night, that she was sure she'd come to this very restaurant once, with her father, when she was a child in the 1960s. Gil Wolf had patiently taught his daughter to hold a pair of lacquered chopsticks at that dinner. But maybe it hadn't been this restaurant at all; there were a few such places in the city, unlabeled, unlisted, unpriced. You just had to be the kind of person to know about them. You just had to have money.

But it wasn't only the food that made Ethan feel the way he did. By rights he ought to have been relaxed. The time to be tense was before today, and he'd been tense then too. Now, with a season of the show ordered, and an entire floor of an office building rented as studio space, the network couldn't take it back. They couldn't suddenly realize the depth and breadth of their error, the fact that they had mistakenly offered *him,* of all people — uncool, unbeautiful Ethan Figman — a very large sum of money to do what he'd always done anyway, at least in his head.

"How does it feel to know that if audiences respond the way we think they will, you're going to be the most lovable Figman in America?" Gary Roman asked.

"I bet you're psyched," murmured Hallie Sakin.

"I think I will actually be the second most lovable one," said Ethan. "My great-uncle Schmendrick Figman is *worshipped,* at least within the Bensonhurst section of Brooklyn."

There was a confused pause, and the executives both laughed with similar bleats, though Ash didn't even pretend to find it funny. Ethan was babbling; this was what he did in times of stress. Of course he did not have a great-uncle Schmendrick, and the joke wasn't even a joke. He knew that Ash didn't like this part of him, but when you were in a relationship you had to take the whole package. By the time Ash came to love Ethan, he had developed so many liabilities: the babbling, the sweating hands, the insecurity, the general ugliness with his clothes on and perhaps the greater ugliness with them off. Ethan Figman needed more sake now in order to talk to these people the way a human talks to other humans. He couldn't only talk to his friends for the rest of his life, though that would have been preferable — particularly if he could mostly talk to Jules. He and the network were now partnered, paired off. Ethan was going to have a show called *Figland* to create and write and do voices for and take part in table reads for and devote all his time to. He would be ringed by many, many people, not just Ash and Jonah and Jules.

Almost three years earlier, Ethan had been hired by a clever if shrill nighttime cartoon for adults called *The Chortles.* He was a few months out of the School of Visual Arts when he took the job, and though before then he'd been able to find work doing industrials, he was curious about what it would be like to be part of a show. Alone among his friends he appeared to be eminently hirable. Everyone else seemed to be circling their desired careers, not inhabiting them yet. Jules was still trying to be a comedic actor; Ash was trying to be a serious one. Jonah, fresh out of the Moonies, was undecided and lost, looking for some kind of engineering job. *The Chortles* was one of the very few TV cartoons for adults, and what made it even more unusual was that it was produced in New York, not LA; this was its biggest allure for Ethan. He didn't actually like the way *The Chortles* looked, and the humor was sort of mean and childish. Characters actually stuck out a foot and tripped one another in a running gag that tested well with audiences between the ages of eighteen and twenty-five, the desired demographic. The animation studio where Ethan drew and wrote *The Chortles* was a big, open space in Chelsea with modular furniture, a Joy Division soundtrack, a refrigerator packed with sodas and juice, and a staff under the age of thirty.

One day someone brought in a pogo stick that left a long line of pockmarks in the beautiful floor. Ethan settled in to the job and more than a year passed, during which he was given a series of raises and compliments. *The Chortles* was doing so well that the producers flew the staff to Hawaii in gratitude.

On the island of Maui in December 1982, sitting in a long-sleeved shirt and long pants — practically full beekeeper regalia — on a lounge chair under the shade of a tree with a book, while everyone else was in the sun or in the water, Ethan realized that he was depressed and not only needed to go home, he needed to leave his job. He didn't want to be responsible for the Chortles with their wide, dumb heads any longer. Ethan went up to his hotel room and called Ash in New York; he hadn't used the phone once since he'd been here, not wanting to rack up any extra expenses, afraid that someone from the network would be mad at him if he did. Even his minibar had remained unplundered. Surely all the other *Chortles* staff were eating fistfuls of Kona coffee–glazed macadamia nuts day and night. Ethan was concerned that when he told Ash he was quitting, she would say, "That's really impulsive, Ethan. Look, stay for the rest of the trip, then come home and we'll discuss it."

But what she said was, "If that's what you

want to do."

"It is."

"All right, then. Let me know when you're coming. I love you so much."

"I love you too." He said it fiercely, feeling her quiet power. Ash never judged. Come home, she told him, and now he would come home, and she would be waiting, and would help him sort it out. Partners and spouses had been invited on this trip, but Ash had chosen to stay in New York to be the assistant director of an experimental play called *Coco Chanel Gets Her Rocks Off*, which would be put on outdoors in the meatpacking district at night. She wasn't being paid for her work, but Ethan's salary supported them both. He packed his bag while the other animators splashed and dove in the Pacific, and he left a note at the hotel's front desk for his boss, explaining that his decision had struck him swiftly but solidly. "It was like being hit in the head with a surfboard," he wrote. "Not that I personally would know what that's like, since as you might have noticed I spent this vacation in the shade reading *A Confederacy of Dunces*. But I have to get out, Stan. I'm not even sure why."

Back at home in New York, Stan called and asked Ethan to come in the following week for a "sit-down," but Ethan declined. He stayed in the apartment obsessively doodling

Figland figures in the little spiral notebooks that he bought in bulk. Sometimes Jonah Bay, who was now overworked at the job he'd recently found designing daily-living innovations for disabled people, came over and stayed for much of the evening, and occasionally even collapsed on the couch and spent the night. Or else Jules came over with her boyfriend Dennis Boyd, a big, dark-haired man who had begun attending ultrasound technology school in the fall.

"I know you see ads all the time on the subway about becoming an ultrasound technician, so it sort of seems like a joke," Jules had said after she'd announced Dennis's plans. "But what he wants to do professionally is actually something important. He's going to be able to see inside people, see the mysteries beneath their skeletons. And with sound waves, no less. It's sort of like being a psychic, but with machines. I think it's a kind of artistry, in a way. He'll be dealing with anatomy. With people's lives. What's inside them. Their entire futures."

"I know that," said Ethan. "And I like Dennis. You don't have to sell him to me."

Dennis Boyd was shy, and there had been some emotional trouble in his background, Ethan knew. But mostly he seemed to be a decent person who would never hurt Jules, thank God; who would only love her. Looking across the room at Jules sometimes,

Ethan felt as if the selves they'd inhabited at age fifteen were still thoroughly present. He could still kiss her, he realized, and then he immediately told himself: *banish this thought.* In her twenties Jules Jacobson wasn't even particularly sexy or sexual — not that she had been at fifteen, either — but he was excited by her to this day because he simply liked her so much. Jules was smart and charming and self-deprecating. No one had ever given her anything, and she hadn't been coddled. Ethan hadn't been coddled either; they had this in common, along with a certain skewed sensibility. Jules didn't care if she seemed dignified or not. Her jokes were often on herself; she threw aside dignity in the service of comedic effect.

Ethan knew that, objectively, Jules wasn't all that hilarious. Right out of college, she'd started coming into the city on the train from her mother's house all the time to try out for funny parts in plays in New York, but she hadn't had any luck. While Ash found her hilarious, Ethan found her funny and winning and wonderful. Why wasn't that enough to make it in acting?

A few months earlier, Ash had come home one night after the acting class she and Jules had begun taking together in the summer, and said to Ethan, "Poor Jules. You wouldn't believe what happened to her."

"What happened?" He looked at his girlfriend with fear, not wanting anything to have happened to Jules. Unless, of course, Dennis had broken up with her. Bizarrely, that idea did not make Ethan too unhappy. It even gave him a prickle of well-being, thinking of Jules as now being *available* — even though, of course, Ethan himself was not available.

Ash dropped her big carpetbag pocketbook and sat down next to Ethan on the couch, her head on his shoulder. "In class tonight, Yvonne just kept riding her and riding her, telling her she wasn't going deep enough. And then at the end, when we were all leaving, Yvonne suddenly asked her to stay. So I waited outside on the street, because you know that Jules and I always go get dinner. And she and Yvonne were in there for like ten minutes, and then Jules came out and her face was really, really red, but just in spots, the way it gets; you know what I mean?"

"Yes." He'd long been a student of Jules's blushing and flushing.

"She looked like she had the measles," said Ash. "She was completely inflamed, completely upset. We went to the restaurant, and she told me that Yvonne had basically said to her, 'My dear, let me be blunt. Why are you acting?' "

"Your acting teacher said that to Jules? 'Why are you acting?' "

"Yes. And Jules said she muttered something like, 'Well, because it's what I want to do with my life.' And then Yvonne said, 'But have you ever asked yourself whether the world actually *needs* to see you act?' That's what she said! This bitchy old lady in a turban. And Jules said something like, 'No, um, I haven't thought of it.' And Yvonne said, 'We are all here on this earth for only one go-round. And everyone thinks their purpose is just to find their passion. But perhaps our purpose is also to find out what *other people* need. And maybe the world does not actually need to see *you,* my dear, reciting a tired old monologue from the Samuel French collection or pretending to be drunk and staggering around. Has that ever occurred to you?' "

"Oh my God," said Ethan. "That's horrible."

"I know. So Jules said 'Thank you, Yvonne' — she actually thanked her for saying this; it was totally masochistic of Jules — and then she came rushing out onto the street and started to cry."

"I wish I'd been there to help her," Ethan said.

The next day, while Ash was out of the apartment, Jules called. It was unclear which of them she'd wanted to speak to; probably Ash, but Ethan acted as though she'd wanted to speak to him, and he settled into the call. "It was humiliating, Ethan," Jules said. "She was just standing there in her turban staring

341

at me like she hated me. Like, 'Get out of the theater!' And I guess she's right. I may be sort of funny. But it's not 'acting' funny. It's just 'life' funny. Like you," she added. "Although, of course, you're also 'genius' funny, so that gives you a lot of options."

Ethan's face burned with good feeling, and he leaned back on the couch, wondering where Jules was sitting right now, whether she was on her own couch too, and if their locations were parallel. "Hardly 'genius,' " he said.

"I'm not even going to dignify that," said Jules, then she said, "I'm willing to keep giving this whole thing a try. But how long do I put myself out there, Ethan? Obviously, I'm done with that acting class. Not that I can ask for any of my money back, even though there are weeks and weeks left. It would be too horrible to ever speak to Yvonne again. And besides, she's already spent my tuition at Turban World. But what about auditioning? Do I say, 'Fuck Yvonne,' and keep on doing it? When do I stop? When I'm twenty-five? Thirty? Thirty-five? Forty? Or right this minute? Nobody tells you how long you should keep doing something before you give up forever. You don't want to wait until you're so old that no one will hire you in any other field either. I already feel kind of worn out by it all and I've basically just started. But I want to get cast in *something*, even an incomprehensible little play in a theater with twelve seats. Do you remember *Marjorie Morningstar*?"

"No."

"It's a famous novel by Herman Wouk from a really long time ago. Marjorie Morningstar grows up always wanting to be an actress; her name is originally Marjorie Morgenstern — Jewish — and she changes it for when she becomes famous, which everyone knows is going to happen. She's the pretty, vivacious girl who had all the leads in the school plays and in summer stock. And then she sets off to make it as an actress in New York, and she has a lot of experiences, but finally it doesn't work out. At the very end of the novel, the story flashes forward to many, many years later, and a friend of hers from long ago comes to see her. And now Marjorie is a suburban housewife living in Mamaroneck. She used to be really dynamic and exciting and filled with promise, but she's become this ordinary, sort of boring person, and her friend can't believe that this is the same person he used to know. I always thought it was the saddest and most devastating ending. How you could have these enormous dreams that never get met. How without knowing it you could just make yourself smaller over time. I don't want that to happen to me."

"Jules, you are many things, but you are nothing like Marjorie Morningstar," Ethan said after a moment of silence. He wasn't being insulting, and Jules must have understood this. She wasn't naturally headed for stardom, and never really had been, and so in all likelihood her story wouldn't have a devastating ending.

Ash was the star; Ash would make it in acting if she wanted, though it seemed lately that she didn't want it at all. She wanted to direct, not act, Ash had been saying to him. In particular she wanted to direct works by women, and works about women, with good female parts in them. "There's an unbelievable imbalance out there," Ash said. "Male playwrights and male directors rule this little duchy, and then they come in and sweep up all the prizes. I swear, if they could find a way to cast men in all the women's roles, they would."

" 'Tommy Tune *is* Golda Meir,' " Ethan had interrupted.

"Theater is definitely as macho as any other field," said Ash. "It's pretty much as bad as . . . wildcatting for oil. The sexism is hateful, and I want to try to change it. My mother got a great education at Smith, but she got married right away and never did anything professionally. I look at her, and think she could have been many, many things. An art historian. A museum curator. A chef! As you know, she's an excellent cook, and an excellent mother, but she could have had a big profession too. They aren't mutually exclusive. I almost feel like I owe it to her to do something woman-related." Ash told Ethan that she wanted to become a feminist director. In 1984 you could describe your dream job in this way and not be made fun of. Of course the odds of success in directing were even lower than in acting — and lower for Ash because she was female — but lately she was convinced that this was what she would do with her life.

Jules, though, had fallen into theater accidentally, and she'd stayed in it maybe a little too long. College had been the last, long gasp of all that, and though in New York she'd positioned herself as one of those loopy character actors, not beautiful enough to get a lead but with a different kind of sidekick charm, she'd appreciated that there were much better people all around her. She saw them perform scenes in acting class; one of them had an amazingly elastic body, and another could do a wide array of convincing accents. Jules had also met them in waiting rooms as they all sat clutching their head shots, and she'd seen them in action during auditions. Though they too understood their lowly place in the theater hierarchy, they were competitive with one another for these small, crucial, occasionally show-stealing parts. They were good at what they did, better than she was.

"No," Jules agreed with Ethan on the phone. "I'm no Marjorie Morningstar."

"So what else can you imagine doing?" he asked.

"Do I have to decide now?"

"I'll give you a few minutes," he said. "Talk amongst yourself."

They sat in silence, and Ethan heard her jaw crunch down on something. He wondered what it was; it made him hungry, and he stretched the phone cord so he could reach a bag of chips on the coffee table. As quietly as he could, Ethan separated the two sides of the bag; trapped air rushed out and he began to eat. Together he and Jules crunched on their chips or their whatever, unselfconscious. "What are you eating?" he finally asked.

"Is that like the platonic version of the phone question, 'What are you wearing?' "

"Something like that."

"Cheez-Its," Jules said.

"Doritos," he said. "They're both orange," he observed for no particular reason. "We both have orange tongues right now. *They will know us by the color of our tongues.*"

They crunched onward for slightly longer, like two people walking through leaves. Ash never ate snack food; her food purity was sort of astonishing. Ethan had once come upon her in their living room when she was sitting and eating a tomato that had been ripening on their windowsill — just holding it in her hand, deep in thought, casually eating it like it was a peach or a plum.

"Well," Jules finally said. "I know this sounds lofty, but I've sometimes imagined doing something that deals with people who are suffering. I'm not joking, in case you think I am. When my father died, I was just so closed up about it. I never really tried to help my mother. It's disgusting how self-involved I was."

"You were a kid," he reminded her. "Comes with the territory."

"And now I'm not a kid. You know how in college I minored in psych? Freshman year, when I was so miserable, I went to university counseling and saw a really nice social worker."

"Okay," said Ethan. "Go on."

"Becoming a therapist could maybe be interesting. Getting a Ph.D. and everything. But my mother can't help out with tuition, and I'd have to pay back student loans forever."

"Aren't there cheaper ways? Could you become a social worker, like the one you went to? Wouldn't it cost less that way?"

"Well, yeah, I think so. Dennis says I should look into graduate school one way or another."

"He likes the idea of it?"

"Oh, he likes whatever I like," said Jules.

"And he's really glad he enrolled in ultrasound technology school. Of course, *his* school," she said in a dry voice, "has a great lecture series, and a wonderful lacrosse team, and an ivy-covered campus. Why, there's even a school song."

"Oh there is, is there?" said Ethan. "My curiosity has been roused. Tell me the school song for ultrasound technology school."

Jules paused, thinking. "It's by the Beatles," she finally said.

"Okay . . ."

" 'I'm Looking Through You.' "

"Perfect," said Ethan, appreciating her wholly, never wanting to get off this phone call.

"Seriously," said Jules, "it was a good idea for Dennis. Before then, he didn't know what to be, what to do. You know he got thrown off track in college when he got sick. Ultrasound isn't something he was burning to do, but it's good for him, it's a relief. So, yes, he likes the idea of me going to school too. But you — I know you'll have a strong opinion about this. Not that it'll definitely be right."

"My opinion is that I agree with Dennis. You'd be good at it," Ethan said. "People would like talking to you."

"How do you know that?"

"Because *I* like talking to you."

Not long afterward, Jules applied to the Columbia University School of Social Work, was accepted on scholarship, and also took out student loans. She would start mid-year, and was relieved not to have to keep buying *Backstage* magazine every week and sitting like a stooge in a coffee shop with a yellow highlighter, imagining that she might be hired for one of these roles, when probably she never would. Acting fell away from her, along with the dream of getting so much attention — too much attention — that you could feel it collect like a fever in your head. Also, she'd had enough of working at La Bella Lanterna, where the tips were poor and she came home at the end of a workday with her hair smelling of espresso. No amount of Gee, Your Hair Smells Terrific shampoo could get rid of the odor. At Columbia her hair smelled neutrally sweet again and classes were going well except for statistics, which was dreadful, but she said that Dennis helped her, sitting beside her in bed reading slowly aloud to her from the incomprehensible textbook.

But for Ethan, although quitting his staff job at *The Chortles* was a good idea intuitively, he was now left with nothing to aim toward. He wished he could use Jules to talk to, the same way she had used him. Talking to her was different from talking to Ash, who essentially trusted his instincts and wanted him to be happy. Jules was much more critical of Ethan; she was the one who told him when something he'd come up with was a poor idea. But he would have had to say to her, "I am completely confused," and he couldn't do that, for Jules would see him as slightly pathetic, and he'd been trying hard to climb up out of the nether region of pathetic ever since he'd made the mistake of kissing her years earlier in the animation shed.

One afternoon, a few days after returning from Maui, Ethan was invited to lunch by Ash's father. "Let's meet at my office," Gil Wolf said. Ethan understood that lunch would require him to wear a tie, and he felt depressed and sunk by this. Wasn't the whole point of being an artist, or at least part of it, that you didn't have to wear a tie? And why was he even going to lunch with Gil, alone? Ethan and Ash had been a couple since the summer of '76, with only one bad stretch of breakup, which had taken place junior year in college. Ash, at Yale, had gotten drunk and slept with a boy in her dorm, or her "college," as they pretentiously called dorms there. The boy was part Navajo, with exotic dark looks — and it had "just happened" after a party, Ash had said. Ethan had been so angry and shocked that he felt as if all his internal organs would come exploding out of him. It was a wonder that he didn't crash his father's noisy old car driving back down from New Haven. Ethan and Ash didn't speak for five weeks, during which time he created an ugly, mean-spirited animated short called *The*

Bitch, about an ant at a picnic that betrays its lover ant.

One weekend in that miserable period, feeling lower than he'd ever felt, Ethan drove up to Buffalo to see Jules, and though he was meant to sleep in a sleeping bag on the floor of her cinder-block dorm room, he'd ended up sitting up in bed with her for half the night while she studied for a psychology exam. He kept trying to talk to her, to distract her, and she kept shushing him and telling him he was making her tense and that she would fail her exam. "I'll give you a back rub," he said, and when she absently agreed, he started rubbing her shoulders, and she leaned forward to let him scoot behind her and get better access.

"That actually feels good," Jules said. Ethan diligently rubbed in silence, and Jules finally put her book facedown in her lap and closed her eyes. His hands moved along the surface of the oversized T-shirt that she slept in, and Jules made noises of approval, which pleased Ethan considerably. His hands moved in rhythmic pulses, and Jules sighed with a pleasure that in turn felt very pleasurable to Ethan. Something seemed to have changed in the room — was he reading this right? — and his hands moved lower on her back. Somehow, one of his hands rounded the corner of her midsection, and he now felt *certain* that something had changed, and in absolute silence he slid his hand upward and

351

cupped her breast, two fingers finding her nipple. Everyone and everything was shocked: Ethan, Jules, the hand, the breast, the nipple. Then Jules moved sharply away from him and his hand and demanded, "Ethan, what is *wrong* with you?"

"What?" he said, both crushed and pretending ignorance of what he had just done.

"Go sleep on the floor in the sleeping bag," she said. He obeyed, crawling back inside it like an animal in a cave. "Why would you think that was okay?" Jules went on. "That's not the way we are, you and I. And why would I possibly do anything with you — my best friend's boyfriend?"

"I don't know," he said, not looking her in the eye. Because we love each other, was the true answer. Because it feels so wonderful, at least to me. Because, oh, even though I have been entwined with Ash for quite a while, when things go bad I revert to the desire I've always held — the desire for *you* — which I will hold until the day I die.

What happened in Jules's dorm room at Buffalo would become something that neither of them spoke about for years; and then, finally, Jules brought it up once when they were alone, casually referring to the event as "the Buffalo nipple," a name which stuck. "The Buffalo nipple" became a secret phrase that referred not only to this specific event, but to any misguided action that a person might perform in life out of longing or weakness or fear, or pretty much out of anything human.

"She'll come back to you," Jules said to Ethan that night in her dorm room as they lay apart. "Remember when she kicked me out of her parents' apartment after I went to see Cathy Kiplinger at the coffee shop?"

"Yes. But Ash was the one who betrayed *me* here. *She* was the one, and now I'm waiting for *her.* How did that happen?"

"That's the way it is with Ash. It's just the way it always is."

Ethan and Ash's separation became unbearable to both of them. Each would call Jules and plaintively discuss the distress of being without the other. "He's a part of me," said Ash, "and I somehow momentarily forgot that, and now I just can't bear not having him here. It's almost like I had to sleep with someone else in order to see how much I need him." All Ethan kept saying to Jules was, "I can't take this anymore. I mean, I just *cannot take this,* Jules. You're minoring in psychology. Explain girls to me. Tell me everything I need to know, because I feel like I know nothing."

Eventually, though, the couple rushed back together, sealing themselves to each other once again. Ash never heard about the Buffalo nipple, and there was no reason that she ever should. Now Ethan and Ash had been living

353

together since college, on East 7th Street, right off Avenue A, a street fully staffed by junkies and dealers. "I don't like this one bit," Gil Wolf said when he and Betsy visited; they promptly called a locksmith and paid for the most expensive titanium lock available.

Ash and Ethan were both twenty-three years old when her father invited Ethan to his office, a perfectly reasonable age to co-habitate and not yet have to turn an eye toward marriage. Ethan was concerned that somehow Gil was going to ask him about whether he had any plans in that direction. But Gil did not want to talk about marriage, or about Ash at all. It seemed that he was simply concerned about Ethan having quit his job at *The Chortles.* Gil seemed only to want to offer himself up as a father figure, knowing that Ethan's own bitter, self-absorbed, and irresponsible father was use-less. Ethan wore a brown skinny tie and a brown jacket that pulled at the sleeves; his hair was freshly moussed. He sat in a brushed steel and distressed leather chair across the desk from Ash's father at the lower Lexington Avenue offices of what was now called Drexel Burnham Lambert. Outside the window the sky looked smeared with clouds, and the city, seen from here, was not quite recognizable, just as Ethan felt not quite recognizable.

"So what do you think you'll do next?" Gil Wolf asked. On his desk was one of those executive ball-clickers, a Newton's cradle, and it was all Ethan could do to keep himself from reaching out and playing with it, but he knew to keep his hands to himself.

"Haven't a clue, Gil," said Ethan. He smiled apologetically, as if the sentiment might be offensive to a man in finance. The men in this place all knew what to do *next*. The offices of Drexel Burnham Lambert in 1982 were as revved up as a racetrack. Everyone here wanted to make money, and they knew how to do it too. Ethan was out of place in the world of investment banking. Today, before coming upstairs, he'd been given an adhesive visitor's badge, and he stuck it on his lapel before entering the elevator, feeling as if instead of VISITOR it said DISPLACED PERSON. Yet he couldn't deny the *tang* of being here, the chemical surge he felt when Gil's assistant came to fetch him from the waiting area upstairs.

"Mr. Figman?" the young guy had said. "I'm Donny. This way."

Donny was only slightly older than Ethan, in a conservative dark suit and starched shirt. No art school for him! Instead, he'd gone to business school. The environment here was perplexingly appealing to Ethan, who had rarely thought about money before. His father's salary as a public defender had paid for their cramped and rent-controlled apartment off Washington Square. His mother was

355

a substitute teacher, though she wasn't very patient with children. In fact, she was a screamer. In the summers there had been just enough money to send Ethan to camp, and then he'd attended the School of Visual Arts on a free ride. In his childhood his parents often fought about money, but they fought about everything else too, and he'd grown up believing that the only thing that mattered, the only thing that would save you from the potential hellishness of your domestic life, was doing what you love. What was better than that?

But maybe the men at Drexel Burnham did what they loved too. Certainly they seemed engaged, and every open office door revealed someone, usually a man, deep in conversation with another man, or on the phone. Ethan followed Donny through the corridors, taking in all the chatter and hum. And now, in the serenity of Ash's father's office, he could have lain down on the cold leather sofa and slept for a few hours. He'd always known the Wolfs were rich, but he'd never before seen where much of their money actually was *made,* nor had it occurred to him to be particularly curious about how it was made. Gil Wolf was primarily the father of Ethan's girlfriend, but here in this world he had a different role, one that was assertive and even refreshing.

"You have no clue what you want to do

next? I find that hard to believe," said Gil kindly, then he was the one to reach out a hand and lift one of the steel spheres hanging from strings on the Newton's cradle. The ball went *click*! and it struck the others and knocked the last ball out of place, and both men impassively watched the little display of the laws of physics.

"I think I was spoiled by Spirit-in-the-Woods," Ethan said. "You were allowed to really be expressive and imaginative there. Working on the show was nothing like that; there was a vision that you had to adhere to. I think I need to get out of animation and do something where I don't have to feel resentful."

"Here's the thing," said Ash's father, and now he stopped fiddling with the toy and laced his hands together and looked directly at Ethan. "I completely believe in you. And I'm not the only one who does."

"Thanks, Gil. That's kind of you to say."

"Not kind," said Gil. "Self-interested too. Because I know that Ash is concerned about you. I don't want to start trouble in paradise, Ethan. I mean that she wants you to be happy too. She wishes you could do what you're most passionate about."

"So do I."

Gil leaned across the desk like a man about to offer once-in-a-lifetime investment advice. "Look, here's what I would do," he said. "Go back to them; tell them what you want to be doing."

"Them?" Ethan laughed, then stopped himself. He had sounded obnoxious. "I mean, there is no them," he said more gently. "The people I dealt with work on that show exclusively. They wouldn't be interested in seeing anything else from me."

"What about the network? Can't you pitch them your so-called *Figland*? As a TV show, like *The Chortles* but much smarter and more satirical and, God knows, funnier. And if they don't want to do it, you can tell them you'll go to the competition. I've done a little research on your behalf. There are black holes in the network's schedule, where shows just won't succeed. They're consistently losing in certain time slots, and they're worried."

Ethan sat back and felt the spine of the ultramodern chair give a little too much, as though it might send him falling backward on his head. Gil Wolf was used to getting things done, made, taken care of; his assumptions and his blitheness were remarkable. He wanted Ethan to go to the network aggressively, confidently, pitch them *Figland* and make them think — no, make them *worry* — that there was a lot of money to be made from Ethan Figman. It would be a mindfuck of some kind, just like in Gil's world. And, just like in Gil's world, sometimes a mindfuck was a satisfying and productive fuck after all.

Looking at Gil's enthused, almost deranged face, Ethan felt himself stiffen and then relent. His own father had been so preoccupied and messed up, and as a result had been spectacularly bad at fatherhood. Now Ethan wanted the love of Ash's father more than anything. After all, he'd even put a pudding-cup's worth of mousse in his hair and donned a monkey suit in the middle of the day in order to get it. The intensity of their eye contact made Ethan suddenly realize that this conversation — or anyway some version of it — was what Gil was meant to have had with Goodman right around now. And now Ethan knew that that was what this whole meeting was really about.

A father who'd lost his son was a desperate creature. Empty-handed, in despair. The tragedy of Goodman's sudden, lurching exit all those years earlier still followed Gil Wolf around, always reminding him of what he'd had, what he'd criticized constantly and probably never appreciated enough, and what he'd lost. The pain was unimaginable. Ash's father needed Ethan to succeed because his own son had taken off and never been found. His own son was dead, for all intents and purposes, and Ethan was not.

Ethan would call the network — what the hell. He would put himself out there like a schmuck and see what they had to say. He could tolerate rejection; he'd experienced it before and survived it.

"And one other thing," said Gil. "If you end up making a deal with them —"

"In my dreams," said Ethan.

"If you do, you've got to give these guys things they can't get anywhere else. They have to need *you.* This is key."

"Oh, I see what you're saying. Sure. Thank you," he said to Gil. "And really, you've been so generous and everything." Both men stood. In his mid-fifties Gil Wolf was still a slim man, a twice-weekly tennis player. There was almost no hair on the top of his head, but he'd developed impressive silver sideburns, and his clothes were natty, picked out by his wife, who had the same good eye for style that Ash had.

"Good," said Gil. "Now let's go to lunch. I want steak. I mean, I want salad." He laughed. "That's what I'm supposed to say. My internist told me that if I eat salad often enough, I will actually start craving it. And my good cholesterol will rise and my bad cholesterol will fade away like the morning dew."

"Salad it is," said Ethan, though at age twenty-three cholesterol was something he'd never given any thought to before. Vaguely, he knew it had to do with fat in the blood, though when anyone mentioned cholesterol, he realized he immediately ceased listening, similar to when someone told him their dream. Gil reached out and lightly pulled Ethan's VISITOR tag off his lapel. It left behind a ghostly rectangle of pollen, which would remain there until the brown jacket was finally taken out of circulation the following year, at Ash's insistence, and replaced with something expensive and not brown.

"Wait. One other thing," said Gil. His face suddenly altered, becoming embarrassed. "I was wondering if you'd have a look at something."

"Sure."

Gil closed the door of his office, then went to the closet and took out a big, brick-colored accordion folder. The string had been elaborately wound around the knob, and he unwound it, saying, "This is my secret, Ethan. I've never shown these to anyone, not even Betsy."

Oh shit, it's going to be porn, Ethan thought, and his collar grew tight around his neck. Some kind of strange fetish porn. There would be images of children, photographed in houses where the windows were blacked out. Gil would want Ethan to be initiated into this world. No, no, that is such a stupid conclusion! Stop it, you're babbling *inside* now, Ethan told himself. He watched as Ash's father removed a stack of drawings on heavy sketch paper. "Tell me what you think," Gil said.

He handed the sheaf to Ethan, who looked at the first drawing, which was done in charcoal. It was of a woman sitting by a window, looking out at the street. It had been labored over, he could see. Through the cloudy gray charcoal it was possible to see all the erasures, the starts and restarts. The woman's head was turned at such an angle that her neck almost looked broken, and yet she was sitting up. It was a very bad drawing; Ethan took that much in right away. But he knew, oh thank God he knew immediately, that this was not a joke, and that he was not supposed to laugh. Thank God, he would often think over the years, that he had not even smiled.

"Interesting," Ethan murmured.

"I was trying for a three-quarter profile," said Gil, peering over Ethan's shoulder.

"I see that." Then, in a very small voice, so small that maybe it was possible Ash's father wouldn't even hear it, and Ethan could have said it without actually having said it, he added, "I like it."

"Thank you," said Gil. Ethan put the drawing on the bottom of the pile and looked at the next one. It was a seascape, with gulls and rocks and clouds possessing sharp outlines instead of the wispy, amoeboid quality that actual clouds had. This drawing was less bad, but it was still quite poor. Gil Wolf wanted to have a hand that could hold a pencil and make it do anything — or, better yet, two ambidextrous hands like Ethan's that could hold pencils equally well and make them do anything. But the problem was that talent couldn't be willed into being. Ethan murmured something appropriate for each drawing he came to. It was like an extremely stressful game show, called *Say the Right Thing, You Idiot.*

"So what's the verdict?" Gil asked, his voice husky with vulnerability. "Should I keep giving it a whirl?"

The moment extended into infinity. If the point of drawing was to bring your work into the world so that other people could see it and sense what you'd meant to convey, then, no, Gil should not keep giving it a whirl: he should never draw anything again. No whirls. It should be *illegal* for Gil Wolf to possess charcoal sticks. But if the point was something else, expression or release, or a way to give private meaning to the loss of your son, your child, your *boy,* then yes, he should draw and draw.

"Of course," Ethan said.

The last drawing in the stack was of two figures, a boy and a girl, playing with a dog. Right away the tangle of their bodies was so tortured that it was like looking at a scene of actual torture. Someone was doing something bad to someone else! But, no, Ethan realized that these children were *laughing,* and their dog, who looked more like a seal, appeared to be laughing too, its lips upturned.

"It's from an old photo," said Gil. His voice was strained, and Ethan didn't want to look up and over at him, for he feared what he would see. Just a moment earlier Ethan had worried that he would laugh; now he knew it was possible that Gil might cry. And then, of course, Ethan would cry too, but he would also need to protect Gil, to make a tender gesture toward him, to tell him he was so glad Gil had shown him his artwork. In the drawing, Ash and Goodman were playing with Noodge when he was a puppy. Gil had done his best to capture a moment in time. Here was a labored scene of Ethan Figman's girlfriend as a little girl, looking vaguely the way she'd actually looked, according to the many photos Ethan had seen on the walls of the Wolfs' apartment. In her father's rendering, Ash and Goodman were happy, the dog was happy and alive, time was stopped, and there was no sense of what the future would be for these children, though, disturbingly, everyone's neck — the brother, the sister, and the dog — appeared to have been idly broken.

After leaving the celebration dinner at the dark and beautiful Japanese restaurant, and saying effusive good-byes to the network executives that included an appropriately

364

solid, manly handshake between the men and delicate cheek kisses between everyone else, Ethan and Ash walked down Madison Avenue in the light rain. It was late, and this street was not meant for nighttime. Everyone out tonight was in a hurry to get somewhere else. All store windows were grilled; the expensive clothes and shoes and chocolates were tucked away into unreachability for the night. Ethan and Ash walked slowly south; he wasn't ready to get into a cab just yet. He put his arm around her and they leaned together as they walked. They stopped on the corner of 44th Street and he kissed her; she smelled a little bit like sake, a little bit like fish. Intoxicating, vaginal, and he felt stirred, right in the middle of everything else he was feeling. She seemed to sense his mood, its many tentacles reaching out unsurely.

"Which one did you like best?" Ethan asked her.

"*Like?* Is that the operative word? And don't you mean *better,* not *best,* because there are only two of them? They're both so slick. And Hallie basically defers to Gary."

"I meant which kind of sushi. And sashimi. Not which network executive. I liked the piece that looked like a gramophone."

"Oh, right. Yes, that one was cool," Ash said. "I think I liked the one that looked like a Christmas present. Red and green. Your show is going to be great, by the way," she said.

"Maybe, maybe not."

"Are you kidding me, Ethan?"

"It's just that there's a dividing line in my life now," he said. "Before and after." Ethan felt convinced that it was easy to become greedy the minute your fortunes increased. Ash had always seemed to take her family's money for granted, which bothered him; Ethan, living first with his squabbling, aggravated, moneyless parents, and then with his careless father, had mostly been indifferent to wealth, but his Socialist tendencies never really developed; he'd been born too late to find enough company for that. "What if it's not right, this show?" he asked. "What if it's a real embarrassment, a total artistic failure? A *mistake.*"

"Ethan, you think everything is a mistake. You have no sense of when things feel right."

"What do you mean?"

"Well, the time you were offered that summer internship after high school —"

"I turned it down for Old Mo," Ethan said hotly. "He was dying of emphysema, Ash, I mean, come on, what did you think I was going to do?" Even thinking about that summer, Ethan felt himself sigh and deflate. Old Mo Templeton, on oxygen and weighing so little, had been unable to eat, and Ethan went out and bought him a juicer. The juicer had been a beauty, the Jaguar of juicers, as futuristic as a spaceship, and he'd pushed carrots and beets and celery into it, and sat by the hospital bed that had been installed in Old Mo's apartment, and held the glass of juice and angled the straw for him.

Once, as Ethan bent the flexible straw, he became aware of the tiny little creak it made upon bending, and he filed away the idea, *straw sound,* for some future endeavor. "Straw sound! Straw sound!" the character Wally Figman demanded of his mother, who'd given him a glass of chocolate milk a few months later in a flashback to early childhood in one of the short *Figland* films. The noisy, brash cartoon soundtrack came to a halt while Wally's mother bent the straw for her son, and the straw made that unmistakable and somehow pleasurable little squeaking creak.

Once *Figland* hit primetime, stoners watching the show would soon say to one another, "Straw sound, straw sound!" And someone might go into a kitchen, or even run out to a store, and bring back a box of Circus Flexi-Straws and bend straw after straw to hear that specific, inimitable sound, finding it unaccountably hilarious.

Ethan had stayed with Old Mo until the last days when the old man was moved to the hospital, and then he'd been there when Old Mo died. He'd inherited everything from his teacher's personal collection of old reel-to-reel cartoons: *Skedaddle, Big Guy, Cosmopolitan Ranch Hands,* and all the others. Sometimes late at night when Ash slept but Ethan couldn't, he threaded the cocoa-colored Bell & Howell projector and sat in the living room, screening the ancient cartoons on the wall, though lately that seemed maudlin and self-pitying, and so he packed up all the reels and stored them at his father's place. One more box in that disgusting apartment wouldn't make a difference.

He'd thrown over the job at Looney Tunes for an important reason, but it was true that he hadn't been able to appreciate what the job might have been like, and what it might have done for him. Looney Toons was a potential nightmare of subservience and adherence to someone else's fixed vision, and yet maybe working there would have been exciting. Of course there was no way to know now. He hadn't gone the showy, Warner Bros./LA route, and had instead stayed in New York after graduating from art school.

"And frankly," said Ash, "it was only a matter of time before you left *The Chortles.* They weren't good enough for you. I said to myself: Where's the subtlety? Ethan's going to hate this."

"You knew more than I did. And then your dad, with his big pep talk that day in his office — without him I would be doing who

368

knows what. Drifting."

For months Ethan had mulled over everything Gil had said, all the while doing industrials again to bring in money. Finally, after a great deal of obsessive thinking, he thought he was ready to present his ideas, as Gil had urged him to do, and to his astonishment the network had said sure, we'll be glad to hear your pitch. He'd brought in a storyboard, and he'd done the voices that he'd always done in the short films, and everyone in the room laughed a lot and called him back for two more meetings with other executives, and somehow in the end they'd actually said yes, and had given him his own show. It would never have occurred to Ethan on his own to have the balls to go in there like that. *Balls.* He remembered the Newton's cradle on Gil's desk. Gil had plenty of balls, hanging from strings, smashing into one another and clicking like mad. He owed Gil everything, and yet even thinking this, Ethan knew it wasn't really the case.

Tonight, after the miraculous, gemological assortment of raw fish, and the raised glasses of aromatic sake that had been knocked together in celebration, the dazzling truth of his success was indisputable. But on the street in the rain after dinner, Ethan felt clubbed yet again, the way he'd felt on Maui. And this time he was doing what he wanted! This time he had gotten everything imaginable! The clubbing came from a different source. Not disappointment but fulfillment. He knew his life would change in a shudderingly radical fashion, and he would emerge different. He would probably even look different. He was like a baby whose head gets elongated as it makes the awful soft-serve ice cream machine trip through the birth canal. Ash was in her coat and scarf, she who had looked so pretty at the low, lacquered table beside him as they sat on the straw mats; obviously Gary Roman and Hallie Sakin had been impressed and surprised by her. Ethan was socially elevated by the incongruous beauty and loveliness of his girlfriend. He hated the fact of this; it insulted Ash, and it insulted him, but the problem was that it was predictable and true.

When they got home that night, instead of feeling weary and damp from the rain they dropped together onto their futon, and without any discussion began to fuck. Ash took off her good clothes until she was wearing only her little sleeveless undershirt that made him incredibly excited for reasons he didn't understand. He slid his hand up under the elastic ribbed cotton; at some point she was on her stomach and he found himself climbing on top of her, and he saw that the T-shirt label was sticking up in back. HANES FOR MEN it read upside down, and these words alone sent new blood rushing to his already filled penis. He wanted to laugh.

Sex was as strange as anything, as strange as sushi, or art, or the fact that he was a grown man now who could fuck a woman who loved him. The fact that he, Ethan Figman, was really fuckable after all, when he had spent the entire first seventeen years of his life certain that this was not the case and never would be. But then, early one morning on a terrible New Year's Day, he'd put his arm around Ash Wolf as they left the police station after her brother Goodman's arrest, and she'd looked over at him with what he'd later thought of as *fawn face,* the expression a deer makes not when it's caught in headlights but when it catches a human looking at it in wonder. The deer looks back, acknowledging not only its own terror but its own grace, and it shows off for a moment in front of the human. It flirts. Ash gave him the fawn face, and he'd blinked in confusion. He'd put an arm around her out of instinct, wanting to protect her because he knew how much she loved her brother and how agonizing this was for her. But there was that *face,* and he decided that he was wrong, it couldn't mean anything different from usual. She was grateful to him, that was all.

For a long time, seven months to be exact, he'd assumed he had misread Ash's expression. But then in the middle of camp again in the summer, away from her family and its nonstop grief at Goodman's disappearance, Ethan and Ash had sat in the animation shed together a few times, and they'd told each other a frank assortment of personal details. Ethan told Ash about the first inklings of Figland he'd had when he was really young. The place had seemed to send him messages about its existence, as if through little smokestacks in his brain. He told Ash he had been positive that the hateful, real world in which we all lived couldn't possibly be all there was, so he'd had to create an alternate world as well. She, when it was her turn, spoke about Goodman, and how she knew they had very little in common other than the same parents, but it didn't matter; she felt as if she *was* him. Ash said she would wake up sometimes, and briefly, literally think she was her brother, lying in a bed somewhere. She also told Ethan about how she'd shoplifted constantly for a full year in eighth grade, and had never once been caught. As a result, she still had an entire drawer full of Coty makeup and L'eggs panty hose in colors and sizes she would never use: "Deep Bayou Blush." "Extra-Plus Queen." It was as though they both knew they were about to commit to each other for life, so they'd better let the other person know all the particulars of what they were getting into and would have to live with. But how could they possibly have understood what was happening to them at seventeen?

When she got up to leave the animation shed one day after a long confessional conversation, Ash said to him, "You can come to the teepee tonight if you want."

"*Your* teepee?" he'd said like an idiot. "What for?"

Ash shrugged. "All right, don't come."

"Of course I'll come." Though Ethan thought he had a decent chance of dying of overexcitement before then.

When he slipped into Ash Wolf's bed that night, he did so in the presence of four sleeping girls, and one of those girls was Jules. He felt extremely unhappy about this aspect; it was almost intolerable for him to be in Ash's bed with Jules so close by. But he had to assume and pray that Jules Jacobson was really, deeply asleep. When he lay against Ash with his shirt actually removed, then later his underpants, just to be nude together, not for full-on sex yet (that would happen another time, without anyone else around, of course), his dick was so hard against his abdomen that it was like a pinball flipper after someone has slammed the button on the side of the machine. He could feel their hot skins touching, almost *ticking.* Ethan was so moved and shocked at the sensation of skin against skin that he was able to forget all about Jules for a while.

Ash Wolf actually desired him. It seemed so unlikely, but then again, so did many things in life. Lying against her that first time, he started making a list:

1) The existence of peacocks.
2) The fact that John Lennon and Paul McCartney just happened to meet each other as teenagers.
3) Halley's comet.
4) Walt Disney's unbearably gorgeous *Snow White.*

That first middle-of-the-night visit in the girls' teepee was so beautiful. It was also extremely sticky, deeply daring, experimental, and almost psychotic in its intensity. But right away both Ethan and Ash knew what this could become, and was already becoming. Across the wooden room, he saw the outline of Jules Jacobson sleeping in the dark: Oh, Jules! He noticed that she was wearing a retainer, which glinted in the moonlight.

He felt tenderly toward her even as he said good-bye to her as his long-term primary love object. He was consciously switching affections, at least outwardly. Ethan was surrounded by girls, and the atmosphere was all about female faces and breasts and fragrant, much-shampooed hair. It was almost too much for a seventeen-year-old male to absorb. But then it regulated itself, became not too much to absorb but *just enough,* and there it remained even now, eight years in.

"Oh fuck, oh fuck," Ethan said as he came tonight in bed with Ash after the Japanese dinner. And then, a few minutes later, when he'd recovered and had the opportunity to take up the delicate and highly enjoyable task of whirling a finger on Ash Wolf's clitoris until she went to pieces before him, she said, "Oh fuck, fuck."

Lying back, then, Ethan said, "Why do all people say 'fuck' and 'oh fuck' during sex? It's so predictable; it's such a cliché! It's like how all paranoid schizophrenics think their thoughts are being intercepted by the FBI. Why aren't people more original?"

"I don't think originality is the issue with you," she said.

"What if the show comes out sort of dumb?" he asked. "What if the way I see Figland, the way I envision it in my head, just can't be made into a twenty-two-minute TV show?"

They lay looking at each other. "I adore you," Ash said, touching his face and his chest.

"That's nice, and likewise, but why are you saying that at this particular moment?"

"Because look at you," Ash said. "You've gotten a huge break. I'm sure the staff of *The Chortles* wishes you were dead. And yet you're harping on this thing again, this fear of yours. This insecurity. You're still worried about getting things artistically right, and making sure they don't come out *dumb.* Nothing you do is ever good enough, in your opinion. Who was it who made you this way, your mother or your father? Or both?"

"Neither," he said. "I was born like this. I came out of the womb saying, 'I'm worried that something's wrong with me. There's this weird *growth* between my legs!'"

"You're insane," said Ash. "You shouldn't be like this. It doesn't make sense. You didn't get pressured by your parents constantly, like I did."

"This is a *Drama of the Gifted Child* thing, right?" Ethan asked.

"In a way, yes. I left it out for you the other day, by the way. Did you actually read it?"

"I skimmed it."

"You skimmed it? It's a very short book, Ethan."

"So short it's like a haiku, right?" he said. "Well, I think I can sum it up in haiku form." Then he said:

"My parents loved me narcissistically, alas and now I am sad."

"Don't make fun of me," Ash said. "It's an important book."

Ash had lately become obsessed with *The Drama of the Gifted Child,* by the Swiss-trained psychoanalyst Alice Miller, which had become a cult hit when it was published several years earlier. Ash said it was the best book she'd ever read. Much of it dealt with the lasting damage done to children by narcissistic parents. Ash had read the book closely, writing in its margins, feeling certain it was relevant to herself and several of the people she knew. The Wolfs, particularly Gil, had always had so many expectations for her, certain that Goodman would never achieve much. He would disappoint them, but she wouldn't. Golden Ash, with her beauty, her thoughtfulness, her plays, her industry, was a narcissistic parent's dream. But Ethan's mother and father had never once pushed him; they'd been too absorbed by their own dreadful marriage and then by their own split to pay too much attention to their son's precocious, burgeoning abilities.

Often, as a kid, Ethan Figman would tumble into short periods of intense unhappiness, but during them Figland had sprouted, and now *Figland.* The elaborated-upon and somewhat altered premise of the witty pilot was that in a chaotic apartment in New York City exists a nerdy and lonely kid called Wally Figman. Wally's parents are always screaming at each other and ignoring him. In art class at school, when he's supposed to be creating a Thanksgiving turkey handprint like all the other kids, Wally creates a little planet out of clay, and, though his teacher brutally mocks him in front of everyone for doing the wrong assignment, he brings it home after school and puts it in a shoebox under his bed. That night, hearing a vague rumbling sound, he opens the shoebox and sees that the planet is glowing and spinning, and that it has become real. Figland, Wally names it, and when he leans closer to get a better look, he shrinks and tumbles into the shoebox. Emerging into the sunlight of planet Figland, his head popping up like a bewildered groundhog, Wally finds himself no longer a weird nerdy kid but instead a clueless grown man.

The pilot tells the genesis of Figland, but the episodes in the first season, as planned, detail Wally's weird and funny adventures in Figland — some political, involving a creepy, corrupt government, and some adventures merely social, or socially inept, and all of it packed with a bang-bang rhythm of smart pop culture references and jokes and clever scatology. At the end of each breathless episode, Wally would be pulled back to earth and screamed at again by his parents.

In his childhood, Ethan closed his eyes every night and returned again and again to Figland, mapping out that world so thoroughly that by the time he pitched it to the network as a wacky but elegantly witty nighttime animated cartoon in storyboard form ("simple characters, complicated situations," an animator friend of his had always sug-

gested was a good mantra), it was a fully realized entity. Figland had given him a lot to
think about as a boy; it had made him into
who he was. As a man Ethan Figman was
neurotic and self-doubting, but he wasn't
traumatized, and the show made the transition into viability.

Ash ran her fingers along the soft white skin
of his arm, even tracing over a rashy patch.
"Look, if the season comes out badly," she
said, "we'll get out of your contract and go
somewhere far away."

"If the season comes out badly, we won't
have to get out of my contract. It'll end. But
in any case," he said, "as you know, I wouldn't
leave the city." It had been a big deal when
the network agreed to open the studio in New
York to produce *Figland.* Of course *The
Chortles* was produced here too, but that was
a much lower-budget show. This, now, was
something new, a very expensive project created by a neophyte, and yet the network was
going all out for it, agreeing to produce it in
New York and giving Ethan the resources he
would need.

"Even in this fantasy you wouldn't leave?"
Ash said. "Because this *is* just a fantasy. The
season's not going to come out badly."

"No, I'd want to stay here. You know that."

New York in the mid-1980s was an impossible, unlivable, unleavable city. The homeless
sometimes lay directly in your path on the

sidewalk, and it was hard not to become inured to them. You had to train your mind to remember: *human being lying here at my feet, not someone to feel contempt toward.* Otherwise you could turn sour and inward-looking, propelled only by disgust and self-defense as you made your way out into the grid each morning.

Hanging over everything like a cracking ledge was the AIDS virus and its certain death sentence. The gay men whom Ethan knew had begun to spend their afternoons at memorial services. He and Ash had gone to several. Many people they knew, gay or straight, were fairly hysterical, combing over the rosters of everyone they'd ever slept with. Ethan knew that the one among them who they should maybe be concerned about was Jonah — not that they even had any real specifics about his sex life. Jonah Bay was the sweetest, mellowest person you could ever meet, but he was partly a mystery. Even Ash, who used to be his girlfriend and still felt great affection for him, didn't know exactly who he was.

But what made life in New York odd — not better, and in fact probably worse — was the impression of *wealth* seeping through everything. New high-end restaurants kept opening; one of them featured lavender in every dish. Ethan and Ash had recently heard from Jules, who'd heard from Nancy Mangiari, that Cathy Kiplinger had gotten an MBA from Stanford and was starting work in "capital markets," whatever that meant. It didn't make sense to Ethan that someone so talented and dancerly could end up sitting in a swivel chair all day, reading spreadsheets about . . . capital markets. Maybe beneath her massive desk she sometimes arranged her feet in first or second position.

In the weeks when Ethan's deal was being put into place, his financial planner, as an afterthought at the end of a meeting, said to him, "If I were you, and this show takes off and becomes a hit, I'd seriously think about collecting Peter Klonsky."

"Who?"

"Those ice cream cone paintings. I keep hearing his name. The work is big and lush and kind of vulgar in a great way, and it's definitely going to appreciate."

"In the past, people *appreciated* artwork. Now artwork *appreciates*? That's what we're coming to? Well, I guess it's always been the case, but I've just been naive about it."

The financial planner had laughed, but Ethan uneasily wondered if he himself was being thought of as an artist whose work would appreciate. Of course he was; Gil had told him as much. The minute he'd pitched his show to that roomful of receptive, giggling network executives, he'd entered the bloodstream of money and commerce. Purity didn't mean anything, and probably never had. The word itself had pious overtones. Ethan knew a woman who called herself a writer, but when you asked her what she'd written, she'd tell you, "I only write for myself." Then she would coyly show you her quilted journal, and when you asked to see its contents, she demurred, saying what was inside was for her eyes only. Could you be an artist if you didn't have *product* to show? Ethan himself was all product, and he was allowing both it and himself to be lavished with the promise of future money. Maybe he would own a Peter Klonsky someday. He hadn't even *seen* a Peter Klonsky, yet suddenly he was ashamed to realize he wanted one.

As for Cathy Kiplinger, off in capital markets, maybe the manipulation of money and markets gave her the same endorphin release that dance had once given her. Ethan had quietly kept in touch with her for a few years. She'd been a needy girl and had become a needy woman. She'd had an on-again off-again relationship with Troy Mason, who had joined the corps of the Alvin Ailey American Dance Theater. Ethan wondered if Troy and Cathy were still a couple, but he doubted it. It was apparently unusual to still be involved with the person you'd been involved with as a teenager; everyone told him and Ash this. Time had passed, and now Ethan and Cathy weren't in touch at all. She didn't seem to want anything to do with him anymore, or with that earlier, bad part of her life. He gathered, though, that she was here in the city, stoking her fortune and the fortunes of others. The city was a paradox, though maybe it had always been one. You could have an excellent life here, even as everything disintegrated. The city at that moment was not a place that anyone would remember with nostalgia, except for the fact that in the midst of all this, if you played it right, your money could double, and you could buy a big apartment with triple-glazed windows that overlooked the chaos.

But exactly because of how hard the city was now, it was a place where Ethan Figman needed to stay. He knew that regardless of how awful it got in New York, the city would excite him. He loved this breaking, teeming, competitive place, where he'd lived his whole life. But there was more to it than that, which he hadn't discussed with Ash yet; and tonight, after the Japanese dinner with the network executives, he did.

"I'm aware that New York is a toilet bowl — but an expensive porcelain one," he said to her. "That's kind of immaterial, though, because anyway, *you* couldn't leave."

"What do you mean?"

"You wouldn't do that to your parents. *I* wouldn't do that — take you away from them. First they lose Goodman, and then *you*? It'd be too much. It wouldn't be fair."

"They wouldn't be *losing* me," Ash said. "It's not the same. I'd only be in LA."

Ethan flopped onto his back on the futon. "I constantly think about your brother, and wonder where the fuck he is right now," he said. "I mean, *right this minute,* where is Goodman? What's he doing? Is he eating dinner? Lunch? Breakfast? Is he taking a crap? Is he working in a falafel joint?" Ash didn't say anything. "Don't you wonder?" he asked. "Of course you do." But still she didn't answer. "*Don't* you?" he repeated.

"Yes," Ash finally said. "Obviously. Though it's not," she added, "like he's Etan Patz." Ethan took in this comment, Etan Patz being the six-year-old boy who had disappeared in SoHo in 1979 on the first day he'd ever been allowed to walk to the bus stop alone. The child was a touchstone, a symbol of an increasingly frightening city. But this wasn't a good analogy, for obviously nothing good had become of Etan Patz. Goodman Wolf, however, could be anywhere, doing anything.

"I know that. You just get so strange about it," said Ethan.

"It's a strange subject," Ash said in a tight voice that he'd only very rarely heard from her, and disliked.

"You know, I dreamt about Goodman the other night; I meant to tell you this," said

Ethan. "He was in our apartment, and he was still a teenager. I tried to ask him why he felt he had to leave, and where he was now. But he wouldn't tell me. He wouldn't talk at all. He was completely mute."

"Hmm," said Ash. "That sounds intense."

"Wouldn't you give anything to know where he is? To know that he's okay?"

"Of course I would."

"Imagine just disappearing one day and then never being seen again. Who *does* that? What kind of person puts their family and friends through that? Sometimes I think that maybe he was much more fucked up than we thought. That he was even, like, a sociopath."

"My brother was not a sociopath."

"Well, all right, but we had no idea of what we were dealing with at the time. We were kids. We were idiots. We listened to what everyone told us."

"Ethan."

He had become unexpectedly agitated — this frustrating subject always did that to him. "It's just that it was all left unresolved," he said.

"Yes, that's true. But he was innocent. And there was going to be a *trial,*" Ash said. "Dick Peddy would have defended him. Successfully."

"Yeah, there was *going* to be a trial, but then Goodman made sure there wasn't. So who knows what happened? That question's always been kind of lurking, right? Just because we don't talk about it doesn't mean it isn't there. And maybe we should really face it."

"Why exactly should we face it?" she asked.

Ethan looked at her, surprised. "Isn't knowing always better than not knowing? I mean, generally in life? It's not like you can change anything, but at least if you have the information, then you can think, 'Well, it is what it is.' Isn't that one of the messages of your little book? *The Drama of the Gifted Child*? That you have to know what really happened a long time ago so you can live truthfully now?"

"My little book? God, you're condescending."

"I'm sorry. But we could hire private detectives. Have you and your parents ever thought of that? Now that I've got this money coming in — I know it's only one season they've committed to, but we've got *plenty*. We could hire someone really top-notch, and it could give you and your family some closure, some —"

"Would you just stop," Ash said, and then her face went messy and soft the way it always did right before she began to cry. "I told you, Ethan, I *don't like* to discuss my brother, it upsets me too much. He was in my life every minute of every day, and then he wasn't. You don't have any siblings, so you can't understand. Goodman had all this potential — he just hadn't put it together yet. He would've made something of himself, I know he would have. But he never got to do that, and it's one of the saddest things I know."

"You don't know that for sure about him," Ethan said.

"What, you think he's off building the next great museum or skyscraper or . . . Fallingwater? I highly doubt it," she said sharply. "Why are you *doing* this to me now? We can't just 'find' him all of a sudden. Even if we did, it would open up a whole new legal thing for him. He'd definitely be sent to jail for skipping out on his court date. They would be very hard on him; there would be no mercy whatsoever. It would only add to what is already most likely a difficult and limited life. Can't you just leave things *alone*? Or do you really want to torture me?"

Then she was in tears, and she turned away from him, which was just not bearable. Once you had what he had, you couldn't ever not have it; he supposed that this was true of all passionate love. So now, having poked uselessly at the ancient question of Goodman Wolf and where he was and exactly what he had done to Cathy Kiplinger, Ethan Figman told his girlfriend he was very sorry; he'd forgotten how painful it was for her. No, no, he amended, of course he hadn't *forgotten*. It was just that sometimes he had trouble distinguishing what should be kept as a thought from what should be spoken aloud.

It was odd, to be sure, that Ash never wanted to talk about Goodman and how he'd run away before there could be a trial. Not talking about it was an absolute denial, and the whole family engaged in it. Once in a while when Ethan and Ash went to the Wolfs' for dinner, either Betsy or Gil might lightly mention Goodman's name, and a suddenly atomized vapor of sadness would hover over them for a few minutes, before dissipating. Maybe Goodman really was dead. He could be anywhere in the world, or nowhere.

Ethan would try never to upset her like that again. He would keep it to himself instead. He'd been on such an idealistic, free-associative streak, and in the middle of it he'd said the wrong thing and had ruined, retrospectively, the whole evening, the celebratory Japanese dinner and the thrilling fucking for dessert, and then, of course, the quiet time afterward, which was always the happiest time for him, though not tonight.

ELEVEN

Dennis Jacobson-Boyd was on a mission. Early one spring morning, he walked to the corner store down the block and picked up a copy of a magazine that had been delivered shortly after dawn. The cover story of the May 1986 issue of *Media Now* was a list of the one hundred most powerful people in media. Dennis quickly flipped through the issue and found what he wanted, then he turned around and walked home to Jules, who had seen him approach from the apartment window high above the street, and was now out in the stairwell in her pajamas as he entered the vestibule down below.

"Well?" she called down as Dennis mounted the stairs. He looked up and laughed.

"You couldn't wait until I got inside?" he called back.

"No."

"Ninety-eight," Dennis announced.

"Out of a hundred?" Jules called. "Is that good? It doesn't seem all *that* good."

"It's very good," he called back. "Just getting on the list means they think he's really powerful."

"And what about the money?" she asked. For this, of course, was the important part.

"That's more complicated," said Dennis.

"What do you mean?" she said, her voice a half-shout.

"Why are you shouting at me?" he called up. "Can't you wait?"

By the time Dennis had arrived at the fifth floor she had already gone back inside. At age twenty-seven, Jules and Dennis had outgrown this walk-up apartment on West 84th Street, just around the corner from where Dennis used to live. Their place had an intractable mouse problem — mice seemed to dance in mockery, like puppets, ignoring the traps left for them. But the rent was manageable, and they couldn't afford to move. Jules had a roster of clients in a Bronx psychiatric hospital, under close supervision. Dennis had been hired as an ultrasound technician by MetroCare, a medical clinic right in the neighborhood. Both of their professional lives were hectic and the hours were long, although between the two of them very little money came in.

They'd gotten married earlier that year in a small ceremony performed by a woman judge in a Greek taverna in the Village, attended by Ash, Ethan, Jonah, Dennis's college friend

Tom, and the Jacobsons and the Boyds. Neither family had any money, and it made sense to hold the wedding this modest way. Jules's sister, Ellen, came from Long Island with her husband, Mark, and Dennis's brothers stood broad-shouldered in dark suits and ties that they could not wait to unknot. Lois Jacobson looked so small and tentative in her turquoise dress. "Dad would have loved to be here," she said, and for a second Jules had thought, *Whose dad?* And then she remembered: *oh, mine.* Warren Jacobson was so rarely thought of by her as "Dad." He was "my father" or, even more often, "my father who died when I was fifteen." It was better to keep him at a distance, and when her mother said this in the taverna Jules had no idea of what he would have loved. He'd never known her as a grown woman, only as a somewhat out-of-synch girl with ridiculous hair. He hadn't even known her as Jules, only Julie. It was too sad to think about him today of all days, when she was joining her life with the life of a man who was vowing to stay beside her over the years. After a reasonable moment Jules turned away from her mother and put her arm around her substantial husband, who had taken off his jacket, and whose back was as warm and broad as a bed.

In the middle of the wedding lunch, Ash stood up at her seat and tapped on her water glass. "We're all here," she said, "because of

Jules and Dennis. I realized, the other day, when I was thinking about what to say during my toast to my best friend and her groom —" The women gave each other a smile at the word *groom,* which was unfamiliar and thrilling. I have a groom! Jules thought, and Ash is sanctifying his presence. "— that Dennis is a solid and Jules is a liquid," Ash went on. "And I don't think there are any scientists among us, but I'm sure there's some chemical explanation for how they found each other and fell in love. And anyway, I'm so glad they did." She looked right at Jules, her eyes wet. "I'm not losing you," said Ash. "Marriage, I don't think, is like that. It's something else. It's a thing in which you get to see your closest friend become more of who she already is. I know Jules Jacobson — excuse me, Jules Jacobson-Boyd, hyphen queen — as well as I've known anyone. The solid and the liquid have joined together to make — well, not a gas, that doesn't sound very nice." There was laughter. "But some powerful substance that all of us need, and that all of us love."

She sat down, smiling and streaming with tears, and Jules stood and kissed her, and Dennis did too. There were other toasts — something from Jonah about how seeing his friends grow up and go off into their lives was an astonishing, beautiful thing, like watching one of those speeded-up-growth-of-a-flower films he'd seen in grade school. "Except the difference is that I never used to get teary eyed about those flower films. But this is really getting to me." One of Dennis's brothers ended with a hardware store joke that Jules didn't understand. But the toast she most remembered was from Ash, who always knew what to say, and who meant it.

Two months later, Ash and Ethan were married at the Water Club, with 200 guests in attendance, and cracked lobsters carried overhead as everyone looked out at the brilliant view over the East River. The Wolfs "went all out," people said, and there was a tacit understanding in the room that the loss of Goodman had probably caused the family to want a bigger, more elaborate wedding than they would have had under normal circumstances. They were celebrating the child they still had, the child who was here. But of course they hadn't lost Goodman in the way that people thought.

The subject of Goodman was vivid and present between Jules and Ash; the secret of Ash's brother living quietly in Iceland had been carried along from adolescence into adulthood. It was huge, Jules knew, to possess this information, and while she sometimes experienced it like a sort of pressure between the eyes, a legal, moral migraine, she often still felt stupidly special to have been included. Ash sometimes needed to talk to her about Goodman; all of a sudden she'd grab Jules and take her somewhere private and quiet, and she would just unspool in front of Jules about her brother. Ash would smoke one cigarette after another and gesture with her hands and tell Jules whatever news there was from Iceland about Goodman's limited but elaborately described life. All Jules could do was listen and commiserate and offer occasional exclamations. She was aware that her role was passive and fixed. She could never change; Ash needed her to listen. She was the only friend who could do that.

Every so often, Betsy and Gil Wolf went to Europe to visit their son. They would be traveling there soon, in fact, and Jules figured that they would bring along photos from the wedding to show him. So really, he wasn't entirely gone, and it could almost be said that he hadn't entirely missed everything. Even Ash managed to see her brother every couple of years. There had been a Wolf family trip to Paris upon her Yale graduation back in 1981, and Ethan had been discouraged from attending; Ash made it seem as though it was a real drag for her to have to travel with Gil and Betsy, and she convinced Ethan that he was lucky not to have to go with them too. Who wanted to go to Europe with his girlfriend's parents? Ash had told Jules all about the plans in advance: the apartment her parents had sublet for the family in the

Seventh Arrondissement, and how Goodman would meet them there. He was fairly comfortable traveling on his false passport throughout Europe, and there were various possibilities for family reunions in the future. When Ash returned home, she was buoyed and sentimental.

Ash would have loved more than anything to have had her brother at her wedding. At one point during the lunch, when she and Ethan were making the rounds of the room, Ash leaned down to Jules, her dress crackling, the wreath of little flowers in her hair brushing against Jules's face, and whispered hotly to her, "You know what I'm doing right now?" "No, what?" said Jules. "I'm pretending he's here." And then Ash was gone, off to talk to other guests. Ash was imagining Goodman at the wedding reception, and now the whole day, in addition to being so beautiful and emotional, was complete.

Jules gave a toast to Ash, saying how lucky Ash and Ethan were to have found each other. "They are the best people I know," she told the large, bright room. Then the moment called for humor. "And now," she said, "I am going to perform *Both Ends,* the one-woman show Ash wrote in high school, in its entirety. If you need to go to the bathroom, please do so now. This will take a little while, maybe, oh, three to four hours." There was a rolling wall of laughter, and Jules's face was as hot as it ever got, and when she sat down she drank a full tumbler of water, ice and all.

Married life proved not very different from premarried life, except now there was the desire for solidity instead of expansion. Jules and Dennis, heading into professional lives that were, respectively, a compromise and a practicality, knew that they wouldn't have an outcome similar to that of their closest friends, but still they thought everything would reconfigure and become something well beyond the low pay and hard work that predominated now. At that moment, early on in their marriage and deep into their twenties, Jules and Dennis were borderline poor together, with significant school loans and in credit card debt already, always anxious about being able to pay the rent, and unable to afford cable, though all of this was fine because they imagined that at some distant point their fortunes would increase.

They both felt that as a newly married couple — and eventually, they assumed, as a family — they would have money and stability. Dennis had learned a trade; his job included a health plan, thank God. He smoked cigars sometimes with a couple of his ultrasound friends, a diverse group, white, black, Hispanic, and he still played football in the park on weekends, coming home grass streaked, sated. He and Jules trusted that everything would come together for them because they were still relatively young, appealing, educated, and had started off their marriage happily, and Dennis's MAO inhibitor was still working well, "knock wood," they said.

The deep friendship between Ash and Jules had stealthily transformed into its adult version, which meant that what they talked about had expanded to include all the new people in their midst, and an increasing political awareness: Ash and feminism as it applied in the eighties; Jules and the economics of mental illness, which confronted her at the psychiatric hospital in the Bronx each day. Their friendship still had a primacy over most other things. Both Ash and Jules saw Jonah whenever they could, but he was busy at his robotics job, and also he was in the early stages of a relationship with Jules's friend Robert Takahashi, and was always slipping off to be with him.

If Jules or Ash needed to see each other, then the two husbands stepped aside. It almost seemed gratifying to the men to step aside in those moments, remembering what women could have together that men rarely could. Ash and Jules felt relief in knowing each other as well as they did. The friendship was like a fortification for their marriages, an extra layer of security. Ethan was so busy with the show — the table reads, the recording sessions, the production meetings, the conference calls with the network — and Ash would always spend some of that time with Jules.

Once, looking through a women's magazine together, they saw an article about a legendary sex toy emporium in New York for women called Eve's Garden. It wasn't that their marriages weren't sexually satisfying to them — both of them had confided that they were — but they got into a discussion about how maybe it was a good idea to have "a vibrator of one's own, to paraphrase the late, great Virginia Woolf," Jules said. Then, to amuse Ash, she went off on a Woolf sex riff, saying, suggestively, "Are those rocks in your pocket, or are you just happy to see me?" Going to the sex toy store would be a weird little adventure, the women decided. The place was famous, but it was unlike almost any other sex store in New York, because it lacked a lurid overtone. Instead, it had been designed as a feminist business celebrating sexual freedom, back in the earnest 1970s when women were joining the workforce and discovering their clitorises. ("Not at the same moment, I hope," Jules had said to Ash. "You'd get fired.") Now, deep into the Reagan years, you could still feel the sad spillover from that quaintly vanished era, and you could go with your best friend to this friendly sex toy store located in an anonymous office building, and stand together, silently shaking with laughter, both teenaged and fully grown all at once, knowing that you would never have to choose between those different states of maturity, because you contained them both inside yourselves.

"May I help you?" asked a woman who had just stepped out of a line drawing from *Our Bodies, Ourselves*. Ash and Jules let her advise them on vibrators, in the end both choosing the same model, a grotesque translucent pink jelly thing called the Joystick, and packs of overpriced batteries. At home, alone, Jules used the vibrator a few times, though tentatively and self-consciously, and once in a while she or Ash would tell the other, "I had a date with the Joystick the other day," or, "You seem a little stressed; maybe you could use some *joy* in your life," or, "Guess who I saw last night? My old friend Joy Stick. Remember her? *Joy Stick?* She was always such a *stimulating* person, don't you think?" And then after a while life became so busy that the jokes slowed and then finally stopped. Jules tossed the thing deep in her closet and never missed it, and the Joystick wasn't found again until a closet purge that took place some eight years later, by which point one of the batteries had exploded, corroding the whole pink and porous thing.

But the friendship was untouchable, uncorrodible; it was the centerpiece of the two marriages, and all four of them knew it. Jules and Ethan's friendship in adulthood was different, less public, less explainable, more unusual and unspoken though quite deep, and harder to articulate, at least to Dennis and Ash. The two couples, side by side, had history and comfort. They had all come up together in New York City, but now the imbalance between the couples was suddenly, jarringly evident. It had been imbalanced for a long time, but having learned, a moment earlier, of Ethan's place on the list in *Media Now* magazine, Jules felt with pinpoint pain that her life with Dennis was not likely to ever feel big enough in order to be tolerable, at least not as long as these two were their closest friends. Jules and Dennis had already understood that Ethan Figman was highly successful and talented — but *powerful*? Ethan? He didn't care about power. He wore Felix the Cat and Gepetto T-shirts and still drew in little spiral notebooks. Powerful was something else. None of them were supposed to be powerful; power wasn't anything they'd ever aspired to. They hadn't aspired to money either, but in this respect they were now in the minority. Slowly, the movement away from the creative, and toward the creativity of money, was becoming increasingly visible.

All around them, making money, and wanting to make money, had grown infinitely more reputable. People spoke about their money managers with great feeling, as if describing artists. And artists themselves were spoken of more candidly in terms of their worth. Gallery owners shared the limelight with their star painters. The newly rich would drop a lot of money on the newly famous; everyone, whether in business or art, almost seemed to be the same, interchangeable, coated with an identical moneyed gleam, as if they'd been licked all over by the same magical dog. And even artists who hadn't made it yet wanted some part of this, jockeying to become the implicit entertainment at certain Upper East Side dinner parties. During the soup course, everyone turned expectantly to hear them talk about what was happening in the art world. But you wouldn't get asked back to those dinners if your career didn't advance fairly soon. These days, if you were a starving artist, you were thought of as *failed;* and even if your work was really, really good, no one would quite believe it. Because surely, if it was *that* good, someone would have discovered it by now. "Van Gogh would never have been invited back to 1040 Park Avenue," Jules told Ethan. It wasn't just the visual arts either. "In the past," a writer friend of Ethan's had recently said, over lots of beer, "everyone wanted to be novelists. And now they all want to be screenwriters. It's like screenplays are the same exact thing as novels, but easier to read and worth a lot more money."

Jules and Dennis were aware of the change

in the climate, and she knew they would need money themselves pretty soon; actually they needed it now. She just didn't want to think about it yet, which she knew was a babyish attitude, yet also kind of admirable. There were so many poor people in the city who required therapy; she couldn't imagine jacking up her fees and treating the rich. She feared that she wouldn't even be able to relate to the rich. Jules had known a boy in college, a very talented tenor, who'd abandoned his operatic yearnings in order to become a stockbroker. Now, he cheerfully announced, he made a fucking fortune, and sang in the Gay Men's Chorus once a week, so he had the best of both worlds. But money as an end product, money as a *creation,* seemed disgusting to Jules, just as it had seemed disgusting to Ethan. Was Ethan changing? Did he feel different now that he was in such a different world? But then she reminded herself that just because he made a lot of money, it did not mean he loved money. Although, she thought, if she had money, she'd probably love it.

Dennis, coming into the living room of the walk-up after fetching *Media Now* magazine at the store, held the rolled up magazine in his hand, as if he was going to swat something with it. "Go ahead," Jules said. "Tell me about the list." Dennis opened his hand and smoothed out the magazine.

"Number ninety-eight is great," he said. "Remember, we didn't even know if he would be on the list at all. He's new to all this." Then he handed her the issue, and together they looked at the page that featured a fairly decent photograph of Ethan, his estimated worth listed beside his rank. The amount was very big in normal-person terms. However, there was an asterisk next to it, and a note at the bottom of the page explaining that the editors were aware that the figure was much lower than the estimated wealth of most of the other people who lolled nearby on the list. But, wrote the editors, they considered Ethan one of the one hundred most powerful people in media party because of what was likely to happen to him over the next several years when *Figland,* already so beloved, would likely — though there were no guarantees — go into syndication.

Ethan had explained to Jules how the truly massive wealth in TV occurred once your show reached five seasons, or roughly a hundred episodes — because that was when it went into syndication. Ethan insisted that he still had no idea whether or not this would happen to his show, and that probably it wouldn't. "The chances are low," he'd said. "It's a crapshoot. I'm amazed that we were even renewed this season. The reviews were good, but the ratings haven't been stellar." But maybe he'd been lying to her in order to seem more modest. Lying because he was embarrassed to be talking to Jules, a clinical social worker married to an ultrasound technician, about the extraordinary direction his own life was surely heading. He never said, "Isn't it *wild,* Jules, what's happened to me? Isn't it *nuts*? I mean, this is me we're talking about, me! Shouldn't we stand on the roof of a building and *scream*?" Or, "Don't worry, I won't become one of those money assholes we hate. There is no Ferrari in my future." He never gloated, or even really referred directly to what was happening, except obliquely, with embarrassment. Mostly he kept his head down and worked on many different aspects of his show.

The future, Ethan said, was always uncertain. But the editors who compiled this important top 100 list were more optimistic. They already expected that *Figland* would go into syndication, and felt confident pronouncing that Ethan's power — though much more significant so far than his money — was pretty formidable even now. The figure that was listed was far more than Ethan and Ash had ever let on to Jules and Dennis, and also far more than their lifestyle suggested.

"Our powerful friend," Jules said. "Fuck."

"Why fuck?"

"I don't know how to think about him anymore."

"Why do you have to think anything?"

Dennis asked.

"We can never tell them we went out and looked at the list," she said. Ash had mentioned the magazine to Jules in passing — she and Ethan knew the issue was coming out, and the list, an annual, highly anticipated event in certain quarters, would probably get a lot of attention, but they didn't know if he'd be on it. "It'd look like we were going out of our way to look him up," Jules said. "To take his pulse without him knowing it."

"Which is exactly what we *were* doing," said Dennis. "But it's okay. There's nothing criminal about it. Just maybe a little creepy. A little stalkery."

"I just wanted to know what we were dealing with," Jules said. "And the money part too, even though I know it's not that much compared with the money of the other people on the list. But obviously it's going to go way up in a few years. Syndication, when it happens. *Assuming* it happens. Ethan says it probably won't. The show is more prestigious than it is profitable. It all involves market share. God, I act like I even know what I'm talking about — 'market share' — but I don't."

"So we pried into our good friend's power and finances," said Dennis, "and now we're done and we can think about something else. Are you going to the Bronx later? Is that girl you told me about still in the hospital?"

Jules had a client, a sweet, mumbling teenager, who had been hospitalized after a suicide attempt. Jules went there every day and just sat talking to her and sometimes even got her to smile or laugh. Yes, she told Dennis, she would go to the hospital later. But she was not yet done with the conversation about Ethan. Probably she would never be done with it. Right now, a straight shot downtown in Tribeca, in the expansive honey-floored duplex loft they'd moved into, Ethan and Ash were probably getting up and padding across those floors to the walk-in refrigerator, a big, extravagant purchase that they'd originally shown off to their friends with embarrassment and childlike pride. "I can't really explain my pleasure in this bizarre appliance," Ethan had said.

"My theory," said Ash, "is that it's because after his mother left his father, the refrigerator was always empty. You know what his father kept in there? Sardines and Parkay margarine."

"And eyedrops," added Ethan. "Don't forget eyedrops. My dad had some eye condition, and the drops had to be refrigerated."

"Yes, eyedrops too. So now," said Ash, "Ethan can actually walk *into* the refrigerator and be surrounded by choices. It doesn't exactly make up for what he missed, but it can try."

"She read all this in *The Drama of the Gifted*

Child," Ethan joked.

Dennis flopped down hard now on the little foam couch beside Jules, the whole cheap thing bisecting slightly; then he took off his shoes and socks and crossed a leg, depositing his bare foot in her lap. "Foot rub?" he asked. "I'll pay you."

"How much?"

"Whatever Ethan gets an hour."

"Sure," she said. "I'd prefer cash, though gold bullion would be fine too." She began to press her thumbs into the bottom and sides of his cold veiny foot.

"Ooh, that's excellent," he said. "Really, really excellent. You know exactly what to do."

Jules Jacobson-Boyd rubbed her husband's foot deeply and, after a minute, a little sadistically. It was thick and callused from the athletic shoes he wore during all those touch football games. Dennis closed his eyes and made a string of contented animal noises. He had gone out and brought home a greater understanding of Ethan's power in the world and the current metrics of Ethan's wealth, which would only expand insanely in due time, if everything went well. But already there was his percentage of revenue not only from the show but from every *Figland* T-shirt, plush toy, beach towel, and pencil eraser that anyone spent their money on.

"What I take away from this," Jules said as she continued digging her thumbs into her husband's foot, "is that he is in some other world, and that therefore so is Ash. And all this time when we keep inviting them over here, they probably say to each other, 'Oh God, we really love them, but do we have to go to that depressing place again with the cheap furniture and all those stairs?' Dennis, why didn't this occur to us before? Obviously we've known they're very very rich, but we should have been embarrassed all this time to let them come here. They don't *want* to come here, but they have to act like they do. They play their wealth way, way down; they're very modest about it. They act like they're in the same world we're in, but they aren't. And all this time when we've gone out to eat with them and Ethan grabbed the bill, and we said, 'No no, Ethan, that's not necessary, let's split it,' it was completely absurd of us not to let him take care of it. It was actually *pathetic* of us, and he knew it but we didn't. He was just being kind by not insisting. He probably doesn't even want to go to those dinners with us anymore at normal-people restaurants," she went on. "Remember how we all went to that Turkish place last month? I kept talking about the kebab special. Oh, whoopee, so it came with a chopped salad and all the microwaved flatbread you could eat. What a thrill for Ethan Figman!"

"What are you saying, Jules?"

"Ethan and Ash don't need kebab specials

in their lives anymore. What I really mean is, they don't need us. If we all met now, we would never become friends. You think they would feel a connection if someone said, 'Here is a very nice social worker and a very nice ultrasound technician?' That's why meeting in childhood can *seem* like it's the best thing — everyone's equal, and you form bonds based only on how much you like each other. But later on, having met in childhood can turn out to have been the *worst* thing, because you and your friends might have nothing to say to each other anymore, except, 'Wasn't it funny that time in tenth grade when your parents came home and we were so wasted.' If you didn't feel sentimental about the past, you wouldn't keep it up. And when Ethan's show goes into syndication, this whole thing will be so much more massive and disturbing. If I was a better person," Jules said, "then I would cut them free. They have other friends; remember those people at dinner?"

Dennis nodded. "They were okay," he said. The friends of Ash and Ethan in question had been a couple of recent friendship vintage. The husband was a portfolio manager, slightly older, and the wife was an interior designer who also ran a literacy program in East Harlem. Both of them were lithe and angled, their clothes made of linen, and the dinner that night hadn't been awkward so much as depressing. The portfolio manager and his wife had had nothing to ask Jules and Dennis. It wouldn't have even occurred to them to ask them anything. The fact that all the interest flowed toward that couple did not seem at all unusual to them. They neutrally accepted the one-way flow, and Dennis in particular kept the conversation going, wanting to know the answers to various questions. Once again, he was interested in other people; it was an admirable quality generally, but in this case it irritated Jules, who didn't want these people to think they should accept other people's interest as their due. She herself, in her mild rage, began to ask them question after question. "What are the literacy rates in our country?" she drunkenly demanded of the wife. And, barely having listened to the answer, she turned to the husband and said, "Since when did 'portfolio' start to refer to money, not artwork? It's like the way if someone's an analyst, it no longer means they're a Freudian, it means they study the stock market." This was the kind of remark she and Ethan sometimes said to each other. She was furious at being ignored, and Ash, usually so sensitive to everyone's needs, was so busy seeing that drinks were filled that she didn't notice the unresponsiveness of the other couple or Jules's anger. Jules and Dennis were the odd ones out that night; everyone else was inside a circle, an enclosure, a walk-in refrigerator of wealth and importance.

It had been an upsetting evening, and an indication of more to come, but Jules and Dennis had never spoken about it before now. They would have had to turn to each other on the way out of the loft building and say, "We are such doofuses." If Jules had been talking to Ethan, she might have corrected herself and said, "We are *The Doofae*. It's like the name of a Greek play that Ash would want to direct."

Jules thought of that couple now, and the other friends that Ethan and Ash had accumulated over a relatively brief period of time. A few of their new friends worked in television or film and easily went back and forth between the coasts as though shuttling between Manhattan and Brooklyn. Somewhere along the way Ethan had become friends with a famous, boyish magician who once, at dinner, made figs pop out of Ethan's ears and nose, and then dusted Ash's long hair in what he insisted was volcanic ash.

"What were that couple's names?" Jules asked Dennis. "The portfolio manager and the literacy volunteer. The ones I interrogated, and who didn't give a shit about us or even ask us anything at all. The prick and the cunt."

"The prick and the cunt?" said Dennis,

411

laughing. "Whoa, listen to you. Their names were . . . Duncan and Shyla, I think."

"Right!" said Jules. "We should let Ash and Ethan go be with Duncan and Shyla, and not make them feel that they have to stick with me, with *us*. The difference between our lives is humiliating, I see that now. Remember the day at the Strand?"

A few weeks earlier, Dennis and Jules had lugged several shopping bags full of books on the subway to the enormous, raw-spaced, famous Strand bookstore, where you could sell your used books. No matter how much you brought in, Dennis said, it always seemed as if they gave you fifty-eight dollars, but even that was enough to make it worthwhile. Fifty-eight dollars in your pocket made you feel a little bigger. As they struggled to drag their bulging, partly ripping shopping bags down the street into the bookstore, they came upon Ash and Ethan, arms linked, headed to the bookstore to browse. "Hey, where are you going?" Ash had said in pleasure when they saw one another. "We'll help you."

"Yes, we'll help you," Ethan said. "I have an hour max, and then I have to go to work. I'm playing hooky now; they're waiting for me to show up."

"They're waiting for you?" said Jules. "Don't keep them waiting to help us bring our books to the Strand. I mean, that's ridiculous."

"But I want to," he said. "I'm dreading going in today. There's a scene that no one knows how to fix. I'd rather be at the Strand with you guys."

So they'd had to endure Ash and Ethan helping them navigate their bags of books into the store, and then insisting on standing on line with them amid all the other people selling their own books. There was a junkie couple on that line, a bedraggled, practically chimney-sweep-filthy man and woman whose teeth chattered and whose bony, ruined arms shook while they held their clearly stolen coffee-table books with titles like *Mies van der Rohe: An Appreciation.* That day at the bookstore, on line with the junkies, was so quietly humiliating that Jules hadn't brought it up again to Dennis. But now that she had, he said quietly, "It wasn't a big deal."

"Yes, it was," said Jules. "Thinking back on it now, with this new perspective because of the list in the magazine, it feels to me as if they saw us selling our blood."

"They would be really shocked to hear this," Dennis said. "Isn't Ash your closest friend? Isn't Ethan your favorite male person — other than me?"

"Yes," Jules said. "But the more I imagine things changing for them, the more I know they would just keep insisting they haven't changed in substance. When Ethan tries to pay for meals, I see now that it's just because

413

he doesn't want to embarrass us by letting us know the truth."

"And what is the truth?" asked Dennis. He took his foot back, suddenly done with being touched by her.

"That in a few years he will probably never have to think about his own income again. That he will be able to do exactly what he wants forever. It's already begun to happen. And Ash will be able to do what she wants too."

"Yes, probably," Dennis agreed. "Because of him."

"Right. Him and his power. Him and his money. I would bet anything that in a few years Ash breaks through in her career too. She won't have to distract herself with a million weird little theater projects anymore." Ash's résumé resembled those of hundreds of young women five years out of Ivy League schools — women who wanted to go into "the arts," and were waiting for the perfect jump-rope moment when "the arts," that nebulous place, became accessible to them. Through her connections from childhood and Yale and the city, Ash continued to take low-paying or no-paying jobs in theater whenever she could, directing a series of one-acts at a depressing nursing home, putting together a performance piece with a few college friends called *Commuters* right in the middle of Grand Central Terminal, while

414

actual commuters, annoyed, had to walk around them to get to their trains. But these jobs were only occasional, and all the while Ash was making notes about feminist performances she wanted to direct — a contemporary *Lysistrata,* an evening devoted to the playwright Caryl Churchill — and reading long, demanding books of Russian theater theory, and living extremely well, without discouragement or financial anxiety.

"You have no way of knowing where she'll be professionally in a few years," said Dennis.

"I do know." It was as though Jules possessed a new clarity she'd lacked until now. She understood that it had never just been about *talent;* it had also always been about money. Ethan was brilliant at what he did, and he might well have made it even if Ash's father hadn't encouraged and advised him, but it really helped that Ethan had grown up in a sophisticated city, and that he had married into a wealthy family. Ash was talented, but not all *that* talented. This was the thing that no one had said, not once. But of course it was fortunate that Ash didn't have to worry about money while trying to think about art. Her wealthy childhood had given her a head start, and now Ethan had picked up where her childhood had left off.

"I feel horrible saying this," Jules said to Dennis. "I love her and she's my best friend and she's very dedicated, and she does the reading and puts in the time, and she's legitimately interested in the feminist aspect. But isn't it true that there are a lot of other people who are talented at the same exact level, and they're all slaving away? She's got some good ideas. But is she great at directing? Is she the theatrical equivalent of Ethan? No! Oh, God will strike me dead right now."

Dennis looked at her and said, "Your nonexistent God, Ms. Atheist Jew? I doubt it." He walked into the kitchen, and she followed him. The sink was piled high with plates from last night's Chinese takeout, and Dennis wordlessly poured yellow liquid soap over the whole mess, and picked up a ragged sponge. He was now apparently going to hand wash all their dishes and stuff them precariously into the drying rack, performing a task that would further illustrate the disparity between them and Ethan and Ash. Jules wondered if Dennis was doing this on purpose.

"Ash doesn't have greatness, I don't think," Jules said over the water. "And she might not even need it. I always thought talent was everything, but maybe it was always money. Or even *class*. Or if not class exactly, then connections."

"You're just realizing this now?" Dennis asked. "Haven't you been seeing examples of it everywhere in the world?"

"I'm a slow learner."

"No you're not."

"I bet she's even going to have her own theater in a few years, devoted to promoting the work of women," said Jules. "The Ash Wolf Athenaeum."

"Her own theater? You're a demented individual," said Dennis. "Here, dry some of these. There's no room to put them all on the rack." He held a plate out to her and she took it and grabbed a dish towel, which felt slightly grimy, almost oily. If she dried the plate with this, they would find themselves trapped in not quite cleanliness. Suddenly she wanted to cry.

"Dennis," said Jules. "Let's leave these dishes and just go out somewhere."

"Where?"

"I don't know. Let's just go out walking or something. Let's do one of those New York things that are free and that make you happy when you're feeling discouraged."

Dennis studied her, his arms deep in the sink, and then slowly he lifted them out, dripping, and unstopped the drain. Water was pulled out with an obscene slurp, and Dennis wiped his hands on the sides of his pants and came forward to collect Jules against him. He smelled of lemon Dawn, and she probably smelled of whatever chemical was released when you became bitter. "Don't be discouraged," he said. "We have a lot of good things. We're here in our little love nest. Okay, our crappy little love nest. But we're here." It

417

touched her that he'd said this. "You are unbelievably nice to me, even when I'm like this. It's just very hard for me," she told him, "when I realize we're at such a different place from them. I knew I wasn't going to make it in acting, finally. I knew I had to stop trying out for all those plays. It wasn't just what Yvonne said to me. I wasn't supposed to be an actor in the first place. Acting, being funny, was my way *into* the world. And then I had to give it up. But it's different for Ash. I feel that she and Ethan are bulletproof; him because he's so talented and so huge. And her because she's with him. And for us to think that somehow what we're left with is enough — well, as of today, I know it isn't."

Dennis's face shifted as he regarded her; the sympathy he'd shown her was retreating. He was tired of her again; it went in waves. "I thought you were winding down," he said. "And I thought, *good,* because I've kind of had enough of this. But now here you are winding up again."

"Not on purpose," she said.

"I just don't have the energy for this, Jules, I really don't. You basically expect me to be this unchanging and totally understanding person, while you have your little fits every once in a while, and then I soothe you. Is that the way it's always going to work between us? Does that sound happy to you? I don't think I signed up for that."

"But the situation has changed," she said. "You 'signed up' for something that's a little different now. That's what happens. Things shift."

"No, 'things' haven't shifted; you've shifted them," said Dennis. "You actually want me to comfort you while you're the one basically coming in here and messing everything up. I cannot comfort you on this. I *like* our life. Is that such a fucking crime? I like our life, regardless of what goes on around us, but you apparently don't." His usually low scrape of a voice had been tightened, and had become unpleasant. This was Dennis angry, which she had rarely seen, or at least she'd rarely seen the anger directed toward her for any length of time. Once, after he'd spotted a mouse in their kitchen and had tried to kill it with a spatula, the only implement within reach, he'd been in a fury, which they'd both admitted later had had a comical edge. But this didn't.

"That is not true!" she said.

"Maybe this whole thing," he went on, his voice unchanged, "is all a secret way for you to tell me you feel really cheated because I don't make a fortune too."

"No, it isn't."

"That you wish I was someone else, so *you* could be someone else."

"No," she said. "Not at all."

"Because that's the way I'm starting to hear

419

it," said Dennis.

"It isn't true," said Jules. "I'm sorry," she said, with feeling. "I know I should stop talking about this, I know it's unhealthy." Please stop being angry at me, she wanted to say. That was what seemed to matter now.

"Yes," said Dennis. "That's exactly what it is. It's very, very unhealthy. You should think about it, Jules. Think about what these unhealthy comments do to us. They create this environment of unhealthiness. Of disease."

"Don't exaggerate."

"I'm not."

"I'm happy with you," she said. "I really am. I don't suddenly think that there's a one-to-one correspondence between money and happiness. When we fell in love, it had nothing to do with whether I thought we'd have some luxurious life. It never occurred to me to think about that. I'm not shallow, you know."

The phone rang exactly then and Jules was relieved to answer it. This was how their arguments had ended a few times; someone called on the phone, and by the time the conversation was over, the imperative to argue had virtually disappeared. But it was Ash on the phone now, wanting to know if they could all have dinner that night. A new Asian fusion place had opened, she said, and the spring rolls with glass noodles inside were amazing.

Ash sounded the way Ash always sounded — enthusiastic, warm — and Ethan was talking in the background, saying that Ash should tell Jules that she and Dennis had to come; the food would not taste good without them there.

Ash asked her, "Will you come?"

Jules pressed the phone against her chest and looked at Dennis. "They want to know, will we come?"

He shrugged. "It's up to you."

So they went. The food was good and their friends were the same as ever. They did not appear different, or richer, or as if they lived in another world. But when the bill came, Ethan reached for it, and Jules and Dennis made an attempt to reach for it too, or at the very least to split it, yet in the end they let him get it. And so, quietly but noticeably, a new part of their lives began. From that night on, Ethan paid for almost all dinners and vacations.

The first trip they took together was to Tanzania, to climb Mount Kilimanjaro in July 1987. Jonah and Robert Takahashi, whose relationship was now serious, came too. Ethan, though he'd been on some expensive vacations since becoming successful, did not love travel, and paid very little attention to it. "We didn't go on a lot of family vacations when I was growing up," he said. "The swankiest place my parents ever took me was the Pennsylvania Dutch country. We looked at people in old-fashioned clothes on horse and buggy, and my mother took pictures with her Polaroid Swinger, even though she wasn't supposed to, and an Amish guy yelled at her, and my parents had a huge fight about it — so what else is new? Then we bought a hex sign and some weird kind of fudge called penuche — that name embarrassed me, it was like 'penis' — and went home." Now, though, Ethan had asked his assistant if she would mind terribly finding a trip for the three couples during a week later on in the year when *Figland* was on hiatus; he wanted a trip that was "outside my comfort zone," as he put it. "Even asking my assistant such a question is outside my comfort zone," Ethan said. "Even having an assistant is outside my comfort zone." The assistant, having read Hemingway in college, suggested Kilimanjaro. The price of the trip seemed exorbitant, and this made Ethan anxious, but Ash reminded him, "You're twenty-eight years old and independently wealthy. You have to get used to it and live accordingly. It actually isn't particularly flattering for you to whine and complain about your good fortune. I don't know who that helps. You're not your crazy, screaming, financially erratic parents' little kid anymore. You can actually go new places and try new things. And you can spend money; it's okay, it really is."

The assistant had booked them all on a climb with one of the top-of-the-line mountaineering outfits. After a couple of months walking up flights of stairs carrying heavy packs, and going on hikes whenever possible, in preparation for the trip, the three couples gathered with the other climbers in a lounge in a hotel in Arusha, where they were asked by the guides to take out their gear for inspection. Jules, Dennis, Jonah, and Robert unzipped their bags and pulled out all the various, slightly alien items they'd had to buy at a camping-goods store downtown. Dampness-wicking underwear, a sleeping pad. "The salesman told me that *wicking* meant that the dampness is drawn away, but why does dampness need its own verb?" Jonah asked the group, but Jules was distracted by Ethan and Ash, who were crouched over their own gear, studying it as if they'd never seen it before. She realized that in fact they *had* never seen it before; someone else had done both their shopping and packing for this trip.

Further vacations taken by the two couples, and only occasionally also with Jonah and Robert, were carefully planned around the production schedule of *Figland,* and brought out other small revelations. On a trip to Paris, Ethan wanted to buy a surprise gift for Ash, "some kind of scarfy thing," he'd said, and so

Jules went with him, going off together on the pretext of getting *croque monsieurs,* which seemed legitimate, because what had interested the two of them most on this trip was the food. In a gleaming boutique on the rue de Sèvres, Jules said, "I want to ask you something that will sound very unsophisticated, but I'm going to ask it anyway. How do you know how to behave rich? Does the knowledge sort of arrive with the money? Or is it the kind of thing you learn on the job?" Ethan looked at her, surprised, and said you don't know, you just wing it. He appeared displeased at the question, or at his own answer, as if it had forced him to acknowledge how his life was turning — the way a ship of state turns, slow and incremental, with great, violent, unseen convulsions underneath.

But then, over time, Jules noticed that Ethan seemed to be winging it less. He dressed better, and he actually seemed to know about wines when the list was handed to him in a restaurant in Madrid. When had he learned about wines? He hadn't told her about his new knowledge. Had a wine tutor come in at night and given him lessons? She couldn't ask him any longer. Ethan wasn't a rube, but was polite and modest and gracious. He had become more comfortable around money than Jules had ever imagined he would be, and she realized this disappointed her.

Their lives were dividing further; even finding time to get away with Ethan and Ash was
difficult for her and Dennis. Clinical social
workers — particularly ones with a fledgling
part-time practice, as Jules now had — and
ultrasound technicians usually had very little
vacation time; Ethan, as frantic as he was with
his complicated, overburdened schedule, and
Ash, far less frantic, sometimes ended up
needing to be the flexible ones.

One morning on a five-day vacation the two
couples took to Venice in 1988, having been
flown there by company jet, which was now a
fairly frequent occurrence, Jules Jacobson,
twenty-nine years old, lying in bed with
Dennis, opened an eye and coolly looked
around the room. This was not the way
anyone else she knew traveled. Her small
group of friends from social work school told
one another about their vacations, recom-
mending an all-inclusive cheap package deal
to Jamaica or a great price on a hotel room
in San Francisco. This hotel in Venice was
the kind of place where wealthy, old-money
European families stayed — "where the von
Trapps might have stayed, had they traveled
other than to escape the Nazis," Jules wrote
in a postcard to Jonah. "Help, Jonah, help!"
she added at the bottom. "My values are being kidnapped!" The hotel did not feel age
appropriate at all. A small slice of canal was
in view out the wavy-glassed window; a fruit

and cheese plate from the night before was wilting on a tray; the ceilings were coffered; and Dennis lay asleep with his head on one of the long, scrolled pillows.

By now, *Figland* had been sold all over Europe and in the UK, and Ethan was conducting TV business here. Dennis and Jules stayed in Venice while Ethan went for a short trip to Rome. Ash had decided that while he was in Rome she would take a flight to Norway to "have a look around," as she said, since she was hoping to direct Ibsen's *Ghosts* at the small Open Hand Theater in the East Village; she'd been strongly campaigning to be hired, and was waiting for their decision. It was true that Ash was going to have a look around Norway, but Jules also knew that she would be with Goodman during the trip. Ash hadn't seen him in a while. Iceland was just over two hours by plane from Norway, and everyone on this vacation other than Ethan understood that Goodman would be joining his sister.

Ash, as her late twenties pressed on, tried to visit Goodman whenever she could, though often the visits seemed to Jules nervy and reckless. As a teenager it had been difficult enough for Ash to keep up a clandestine long-distance relationship with her fugitive brother, and then in her early twenties, living with Ethan had made it even harder. But after Ethan became so successful there was a little more latitude for Ash to be in touch with Goodman and see him sometimes when she traveled. Still, it was always a complicated and anxious proposition. Once in a while, every few weeks or so, when Jules and Ash were alone Jules might suddenly ask, "Anything new with your brother?"

Ash's face would turn excited and she would say something like, "He's doing okay, he really is. Working part-time as an assistant to an architect, actually. Well, not really as an assistant, more like running complicated errands, but he feels he might get more responsibility soon, and even be allowed to do some drafting. He just likes hanging around that world. And he's still trying to get construction jobs."

Once, nearly a year before Norway, Ash had told Jules that her parents had been to see Goodman, and that he'd seemed "unwell." What did that mean? Jules asked. Oh, said Ash, it meant that Goodman had been staying out all night in Reykjavik's drinking, drugging scene, and had started showing up for his construction job late and had been fired. Frustrated and idle, he'd spent his parents' money on cocaine, then confessed the whole thing to them in an emotional phone call. After a month spent in a no-nonsense Icelandic rehab, Goodman returned to his flat over a fish store in the center of town. He hadn't lived with Gudrun and

Falkor for some years; they had their own child now, a daughter, and had needed Goodman's room as a nursery. Eventually they moved somewhere much better, for Gudrun had rapidly built a very successful career as a textile designer; the money the Wolfs had sent all those years had allowed her to perfect her craft. It was amazing to realize that there were so many worlds within worlds, little subcultures that you might know nothing about, in which someone's art could make them stand out. Though it was wonderful, certainly, it also seemed like a punch line to say that Gudrun Sigurdsdottir was apparently a superstar in the world of Icelandic handicrafts.

Keep what we've told you to yourself, the Wolf family had commanded Jules originally in the summer of 1977, and like the coweyed girl she was and would maybe always be — the funny but obedient one, the dope, the dupe — she'd obeyed them for years without much difficulty. The family's belief in Goodman's innocence was an organizing principle, and their belief became interchangeable with her own. Only later was it striking to Jules how she'd allowed herself to stay in this haze of certainty that wasn't certainty, a state that could easily occur if you'd been thrust into it when you were young. In social work school, an old female professor in a cardigan with a balled tissue forming a lump beneath the sleeve spoke about the way people could often "know without knowing."

For the first few years after Goodman had run off, Jules had had no one to talk to about the situation, other than Ash. She'd never said a word to Jonah. But then, starting in the early weeks of 1982, she had Dennis. Jules told Dennis everything important, and finally, only a couple of months into their relationship, when they were joined in a way that seemed to her permanent, this included telling him about the Wolf family's ongoing secret support of their son. Of course he was shocked. "They just send him money?" he said. "They know where he is and they never told the police? Whoa, unbelievable. Unbelievably arrogant."

"I think most parents would do that for their son if they were sure he was innocent," Jules said, but she was only repeating something Ash had once said.

"Why were they so sure?"

"Well, because they *know* him," Jules said.

"Still," Dennis said, "didn't you ever think about, you know, turning him in yourself?"

"Oh, well, vaguely," she said. "But I just never wanted to get involved in that way. It's not my place."

"I can understand that," said Dennis. "There was a family in my old building, right upstairs from Isadora. The mother verbally abused her five-year-old, calling her a worthless piece of shit and other terrible names.

Finally someone in the building called Child Protective Services, and the girl was taken away from her mother, who she apparently loved despite everything. And then Isadora told me she'd heard that the girl was sent to foster care, where she was molested by a much older foster brother. So you never know what you're setting in motion. Though I have to say," Dennis said, "it's still wild that the Wolfs did this. That they *do* it. But what's really wild is that they keep it from Ethan. That Ash does. I mean, *whoa.*" He shook his head at the nerve of it all, the entitlement. He was not under the influence of that family.

"I shouldn't have told you," Jules said. "But I had to. I'm never going to tell Ash that I did, so you can never ever mention it to her in any way. Seriously, even if you and I break up one day and you hate me for the rest of your life, you can never tell anyone about Goodman, okay?" She realized that she sounded the way Gil Wolf had originally sounded when he had spoken so sternly, almost threateningly, that night in the Café Benedikt. "I can't even believe I told you, Dennis," Jules went on. "What does it mean that I needed to tell you?"

He smiled happily. "It means something big!"

"Yes, I guess it does," she said. "But you could call the police right now and have

430

Goodman arrested. And the entire Wolf family too, probably."

"And *you,*" Dennis added. "Time to get a lawyer." They were both silent; he'd gone too far. "I was kidding," he quickly said. "I would never do that to you."

"I know you wouldn't."

"I just love you," Dennis said. "And now that you've told me this, I even love you more."

"But why?" she asked. "What does it have to do with anything?"

"Because we're still pretty new to each other, like two months' new, and even so, you told me this thing. I am awed by it. It's like . . . a declaration. I feel sorry for Ethan, though," Dennis went on, thoughtfully. "He's the genius, but he doesn't even know this basic, major fact about his girlfriend and her family. I don't like the Wolfs," he added. "I like Ash, of course, she's a good friend to you and everything, but I don't like her and her family as a thing. A unit."

"You don't have to like them."

"You're sure?"

"I'm sure."

Dennis had never been seduced into anything by anyone other than Jules. He was grateful to have been folded into her life, and as far as he could see, the backstory of Goodman Wolf, someone he'd never met, had nothing much to do with anything anymore.

Now, in Europe in 1988, Ash hadn't entirely lied to Ethan about where she would be for the next two days in Norway; she'd only omitted key parts of her plans. It was true that she was staying at the Grand Hotel in Oslo. While Ash was in Oslo and Ethan was in Rome, Dennis and Jules spent the weekend by themselves in Venice. But she felt uneasy on her own with Dennis in this unnervingly expensive hotel room. She placed a hand on Dennis's arm as he lay beside her in the bed, though he was still asleep. "Dennis," she said. "Dennis."

"What?" He opened his eyes and came closer to her, and she smelled his breath, which was strong but not bad. *Oaky.* Cork breath, from last night's drinking. He was hardly awake, but he instinctively moved on top of her, and she felt the automaticity of his a.m. erection, for which she didn't take any credit. He arranged himself, and though she'd only been self-conscious about the lavish surroundings and obscurely worried and had wanted just to talk to him about anything at all, this was as good or maybe better. Sex in an Italian hotel room had a specific effect on Americans: it made them feel Italian. Dennis at twenty-nine almost looked Italian, with his now slightly heavier-set, shadowed face and dark eyes, and the scramble of chest, underarm, and pubic hair. One of the scroll pillows dropped to the floor, heavy as an anchor. Half asleep, Dennis lifted Jules up as if she were weightless and planted her on top of him, but she reached down with both hands, not wanting this to turn into a moment when the positioning was wrong, and the woman had to make adjustments while the man looked away discreetly or else watched openly. Making sure a penis was inside you correctly so that it wouldn't hurt when it pushed in was like the moment in a car when you struggled to connect the metal part at the end of the seat belt into its little groove. You waited for the click of a seat belt, just as here, in an Italian hotel bed, you waited for a different kind of click that came from interior mysteries. There was only a momentary resistance, and then none at all, and finally you were absurdly happy at how it had worked out, as though in arranging a penis inside your body, you had done something important, like successfully completing the critical repair of a space shuttle.

Below her in the hotel bed, Dennis closed his eyes, and his mouth hung open a little, the tongue slightly revealed. She thought of Ash and Goodman in separate beds in adjoining hotel rooms elsewhere on the continent, and then she thought of how, in the living room of the Wolfs' apartment in the Labyrinth, Jules had once kissed Goodman, her own tongue seeking his and finding it, until he got bored and shut the kiss down. She leaned down now, her mouth covering Dennis's, and he responded without mockery or ennui, and instead with his full self, the oaky, tannic mouth, half-closed eyes, and the unshowered body with its pheromones that drew her toward him even though the appeal could never fully be explained.

Afterward, they had breakfast downstairs, one of those strange European hotel breakfasts that feature hard-boiled eggs and Weetabix, and then, right between the two, as if it were perfectly normal, organ meats. In the Babel of the breakfast room, she and Dennis sat at a table among Spaniards and Germans. Jules said to Dennis, "I wonder what Goodman looks like. He's *thirty* now. Jesus, Goodman at thirty! It's really hard to picture."

"Well, I've obviously never met him, but he's probably a lot more weather-beaten," Dennis said. "Isn't that what happens to people who smoke and drink and do drugs? It beats up their skin so it looks like — what's that called? — distressed leather."

She imagined Goodman lined and weathered and distressed, sprawled across one of the two double beds in his room at the Grand Hotel in Oslo. His long body took up the whole bed, and his sister lay on the other bed, both of them smoking and laughing. Ash would be so relieved to be with him again, to have a chance to check in on him and see that he was at least broadly okay, and hear his drawn-out, sardonic voice, and gaze at the face that had once hewed close to hers. The love between a brother and sister just over a year apart in age held fast. It wasn't twinship, and it wasn't romance, but it was more like a passionate loyalty to a dying brand.

My little sister, let me in.

Jules and Dennis took a high-speed train back to Rome to meet up with Ethan and Ash. On the last night of the vacation, the two couples had dinner near the Piazza del Popolo, during which they compared notes. Ethan described the meetings he'd had with the executives from the Italian public broadcasting service Rai, which took place over multicourse meals and a parade of wines that roiled inside him as he and the Rai people stayed out until two a.m., celebrating the continued Italian ratings success of *Figland,* which was known here as *Mondo Fig!*

Jules and Dennis described their lazy weekend in Venice. "Dennis in Venice," said Ethan. "A new comic strip." They talked about the walks they'd taken through drizzly, impossible little streets.

"How was Oslo?" Ethan asked Ash.

"I like it there," Ash said, shrugging lightly. "I just wandered around, imagining the atmosphere of the play."

Jules had to remember: Oh right, *Ibsen,* the putative reason Ash had gone to Oslo. Ibsen's

Ghosts. Women briefly walking across the stage bare-breasted, in this version the nipples painted in Day-Glo colors, which would provide a strong effect with the lights down. Was Ash having a little fun, choosing that particular title? Goodman had slipped over into the land of the ghosts by now, twelve years after he'd run away from New York and the U.S. and his trial, but he was intermittently revivable, shuttling back and forth between ghost and living human. His mother sent him care packages, the way she used to do at Spirit-in-the-Woods, but instead of 6-12 insect repellent and cheese in a can she sent him protein powder and amber bottles of vitamins. Ash sent her brother books, recalling the tastes he'd had as an adolescent, and extrapolating from them into adulthood. She sent him a recent Günter Grass, and Thomas Pynchon and Cormac McCarthy, and a novel by a young genius named David Foster Wallace called *The Broom of the System.* She once threw in her favorite book, *The Drama of the Gifted Child,* with a note saying that this book was relevant to her life, not his, but she thought maybe he would find it interesting anyway, given that they'd had the same parents. Goodman read everything his sister sent, and dutifully mixed the protein powder into his skyr and swallowed his mother's vitamins, and he found construction jobs when he could — the job helping out in that architect's office hadn't worked out — though he had bàck problems now and was sometimes incapacitated for weeks. He smoked pot most evenings and some mornings, and he retained an intermittent interest in cocaine, requiring another stay in rehab.

"Here's to our vacation, and to *Mondo Fig!* and to your generosity, as always," Dennis said at dinner, raising his glass the way, in recent years, he and Jules had learned to do. Once you started toasting people, you had made the complete transition to full-throttle adulthood.

After the long flight back from Rome, a car dropped Jules and Dennis in front of their building on West 84th Street. Ethan and Ash took a separate car; he had to race off to the studio immediately, and didn't even have time to go home. Everyone at the show was waiting for him, he said, as they always seemed to be. Standing before their narrow tenement, Jules and Dennis both looked upward and made a face at the same moment, then laughed. There were no bellmen to carry their suitcases, no sherpas. No trays of fruit and cheese awaited them upstairs, no robes. They wedged their suitcases through the narrow vestibule, and angled them carefully in order to drag them up the four flights of stairs, hearts thudding hard. In the apartment, the answering machine blinked fiercely, two gnats drag-raced around the apparently sweet, rotting hole of the kitchen drain, and life was difficult once again, and familiar, and a disappointment.

Now there would be no vacations for a long while. Both of them had used up their vacation days. In time, Jules began to build up her private practice and ease out of working at the hospital. All her clients were low fee at first. An obese man wept about his wife leaving him; a teenaged boy only wanted to talk about Sid Vicious. It was like opening a novel whenever a new client walked in, Jules told Ash. She was never bored seeing people in therapy, even if she feared that her own powers to help them were small, tentative. Ash and Jules discussed their work all the time — Ash's fears and excitement about actually getting to direct her first full production at Open Hand, and Jules's interest in and worry about her clients, and her worry about her own abilities. "What if I say the wrong thing to them?" she said. "What if I give them bad advice and something goes wrong?" Ash told her she was sure Jules was a good therapist and wouldn't do anything dreadful. "I remember when I came and sat on your bed at camp," Ash said. "I can't explain it, but it was just such a relief. I bet they feel that way."

But also, at the same time their careers were really taking form, both women began to talk about having children. It wasn't the right moment yet — Dennis was working long hours

438

at MetroCare, the clinic on the Upper West Side where he'd been employed since leaving ultrasound school — but maybe in a year? Sometimes Jules and Ash shared a fantasy of having children within months of each other so that they could be mothers together, and their kids could be friends — best friends. Maybe both kids could attend Spirit-in-the-Woods!

For now, no one wanted to disrupt the way life was being lived, the opening of this new era, in which everyone was given a chance to vaguely start to catch up with Ethan. No, not catch up exactly, Jonah said; they could never do that. "I don't even care about catching up, personally," Jonah went on. "I grew up around really successful people, famous people. None of it impresses me. I don't want any of it for myself. I'd just like to enjoy what I do for a living more. To actually look forward to going in each day. I keep waiting for that to happen, but it doesn't."

Ash liked her own work now. Ibsen's *Ghosts* opened for a short run at the Open Hand Theater in the fall of 1989. Jules went with Ash to a rehearsal and saw that everything Ash had learned in the theater at Spirit-in-the-Woods had reappeared here, in adult, substantial form. The production she directed was well researched, earnest, and ambitious. It wasn't witty, because Ash wasn't particularly witty, but it was smart and careful, clever with its background use of women's bodies. The Day-Glo nipples were a hit. *Ghosts* wasn't some vanity production that Ethan's wealth and success had made possible. You sometimes heard about the marginally talented wives of powerful men publishing children's books or designing handbags or, most commonly, becoming photographers. There might even be a show of the wife's work in a well-known but slightly *off* gallery. Everyone would come see it, and they would treat the wife with unctuous respect. Her photographs of celebrities without makeup, and seascapes, and street people, would be enormous, as though size and great equipment could make up for whatever else was missing.

This wasn't that. On the opening night of Ash's play in September, the second-string reviewer from the *New York Times* came to see it. In a small but positive review, the production was praised for its "fidelity," "verve," and its "thoughtful look at nineteenth-century morality, with a compelling emphasis on the meanings of femaleness. The reviewer wrote, "That Ms. Wolf is the wife of Ethan Figman, the creator of *Figland,* should be of no consequence. But it reminds us that this handsome production — with its colorful, startling anatomical flourishes — is anything but a cartoon." The run was extended; Open Hand hadn't gotten a reviewer from the *Times* to come to one of their plays in a long time, and nothing they'd produced had ever received such an important and positive review, and they giddily asked Ash what she was interested in directing next. Did she want to write something for them too? She could be their resident feminist play-wright *and* director. Men still dominated the theater, and Open Hand said it was commit-ted to changing that; Ash could make a dif-ference.

A celebration dinner in honor of Ash was quickly arranged by Ethan, who invited Jules, Dennis, Jonah, and Robert. They gathered at Sand, a tiny East Village restaurant that had also recently ascended after its own positive review in the *Times*. The restaurant was a skinny room with sand on the floor that crunched when you moved your chair or your feet. With sand beneath their shoes and complex tastes popping in their mouths, they ate their expensive, fussy-looking, last-days-of-the-eighties drizzled-plate dinner and talked about what was next for Ash. "I told her she should definitely take them up on their offer and write something original," said Ethan. "She can be a double threat. Hey," he said, turning to his wife with a droll face, "why not revive *Both Ends*?"

Everyone laughed, and Robert Takahashi asked what *Both Ends* was, and said it sounded like the name of a gay S&M play.

441

Jonah had to explain to Robert that *Both Ends* was a one-woman show about Edna St. Vincent Millay that Ash had written when she was in high school. "A *terrible* one-woman show," said Ash. "With, apparently, an unfortunate name. And these guys had to see multiple performances of it." She turned to them and said, "I'm so sorry. If I could give you those hours back, I would."

"Do the opening scene," said Robert.

"I can't, it's too awful, Robert," Ash said. "I finally get that, though it took me a long time. My parents said everything I did was wonderful."

"Come on," Robert said. "I have to see it." He smiled charmingly at her; he and Jonah were so good-looking individually and together that Jules sometimes just surreptitiously looked at them for a while when they all got together for a big dinner.

Ash said, "Okay. So I'm Edna St. Vincent Millay. And I come out onstage by myself in a nightgown, carrying a candle. Otherwise the stage is completely dark. I stand in the middle and I say, 'My candle burns at both ends; / It will not last the night; / But ah, my foes, and oh my, friends — / It gives a lovely light!' Then I step forward to the edge of the stage and I kind of beckon to the audience. I say to them, 'While my candle stays lit, won't you sit and listen? We'll talk until the light dies away.' "

Everyone laughed, including Ash. "You said that?" said Robert. "You actually said that without cracking up? I wish I'd been there for it."

"I wish you had too," said Jonah.

"Dennis," said Robert, "you and I came in to the story way late. We were supposed to have been here long ago. Look at what we missed. *Both Ends.*"

"I think I really will write something new for Open Hand," said Ash. "I have no idea what. But if I start it right now, coming off *Ghosts,* it would come out sounding morose and Scandinavian." Jules thought again of Goodman and Ash in Oslo together, sprawled out in a hotel room, talking all night.

"You don't have to begin it now, that's the good thing," said Jonah. "You can take your time."

"I like the idea of being able to take your time," said Dennis, who'd never been *fast* like these friends here. "Not having to plan everything. Just waiting for things to fall into place," he said, and maybe these were the last calm words he spoke that night. Or maybe this was more of a stage-play memory of the evening — the scene in which a woman's husband contemplates the pleasures of taking one's time, and within the hour it's all ruined. Maybe he didn't say this at all; later on, Jules wasn't sure. There was so much drinking, and Ethan had arranged for a succession of amuse-bouches to be brought to the table before the meal. Little delicious items adorned with squirts of colorful gel kept appearing, and it was too dark in the room to see exactly what any of them were eating. Texture was everything in 1980s fine dining; specifics were often less meaningful.

Dennis, because of the MAO inhibitor he took, now referred to commonly as an MAOI, was always careful with what he ate; at the beginning of the evening he'd quietly told the waiter his food restrictions. But tonight there was an unusual force field around the table, in part because of Ethan's presence in the restaurant, which had excited the owner, who was a big fan of *Figland,* and whose recitation of entire chunks of dialogue from the show was actually touching to Ethan, who agreed to draw Wally Figman on a tablecloth as a favor. Everyone at the table was talking a lot, excited for Ash about her first real success, feverish about their own possibilities, aware that thirty was a significant age and a good age. It might have been that Dennis's tone, when speaking to the waiter, had made it sound like he just disliked smoked, pickled, and preserved meats and aged cheeses and liver and pâté; not that any of those foods could potentially kill him.

A shallow ceramic spoon arrived for each of them with something called "tomato water" in it and a single scallop like a big tooth. A bottle of wine appeared, and the presence of *Pouilly* on the label made it clear to Jules that it was good. They consumed everything given to them. Did some of the food taste smoked, pickled, preserved, *poisonous*? It was hard to say; it all tasted good, and Jules had no reason not to assume that Dennis was alert to his own food restrictions tonight, as usual. But near the end of the meal, in the middle of an array of free desserts, including a plate of cookies that were described by the waiter as "Serrano pepper molé *ducats,*" Dennis leaned over to Jules and said, "I'm not feeling great."

"Did you eat something you're not supposed to?" she asked, but he shook his head. "Do you want to leave?" she pressed, and in the candlelight she saw that he was sweating; his whole face was streaming. "Dennis," Jules said sharply. "Dennis, I think something's really wrong with you."

"I think so too." He pulled at his shirt collar and said simply, "I have a bad headache. I think I'm going to die."

"You're not going to die." Dennis didn't say anything, but just craned his head forward and began to vomit onto his plate.

"Oh my God," Jules said, and she turned frantically to her friends, who were still looking at one another and laughing and eating. Robert was feeding Jonah a crab cake, for some reason. *"Ethan,"* Jules said without thinking; he was the one she wanted to help her. "Ethan, Dennis is really sick."

Ethan looked up with his mouth half-open, and he saw Jules's panic, which made him swallow his food quickly and practically launch himself across the table, his shirt nearly skimming the candle in its glass. "Dennis, look at me," Ethan said, and Dennis, who'd stopped vomiting, looked at him but his expression was dull. Then somehow — had he flown? — Ethan was right beside Dennis, opening his shirt collar, and lowering him onto the floor between this table and the next one, which meant Dennis was lying on a bed of sand. On his back, his body made an imprint, a sand angel, a police outline foretelling an imminent death. Jules knelt on his other side, crying onto his neck and slack face. She found the pulse in Dennis's wrist, and it was wild — "tacking," the EMS technician would say a few minutes later.

Hovering over him, waiting for help, Jules thought that here was her dying husband, the ultrasound tech still ambling along, not a star in his field or any other. God, all the *stars* out there, she thought, and all the worlds those stars existed in; and all the non-stars too, the strivers, everyone worried about their own careers, their own trajectories, how it looked, what it meant, what other people thought of them. It was just too much to take in; it was just so sickening and unnecessary.

446

Leave success and fame and money and an extraordinary life to Ash and Ethan, who would know how to use it, she thought as the EMS technicians strode through the narrow space, crunching purposefully along the floor with their heavy shoes, surrounding her husband. Leave everything to Ash and Ethan, for they deserve it. Just give me what we had, she heard herself thinking, or maybe saying. It's enough now.

TWELVE

Jonah Bay, heading home from the Beth Israel Hospital emergency room in a taxi just past dawn with Robert Takahashi beside him, said, "Did you hear what she said? In the restaurant, right after it happened, when she was sort of talking to herself, sort of praying?"

"Yeah."

"Jules doesn't pray; she's always been an atheist. Who would she pray to?"

"No idea," said Robert. They leaned against each other in weary silence as the streets flew by, the taxi making every green light in the absence of traffic at this unlikely and disconcerting hour.

"Well, apparently it worked for her, whatever she did," Jonah said.

"Oh, come on, you're saying that to *me*? Don't you know how many ERs I've sat in with friends with pneumonia or cytomegalovirus? Their relatives were always praying for them, and it never did a thing. One guy from the gym, all his aunts and great-aunts came — this big, terrific black family from North Carolina — and they formed a prayer circle and said something like, 'Please, Jesus, protect our boy William; he has so much he still wants to do here on earth,' and I swear I thought it was going to work that time, but it didn't. I haven't seen any miracles. All the stories end the same fucking way." Robert looked out the window as the taxi bumped over the pocked streets. "You know, one of these days," he said, "you're going to be the one sitting in an ER for me."

"Don't say that," said Jonah. "Your T-cell count is good. You've been mostly fine. You had shingles, but almost nothing else."

"Yeah, that's true. But it can't last. It never does."

"Well, I guess I still have a little of that miraculous-religion thing in me," Jonah said.

"Oh yeah? I thought the deprogrammer knocked it out of you for good back then."

"No, I still held on to a tiny little piece. Don't tell Ethan and Ash. They put so much effort into that."

They got out of the cab in front of Jonah's building on Watts Street, which in all kinds of light — dawn, dusk, the alarmingly violet moments before a major snowfall — looked tilted and slightly scorched, but still remained habitable. What had happened to him, and to his mother, leaving him the legal occupant of her loft, still astonished him. But at the time, it was just what had happened; it was just their story. It made very little sense now to think that for nearly three months way back in 1981, Jonah Bay had been a member of Reverend Sun Myung Moon's Unification Church. The Moonies were at the time often considered a punch line, occupying the same zeitgeist territory as the Hare Krishnas.

Jonah had been drawn into the church in the way that many people were: accidentally, not even knowing he'd wanted a church. He had had no natural churchiness in him whatsoever. Sometimes in childhood, his mother had taken him to the Abyssinian Baptist Church in Harlem to hear her gospel-singer friends perform. "Just close your eyes and let yourself be transported," Susannah would say. Jonah responded to the music, but he'd had no use for Jesus, and during the sermons he would refuse to close his eyes, but would instead look at his hands, at his shoes, or often at other boys in the pews.

In college, fiddling in the laboratory for his robotics class on a Saturday night, Jonah breathed in the scent of machine parts and electrical wiring and, especially, underwashed MIT undergraduates, who definitely had their own scent; and it seemed to him that an unspiritual life engineered solely by humans, busy in their fluorescent academic hive, would be perfectly acceptable. He had a brilliant friend in the lab, Avi, who was an Orthodox Jew, and Jonah could never understand what that deep layer of observance gave him. "Your work is scientific," he'd said to Avi. "How can you believe in the sublime?" "If you have to ask, then I can't tell you," Avi said. Was a spiritual life like a special cloak? Jonah had gotten intimations of the sublime in brief bursts: some of the gospel music at that Harlem church had been celestial, and so was a good deal of his mother's folk music. The song "The Wind Will Carry Us" was exquisite, and Susannah's younger voice on that record was so achy that maybe it qualified as sublime. What seemed most otherworldly to Jonah Bay was the sensation he'd had as a boy, his brain cells repeatedly messed with by a grown man who had behaved like God.

During those involuntary, never-confessed-to or alluded-to drug trips, Jonah's body had been alert and taut, his mind running all over, hyperactive and on a mission. The sensation of being overstimulated was so tremendous that he almost couldn't bear it. He'd felt it again, in a completely different way, the first time he'd ever had sex with a man, at age eighteen at MIT. He'd ejaculated in about twelve seconds, much to his horror, and the other guy, a brain and cognitive sciences major with a boxer's blunted face, had said it was fine, fine, but it wasn't. Jonah couldn't say to him, Look, I get overstimulated really fast, and then *ker-splash.* It all started when I was secretly fed a lot of acid as an eleven-year-old. Yeah, *eleven,* isn't that wild? Now, whenever I get excited, I get afraid that I'm basically about to go crazy. Exciting sex still scares me to death.

But Jonah wouldn't say any of this, because he'd never told a single person, including his friends from Spirit-in-the-Woods, about what Barry Claimes had done to him. It would have been too mortifying. It had been easy to come out as a gay person to everyone, which Jonah did the week he arrived at MIT and had had sex — real, going-the-distance sex — for the first time. He'd wanted to wait until sex had taken place in order to be sure that he was right about himself. Yes, he was right. When he made the phone calls to tell people, none of those people seemed shocked or particularly surprised — not Ethan, Ash, Jules, or even his mother. But telling them about Barry Claimes was something Jonah couldn't do, even though he often thought about the folksinger, a man who had been without inspiration, and who had found a source of it in Jonah; a man who had lost his musical cash cow when Jonah made the decision to stop speaking to him at age twelve. But despite Barry Claimes being mostly gone (his visit to Spirit-in-the-Woods in 1974 with Jonah's mother had been *excruciating*), the singer had continued to feel like a real presence to Jonah, and never more so than in adolescence, when sexual feelings took hold. Jonah had had feelings for boys long before the era that Barry Claimes was in his life. When Ash became Jonah's girlfriend, he already mostly understood he was gay, and he often fantasized about boys, but the fantasies were too exciting and he barely knew what to do about them, or even how to think about them, so he hardly articulated them to himself. Ash had *understimulated* him, which had been a great relief.

Later on, in college, each time that sex with a real, naked, panting man became an actual act looming in front of Jonah like a meal set before him on a table, he grew afraid that he would be overcome and would almost start to hallucinate. Being highly aroused made him feel hopped-up and *sick,* made him want to turn away and go to sleep for hours. Barry Claimes's drugs had done this, the stream of hallucinogens slipped to a child by a powerful and opportunistic man.

Jonah had met Robert Takahashi at a dinner party at Jules and Dennis's apartment in 1986. Robert had long since left the copy store where he used to work, and had gone to law school at Fordham; by 1986 he had begun practicing AIDS-related law. At the dinner he took an immediate interest in Jonah, wanting to hear about his stint in the Moonies, the way everyone did, and about his job designing and perfecting technologies to help disabled people in their daily lives. Jonah described an innovative device, a sort of piece of scaffolding that allowed a paraplegic person to take a shower, wash himself and dry himself, all on his own. These were simple tasks that able-bodied people took for granted, Jonah said at the table, but the disabled had to rely on everyone for everything; they had to give up the idea of modesty. They had to somehow learn not to feel shame about their bodies and their need for help, which was something that Jonah himself was sure he would never have been able to do. "That all sounds great," Robert said about Jonah's work, and Jonah explained that, yes, it was fairly intense, but he felt he had to add, "I just never saw myself doing this for a living." Robert questioned him further on this, but Jonah was vague. "Is it compelling, and does it have meaning?" Robert asked. "Those were the criteria I set for myself when I took my job at Lambda Legal."

"Yeah, I guess it meets those criteria," Jonah admitted, though it still surprised him that this was what he did now, and this was who he was. Music was gone completely. He rarely even listened to music anymore. His album collection was in crates, and he'd barely bought cassettes or CDs. His guitar languished in his closet. The work Jonah did at Gage Systems actually could be very absorbing, but he was reluctant to say this to the buff Japanese-American guy who leaned forward in his chair at the dinner party at Jules and Dennis's apartment, directed toward Jonah like a plant toward sunlight. Jonah was *sunlight*? Men had been drawn to him frequently over the years, in bars, at parties, on the street, but rarely this cheerfully and directly. Usually, sexual attraction had an air of cloaked menace about it; that was part of the excitement.

Robert Takahashi also talked about himself a little, lightly referring to himself as "a poster child for the AIDS virus," which made Jonah feel shocked and sorry for him; but everyone else in the room, who already knew about Robert's recent diagnosis, acted like being positive was no big deal. The two men happened to leave the dinner party at around the same time; or at least, Robert got up to go almost immediately after Jonah said he was leaving. As they walked out of the building, Robert said, "So I've been trying to get a handle on you all night."

"What do you mean?"

"I can't tell if you're flirting with me."

Jonah said stiffly, "I'm not."

"Well, okay, fine. But can I ask you something? Are you queer?" It was a genuine, not hostile, question, but somehow Jonah was shocked to hear this word used this way. "Faggot" he'd grown used to hearing spoken by gay men in a friendly context, not to mention "faggotry," the state of being a faggot, but "queer" hadn't been said to Jonah before. "Because I don't want to get myself into one of those situations with a straight guy who's slumming," said Robert. "I mean, you definitely give off a queer vibe, but I have been wrong before. Famously wrong." Robert was smiling at him the whole time, and Jonah thought maybe "queer" was actually an appropriate word here; he did feel so *queer* when he got excited.

So here was the compact, slender, handsome, and unapologetically queer young Japanese-American lawyer Robert Takahashi out on the street, asking him a startling, exciting question, and Jonah Bay could not bring himself to answer. Instead, he became exceedingly shy. He didn't say no, and then, curtly, "Well, good night," and just keep walking. He also didn't say yes. Instead Jonah went into his default mode, which was pensive, wooden, and taciturn.

"That's personal," he said.

"What's personal?"

"My so-called queerness. Or lack thereof."

Robert laughed, which sounded like three sequential, appealing hiccups. "I have never heard anyone answer that way."

"You go around asking people if they're queer?" said Jonah. "Is it like taking the census?"

"Usually I don't have to ask," Robert said, "but you're a difficult case. A tough nut to crack." He smirked again, this confident man with a fatal diagnosis.

Jonah apparently could not be figured out by Robert Takahashi. So Robert, trim and sexually appealing in his old black leather jacket, unlocking his lime-green motorbike from where it was chained to a parking meter, said, "Well, I suppose it'll have to remain a great mystery. Too bad." Then he hopped on, kicked off, and puttered away as Jonah headed for the subway. All Jonah could think was that he felt terribly disappointed. But moments later there was Robert again, right beside him, and his reappearance felt like an enormous relief, a *delight.* Robert idled the bike and asked, smiling again, "Have you decided yet?"

Yes, the queerness question had been decided long ago, but Jonah was protective of his own predilections, cupping them and holding them close. He didn't want to be overwhelmed by sex and lose control. Slim little Robert Takahashi, a gym rat and a quick legal mind, had tested positive for the AIDS virus, and what kind of sex could you possibly have with an infected person? Maybe you could have *controlled* sex — which was, to Jonah, good sex.

They went to bed together in the loft on a rainy afternoon a week later. Robert had come over, and while Jonah dragged out his records and spent too much time at the record player trying to make a good choice, knowing that most people saw music as crucial to establishing a mood, Robert lay back against the pillows on the bed with his shirt off. Seeing his planar chest was like being allowed entry into a new dimension. Robert was slight and nearly hairless, but he was muscular; he put time into his body, hoping to keep it in as good shape as he could for as long as possible. "Enough music," said Robert finally as Jonah obsessed. "Just come here."

Rain pattered the old, loose windows of the loft where Jonah had grown up and still lived, and there was something exquisite about rain accompanying a long, first kiss. Robert Takahashi's mouth was hot and assertive; they pulled back now and then as if to check in, to make sure the other person was still there, and that they weren't just two disembodied mouths. But the kissing spoke to the larger question of what was allowed and what wasn't. "What can we do?" Jonah whispered awkwardly, not at all sure of what was safe and what might one day kill him. Robert Takahashi's body was in need of being explored, and yet there were parameters in going to bed with a man who had tested positive. You couldn't just do whatever you desired. You had to pay attention, or else some years from now the nodes in your neck would swell like marbles in a bag because of a bout of sex you'd had long in the past, which might well have been ecstatic then, but which you could barely remember now.

Robert looked at him with focused eyes; how beautiful they were, with their epicanthic folds. Jonah didn't even remember where he had learned that term — maybe a genetics class at MIT? — but it appeared now, summoned for the first time in his life, as he looked into these dark and marvelous eyes. "We can do a lot," Robert said. "But carefully." Those were the words that became Jonah Bay's password phrase into the kind of sex he liked and could tolerate. *A lot, but carefully.* Robert ripped open the wrapper of a Trojan with his sharp teeth, and took out a tube of a water-based lubricant called, lasciviously, Loobjob.

"This is really okay?" Jonah asked. "I mean, you're sure? Have you asked any experts?"

"Well, no," said Robert, "but I've read about it pretty extensively, and I assume you have too. Do you want to talk to an expert?"

"Now?" Jonah laughed.

"Yes. Now. If it'll make you feel better."

"It's a Sunday afternoon. Where are these experts? Aren't they all at brunch?"

Robert was already on the phone, calling Information and asking for the number of a hotline he knew about. The operator connected him. Lately the hotline had been in constant use, with everyone calling in terror, afraid of what they'd already done, unsure of what they could now do, tortured with knowledge and ignorance, palpating their own necks for swollen glands.

"Hi," said Robert. "I'm here with a friend, and he has a question for you." Then Robert thrust the phone at Jonah, who was appalled, and said, "What? Me?" moving away from it. "Yes, you," said Robert, clearly enjoying himself. Jonah reluctantly took the phone, the cord stretching tight across the bed, bisecting it, keeping the men in separate sections. "Hi," he mumbled flatly into the receiver.

"Hi, my name's Chris. How can I help you?"

"I just want to know what's, you know . . . safe."

"You're talking about sexual safety between two partners?" asked Chris. "Two male partners?" Jonah imagined him blond-haired, early twenties, sitting in a shabby office with his Keds up on a cluttered desk.

"Yeah."

"Okay. We can't say for certain that any sex act carries zero risk, but some acts are clearly safer than others. For instance, oral isn't risk-free. While we can't prove anybody's gotten it this way, we can't prove they haven't, either. If you have cuts, sores, or abrasions in your mouth it makes it riskier. Some people choose to pull out before coming. And then there's mutual masturbation. Maybe you've heard the phrase, 'On me, not in me.'"

No, Jonah had never heard the phrase. While Chris was talking, Robert had come forward and begun to kiss Jonah's neck, which tickled and made Jonah strain away from him; and then Robert put his hand on Jonah's thigh in a proprietary gesture. "As for intercourse," Chris went on as if he were a waiter winding up as he described the nightly specials, "without a condom there's a high risk of transmission if the active partner is infected. And even *with* a condom, the risk isn't reduced to zero, given the fact that theoretically it could break. That said, with condom use between two partners, only one of whom tested positive, to my knowledge there haven't been any reported incidents so far of seroconversion. This doesn't mean there haven't been any that *haven't* been reported, or that there won't be any in the future. But it's important to use latex only, no natural skins, and also to use a water-based lubricant containing the spermicide Nonoxynol-9. Oils and petroleum jelly can weaken the latex and make it prone to breakage."

Was Chris reading from a script? Was he bored? Excited? Did he suspect that on the other end of the phone line, two men were

461

poised on a bed, waiting to spring into action once one of them received reassurances from a stranger on the telephone? Did Chris know that his name and his voice, so bland and young, were in themselves arousing to these men? "Chris," whoever he was, was like an epidemiologic porn star.

"So you think it's okay for my friend and me to try to do some things together?" Jonah asked in a constrained voice.

"I can't say that. To achieve zero risk, cuddling is a good bet."

"Cuddling?"

"Tell him you have to go," whispered Robert.

"I have to go. But thank you."

"Okay," said Chris. "Have a good day. Stay dry," he added, and then he hung up.

"What did he mean, 'Stay dry'?" said Jonah with alarm.

"What?" said Robert.

"There at the end, he said, 'Stay dry.' Was he referring to *fluids*? Was he giving me his honest opinion, even though he wasn't supposed to?"

"He meant that it's raining out."

"Oh. Oh. Right," said Jonah.

"You are adorable," said Robert. "I even like your anxiety."

"I don't. I hate it."

"We don't have to do anything, today or ever," said Robert Takahashi, but the idea of

462

this was unacceptable to Jonah Bay, who couldn't have explained that although he was anxious and afraid, he wanted to partake of encumbered, restrictive sex, the only kind that wouldn't threaten to bury him in sensation. Maybe he had found a perfect way to manage his problem of overstimulation, yet not deny his essential, exuberant queerness.

Over time, on gray, moody days in the loft or on days that fractured the loft into various columns of sunlight, or at night, in near darkness, he and Robert Takahashi, one pale-skinned, the other a kind of grain color, ripped open Trojan wrappers and slowly fucked each other. It amazed him the way body parts could fit together with the precision of Lego. Sex with Robert was a tense, highly careful experience that invariably led to great pleasure. Robert appeared to have bought out the entire mid-Atlantic supply of Loobjob, and he stored a couple of tubes in Jonah's night table drawer, where Susannah used to keep dozens of guitar picks.

As a couple, Jonah and Robert didn't look into their shared past, which didn't go far back, nor did they look into the future, where they couldn't see too far ahead. Robert Takahashi needed to keep his T-cell count up as long as he could. Neither of them wanted to discuss his condition very much, but the fact that Robert would in all likelihood die young could not be ignored. So far, he was mostly asymptomatic, and his T-cell count was good. Later, some friends were put on AZT, a drug that reduced their lives to a round-the-clock frenzy of beeping pill reminders and bouts of diarrhea and other indignities. The same frenzy would likely eventually arrive for Robert; but under the guidance of a somewhat renegade physician, he took bee pollen and wheatgrass shots and vitamin B_{12} and worked out at the gym for a solid, belligerent hour before work each day, each grunt a battle cry. His job at Lambda Legal was the center of his life. Jonah envied him this; his own job at Gage Systems, as he told people, was fine but left him feeling slightly empty. His design team had recently received a very emotional letter from a man whose upper body had been paralyzed in a car accident long ago, and who was now able to make himself breakfast each morning because of the robotics arm that Jonah's team had perfected.

Yes, this work had meaning, but Robert's work seemed to be a calling, which was different. A year or so into their relationship, back in the spring of '87, Robert had invited Jonah to come down to D.C. with him to take part in an act of civil disobedience in front of the White House. They made posters before they left, and much later, when Jonah thought about that day and that time in life, he remembered the smell of Magic Marker, sharp and strong like a draft of smelling salts held under the nose. Reagan's actual presence could be felt; though he wasn't there, Jonah pictured him in a big-shouldered coat, being ushered past the protestors, barely looking at them. Reagan wasn't even a real person to Jonah, just a feelingless object, and though he'd been reelected in a landslide, he had not been able to bring himself to say "AIDS" for the longest time, had not even seemed able to imagine gay men in their beds or at the funerals of their lovers.

As the crowd at the White House began to chant, and the signs waved and bobbed, the police closed in wearing rubber gloves. Jonah had lain down on the ground, and in the chaos a heel went down on his thigh and he cried out. When he turned to Robert, he saw that he was no longer there. Frantically Jonah called Robert's name, but there were too many people crushing in and too much movement. He had lost Robert Takahashi, and instead found himself pressed face-to-face against an old muscleman who looked like Popeye. "Robert!" Jonah called again, and then a hand was on his back, and Jonah looked up to see Robert standing directly above him. Robert's powerhouse arms scooped Jonah up and staggered off with him.

Tonight, after Dennis Boyd had collapsed in the restaurant, Jonah and Robert had sat side by side in the ER waiting room at Beth Israel with Jules, Ethan, and Ash; and the awful, dislocating institutional scene had reminded Jonah of an image of himself and his friends sitting on molded plastic chairs in another brightly lit space. What *was* that space? At first he couldn't remember. He thought hard, and there it was: the police station on the Upper West Side in the earliest hours of 1976. Jonah and the others had waited there all night; it was so long ago now that Jonah could barely recall it, and it had all been left unfinished. Cathy Kiplinger had simply been *erased* from the group of friends, hustled out by adult forces. He'd always liked Cathy; it was true that she was kind of hysterical, but he had also admired how expressive she was. He could never express anything, but she had often cried and yelled and was full of opinions. Also, she had always responded sardonically to Goodman, who needed it. Cathy had seemed brave in her own way, unafraid to make demands, carrying around a woman's body when in fact at the time she was still pretty much a girl.

What had ever happened to her? Sometimes in the first several years after that night Jonah had wondered, but no one ever had a detailed or reliable answer to give. It was like hearing what had happened to former child stars from TV sitcoms; almost all of them had supposedly died in Vietnam. The reports were not to be trusted. Someone had "seen" Cathy, and had said she was doing okay. First they had seen her in college; then business school. Then, finally, Jonah had no idea where she was. No one had seen her or heard anything about her for years. Jonah occasionally felt a ghastly unease about Cathy Kiplinger, and about his own role in getting Goodman and Cathy a cab that night, when they were so stoned on the hash that Jonah had provided. Over and over his friends had insisted he was absolutely not responsible for anything that had happened. "Jesus, Jonah, do I have to hit you over the head with a frying pan?" Ethan had once said in exasperation, in the first few weeks after that New Year's Eve. "I don't know how to convey this to you any better than I already have. You had nothing to do with what happened between them. Nothing. You are innocent. You were not an 'accessory,' and you didn't 'drug' anyone, okay?"

Over time Jonah began to believe that Ethan was right. He became preoccupied with other thoughts: fantasies about how certain teenaged boys might looked undressed, and certain men; and thoughts about what he wanted to do with his life now that he'd decided he definitely wasn't going to be a musician. As the years passed he wondered about Cathy far less often than he used to. He went to college, he graduated, he got sidetracked by the Unification Church briefly, he took a robotics job at Gage Systems, and by 1989, even brash, exciting Goodman Wolf had completely faded — Goodman, who had been as sharply defined and as erotically charged as anyone on earth.

In the ER tonight, Ethan was the one who felt needlessly guilty; he kept pacing and saying to Jules in an agitated voice, "But don't you get it? *I arranged the dinner.* I told them what Dennis couldn't eat, but I should have made double sure." Jules had told him, "Ethan, stop, it's not your fault," and then Ash had gotten upset with Ethan and said to him, "Would you please leave Jules alone about this? She has enough to deal with." Everyone tended to believe everything was their fault; maybe it was just hard to imagine, when you were still fairly young, that there were some things in the world that were just not about *you.*

Finally a young doctor had come out and said, "I can tell you that Mr. Jacobson-Boyd had a very mild stroke. We do think it was caused by eating something contraindicated by his MAOI." At dinner Dennis had apparently ingested a food that contained a substantial amount of tyramine, though no one would ever be able to figure out exactly which food it had been. His blood pressure had been "through the roof," the doctor said. Dennis would recover, but he would need constant monitoring for a while. "We're taking him off the MAOI immediately," the doctor said. "There are much better anti-depressants now anyway. At the time he was prescribed this one, back in the seventies, no one knew anything. Personally, I'd try him on a tricyclic. What does he need an MAOI for? It's got so many problems, as you saw tonight. One piece of smoked cheese, and you're having a hypertensive crisis at age thirty. We'll keep him here for a few days, and we'll worry about the depression later. And maybe he won't even need treatment for that. It's kind of a wait and see."

"So he's not going to die?" Ash said. "He'll be okay? Jules, did you hear that?"

"Yes, he'll survive this," said the doctor. "You got him here in time."

Jules began to cry in a sharp burst, and Ash did too, and they hugged each other and then Jules composed herself a little and said she had to go call Dennis's parents in New Jersey. His mother would no doubt be beside herself, his father gruff and monosyllabic. Jules said she also had to go to hospital admissions and give them all the insurance information. There was so much to do; as a social worker she knew how much paperwork there would be. This was just the beginning, she said. But Ethan said to her, "You're not doing any of that."

"I'm not?" said Jules.

"No," Ethan said. "Just go to Dennis now. Seriously. I'll take care of everything."

■ ■ ■ ■

Jonah had been walking down a side street in Cambridge, Massachusetts, one afternoon in June 1981, when a couple of members of the Unification Church came to him with a message. They didn't say "God is love," or anything similar. That wouldn't have worked on Jonah Bay, who was deeply agnostic. Their message, though not stated directly, was that they recognized he was lonely, and they wanted to help him. Somehow, they were able to perceive his loneliness, though he had no idea how. He was leaving Dr. Pasolini's mechanical engineering lab, where he was working for minimum wage. He'd just graduated from MIT and was living in one of the summer dorms until the fall, not sure what kind of job he would ultimately take or what city he would wind up in. Unlike almost everyone he knew at college, Jonah was not particularly ambitious. When people inquired about his ambitions, he told them that his mother's non-acquisitive folksinger's values must have rubbed off on him, because he didn't feel the need to have his life figured out. But the truth was that he didn't want to deal with it.

An old purple VW minibus was parked on the sloping street, and a man and woman, a few years older than he was, both dressed in generic leftover hippiewear, were sitting in the open doorway with a big Labrador retriever between them. Jonah smiled politely and the man said to him, "Nice shirt."

Jonah was wearing a vintage bowling shirt that read *Dex* on the pocket.

The woman said, "And nice smile too, Dex."

So Jonah smiled again for them, not bothering to say his name wasn't Dex. "Thanks," he said.

"Do you know where we could get some water for Cap'n Crunch?"

"You mean milk," Jonah said.

They both laughed as if he were deeply witty. "Cap'n Crunch is our dog," said the woman. "We've been in the car a long time, and he's extremely thirsty. I'm Hannah," she said. "And this is Joel."

It was a reasonable act to bring them into the summer dorm with their dog and let them fill the dog's bowl with genuine MIT tap water. The dorm was quiet, and the dog's toenails clicked ostentatiously along the floors. The place felt melancholy, with whiteboards left up on some of the students' doors, their once-relevant erasable-marker messages still visible. "Amy, we are going to see *The Howling* at 12!!!" Or, "SORRY, DAVE, ALL YOUR DROSOPHILA ARE DEAD AND I KILLED THEM!!!! HAHAHAHA — YOUR EVIL FUCKING LAB PARTNER." The third floor was echoey, overly warm, but the man and woman looked around approvingly, as though they'd never been in a college dormitory before, and perhaps they hadn't. Cap'n Crunch scarfed up the water Jonah got him, and looked beseechingly for a refill, his loose drape of lips still dripping.

"Easy there, Crunch," Joel said, stroking the long black side of his dog. "You don't want to get bloat."

"What's bloat?"

Hannah and Joel explained the sometimes fatal condition that dogs could develop. "I'm thinking about becoming a veterinarian," Hannah said. "That's just one of the things we study at the farm."

"The farm," Jonah repeated.

"Yes. We live on a farm in Dovecote, Vermont, with a bunch of our friends. We've got some animals up there. It's a pretty amazing setup." She looked around her. "But it seems like you've got a nice setup here yourself."

"Not exactly," said Jonah. He opened the door of the room where he was staying, in order to show them the minimalism of his summer living conditions. They took in the narrow iron student bed, the desk with the Tensor lamp, and the pile of books about principles of mechanical engineering and robotic design and vectors. "Vectors!" said Joel, picking up a book. "I have no idea what they are, but I'm sure I wouldn't understand them."

Jonah shrugged. "If someone explained them to you, you probably would."

The couple sat on the bed, the springs straining, and Cap'n Crunch leapt up between them, while Jonah sat in his desk chair. No one else had been to visit his room since he'd been living here this summer. Even at college for the past four years Jonah hadn't been overly social; he'd gone to parties in large groups of friends, and had had a few sexual encounters, but as far as he could tell he hadn't made any lifelong friends. His closest friends were still Jules, Ethan, and Ash; they all got together in New York over breaks. For a while in college he'd played guitar and sung vocals for an MIT band called Seymour Glass, and all the musicians were extremely talented. But when they arranged to get together in the music studio senior year to cut a demo tape and "take it around," Jonah decided he didn't want to be in the band anymore.

"Why not?" asked the bass player. "You're so good."

Jonah had just shrugged. He'd been squeamish about music ever since Barry Claimes. Not squeamish enough to have given up playing a little on his own, but he never tried to write songs. Whenever he picked up his guitar he recalled sitting around making up music

473

for that grotesque man, who had stolen it from him.

As it turned out, Seymour Glass had signed with Atlantic Records right before the school year ended, and the other band members were going off to LA now with a session guitarist in Jonah's place. Jonah wished them well, and even though it was painful that they might become really successful (as it turned out, they did, getting known as the cool MIT-grad nerd band), he was relieved to have nothing to do with them. He'd abdicated his talent, he knew, which was depressing when he really thought about it, but also a relief. He'd gotten a reputation in college as a shy, attractive, long-haired boy whose mother was "that folksinger," as people said, though no one expressed real interest anymore in Susannah Bay. She was over. She'd been over for a while. Talking Heads were big when Jonah was in college, along with the B-52s, whose female band members sported retro hairdos. Susannah Bay had never used hair spray in her life, and the women of the B-52s seemed to offend her sensibility, even though the hairdos were clearly meant as a strange and campy aesthetic. Susannah's long black hair was her "signature" look, journalists had always said, just as "The Wind Will Carry Us" was her "signature" song.

You had only one chance for a signature in life, but most people left no impression.

Quietly, Jonah had done excellent work in mechanical engineering in college, writing a thesis on robotics and graduating with honors. He was adept at this work, and was frequently praised by Dr. Pasolini, who wanted him to meet the people at Gage Systems in New York for possible employment, but Jonah already felt isolated this summer. He didn't know what he wanted to be, or do, and he wasn't planning on spending the summer in the loft with his mother, who had grown increasingly discouraged as her career appeared to dry up like an old seedpod. When Jonah had come home for spring break, she had put his B-52s album on full blast and shouted, "Just listen to that! It's so *bizarre*! Do you actually like it?" Of course he liked it, and he'd danced to it all night at the post-midterms blowout his suitemate had forced him to attend, his body bumping up against a sophomore with a key ring in his pocket that crunched pleasingly against Jonah's hip bone, but he'd told his mother he could take it or leave it.

"So explain vectors to us," said Joel, and for some reason Jonah found himself wanting to comply.

"Well, there's Euclidean vectors," he began. "Does that interest you?"

"Absolutely," said Hannah with an encouraging smile.

"A Euclidean vector is what you need when

you want to carry point A to point B. *Vector* is from the Latin. It actually means 'carrier.' "

"See, we're getting an MIT education," Hannah said to Joel.

"We'll have to tell everyone at the farm that we went to MIT and had a seminar in vectors," Joel said. "But they won't believe us. You'll have to tell them, Jonah."

Jonah tensed upon hearing his name spoken. Just a little while ago, they'd been calling him "Dex." How did they know his name? Oh, of course; there on one of his textbooks from the school year on his desk, across a large piece of masking tape, he had written "JONAH BAY, '81."

"Do you have any interest in spending a rural weekend up there?" Hannah asked. "Pitching hay? Explaining vectors to other people? It would use your brain *and* your body. Plus, the food is super delicious."

"No, thanks, I don't think so," Jonah said.

"Okay, fine; if you can't you can't," said Hannah, and she smiled at him with what appeared to be genuine regret, and maybe it really was. They weren't pressuring him to go; he felt no pressure whatsoever, merely a desire on their part for him to be with them.

"Well," said Joel. "We should hit the road. I enjoyed talking to you, Jonah, and I hope the rest of your summer goes really well." He stood up and motioned toward the dog, who scrambled to its feet.

Jonah thought of how the room was filled with human life and canine life right now, and that when these strangers left they would take all that life with them. He suddenly wanted to stop that from happening. On impulse, he who rarely followed impulses said, "How long is the drive?"

Before he left with them, he grabbed the mushy-wicked Magic Marker from the message board on his door, and quickly wrote in dry, milky gray letters, "GONE TO FARM IN DOVECOTE, VT. WITH PURPLE MINIBUS PEOPLE. BACK MONDAY." In the unlikely event that they were planning on murdering him, there would be clues.

The farm was enjoyable, if in a slovenly way. Some of the people who lived there seemed to have been slightly damaged by life: they spoke a little too slowly; they appeared to have been burned out or, in one extreme case, had no legs and rode around the bumpy dirt in a little motorized wheelchair. Yet the food was soft and warm, with an emphasis on rice and potatoes and novel grains like spelt and bulgur. Jonah found himself wanting to eat and eat, and a very kind woman kept refilling his plate until he felt that he might turn into a snowman made of mounds of food. Everyone was so incredibly *nice* to him; it was different from MIT, where people were involved in what they were involved in, and sometimes at dinner it could seem as if the person sitting across from you was in another dimension. Even while they ate, the engineers were engineering, and the mathematicians had set up little invisible blackboards in their brains; and though the conversation was friendly, it could be remote. Also, by senior year everyone was already planning their next moves, as cunning as double agents.

But here on the farm no one seemed to have any ambitions beyond preparing hearty foods in creative ways; discussing an old sheep that had wandered from the meadow; and welcoming their new guest, Jonah, whom they said they felt blessed to know. Toward the end of dinner, when the women spooned a brownish carob agar pudding into flea market cut-glass cups like a pile of giblets, Joel bent his head in prayer, and everyone else did as he did. The prayers were brief, followed by a few unfamiliar songs, one of them in Korean. Looking back at this scene, Jonah appeared so *innocent.* He was astonished at how he had allowed himself to be led like that old sheep back into the meadow.

Dinner was followed by a visit to a converted barn, where there was more singing and more prayers. Then Tommy, the man with no legs, locomoted himself to the front of the room, and everyone got quiet. "In 1970," Tommy said, "here was my situation. I got drafted and sent to Vietnam, where within two months my legs were shot off by a bouncing Betty. I managed to get pulled out of the river and sent back to the U.S., but I spent a year in the V.A., and when I got home my wife said, 'Hell no, bub, I'm not staying married to a fucking cripple who can't even walk across the room to fetch me my pack of cigs.' " There was mild sympathetic groaning, but Jonah sat silently, appalled. "I was down on my luck," Tommy continued. "Became very bitter. My friends all gave up on me, each and every one, and truthfully I don't blame them. And then one day I was sitting in my pathetic little wheelchair on the street in Hartford, Connecticut, begging for change — that's what my life had come to — when a van pulled up at the curb. And the loveliest people in the world stepped out. They said to me that I looked like I didn't have any family to speak of, and I admitted that this was true. And they said we are your family. And this turned out to be true too." He wiped his eyes with the back of his hand. "They recognized that I needed them, and that they needed me. Just the way everyone in this barn is family, and needs one another, because Satan is all around us. As you know, Israel was God's chosen nation. But it seems that the Jews, falling under the sway of Satan, turned away from Jesus. God did what he could to show them how dangerous their path was," Tommy went on casually. "For century after century

479

he made them suffer, and finally, to make a point, he took six million of their people and extinguished them in one fell swoop. But it's been said that the Jews had made a fatal error in leaving Jesus, and that God needed to look elsewhere to find a new Messiah and a new place to establish himself. So where did God turn?"

The question was rhetorical. Tommy pushed a lever on his wheelchair and made it spin in place. "Where he lands, nobody knows!" he called, and then he stopped sharply, facing the room again, and said, "But actually, God *did* know. Korea was a perfect location. And because it is a peninsula, it resembled the male sexual organ, the organ of *power.* It proved to be an ideal place for the battle between God and Satan. And Reverend Moon proved to be the ideal reincarnation of Jesus Christ, only without the flaws."

Jonah would have laughed at this absurd monologue, but he was alone among these strangers, in a barn on a farm far from anyone he knew. No one would look kindly on him if he mocked this Vietnam vet in the wheelchair. Everyone was listening politely, indulging the man, probably because he was so badly disabled. When Tommy was done speaking, there was applause, and more singing. Jonah quickly learned the words, and the tunes were catchy. Then suddenly a couple of

480

guitars appeared, and Hannah handed one to him, shyly saying, "I know you play, Jonah. I saw the guitar in your dorm room." But the guitar she gave him was the worst instrument he'd ever played in his life, a totally out-of-tune piece of shit that ordinarily would have been thrown away, yet Jonah spent a few hopeless minutes tuning it, then played while the twenty-five or so people who had now gathered around all sang. They complimented his playing, having no idea of his lineage.

By the time he fell asleep in the men's communal living quarters, a large loftlike space with rows of bedrolls on a floor of cheap carpet, Jonah realized he was content and exhausted. He had traveled a couple of hours to get here, and then he had eaten great quantities of starch. He had sung song after song. He had been passive, and had listened. He had prayed, in a fashion, though he didn't believe in God. He had played guitar on command. His eyes now flickered and shut, and he slept undisturbed on his back with his hair spread out around him on the pillow. In the morning there was more soft, plentiful food, now served with syrup. Also, more prayers and teachings, and more warmth and love and kindness. Jonah was a skeptic, the way all decent scientists were, but his skepticism was outmaneuvered by the good feelings that he now connected with being here among these people. This was what a family felt like;

this was what a family was.

It did not seem so strange, three weeks later, for Jonah Bay to find himself selling dyed pink and blue flowers out of a plastic bucket on a street corner in nearby Brattleboro, Vermont. Or if it did feel strange, he was defiant in the face of strangeness, and besides, he liked Lisa, the girl he sold flowers with, though "selling" wasn't the right word, because no one was buying. The people they approached regarded them with annoyance or open hostility. Here, as at earlier points in his life, Jonah felt he knew what he was doing, but he seemed to be watching it all in third person, neither approving nor disapproving, and unable to affect the outcome.

Naturally, his mother was hysterical about his change of plans. He had gone back to Cambridge in the minibus with Hannah and Joel and Cap'n Crunch, in order to pack up his summer dorm room, and from there they had driven down to New York to drop off his worldly belongings, which he would no longer need on the communal farm. All he would need was a pillow, a blanket, and some clothes. In the loft on Watts Street, his mother angrily said she thought he had more of an independent mind than to join what she called "a common cult." She had one of her musician friends with her that day for moral support, and they both tried to argue with

Hannah and Joel, who were expert at not engaging with irate parents. The more Susannah Bay became upset, the more calmly Hannah and Joel talked. At one point, Hannah said to Susannah, "I have to tell you, we may come to this from different angles, but I really admire your music." When Jonah had casually mentioned to them who his mother was, Hannah had said she really wanted to meet Susannah, which he suspected was part of the reason for the return to the loft.

"Oh," Susannah said, a little surprised. "Well, thank you."

"I grew up listening to your songs, Ms. Bay," said Hannah. "I've bought every record you've ever made."

"Even the disco folk one?" Jonah asked, unnecessarily cruel.

His mother quickly said, "That was a mistake, that record. And this, Jonah, this is a mistake too. We all do things we later regret. Come on, you just got a degree from MIT. You're such a bright person, and you can do anything you want, yet you're choosing to live on a farm with people you barely know who follow the teachings of a Korean man who says he's the Messiah?"

"Yes, that about sums it up," said Jonah, and he grabbed his old blanket and pillow and slung them over his shoulder. He both knew and did not know that what he was choosing to do was radical. He felt grateful to have decisions taken away from him for once, and to know that he would not be overcome with feeling in ways that were always hard for him to manage. He and his new friends and their black dog sauntered out of the loft and got back into the minibus with the shot springs, and headed back to Vermont, reaching the farm by sundown, in time for prayers.

Within three months Jonah had been so absorbed in life there and in the teachings of the church, as conveyed to him by some of the other residents of the farm, that it was as if he had been triple-dipped in a bath of ideology. His mother remained distraught and contacted a few of Jonah's friends, essentially saying, "Do something." So in the fall, in consultation with Susannah Bay, Ash and Ethan quietly arranged for a deprogramming of Jonah that would take place in a midtown hotel room in New York City. Ash's father "knew someone" — of course he did, he knew all kinds of people. The guy had been recommended by a colleague of Gil's at Drexel, whose daughter Mary Ann became a Hare Krishna, shaved her head, and changed her name to Bhakti, which meant "devotion." It was set, and Susannah agreed to pay the shockingly high fee.

What they needed to do first was get Jonah away from the farm; that part was apparently often harder than the deprogramming itself.

Ethan, Ash, and Jules drove Susannah up to Vermont to see Jonah and have a look around, and then, the following day, to somehow find a way to get him home. The four of them stayed for dinner and spent the night on the farm. Unlike Jonah when he first went there, none of them were interested in learning more about what they'd seen and heard at dinner and in the barn. All they wanted was to take him out of there. "Listen, Jonah," Ethan said the next morning after breakfast. "I did a little reading before we came up here. I went to the New York Public Library and I asked them for everything on microfiche that I could find. In my opinion, Moon is a megalomaniac."

"No, Ethan, that's not true. He's my spiritual father."

"He isn't," Ethan said.

"I seem to remember something about *your* father," said Jonah, using the only retort he could think of, "and your mother, and your pediatrician."

"Well, at least you remember the conversations we used to have," said Jules. "That's good. It's a start."

"Apparently Moon's followers give up their individuality and creativity, which is something we've all valued above everything else," said Ethan. "If the Wunderlichs taught us anything, it was that. Is it that you're afraid? Is it because it was hard for you to come out as a gay man? No one cares if you're gay, Jonah; I mean, big deal! Don't give that up; don't take it back. Be yourself, fall in love, have sex with guys, do all the things that make you you. Don't be guided by some rigid external philosophy. *Make* things. Play your guitar. Build robots. This is all we've really got, isn't it? What else is there but basically building things until the day we die? Come on, Jonah, don't fall in line. I just can't understand this; why are you even here?"

"I've found my place finally," Jonah murmured, and then someone called him to tend the hydroponic lettuces. "I've got to go," he said. "And you should all hit the road. You don't want to run into traffic heading back. Where's my mother? Someone should tell her it's time."

"You're under the *influence,* Jonah," said Ash. "Please don't say that this is the sum total of who you are." She came close and took him by both wrists. "Remember when we were involved?" she asked shyly. Then she whispered, "I know it never became anything big. But it was an unspoiled, delicate thing, and I'm glad it happened. You were the most beautiful boy I'd ever seen in my life. I don't know what happened to make you so vulnerable to this kind of thing. You should be an artist, Jonah."

"I'm not an artist," Jonah said flatly. "That didn't happen."

"You don't have to be one," Jules suddenly put in. "You can be whatever you want. It just doesn't matter."

Jonah looked around at all of them. "I needed something, okay?" he said. "I didn't even know I did, but I did. Ash, you and Ethan have each other. Me, I'm totally on my own." He was almost in tears as he spoke, confessing his isolation to his oldest friends. "Maybe I needed a deep love that was more powerful than any other kind. Didn't any of you ever feel you needed that?" he asked them, but he had turned his head now and was looking right at Jules. She was the other unattached one here, the one who seemed to be quietly waiting, standing in the river of her life, the way Jonah had been. Jules looked down at the ground, as if it hurt her to make eye contact with him.

"Sure, sometimes," Jules said, and it was the strangest thing, but Ethan was now looking at Jules too; he and Jonah were both regarding Jules Jacobson attentively. Ethan, looking at Jules, seemed to have fixed himself upon her the way people fixed themselves upon the Messiah. Jonah could almost see the ragged edges of light that Ethan certainly saw around her — the coronal fringe light that was sometimes created by diligent, applied love.

Ethan loves her, Jonah thought. This was an epiphany, one of many that he'd experienced on the farm. Ethan Figman loves Jules Jacobson even now that he's bound his life to Ash Wolf, even now that so many years have passed since that first summer. He still loves her, and because I am now a devotee of the Messiah, I can see such powerful and radiant light.

"You love her," Jonah said to Ethan indiscreetly. He'd seen it, and he felt he had to say it.

"Who, you mean Jules? Yes, of course," Ethan said in a curt voice. "She's my old friend." Everyone looked in all sorts of directions, trying to sever the moment from the meaning that Jonah was giving it. Ethan walked back over to Jonah now and put an arm around his shoulder. "Listen," he said, "if you let us, we'll get you some help."

"What kind of help do you think I need?"

By now, a few residents of the farm had begun paying attention to the agitated scene between Jonah and his visitors. Hannah and Joel came over to intervene, and Tommy hummed up in the wheelchair, his baseball cap backward on his head. "Is there something distressing going on here?" asked Hannah. "Some conflict?"

"No, we're just talking," said Ethan.

"Jonah was asked to tend the hydroponic lettuces," Joel said.

"Seriously, you can go fuck the hydroponic lettuces, Joel," Ethan said. "I mean, really,

are you going to compare the need for lettuces to be tended with the need for this
person, this great friend of ours, to have an
actual life out there in the world? Doesn't
everyone deserve a chance to live in the
world, instead of hiding away on a farm, selling dyed flowers that no one wants, and that
everyone *runs away from* when they see the
dyed-flower bucket coming their way? What
is it with you guys and selling flowers? The
Hare Krishnas do it too. What, did everyone
see *My Fair Lady* and think, ooh, that looks
like a good idea?"

"I don't know what you're talking about,"
said Tommy. "But you're being disrespectful,
and it's time for you to go." He pressed a
button and reared slightly backward in his
chair.

Then Susannah Bay, who'd been giving a
guitar lesson in the barn to two young
women, suddenly appeared with her guitar.
"We're ready to take a little trip to town, Susannah," Ethan said, his face full of meaning,
trying to tell her, *we have to move now.* To
Jonah he said, "I tell you what. Let's go for a
ride. You can show us around the town. Your
mom will come too."

"Oh," said one of the wide-eyed young
women who accompanied her, "Susannah
was teaching us 'Boy Wandering.' The chords
are actually easy. It's mostly A minor, D
minor, E."

"And she showed us the open D tuning for 'The Wind Will Carry Us,' " said the other woman.

For someone who had been so upset since her son had moved to the farm, Susannah Bay now appeared calmer, as if what she'd seen here wasn't nearly as dire as she'd imagined. She'd had a tour of the gardens and the crops and the sheep in the meadow. She'd given an impromptu guitar lesson to people who still knew who she was and still cared about her music. Time stood still here on this commune in Dovecote. Everyone dressed as if they were at a three-day music festival; no one owned more than a few material possessions. The income they'd earned in the past, or that they marginally earned now, went to the church. Susannah Bay found herself and her work *cherished* here. It had been a surprise, and now she was going to have to give it up?

"We've been talking to Susannah," said the first young woman, "and we've asked her a favor."

"What?" said Ash. "What could you possibly want from Jonah's mother?"

"Reverend Moon is holding a spiritual gathering this winter in New York City, in Madison Square Garden," said the woman in a casual, confident voice. "We all just love 'The Wind Will Carry Us,' and we wondered if we could possibly get our chorale — a

490

chorus of five hundred of the best voices from around the world — to sing it at that event. With different lyrics, slightly."

"Different lyrics?" said Jonah. "What do you mean?"

"Well, I'm not a musician myself," said the woman, "but I was thinking it could be something like, 'The Reverend Moon will carry us / Carry us . . . apart.' "

They were all silent, horrified. "Oh yes," said Ethan finally, in a voice thick with irony and condescension. "That's exactly what he'll do. Carry everyone *apart.*" He and Jules looked at each other and smiled slightly.

"Pardon?" said one of the women.

"Nothing. Look," said Ethan, "obviously Susannah Bay is not going to allow her lyrics to be messed with. It's not negotiable."

But Jonah's mother appeared contemplative. Was she faking them all out? It was impossible to tell. After a moment she quietly said, "I'd consider it."

One of the women asked if Susannah would also consider staying on the farm for a few more days to work on the song with them, and on guitar and vocal technique in general. It wasn't as if she had any pressing engagements, right? To everyone's bewilderment Susannah agreed that she would stay here until Wednesday, when someone would drive her to Brattleboro to take the bus home. But Jonah, Ash insisted, should come for a ride into town now. If they'd told him they were taking him back to the city, surely he would have bolted. Jonah, Susannah, and a few key residents of the farm walked away to discuss the situation in private.

"I really don't like the idea of this," Ethan whispered to Ash and Jules as they stood watching the group of people talk among themselves. "It feels like a hostage exchange."

"They said it's just for a few days," said Ash. "Apparently Jonah's mom is into the idea of working with them, maybe even letting them use her song, though I honestly have no idea why. It seems like a terrible mistake to me."

"I think she's just so grateful that someone's thinking about her music again," said Ethan. "It's one thing to have a voice like hers, but if nobody appreciates it anymore, then it's depressing. This is probably giving her a big lift. But this way, at least we get Jonah to come with us. We'll deal with his mother later."

It occurred to Jonah during all the confusing, complicated negotiations — Why did they want him to go into town with them so badly? Why were they even *here,* exactly? — that he'd never wanted to run away from home, but instead he'd wanted to have *his* home, in the person of his mother, run after him. Here she was now, and he was within reach, but she was wavering. He didn't really mind it, though. She was appreciated here, the way she'd been appreciated in the past, but now in a much smaller and more concentrated form. She was making a decision to go where the audience was.

Jonah agreed to drive into town with his friends. He could get an ice pop at the general store; he hadn't eaten anything with artificial color or even sugar in it in a very long time, and he still had a taste for such foods. But when Ethan's father's beat-up old car sped past "downtown" Dovecote, and Jonah said, "Why aren't you stopping?" he supposed he'd already known the answer. He scrambled for the door handle, and Ash and Jules put their arms around him in the backseat and hugged him. "It's okay," said Ash, and Jules said, "Everything's going to be fine," and then Jonah began to cry, because he was confused, and very, very tired, and felt an underground tremor of nameless, swelling emotion that might have been — though he wasn't sure, and couldn't admit it — relief. He was desperate to sleep like a newborn baby squished between his old friends in the tiny car; he had barely slept since he'd been living on the farm. Chores started at dawn every day, and prayers lasted until late at night.

In the city, the deprogrammer awaited him in room 1240 of the dreary Wickersham Hotel half a block from Penn Station. His services were needed for three full days and nights; by the end of it all, Jonah was so worn out from the sleep deprivation that was part of the drill, and from being fed very little other than cold Burger King fries as sunrise broke over the city, and from the constant playing of taped negative testimonies from former church members, and from being repeatedly told that everything he'd heard on the farm was untrue, that Ash and Ethan insisted Jonah stay on their couch in the East Village for a few days, and this he did, gratefully.

It was funny, looking back on this so much later, that Ethan and Ash didn't even have a guest room in their first apartment. The place was ordinary, with an old rag rug that Ash had taken from her childhood home. They were still, in 1981, like everyone else. And in 1981 they were thoroughly entwined, despite the love that Jonah had seen in the air around Jules when Ethan had looked at her. Because of the deprogramming, and the relatively brief period of time he'd been a member of the church, Jonah eventually forgot most of what he'd felt and learned on the farm. The teachings themselves were slowly leached from his consciousness, as if they were the subject matter of a required college course that hadn't been of great interest. But he never forgot how he'd seen the ongoing love that Ethan still felt for Jules, and that Jules perhaps still felt for Ethan. He never forgot it, but he knew enough never to mention it again.

As it turned out, Susannah Bay stayed on the farm in Vermont for a few more days after her son left, singing to a circle of delighted, awed listeners. Their awe would not change over time because of fashion. They would not lose interest in Susannah's talent, which as far as they were concerned was a fixed thing; instead, they just wanted to bask in it. Susannah returned to New York briefly, not by bus as planned, but in the purple minibus, in order to gather a few of her own essential belongings from the loft, which were then transported with her back up to the farm. A few months later, when Reverend Sun Myung Moon gave a speech at the World Mission Center in New York City, Susannah Bay was called onto the stage to sing her signature song with its newly written lyrics. Her voice was as strong and clear as it had been when she was starting out, and some of the listeners cried, thinking of how they used to listen to her when they were younger and how their lives had changed so dramatically since then. Many of them had broken with their parents, and with their soft suburban lives, and had taken up a greater purpose. This singer, so special, so talented, seemed to be singing right to them, and they were grateful.

The following year, Susannah, along with more than four thousand others, was married in a blessing ceremony in Madison Square Garden. The groom, Rick McKenna, twelve years her junior, a professional carpet installer and a member of the Unification Church from Scranton, Pennsylvania, was a stranger to her until the moment they joined hands in front of the Messiah. Directly following the ceremony, Susannah Bay and her husband got into the minibus and headed back up to the farm, where they would live together for the rest of their earthly lives.

THIRTEEN

If you name your daughter Aurora, there is a good chance that eventually she won't be able to carry the weight of that name with total ease and grace, unless she is very beautiful or very confident. Dennis and Jules hadn't understood this when their baby was born in 1990. There had been many typical conversations in advance about baby names, discussions about what sort of name would work best preceding the clanking tin-can trail of "Jacobson-Boyd." These discussions had mostly taken place between Jules and Ash, not Jules and Dennis. Ash had grown up in a family in which both children had been given unusual names. Unusual names was her *beat,* and Jules let her own aesthetic shift and settle accordingly. She would give her own child an unusual name too. Dennis was too cheerless and distracted to concentrate on this topic for very long. He tried, but soon the effort was too great, and one day he finally told Jules, "Oh, you decide."

She had not meant to get pregnant, not now; it was the wrong time for this. Depression had sandbagged Dennis in the weeks after his release from the hospital following his small stroke. He'd been started on another antidepressant right away, but he said that he might as well have been taking Pez. The MAOI had kept him well since college, but now he was in a shaky, low-slung state. Various drug combinations were tried, yet nothing lifted his mood. Dennis went back to work at MetroCare a month after the stroke, but found himself unable to concentrate or follow the directions he'd been given; or else, sometimes, he became overly involved with the narratives revealed through the gray dimensions of ultrasound.

The day Dennis lost his job was a typically busy day at the clinic, and after seeing a few patients, a young woman came in who'd been experiencing pain on her right side. She was lovely, talkative, twenty-two years old, a recent college graduate from Kentucky who'd come to New York City in a tide of graduates, and who was working as an usher at Radio City Music Hall. "I get to see everything for free," she said as she lay on the table, her head turned away from him. "Even the Rockettes. And all those concerts, which is pretty amazing, because we never had anything like that where I come from." Dennis gently ran a transducer below her rib cage. "Oh, that tickles," she said, and then suddenly on the display screen her liver came into view, looming up like the wreck of an old ship.

He saw the mass at once; it was unmissable. Without thinking, Dennis said, "Oh God." The technicians were never allowed to offer any kind of opinion about what they saw, not even to give a hint as to whether it appeared normal or abnormal. Every other time he'd performed an ultrasound — and he'd performed thousands — he'd been poker-faced, mild, and cheerful. When patients had murmured a question, or searched his face for reassurance, he'd told them not to worry, that the doctor would read the results very soon, that it wasn't his job to interpret. But of course he always tacitly interpreted; all the technicians did. He had never reacted this way before, but the young woman was an innocent in the city, and he couldn't bear the idea that there was a significant chance she had cancer, and would die of it.

"What?" she said, turning her face toward him.

"Nothing," he said. "I didn't say anything."

"Yes you did," she said, her mellow Kentucky voice becoming accusatory. "You said, 'Oh God.' "

"I said it about tickling you," he tried, but he knew it was no good. The world engulfed

Dennis Jacobson-Boyd in all its shades of gray, its vulnerable soft organs, and he lifted the wand off the young woman's body, placed it on the cart, and put his hands to his face, for now he was crying. He could not believe he had done this! But he knew that putting a person with untreated clinical depression in this position could easily lead to a bad moment of some kind, and here it was. The young woman pulled her paper gown around herself, but she was all wet with gel, and frightened of him, and frightened for her life. She lifted herself carefully off the table, and swiftly rustled out into the hallway, calling for assistance.

Two of the other ultrasound techs, Patrick and Loreen, immediately crowded the doorway. "Dennis," said Patrick in a sharp voice, "what did you say to that patient?"

"Nothing," he said. "But she has a mass. I could see it. It was like a monster in there."

Dennis," said Patrick. "You have no idea if it's malignant. And it's not your place to get involved in this. You were sitting here crying? She heard you cry? What the hell is wrong with you?"

"I don't know," he said. Then, "I do know."

"Look, a stroke is a big deal," Loreen said. "My grandpa had one. It takes time to recover. You're not yourself. You need more time, Dennis."

"It's not the stroke. That was minor; I

recovered from that."

"Then what?" she asked. Patrick and Loreen would smoke on the street outside the clinic during breaks, and Dennis would stand happily with them in the draft of their smoke. Patrick was a big guy, a former Marine, with a shaved head and a saintly manner, married with four kids; Loreen was black, small, dreadlocked, single, full of ambition. The three of them had nothing in common, but until Dennis's stroke and the return of his depression, he'd enjoyed their company. They'd all become real friends, joined together by sound waves, and now, apparently, separated by them.

He didn't answer Loreen, but unbuttoned his white coat and somberly folded it into a soft pile, like a military flag. "I've got to go," he said.

"I'll say," said Loreen. "Mrs. Ortega is going to fire you the minute she comes down here."

"I behaved inappropriately," said Dennis. "I know I did. I just felt so sad. I was overwhelmed by the futility of everything." He nodded good-bye to his friends and walked past them, out into the hallway where the hefty, determined Mrs. Ortega was striding toward him.

His pharmacologist, Dr. Brazil, still did not want to put him back on the MAOI. "Not when we have so many sharper tools in our

501

toolbox," he said. But it seemed that even these sharp tools were too dull for Dennis, or else Dennis was the one who was dull, for he lay around the apartment in the mornings when Jules got ready to go to her office, or for a meeting with her supervisor, and he watched her through a kind of clinically depressed person's thick cheesecloth.

"Dennis," Jules said, wagging her foot back and forth as she stepped into a flattened shoe. "I do not like this current state of yours."

"I do not like this current state of mine either, Jules," he said, simply imitating her diction but sounding hostile. Why was he hostile? There was no reason, but he just was.

"I keep thinking you'll snap out of it," she said. "I know that's babyish and obviously unrealistic."

"I'm sorry," he said, and he got up from the bed to give her a perfunctory hug, not because he felt loving, but because he was probably scared to not feel loving. Jules was clean and showered and dressed, smelling of the various floral and fruit cleansers and lotions that started her day; Dennis still smelled like an attic of sleep, and at the moment she wanted no part of him.

One day Ash, concerned about the bad situation, met Jules for lunch at a place on Amsterdam where the popovers were as large as a baby's head, and the two women broke them open, steam rushing upward into their faces. Ash's driver waited outside in the car, and would wait for her as long as was necessary. "Talk to me," said Ash.

"You already know what's happening."

"But talk to me more."

"I just don't know what I'm going to do," Jules said. "He's diminished. He's like some vague, irritable version of Dennis. It's like they took him for a while and then returned him to me, but now he's only an approximation of himself. Like he's a member of Jonah's cult back then." Ash just shook her head and squeezed Jules's hand, which was all she really had to do. The two women felt guilty eating their eggy and decadent popovers and talking about Dennis as if he were a particularly recalcitrant client of Jules's. Dennis would hate the way they were talking about him, Jules thought; he would be horrified. "I shouldn't be saying all this," she added, but she needed to say it.

"No, it's okay. You're not gossiping or anything," said Ash. "You love him, and you're talking it through. And anyway, you're telling *me*. It's just me, Jules."

Still Jules pictured Dennis's mortified face, and she knew she had betrayed him. But Ash kept trying to help, wanting to listen and make suggestions. "Maybe he'll just come out of it, like a person in a coma," said Ash, not knowing at all what she was talking about. Dennis's depression divided the two women. Jules could describe Dennis's state to her, and what marriage was like with a husband in that state, but the descriptions weren't vivid enough. You had to be there; Jules was there and Ash wasn't.

At work, Jules's clients somehow seemed to lift themselves out of their worst moods, as if they intuited that she needed them to do this. She cheered them up in ways that she couldn't cheer up Dennis. Her wry running commentary was no good to him now, but only made him feel worse, as did everything else. Even talking to him seemed to grate, but she couldn't help herself, and she chattered about what had happened in therapy, as if he might get some kind of secondhand usage out of it. "This client of mine, a married woman, a grade-school reading specialist, she got into a rut for a while. She's just now coming out of it," Jules told him. It wasn't untrue, but Dennis had no response. At night he would fall asleep early, and she'd go into the living room to call Ash and Ethan, whispering to them from inside her gloomy marriage and imagining them off in their world of light. She felt almost *ill* from the claustrophobia of living with a depressed person, someone who didn't have a job now, and who slept too much, and who shaved only when he couldn't bear not to. Dennis now had the faint beginnings of a mountain-man appearance; no, a Rip Van Winkle ap-

pearance, for he'd been sleeping, not climbing.

"I don't know what I'll do," she said to Ash.
"I mean, I'm not going to do anything. I just
feel horrible. I can't help him; nothing gets
through to him. He's really suffering." Also, I
am too, she stopped herself from adding,
because it sounded so selfish.

Dennis's parents came in from New Jersey,
and his mother looked around the apartment
with a suspicious eye, as if living here with
Jules had done this to her son. "Where do
you do your ironing?" she wanted to know.

"Pardon?" They hardly ironed anything, but
whenever they absolutely had to, they laid
the items on a beach towel across the bed.
This is how we live, she wanted to say to
Dennis's mother. We don't care about ironing, we have no money, and now thanks to
genetics your son is losing the traits that I
loved in him. But the Boyds seemed to blame
Jules for his depression — because there was
no ironing board, or maybe because Jules was
Jewish. (Dennis had pointed out more than
once his father's absorption in Third Reich
documentaries.) But she also saw that the
Boyds were people whose love came with
added sourness — and maybe, as a result,
their son had developed the capacity for
unspeakable sadness, and who could blame
him? Dennis and Jules had both come from
families that hadn't really *felt good.* This

505

they'd shared, and when they'd come together it was to make a home that did feel good, and even sometimes to say: *Fuck you, disappointing families.* The Wolf household in the Labyrinth had proved to Jules that a densely textured, emotionally fulfilling family was a possibility. She'd wanted to create a new, modest version of that with Dennis, and they'd seemed to be accomplishing that just around the time that Ash and Ethan rose up into a life that no one else could remotely approximate. And then, later, Dennis became depressed, and so modest fulfillment still could not take place.

One morning when Jules woke up and saw how relaxed and neutral Dennis's face was in sleep, she thought that soon he'd be awake, and would remember how it felt to be in his skin, and the day would be shot. It was too bad he couldn't just sleep and sleep, for he seemed almost happy then. Thinking about it, Jules realized she was so unhappy that she actually needed to vomit, and hovering over the cold bowl she recalled how few times she had vomited in her life. Most memorably she'd vomited in the hotel in Iceland, and later there were a few drunken, sick experiences in college. This time was different. She considered this to be *unhappiness puking,* but of course there was no such thing. An hour later, a tiny electrical zap struck one of her nipples, and then, a little later, the other one.

Vaguely, uncomfortably, Jules thought about how her last period had been particularly light, a fact that she hadn't worried too much about at the time. This had happened at different points in her life; it was no big deal, and she'd attributed it to stress.

Jules, taking a home pregnancy test at the earliest date and staring at the result, sat in the little bathroom with a pulse pounding in her head, and tried to think about how and when this had occurred. That light period had obviously not been a period at all, but must have been what the books called implantation bleeding. Since Dennis's stroke and recovery they'd had sex infrequently; he was mostly though not completely uninterested in it now. Jules's new client Howie, a computer programmer with big transference issues, miserably but bravely told her he'd once masturbated to thoughts of her when he lay in bed with his wife; he'd made the bed tremble so much, he said, "that my wife woke up and thought it was an earthquake." And yet Jules's own depressed husband was uninterested in touching her.

She tried to do the pregnancy math, thinking back to the weeks before Dennis's stroke, and then before the return of the depression that had made him shapeless and slow. She remembered one night, shortly before Ash's play *Ghosts* had opened, when they'd been at the Museum of Television and Radio for a black-tie opening of an exhibit called *This Land Is Figland.* Ethan stood somewhere in a corner of the main gallery with Ash beside him, in a mass of museum donors, animators, friends. Jules watched Ethan in his tuxedo, his arm around Ash, who wore a partly diaphanous and very short dress, with tiny mother-of-pearl buttons running up the length of the back, like a costume from *A Midsummer Night's Dream,* which coincidentally she actually hoped to direct in the near future. The dress was "a Marco Castellano," Ash had said before the evening, which hadn't meant anything to Jules. Ethan noticed Jules looking at him, and he smiled from across the room.

What did the smile even mean? Probably just, *Isn't it humiliating, all this attention?* Or else, *I know you're bored, and I am too.* Or else, simply, *Hello, over there, Jules Jacobson-Boyd, friend of my youth, soulmate, pal.* But whatever it meant, it caused her once again to feel that old, familiar, pressurized sensation that what she and Dennis had was small and sad. By the time they took the subway home and walked up all those flights, Jules's narrow high-heeled shoes had sliced up the tops of her toes. Inside the apartment they both pulled off their clothes and Jules stood in the bathroom with one bloody foot in the sink, jamming it under the faucet. Dennis came in and said, "You look like a crane."

"I feel like a crane. Sort of awkward and stupid. The opposite of Ash's enchanted sprite. That was a Marco Castellano, by the way."

"What?"

"That's my point." She thought of how they were living a life now that was still in the end of its early stages, that was full of friends and love, and the tendrils of two careers, all of which would have been absolutely fine, if it weren't for their best friends, whose life was so much finer.

But Dennis said, "You know, if I had wanted an enchanted sprite, I would have gone into an enchanted forest and found one."

In the bathroom doorway his tie had been sprung, his cummerbund opened. Dark, strong-bodied Dennis was much better looking than Jules was, but it never bothered her, because he was not someone who would betray her with another woman. Now his bigness, his handsomeness, his dignity, his refusal to be intimidated by the glamorous evening and by a Marco Castellano impressed her. She didn't have to compare their lives with their friends' tonight; she didn't have to do that at *all,* she realized, and it was an astonishing relief. Instead, Jules was drawn toward the hypnotic, inexplicable powers of her husband, who was so beautiful and

509

unquestionably directed toward *her,* his dark eyes sweeping up and taking in the length of her. The bathroom usually seemed so small and inadequate; now it felt filled up with Dennis, a substantial man over whom she had claim. This had nothing to do with Ethan and Ash; this was for her alone. Everyone else was banished, and the private scene was beginning.

"Oh yeah?" Jules said, just for filler. "You'd have gone into an enchanted forest?"

"Yes, I would have," Dennis said, and he took her by her arm and pulled her out of the microscopic bathroom, with the aqua shag carpeting that the previous tenants had crudely installed with a staple-gun, and into the moderately larger bedroom, where he lay her down on their bed. She smiled up at him as he pulled off the remains of his tuxedo, an outfit that he only ever needed to wear for events that had to do with Ethan and Ash. Then he helped Jules unzip her dress, which had left a pink zipper mark up her back, as if demarcating the place where the two sides of her body had been assembled in a factory. They were freed from their Ethan-and-Ashwear, those outfits that seemed much more mature than the people who had worn them, even though they themselves were not too young anymore.

They had to have used a condom that night; they must have, they almost always did, though they'd had a lot to drink on this occasion so it was possible they hadn't. Jules wasn't planning on getting pregnant yet. The sex that night, she later remembered, was unusually gripping, employing all four corners of the bed, with the sheet ending up twisted like a rope. Dennis was ardent, magnificent, and purposeful, pushing the scene forward, keeping each moment turning into another moment. A book that had been lying splayed open on Jules's night table — a series of case studies about eating disorders that she'd checked out of the social work library at Columbia, where she still had privileges — somehow ended up across the room, accidentally thrust into the dusty space beneath the bureau. It wasn't found until nearly a year later, at which point more money was owed in fines than the book was worth. But she had already stopped looking for it, because by that time Aurora Maude Jacobson-Boyd had been born, and life was different.

In September 1990, three months after Aurora arrived, Ash gave birth to her own daughter, Larkin Templeton Figman. At first the two women enjoyed the animal haze of motherhood together, and for once Jules got to be the expert, giving Ash nursing tips and sleep advice. She tossed off phrases like "nipple confusion" with pleasing authority.

One morning, though, Ash called very early and sounded different. She didn't seem overwhelmed in the way she'd often been since Larkin was born. This was something else. She said she'd like to come over, if that was okay. She had the driver take her uptown, and she brought Larkin with her in one of those Swedish papoose-style pouches. Jules still felt self-conscious when Ash or Ethan came to the apartment, though lately she'd perfected a false attitude of seeming not to care how the place looked — how disheveled it was, how crammed with baby goods, the stroller blocking the hallway, the onesies drying on the shower rack until they were crisp. Ash sat tensely in Jules and Dennis's living room, refusing the offer of a cup of coffee or anything to eat. She settled onto the couch, arranging herself and the baby, and looked at Jules intently.

"You're scaring me a little," said Jules. The apartment was otherwise empty; Dennis was in Central Park with Aurora and the gang of mothers and nannies and babies with whom he sometimes spent the entire day. Jules had seen two clients in the morning, and was now home for the day. She would do a phone session later on with a woman who had broken her ankle and couldn't go out.

"I'm sorry. I don't mean to do that. Look, I know you're having a bad time yourself over here, what with Dennis and all." The way Ash spoke, her voice so cautious, made Jules think this was going to be another Goodman conversation. They hadn't had one of those conversations in many weeks; the babies had mostly distracted them from all thoughts of him. Now Jules felt that Ash might say something like, I just wanted to tell you that Goodman is in rehab again. Or, Well, get this: Goodman actually got himself into architecture school. Or, Goodman is dying. Or, Goodman is dead. Instead, Ash said, "I really need to tell you something, Jules. I have to tell someone, and you're the only one."

"All right."

"Well, you know how my parents were really upset when everything started falling apart at Drexel? The investigations and all that?" Jules nodded. "And then after the bankruptcy, my father retired early and got that payout?"

"Yes. But you said things were okay," said Jules.

"They are okay."

"All right," she said, waiting.

"I think my father's been enjoying retirement, actually. And, well, my parents apparently started *thinking*. And they called me over to their apartment and began saying things about how their money flow was going to be different now. It'd be fine, they assured me, but it wouldn't be so liquid. I didn't understand why they were saying this; it took

513

me forever to get it, because they just didn't want to come out and actually say it. But finally I realized where this was going. Finally I *got* it. I said to them, 'Is this about Goodman?' And my parents looked at each other kind of sheepishly, and I knew that that was exactly what this was about. My mother said something like, 'We weren't going to say anything, but we've been taking care of him for a long time, and he can barely work, and he has certain expenses, like anyone. And you and Ethan are so extraordinarily financially secure now, I mean, that's an understatement, and if it were at all possible to transfer this responsibility over to you, it would really make a difference to us.' 'But only if you really want to,' my father actually added, as if it were all my idea."

"So what did you say?" asked Jules, though this whole family scenario was so far beyond her understanding. Her own mother cut out coupons for frozen yogurt and sent them to her.

"I said, 'Well, if it's important to you, I guess I could figure it out.' Goodman can't get a steady job, as you know, nothing professional, nothing that pays well. Plus, he isn't trained to do anything. And as for his pickup construction jobs, his back problems are pretty bad. He got a stress fracture in his lumbar spine not too long ago, and he can't really do much physically anymore. He needs physical therapy, and he doesn't have a steady income. Plus, someone has to pay for his plane tickets when he visits us. And pay for all his little occasional habits, shall we call them. It all adds up."

"Wow," said Jules. "I'm shocked."

"I know. Me too. Obviously I can't ask *Ethan* for the money. My parents know that. They were always impressed that I never told him."

"Are you sorry you didn't?" Jules asked. She'd always wanted to ask this, but there had never been an acceptable moment before.

"Oh, sometimes, sure," said Ash easily. "Because we talk about everything. Everything but that. And I can't ever go there with him. It's way too late for that, and I don't know that he would recover. I want my life and my work to be *honest,* but I had to be faithful to my parents when they asked me to, you know I did, and now I can only go so far with the truth about this. Ethan and I barely talk about Goodman in any context anymore; he assumes it's too painful for me, and that's not completely untrue. It is painful. All of it, the way it happened. What Goodman might've become."

"I wish Ethan knew," Jules said in a low voice. "He just makes everything better," she added before she could think not to.

"I know what you mean," said Ash. "He's the person I always want to go to when something's wrong. I really wish I could tell him every detail from the start. But I can't. I did what they wanted. I was their good child, their *gifted child*. I went along with the whole package, and it's not like I can suddenly say to Ethan, Oh by the way, love of my life, person whose child I've given birth to, I've been in contact with my brother all these years, and my parents and Jules know about it too, but you're the only one I neglected to tell."

Jules said, strongly, "Tell him, Ash. Just do it." Dennis had sometimes said that one day Ethan would probably find out anyway. "Life is long," Dennis had said.

"You know I can't," Ash said. "He's the most moral person, Jules, which of course is generally a quality I love about him. And he doesn't hold back."

"So what are you going to do? Do you have access to money that he wouldn't know about?"

"The short answer is yes. And it's not as if Ethan sits around and does the *bills* each month. We have someone who does that. There's so much coming in, and so much going out. I don't need to answer to him, or to Duncan, who handles our money now. Obviously, the main thing is to do it with an invisible hand. It makes me extremely nervous, because I'm not very good with money, or with anything that has to do with numbers,

516

but I guess it'll work. I have to make it work."
She shrugged, then stroked the flattish back
of her baby's head and said, "Somebody has
to look out for Goodman now. And I guess
it's me."

In the early years of motherhood, Ash and
Jules continued their fantasy of a close friendship growing between their daughters, imagining it as a mirror of their own friendship.
The girls did become friendly, and thought
fondly of each other throughout their lives,
but they were so different from each other
that a close friendship between them eventually was more of a gift that they tried to give
their mothers than something arising naturally.

"*God* are they different," Jules said to
Dennis after spending a day at Ash and
Ethan's. The girls were four years old then;
Ash and Ethan had recently moved into the
large brownstone on Charles Street, a graceful plaque house that rested in the sun in a
choice part of Greenwich Village. Inside the
house, despite the presence of a four-year-old
daughter, and now a difficult two-year-old
son, Morris Tristan Figman, known as Mo,
calm and order were commonplace. This had
a great deal to do with the Jamaican couple,
Emanuel and Rose, who were employed as
houseman and nanny, and oversaw most
aspects of the family's daily life. They were

517

the most unobtrusive staff, a courteous husband with a shaved head, and his attentive but playful wife. The rooms were immaculate, the children were clean and looked after, and so were their parents.

A big playroom upstairs resembled a first-class airport lounge — carpeted so no one could get hurt, and decorated not in the garish colors that children were supposedly drawn to but in muted tones, softly lit. There was a trampoline and a vat full of balls. There was a slide and a bouncer and life-sized stuffed animals. Jules imagined one of Ethan's assistants having called FAO Schwarz, saying, "Give us what you've got."

What a place to grow up, she thought — to have such surroundings and such inventive, unruffled parents. Jules sat on one of the pale couches with a glass of wine handed to her by Rose, and she took a long drink, wanting to feel a softening and polishing along her throat and chest, so that she did not have to create a depressing split screen in her mind: *this* place, *this* life, and her own apartment, the walk-up on West 84th Street where she and Dennis and Aurora now lived in chaos and tight finances and the dominating blur of one person's clinical depression.

Aurora tore through the Figman and Wolf playroom, yelling, "I am an army sergeant! I am the king!" The sergeant/king thrust herself deep into the pool of balls while Larkin, sitting on a window seat with an actual chapter book, watched her, impressed. Mo was asleep in his nursery, Ash had explained, which was an amazing feat, but then again, Rose was a genius with Mo, who was generally miserable at two, always shrieking and unable at naptime to give in to the necessary bonelessness of sleep. Though Jules tried to shush Aurora so she wouldn't wake him up, Ash said she could be as loud as she wanted, because the walls were extremely thick here, and no sound ever penetrated.

Ash noted, "I see that Aurora likes to take control. Maybe she'll run a network."

"No!" said Aurora, her face flushed and triumphant. "I am the army man! I run *everybody*!"

The two women laughed. Aurora was "very much herself," as Ash had said. Jules felt a kind of demented love for her daughter. Aurora was clownish in a very open way, which was different from being witty, and Jules was obsessed with her, and so was Dennis, who was able to ignore the hum of his depression when it mattered and be expressive toward his little girl. It was, maybe, like the equivalent of a parent lifting a car off a baby. He was depressed, but still he was able to rise from depression's weight well enough to take good care of Aurora. Atypical depression sometimes allowed for such inconsistencies, said Dr. Brazil.

Jules observed that over the rest of the afternoon, whenever Larkin joined Aurora in physical play, Ash's daughter mostly seemed to be doing it to be polite. Larkin dipped herself into the vat and graciously let Aurora pound ball after ball against her; she went on the slide headfirst, but after she'd landed at the bottom, she dusted herself off and returned to her place on the window seat with her book.

Aurora sat beside her. "What's that book?" she asked.

"*Little House in the Big Woods*," said Larkin. "Does it have jokes?"

Larkin considered this. "No."

"You can read it yourself?" Aurora asked.

Larkin nodded. "When I learned to read," she confided, "it changed everything."

Larkin was mature, but she was neither mean nor superior-seeming. She was an open little girl who'd inherited her mother's fragile beauty, intelligence, and kindness, though from her father she'd inherited a predisposition for eczema, and already needed special creams. Did she have her father's imagination? It was too soon to tell, but the depressing answer was, oh, probably.

"Are you going to get all bent out of shape about Larkin?" Dennis asked that night, when at bedtime Jules was still describing Larkin's grace and precocity and delicate elegance, and the work being done to the regal house on Charles Street. "Or is that a stupid question?" he went on. "Is the real question, 'How long will it take you to get unbent out of shape about this?' "

"No," said Jules. "I wouldn't trade Aurora for anything."

"I see," he said. "You're saying it that way to draw a distinction with me. You'd trade me."

"No," she said, "not at all."

"Yes, you would. I understand." This conversation almost seemed to have perked him up, as if he thought that he could finally see the world the way Jules saw it again; he could see it through her vivid lens, as she made preparations for leaving.

"Well, stop understanding. This is very fucked up, Dennis," said Jules. "This whole conversation. Would I get rid of your depression? Would I trade you in for a version of you that wasn't depressed? Yes, all right, I would. But isn't that what you would do too? Isn't that what we want?"

Ever since he'd been taken off the MAOI five years earlier, Dennis had rarely returned to buoyancy. Instead, he still struggled with what his pharmacologist variously referred to as "low-level depression," "atypical depression," and "dysthymia." There were some people who were just very hard to treat, Dr. Brazil said. They were able to live their lives, sometimes to a fairly full extent, but they never felt good. Dennis's atypical depression wasn't making him break down, as it had done in college, but it also wouldn't go away. He felt its presence like a speck in the eye or like a chronic, rattling cough. Different drugs were tried, but nothing worked for very long, or if a drug did work, the side effects made it untenable. Early on in the rotation of drugs, the discarded MAOI had been returned to, but it no longer even worked. Dennis's brain chemistry seemed to have changed, and the MAOI was like a former lover who doesn't look good anymore in the light of a new day.

After enough time seemed to have passed after losing his job at MetroCare, Dennis had made a diligent search for work and found nothing. He couldn't get a good reference from the clinic after his "outrageous behavior with a patient," as Mrs. Ortega promised to describe it in any letter she wrote to a potential new employer. But even so, Dennis admitted to Jules that when he eventually did go back to work, he was afraid of what he might see now upon looking into the human body. He and Jules lay in bed at night once and talked about this. "What do you think you'll see?" she whispered.

"All kinds of things."

"I never know what I'm going to see when someone walks into my office," she said. "I wish I had a piece of equipment for looking. I envy you that thing — what's it called, a transducer? — but you can't even bear to use it. Your *wand.* Your magic wand. What I do feels so crude. I know that therapy can actually change the brain; they've done amazing studies. But so much of it involves just sort of waiting things out, and tolerating the same unconstructive ideas being repeated. You have a good eye, Dennis. You know your stuff; don't forget that. And you get to use equipment too. It'll still be there when you're better, when you're ready to go back."

Dennis lay with his eyes open and said, "I did know my stuff. I don't want to know it now. I can't bear the idea of looking deeply. Because you inevitably turn up horrible things."

"I don't know, for someone who can't bear looking deeply, that's sort of a deep observation," Jules said. "A lot of you is here, Dennis, more than you think. If you were gone, that would be a whole other story. But you're not gone." She wanted to perk him up somehow, to turn even her modest curative powers on him. Just a few days earlier her most recent client, sixty-year-old Sylvia Klein, who had essentially been crying for most of every session, had smiled when she described the way her grown daughter Alison, dead for three years of breast cancer, had been obsessed with Julie Andrews as a child, and had insisted on seeing *The Sound of Music* multiple times, and even went around speaking in a British accent, asking her mother, "Mummy, does my accent sound real?"

"You smiled, telling me about that," Jules had said to her.

"No, I didn't," said Sylvia Klein, drawing back, but then she tilted her head and very tentatively smiled again. "Well, maybe I did," she said.

But Jules couldn't do much for Dennis except eat meals with him, rent movies from Blockbuster with him, lie in bed with him, and listen to him talk about the intractability of his dysthymic state. Then, when Jules found out she'd accidentally become pregnant, they were both similarly shocked, and anxious about how they would have enough money to support a baby, and what it would be like for Dennis with a baby in the apartment. What it would be like for the baby to have a depressed father — *a dysthymic father,* Jules insisted on saying, because that sounded less threatening. Would a baby be able to tell? Dennis had an additional worry: What if something was wrong with the baby? "There are so many things that can go wrong," he said. "Weird DNA, anatomical abnormalities. The baby could be missing part of its *brain,* Jules. I have actually seen this. A whole big *chunk* can be missing; it just doesn't grow. Or else there's hydrocephalus, water on the brain, that's another good one." He exhausted her with his fears about the baby, and frightened her as well. At twenty weeks, when Jules was scheduled to have a level 2 ultrasound, the big anatomy scan, she asked Dennis to go with her, though he had declined to go to any appointments with her in the past, saying that he wouldn't be very good company, which was probably true, so she hadn't pushed him.

"I can't," he said.

"I need you there, for this one," said Jules. "I cannot keep doing everything on my own."

So he went with her, and sat beside her in the dim light of the small room, where a young ultrasound technician squirted a mound of gel onto Jules's convex stomach, and began to move the transducer. Suddenly the baby corkscrewed into view. Dennis didn't breathe. He stared at the screen as the young woman pressed some keys, and he asked her a few tense shorthand ultrasound questions. Jules remembered how, the day after the first time she and Dennis had slept together, they had gone to the Central Park Zoo, where they'd talked about his depression in the penguin house. Here they were in another darkened place, looking at a creature behind glass. The technician took measurements, and smiled reassuringly, and pointed.

"Oh, look at her move," said Dennis, his face close to the display now, studying the shifting grainy image that only he and the technician could read, and which, to Jules, was a mysterious play of light and shadow.

"Her?" said Jules. "Her? We weren't going to find out the sex."

"I meant 'her' generically," said Dennis quickly. "I can't tell the sex." The technician swiveled her head discreetly away at that moment, and Jules knew Dennis wasn't telling the truth. Once again he had inappropriately given away big news in an ultrasound room, but this time no one was really upset.

The baby was a she, born to an anxious mother and a precarious father. After Aurora's birth, they jointly decided that Dennis would stay home and take care of her during the day. If they did it this way, they realized that they wouldn't need to put her in daycare, or hire outside child care, which they certainly could barely have afforded anyway. Instead of continuing to look for work, in hopes of finding another clinic job, taking care of the baby became what Dennis did for a living. He and Jules had sat down and addressed the question of whether or not he was too depressed to be with their daughter all day; Dennis said he wanted to try it and at least find out. It interested him, he told her cautiously. Jules also talked about this with Ash and Ethan. Ethan said, "What do you think, he's going to read to her from *The Bell Jar*? I bet it'll be okay."

But not long after Dennis started taking care of the baby full-time, Jules realized that the days were often soothing to him. Curiously, even the tedious parts didn't bother him, and neither did the frankly unpleasant parts, such as going down to the hot laundry room with Aurora in a carriage, dragging a cart swollen with dirty clothes and crib sheets behind him. He was relieved not to have to make conversation with other adults all day about topics like the sudden Gulf War that sprang up in August — the first televised war, viewed in fits and starts like an awful football game, with General Norman Schwarzkopf as the quarterback. Every time this sudden new war came up in conversation, you felt dread, thinking: What will happen next? Will it spread? Will it *come here*?

But in the separate, zipped-up universe of being with young children, the mothers and the nannies and Dennis talked about baby monitors, baby carriages, the comparative quality of different pediatricians. The television channel was turned away from news of the war, and instead there was always a gentle video playing or soft music, and this seemed to be what Dennis needed, as much as Aurora did. Somehow this was the life they'd created without planning it: a single-earner family in which the breadwinner was the mother and the caregiver was the father. Over time, there were many more stay-at-home fathers out with their babies in the city during the height of a workday, whether because of progressive thinking or the tanking economy, but in 1990 it was still an uncommon enough sight that, until they got to know him, mothers and nannies looked Dennis over carefully in the park and on the street, suspicious and curious about what exactly was wrong with him.

Dennis had a lasting but apparently tolerable depression, and Jules had found ways to tolerate it too. As Aurora came into herself, she was demanding and loud, but she gave Jules real joy; and if *joy* was too strong a word to apply to what Dennis felt, at least Aurora moved him, touched a place inside his depression. Jules imagined Dennis's mind like the vat full of colored balls in the Figman-Wolf playroom. Once in a while the balls were stirred and shifted, and a few of them flew into the air when something got through to him.

When Aurora started kindergarten she threw off her first name as if it had been a dreadful affliction, a hair shirt festooned with overly feminine sequins and bows. Then she neatly turned herself, like one of the Transformers robot cars she played with for hours, into Rory — not unlike the way Julie had long ago simply turned into Jules.

Meanwhile, Larkin stayed Larkin forever, a study in pink and cream, and she often slipped envelopes under her parents' bedroom door, or beside their plates at breakfast. In her early handwriting, advanced and shaky and charming, she wrote:

> Mommy and Daddy wod you be my gessed at a dolls tee party it is in my room at 4 oh clock. From Larkin your doter.

"Oh you have to save these," said Jules dully when Ash showed a few of the notes to her. Rory had no interest in writing, but wanted to be in motion at all times. Jules and Dennis bought her every kind of ride-on vehicle they could find: orange and yellow plastic things with wheels the size of inner tubes, which had to be lugged up all their flights of stairs, just as the stroller had had to be lugged up when Rory was a toddler. "We are too old to raise a kid like this in a place like this," Jules said to Dennis. Rory didn't even have her own room, but still slept on a fold-out bed in a corner of the living room. But Jules remembered what Cathy Kiplinger had said in the girls' teepee long ago, referring to her own oversized breasts: "You get used to whatever you get." Still, it was hard. Sometimes when Rory was asked to use her "inside voice," or sit quietly doing a maze while Jules read over the notes from a therapy session, Rory would be unable to comply.

"I can't sit still!" she shouted, as if in great discomfort. "I have an itch inside my body!"

"She has an itch inside her body," Jules relayed to Ash on the phone.

"Can she scratch it?" Ash asked. "That seems to be the important part, don't you think? That she should be able to scratch it."

"I think she means a metaphorical itch."

"I know what she means. And I'm just saying that she should be able to express herself, not for you but for her. You don't want to end up with a situation like in *The Drama of the Gifted Child.*"

Larkin Figman was beautiful, creative, sensitive about everything. At the ivy-strung Tudor weekend house that Ash and Ethan had recently bought in Katonah, an hour north of the city — and sold several years later (they'd ended up rarely using it) for much more money than they'd paid for it — she ran toward her parents with her hands cupped, and inside them there might be a small wounded animal or a livid cricket trying to bang its way out. Larkin inevitably wanted to build a hospital for the creature, and then, if it recovered, hold a tea party in its honor. The tiniest cups in the world were fashioned.

"We get a lot of acorn-cap usage around here," Ethan would say when Dennis and Jules took the train up for the weekend and he'd actually found the time to get away from the studio. "Do you know how hard it is to pry those fuckers off? I have acorn thumb."

Ethan's and Dennis's love for their daughters wasn't complicated, but in both instances was massive and wild. Ordinary father-daughter love had a charge to it that generally was both permitted and indulged. There was just something so *beautiful* about the big father complementing the tiny girl. Bigness and tininess together at last — yet the bigness would never hurt the tininess! It *respected* it. In a world in which big always crushes tiny, you wanted to cry at the beauty of big being kind and worshipful of and *humbled by* tiny. You couldn't help but think about your own father as you saw your little girl with hers. The sight of them was overwhelming to Jules, and she had to look hard, then finally look away.

Something Rory wanted, when she was a young child, became obvious to Jules, but because it was not usually said aloud, she ignored it. It was darkly fitting that Jules herself, who envied her friends so powerfully, would have an envious daughter. But unlike her mother, Rory didn't envy the enormous life of Ash and Ethan and Larkin. Instead, she envied boys. She came home from kindergarten talking about the boy whose cubby was beside hers. "Oh, Ma, Andrew Menzes stands up to go pee. The pee comes out in a curving string. A curving *golden* string," she embellished, and then she cried.

And Jules could have cried too — two jealous crybabies — but she remained mute, and downplayed the importance of the curving golden string. "Your pee comes out in a golden string too," she said lightly. "It's a straight string, that's all."

"Andrew Menzes's pee comes out of a *rocket*," Rory said passionately, and her mother was left with nothing to reply. Some dreams in life were attainable, and others weren't, no matter how much they were desired. It was all unfair, having more to do with luck than anything else. But sometimes, right after Jules had made a comment to Dennis with particular harshness about Ash and Ethan's great good fortune — which included their wealth, their specialness, Ethan's outsized talent, and now even their daughter — she felt sharply revived. Then everything settled down again, the current world returned, along with an image of her own wonderful daughter, and she imagined her friends' kind faces — Ethan's homely, flattened one; Ash's lovely, sculpted one — puzzling over Jules's light meanness.

Then, coming down further from the nasty little high, she felt even guiltier as she reminded herself that Ash and Ethan's life might be vast and miraculous, but their marriage had a locked room in it, inside of which was not only the withheld information about Goodman but also the full freight of Ash's ache about Goodman. The brother from her childhood was gone, even if Ash did get to slip off to see him once a year or so in

Europe, and even if she did speak to him on a dedicated cell phone that Ethan knew nothing about — "my Batphone," Ash called it — and write him letters when Ethan wasn't home; and even though she was now supporting him with a very small fraction of the money her husband earned from the astonishing profits from *Figland.* The loss of Goodman was made almost manageable by the Wolf family's elaborate and underground involvement and love; but still.

"Everyone suffers," one of Jules's favorite instructors in social work school had said on the first day of a seminar called "Understanding Loss." "Everyone," the woman added for emphasis, as if anyone in the room might think that some people were exempt.

Sometimes there would be a sudden, surprise reminder of that earlier life, before marriage, and before wealth or its absence, and before the addition of children. A life when Jules was still a girl, in awe of another girl and her brother and their parents and their big apartment and their gracious, splendid life. Even if she didn't drop into sadness thinking about that early time, she still remembered what had once been. In the fall, at the annual psychotherapy convention held at the Waldorf Hotel, Jules had been standing in a banquet room among a cluster of social workers she knew, drinking a cup of coffee between lectures, when the past suddenly made a cameo. The place was crazed with therapists of all stripes — MSWs, CSWs, Ed.D.s, Ph.D.s, M.D.s — their voices rising as one tidal chorus in the bright, bland room. She noticed a frail elderly man being helped through the crowd by a younger woman. He must have been ninety, and as they slowly passed she read his nametag, LEO SPILKA, M.D., and with a quiet gasp she remembered the name. Without thinking about doctor-patient confidentiality, or even what the point might be of saying anything, she went up to him.

"Dr. Spilka?" she said.

"Yes?" The old man stopped and peered at her.

"My name is Jules Jacobson-Boyd. May I speak to you?"

He turned to the woman he was with, as if for approval, and she shrugged and nodded, and Dr. Spilka and Jules moved a few feet away, near a table of picked-over pastries.

"I'm a clinical social worker," Jules said. "But when I was a teenager I was friends with a boy named Goodman Wolf. Does that name mean anything to you?" Dr. Spilka didn't say anything. "Goodman Wolf," she repeated, a little louder. "He was your client, your patient, in the 1970s. He was in high school then." The doctor still said nothing, so Jules added, "He was accused of raping a girl at Tavern on the Green, on New Year's Eve."

Finally Dr. Spilka mildly said, "Go on."

In a quicker, more excited voice, Jules said, "Well, it's just been this unfinished thing for all of us who knew his family, and knew the girl who accused him. It's been this thing we don't really talk about openly — it was complicated — and then so much time passed that it was hard to bring it up. But I wondered whether there was anything you felt you could tell me, to just, you know, put it in perspective. Whatever you say, it would be between us. I know it's not right of me to ask about a former patient. But it's been so long, and I suddenly saw you here, and I just thought, okay, I have to ask."

Dr. Spilka regarded her for a while, then he nodded his head, slowly. "Yes," he said.

"Yes?"

"I remember that boy."

"You do?"

"He was guilty," said Dr. Spilka. Jules stared at him, and he stared right back. His gaze was even and cool, a tortoise's ancient gaze; hers was shocked.

"Really?" she said in a small voice. "He was?" She hardly knew what else to say. The thought of having to report this conversation back to Ash created a thick presence of something in her mouth, a congestion, as if she was biting down on a gag. She hadn't thought to wonder too often about Goodman's innocence or guilt over the years; his family had known he was innocent, they were secure in this, and that was what she knew.

The psychoanalyst said, "Yes, he murdered that girl."

"No, no. No, he didn't," Jules said. "She's alive, she's some kind of financial person now. She accused him of rape, remember?"

But Dr. Spilka insisted, "Oh yes he did. He raped her and he strangled her until her eyes bulged out. She may have been a slut, but he was a punk, and they put him in a maximum-security prison, where he *belongs,* that punk with the big jutting chin."

"No, Dr. Spilka, no, you're confusing him with someone else — the Preppy Murderer, I think. That happened about ten years later. Another Central Park story. There have been so many by now; maybe they're kind of blurring together for you. That's totally understandable."

"I am certainly not confusing him with anyone," said the old psychoanalyst, standing straighter.

The woman who'd accompanied him and was waiting nearby, observing, came over then and said she was his daughter, and that she hoped Jules would excuse her father. "He has dementia," she confided easily, right in front of him. "He gets things mixed up. Right, Dad? I bring him to this conference every year because he used to like coming to it so much. I'm sorry if he said something that upset you."

"He killed her," Leo Spilka insisted with a shrug, and then his daughter steered him away.

FOURTEEN

What was later referred to by Ethan, somewhat ironically but not entirely, as the Jakarta transformation was originally supposed to have been a restorative vacation. Mo had recently been diagnosed at the Yale Child Study Center as being on the autism spectrum, and Ash decided that the whole family needed to be together somewhere far away from the usual routine. Mo's diagnosis had made Ash cry often in the beginning, but she'd also said, "I love him, and he's ours, and I won't give up on him." For now, she wanted the family to be together in their "new reality," as she put it.

Ethan, stunned into a flat coolness after the diagnosis, said, "Sure, fine." Ash had chosen Indonesia because they'd never been there before, and it seemed like a beautiful and restful place, and also because she was thinking of directing a play for Open Hand that involved Balinese shadow puppets, though who knew when she'd be able to direct again;

she wanted to be there for Mo now. Mo's autism-spectrum disorder was not something that Ethan liked to talk about, even with his wife, because it was like staring into an eclipse. He felt as if he would burn up and disintegrate when he thought of his son. Ash was her usual self, emotional and fragile but finally the one who'd taken the initiative to make the appointment for the two-day diagnostic at Yale — and then, despite her sadness and shakiness, the one who had pressed ahead further and put Mo's team of teachers and clinicians and caretakers in place. She was the strong one, and he never doubted that she would be able to tend their son with a mother's warrior love. Ethan didn't hide his deep sorrow from Ash — she felt her own sorrow, she said — but he kept from her his anger and indifference.

Whenever he started to think about Mo and all the possibilities for him that were now blocked off for good, Ethan's thoughts turned elsewhere, usually toward his work, which was like an endless, interesting problem to be solved. The only place he wanted to be these days was in the studio, working. Over the past couple of years, he'd been referring to the studio unofficially as the Animation Shed, and recently the network had made the name official, with a sign on the glass wall when you arrived at the eighteenth floor of the office building in midtown on Avenue of the

Americas. The actual animation for *Figland* was now produced in Korea, but preproduction and various other projects kept this place busy, hectic. Since Mo's diagnosis, and even before it, Ethan had often stayed on at work after hours; he was rarely alone there. Someone was always in the middle of something and just couldn't be pulled away. One night it was just him and the director, who was correcting timing on exposure sheets; they blasted old Velvet Underground music across the entire floor, and a security guard came up to see if anything was the matter. Late at night in the Animation Shed, Ethan Figman, the father of two young children — one delicate and brilliant, one compromised — offered suggestions and criticisms to staff members on points both huge and trivial. He was overworked from the discussions with network people and the table reads and recording sessions and all else, and was now suffering badly about his son; but still he would have liked nothing more than to remain at the studio for days on end, hiding out in the small private space that had been designed for him in an annex one flight up. Occasionally he even spent the night there, despite Ash's protests. But she'd insisted on this family vacation, this bonding time among three people who were already bonded, and one who wasn't but who needed to be bonded to the others and to the world.

Ash had a solid, reliable career now as artistic director of Open Hand. She had revived the ragged little East Village theater company and made it a place where young playwrights got their start and where young women in particular were given a shot in the still intractably sexist world of contemporary theater. Male playwrights and directors continued to dominate. ("Look at the studies," Ash told everyone, handing out stapled Xeroxes that detailed the unfairnesses. "I know I look like a lunatic," she'd said to Ethan, and, no, she did not look like a lunatic, but, yes, she could get repetitive, even though what she said was accurate, the facts disgraceful.) Open Hand had bought a larger, more elegant space around the corner on East 9th Street, and the first production that would be performed there, a two-hander by a young African-American woman about the estranged daughter of a Black Panther coming to visit her father on his deathbed, had won a few Obies and was in talks to move to Broadway. Ash was sometimes profiled in the arts sections of newspapers and in magazines; the respectful, praising pieces inevitably mentioned her marriage to Ethan — a fact that everyone already knew — and also referred to her physical beauty and grace. Both of these inclusions always bothered her.

"What do I have to *do*?" Ash said. "I mean, really? Or maybe the issue is, 'What does a

541

woman have to do to be seen as a serious person?' "

"Be a man, I guess," Ethan said, and then he added, "I'm really sorry; I know it sucks," as if sexism in theater and everywhere else was his fault. He was known for hiring women at all levels, and for supporting women's causes, but still he felt bad. Everyone knew most people gave authority more easily to men. "There is no expression 'girl genius,' " Ash had once said. Ethan was relieved that Ash was finally being given responsibility and attention, though the world of an off-Broadway theater in the East Village was always going to be so much smaller and less splashy than that of television or film. Still, Ash didn't require splashiness. Neither of them did. But splashiness had happened to Ethan.

The vacation was planned, and the resort on Bali was unsurprisingly luxurious. The last time Ethan had slept in a bed like this, with mosquito netting and the open sky beyond it, he and Ash had been on the island of Kauai with Dennis and Jules, both couples childless then. He realized how much he missed that. But it was also that he missed Jules, which never stopped. For while they'd stayed close during the absurd years of his sharp rise, having children had knocked it all into a different arrangement. The minute you had children, you closed ranks. You didn't plan this in advance, but it happened. Families were like individual, discrete, moated island nations. The little group of citizens on the slab of rock gathered together instinctively, almost defensively, and everyone who was outside the walls — even if you'd once been best friends — was now just that, *outsiders.* Families had their ways. You took note of how other people raised their kids, even other people you loved, and it seemed all wrong. The culture and practices of one's own family were the only way, for better or worse. Who could say why a family decided to have a certain style, to tell the jokes it did, to put up its particular refrigerator magnets?

Since having children, not only didn't Ethan see Jules as often as he used to but he hardly ever saw Jonah at all; Jules had said the same thing to Ethan about Jonah. There was a further divide between those with children and those without, and you had to accept it. And now, having a developmentally disabled child like Mo seemed to have knocked everything into a more extreme arrangement. You and your family needed to *heal,* and you couldn't do that with any of your friends around — neither the childless ones nor the ones with children — even though Ethan fervently wished you could. He would never tell Ash what he really felt about Mo, but he ached to confess it to Jules. I don't know if I love him, Jules, he would say.

I'm stubborn about my love, stingy about it. It comes and goes at all the wrong times.

In the big open-air bed of their villa, Larkin dive-bombed her parents, and Mo, age three, lay on his side, his thin body almost deliberately facing away from all of them. The whole family lay under purple Balinese fabric. Was any healing taking place yet? Let the healing begin, Ethan wanted to intone to Ash snidely. They'd been here for less than forty-eight hours. Was the "new reality" settling in? How in the world were you supposed to tell if it had started?

On the morning of their fourth day, Ash was asleep in bed in the breeze, and the children were eating breakfast on the terrace with Rose. Ethan sat in the shade of a big, shaggy-topped tree writing a postcard. He had addressed it to both Dennis and Jules to be considerate, but he really meant it for Jules, and of course she would know this.

"Dear D and J," he wrote.

It would be so nice if you were here. But this is strictly family time, what with M's diagnosis. All I can say is thank God for Rose, or else family time might become a little too much, and we might be inclined to leave Mo with the kindly fishmonger down the road. A JOKE! Mostly the trip has been peaceful. Ash was right, we did need to be away together for a while.

I've been thinking about you both a lot and I hope things are a little better than when we left last week. Please reconsider what we said, okay? More soon.

Love,
Ethan

Ethan knew that Dennis didn't like to discuss his depression with their friends — he was embarrassed by it, and he wasn't open about it with anyone but Jules — but though Rory was in school now, and Dennis's stay-at-home services weren't required full-time anymore, he still wasn't ready to get a job outside the home that would require energy and focus and exactness and calm. Jules alone couldn't earn enough money to support their family as well as she needed to in New York City in 1995. She had a close to full practice, but it didn't pay nearly enough. Their apartment was the kind of place where you were supposed to live when you were starting out and childless; a place where you leapt up four flights of stairs to see your beloved, and where you clattered down those same flights to head out into the night with your gang of friends, all of you in your twenties, free agents, needing almost nothing. The Jacobson-Boyds didn't belong there now; Rory didn't even have her own *bedroom.* The small, difficult quarters made their situation — Dennis's depression, the lack of money, the mostly

unchangeable clients in Jules's practice —
seem only worse.

"We want to help you out," Ethan had
recently told them in a crowded restaurant.
He'd said it before, but had always been
shrugged away. The two families had gone
out for one of those chaotic Sunday brunches
young parents take with their children.
Nobody has a good time, but everyone needs
to find something to do with their kids on
the weekend. Mo was in a booster seat, crying as usual — he always cried, it was just
unbearable, but now they knew why. Everything grated against him, made him feel *raw.*
Ash stood and went over to Mo, as she often
did when he began to be upset. She was so
natural and unflappable with him. Such an
entitled girl she'd been, and yet she'd grown
up into the kind of mother who could handle
having a child with what people referred to
now as "special needs." Her ego hadn't been
fatally wounded by his diagnosis. She was a
thoughtful mother to poor Mo, just the way
she was a thoughtful lover to Ethan and a
thoughtful friend to Jules and Dennis and
Jonah and his boyfriend, Robert. Just the way
she was thoughtful with the cast and crew of
a play. "Gather round, everybody," she said
in her quiet voice, and even people in the
farthest reaches of a theater would put down
their hammers or scripts and come to her. At
brunch, Mo, too, stopped his crying as

though a switch had been thrown. His mother's hand resting briefly on his stiff, coral-spined back made him look up sharply, squinting at her, remembering that she loved him. Remembering that there was such an element in the world as love. Ethan hadn't been able to do that; or anyway he hadn't thought to do that. Ash whispered magic words to their son — what did she say, *"Shazam"?* — and Mo's body relaxed a little. Even Ethan's body relaxed. Then she returned to her seat at the table, and Ethan just looked at her in wonder.

Rory was standing beside her own chair, shout-singing. Larkin sat quietly, drawing on her place mat with the crayons that the hostess had handed around to the children like bribes. Idly, Ethan glanced over to see what his daughter was drawing. On the place mat, she'd made an extremely accurate rendering of Wally Figman and a recent addition to the *Figland* cast, the opinionated love interest of Wally on the planet Figland, Alpha Jablon.

"Nice," he said to her, startled by her skill.

Larkin glanced up, as if returning from very far away. "Thanks, Dad," she said.

Oh, he thought, *I see, she's an artist.* He felt sorry for her right then, as he sometimes felt sorry for himself. Though he was often so proud of Larkin, he wondered about early talent and the different fates it could meet. In his mind he checked off what had become of the six friends from that early summer, all of them meeting under the auspices of talent. One had become an artful, earnest stage director, finally breaking through, though would that have happened if she hadn't had the ladder of her parents' money and then Ethan's money? No, not likely. One had closed down his musical talent for unknown reasons, remaining enigmatic to even the people who loved him. One had been born with a deep talent for dance, but by an accident of biology had been given a body that did not correspond to that talent past a certain age. One had been charming and privileged and lazy, with the potential to build things but also a longing to destroy them. One — Ethan himself — had been born with "the real thing," as people wrote in reviews and profiles. Though he hadn't been born into privilege, he too had been helped up the ladder over time, though the talent he possessed was squarely his. It had existed before the ladder ever appeared. But he didn't even feel that he could take credit for his own talent, because he'd been born with it, and had simply discovered it while drawing one day, just the way Wally Figman had discovered that little planet, Figland, in a shoe box. And then there was the last of Ethan's friends, who hadn't been good enough at being funny onstage and had had to switch to another field, developing a skill more than an art.

Jules's clients apparently loved her; they were always bringing her gifts, and they wrote her moving letters after they no longer came to see her. But still Jules was disappointed in how she had ended up. Even now, Ethan wanted another outcome for her, and maybe it could still happen. Talent could go in so many directions, depending on the forces that were applied to it, and depending on economics and disposition, and on the most daunting and most determining force of all, luck.

"Look, I'm just going to put this out here pretty openly," Ethan said to Dennis and Jules at brunch. "Will you let us help you?"

"No," Dennis said. "We've already been through this."

There was a moment of contemplative silence at the table, and it almost seemed as if even the children were listening to this adult conversation and understanding it, which Ethan strongly hoped was not true. He waited until the little girls started talking to each other, and then he quietly said to Jules and Dennis, "I'd like to think that if the situation were reversed, I'd be able to accept your help."

Dennis looked at him for a long time, his eyes narrowing slightly. It was as if he was trying to imagine a situation in which Ethan Figman might actually need him. But he couldn't, and neither could Ethan. Now both men were embarrassed.

Ash said, "Jules saves my life virtually every day," and when Jules began to protest, Ash turned to her and said, "No, it's true. You must be a wonderful therapist; I don't care what you say about how your clients don't really seem to break old patterns. You're compassionate and loyal and witty and understanding, and they get so much from you. I don't really know what friendship means if I can't come in and help my closest friends when it's called for. We've all been through a lot together already. Our lives are different now, I get that, but who's the one I go to when I need someone to talk to — Shyla?"

"Who?" asked Dennis.

"You know," Jules said to him quietly. "Shyla. Of Duncan and Shyla. Their good friends."

"Oh, right," said Dennis, and Ethan thought he saw a look pass between Jules and Dennis, but he wasn't sure, and he couldn't decipher it anyway.

"You're the rock, Jules," Ash said. "From the start." She broke off and her face began to contort. At once, seeing her crying, Ethan thought of the loss of Goodman, and probably so did Jules; this was a moment of acknowledgment of the lost brother and how Jules had helped Ash cope with that. "And not just that, but also recently, with Mo," Ash went on, and she looked right at Dennis, making her case directly to him. "Having her

550

there with me when I went up to the Yale Child Study Center and Ethan had to be in LA — it saved me, it really did. And then afterward, when she came to the house for the night, it calmed me down. We're just now dealing with Mo and the future. And knowing that I have Jules here for that is a big relief. So turn it around for a second, Dennis, and see this from our perspective. Our lives, Ethan's and mine, have their own sadness; everyone's does, you know that. But we also have resources that most people don't have. I'm not trying to boast; it's just true. I know you're strapped, and going through a difficult patch in your life, and that the three of you are sort of on top of each other in the apartment. I realize it's not the most fun time. Jules has told me what it's like."

Dennis looked at Jules impassively, and then Jules looked down at her plate of probably now unwanted, sickening brunch food under its slick of syrup. Ethan felt that Ash had misjudged, and had as a result inadvertently gone too far. He couldn't bear upsetting Dennis or embarrassing Jules. He colored slightly just imagining Jules's embarrassment. "The thing is," Ethan quickly put in, "this is much more about us than it is about you. You may not feel you should take any help, but we need to give it. Can you really deny your oldest friends their deepest needs?" He gave them a deliberate expression of wide-eyed neediness, but nobody laughed. "Look, think about it while we're away on our trip," he said, and finally, if only to end the awkwardness, they agreed that they would.

Ethan didn't want Jules to worry about money. He didn't want Jules to worry about anything, even though part of his continuing love for her over the years was due to the fact that they could worry freely in front of each other, seeming foolish, idiotic, neurotic, all the while making jokes as they fretted and complained. Now, having been hustled off to Indonesia by his wife, Ethan walked down the path from their villa at the resort on Bali, clutching his postcard to Jules and Dennis. In the lobby, on one of the brown, cracked-leather couches, another guest of the resort sat reading *The Financial Times.* Ethan had seen him on the beach over the course of the week; he was American, in his fifties, shiny, trim, with a confident businessman's sunniness. Ethan recognized that attitude from his father-in-law, back when he was employed. These days Gil Wolf sat in the apartment in the Labyrinth in an ergonomic chair, staring with cowed awe at the World Wide Web on his new Dell home computer.

The reader of *The Financial Times* put his paper down and smiled. "You're Ethan Figman," he said. "I've seen you around with your family."

"Ah."

"I'm glad even someone like you takes a break now and then. They say you're a work-aholic."

"They?"

"Oh, chatter," said the man. "I'm a worka-holic too. Marty Kibbin. Paine and Pierce." The men shook hands. "I'm glad you're not here for some work thing. Some *reconnais-sance* mission. Checking out the child labor scene in Jakarta, that sort of thing."

"Excuse me?"

"You know, the merchandise."

"Right," said Ethan.

"It's god-awful, no matter how you look at it," the man went on easily. "Those subcon-tractors with the manufacturing rights can give you a real headache, but when CEOs get all pious, they need to go to, reminded that no one can police the world. No one. Things happen along the supply chain that you have no control over. Just give out the licenses to places that check out and seem decent, you know? And run your own company with the ethical code you were raised with."

"Yes," said Ethan. "Well, I should go." What a lame excuse that was; no one at this resort had anywhere they had to go to, unless they had an appointment for a four-handed mas-sage. He smiled thinly, and walked off. He must have dropped the postcard to Jules in the brass mail slot by the concierge's desk, but later on he would have no memory of having done that. He was upset by the man's self-assured words, and hoped he hadn't just let the post-card fall from his hand onto the rush-covered floor.

Back at the villa, Ash stood in the teak shower with various nozzles shooting water at her from all directions. Through the open door he could see the moving lines of his wife's young-seeming body, and also her head, which, whenever her hair was wet, appeared as small as an otter's. He could also see the children and Rose and Emanuel out on the beach beyond the villa. Mo was crying again, his arms gesturing awkwardly and broadly; Rose and Larkin were attempting to comfort him.

Everyone considered Ethan a good person — "moral," Ash always said, but they had no idea. No, you couldn't police the world, but you told yourself you were doing the best you could. He had sat in on several meetings each year about the production of *Figland* merchandise. PLV Manufacturing was theoretically one of the cleaner operations, but they subcontracted all over China, India, and Indonesia, and all bets were always off when everything was handed to an overseas factory. It made Ethan seriously uneasy whenever he thought about what went on there. Maybe, he thought, latching on to a ludicrous idea, that was why Ash had unconsciously chosen this place for a vacation, and why he was here now.

Ethan got on the phone, placing a call to LA, where it was fourteen hours earlier. It was still last night in LA, but the executives he dealt with always worked until very late, so he knew he could reach them. Even if it was *last year* in LA now, someone would patch him through.

Jack Pushkin, who had replaced Gary Roman some years earlier, got right on the line. "Ethan?" he said, surprised. "Aren't you in India?"

"Indonesia."

"They're the ones with rijsttafel, right? The rice dish? I've always wanted to try that."

"Jack," he said, stopping him.

"What is it, Ethan? What's wrong?"

"I want to see what's what."

The conditions at the Leena Toys Factory at Kompleks DK2 in Jakarta were dismal by anyone's reckoning, but nothing seemed extraordinarily outrageous — not that "extraordinarily outrageous" was a legal, technical, specific description. Ethan, dressed in the one nice linen shirt that Ash had had Emanuel pack "just in case," followed the short, imperious Mr. Wahid, who took him through the squat, fused-together yellow industrial buildings where textiles were manufactured, and onto the floor. He saw the women, many in headscarves, huddled over their old sewing machines in an exposed-pipe, overheated space, but the scene didn't seem all that different from the garment district in New York City where Ethan's grandmother Ruthie Figman had once labored. Some of the machines here were unattended. "Slow day," said Mr. Wahid, shrugging, uninterested, when Ethan inquired.

A skinny old man was trotted out to show Ethan what he was making: a shiny satin throw pillow decorated with Wally Figman's face. Like everyone, Ethan was appalled that the workers earned what they earned, and he couldn't call himself content after his brief tour of the depressing Leena Toys, a place you couldn't help but never want to think about again. Yet after visiting he was also somehow not beside himself with guilt and self-hatred. He'd asked to see what one of these factories was like, and now he knew, and he could report back to everyone at the studio and the network about what he'd seen, and urge them to look into what could be done to increase overseas workers' wages. Ash would want to get involved too, though of course she'd have no time, between running the theater and now starting to manage Mo's complicated regimen.

Ethan had hired a pilot and a small plane to take him from Bali to Jakarta this morning, and before he made the return flight he thought he would spend a little time on his own in Jakarta; he was in no hurry to return to the healing of his family. He walked around the streets of Old Batavia, wandering in and out of little shops; he bought a snow globe for Larkin, and then he was at a loss as to what to bring Mo. What did you get for the boy who wanted nothing, and who gave his father nothing? It was a cruel question, but he knew he was the wrong father for this little boy, whose problems had become more obvious with each passing month, leading Ash to ignore the pediatrician's blasé observations that some children need a long time to "settle." Ash had taken action and made the appointment at the Yale Child Study Center. "Whatever they say, I know we can trust," she'd said to Ethan. "I've read up on them."

Those were the words that did it. Ethan couldn't bear the idea that Mo would get an *incontrovertible* diagnosis, and that from then on, assuming it was bad (and he did assume it) they would have to reduce their expectations of him down to a sliver of soap. "The appointment is at ten a.m. on the twenty-third," Ash said. "We drive up and spend two full days there, staying in a hotel at night, and they watch Mo, and they also watch us interacting with Mo, and they give him a battery of tests and do some physical exams, and at the end of the whole thing we sit down with the team and they tell us their findings and their recommendations."

"I can't make it," Ethan said reflexively.

"What?"

He was shocked he'd said it, but now it was too late to take it back. He had to keep going. "I can't, I'm sorry. The twenty-third? Two days? I have meetings in LA. People are flying in from overseas. If I don't show up, then I'm insulting them."

"Can't you postpone the meetings?" she asked. "I mean, you're the top person."

"That's exactly why I can't. I'm sorry, I wish I could. I know, it's horrible of me, but there's nothing I can do."

"Well, I'll try to change the date at Yale," she said unpersuasively. "It generally takes a long time to get these appointments — some people wait a year or more — but, you know, I pulled strings. I guess I can pull them again, though I don't want to seem ungrateful by rejecting the date they gave me when there supposedly *were* no dates."

"You need to take him. Keep the date." He thought fast, then said, "Can Jules go with you?"

"Jules? Instead of you? You're Mo's father, Ethan."

"I feel terrible," Ethan said, and this was actually true, interpreted loosely.

So he had told his wife a bold and monstrous lie, and then, when the twenty-third arrived and he supposedly had to be in LA, he hid out instead for two nights in the Royalton Hotel in New York, in a room that was chic but small, with a shower that was difficult to operate and a stainless steel sink that resembled a wok. Ash called Ethan's cell phone at the end of the first day, when there was nothing conclusive to say yet, and then again late in the afternoon at the end of the second day, when the diagnosis of PDD-NOS had been given — a diagnosis that meant Mo was on the "spectrum." She spoke to Ethan from the car, crying as she talked, and he kept extremely calm and told her he loved her. She didn't ask whether he still loved Mo; that question wouldn't have occurred to her. Ethan spoke to Ash for a while and then asked to speak to Jules, and cool as anything he asked Jules whether she could stay at the house that night with Ash, to comfort her. When Ethan got off the phone, he ordered room service for himself, and when it came he quickly gobbled the steak and the fingerling potatoes and the creamed spinach and drank half the bottle of wine. After pushing the cart out into the hallway he watched a porno film about cheerleaders and pathetically jerked off to it, and then he slept, his mouth open, barnyard loud.

Now he decided on buying a pinwheel for Mo from a shop, and he carried it through the streets, actually liking the clicking it made as the spokes turned. Ethan sat in a sleepy-looking restaurant in a very old building, eating noodles in broth from a blue bowl, loudly sucking each one up in a way that would have embarrassed his wife if she was here, which luckily she wasn't. He sucked away. He was reading the book he'd brought with him on this vacation: Günter Grass's *The Tin Drum,* which had been Goodman's favorite back when they were teenagers. This copy — Goodman's copy, he knew, for the name was written clearly on the flyleaf in superslanted high-school handwriting — had sat on Ash and Ethan's bookshelf all these years, and he'd never thought to read it. Ethan barely had time to read books anymore. He had recently found himself reading an article on the Web about hedge funds, absorbed in this subject as thoroughly as if it were *literature,* thinking about his own money as he kept reading, wondering whether he should invest with the charismatic guy who was being profiled — and he caught himself doing this and was shocked. He'd been lulled and snared by the pulsing screen and the promise of money begetting more money. It happened to people all the time; it had happened to him.

So when he saw the Günter Grass novel on the shelf at home he'd felt a tremendous and sad longing to connect with the book, and with Ash's brother, his old, lost friend. Goodman had been torn away, taking *lightness* with him. Ethan wanted that early lightness back — he wanted schmucky, lively Goodman back, and all the goofing around they'd done, and then the talks after lights-out in the teepee, the discussions about what they'd like to do to Richard Nixon, what they'd *physically like to do* to him, which wasn't pretty; and about sex, and fear of death, and whether there was an afterlife. Ethan wanted all that back, but instead what he had was Goodman's copy of *The Tin Drum,* and he handled it reverently, making sure not to splash broth on it as he sat in that Jakarta restaurant. He was sitting with his noodles and his novel, feeling sorry for himself, when he suddenly imagined how others saw him. The people at the factory this morning must have thought of him as just another rich American idiot who wanted to reassure himself that everything in the world was fine. Everything is fine, rich American idiot, Mr. Wahid had essentially told him as he gave Ethan the nickel tour, and then showed him the door. As soon as he left, did they all cheer? Did the workers take out a pillow with Wally Figman's face on it and kick it around like a football, then stomp on it and shred it to bits?

Ethan stood up suddenly, breathlessly, knocking his shin against the table leg. He paid for his meal quickly, leaving too many bills, and then he headed outside into the street, where he waved his arms clumsily to hail a *bajaj,* one of the orange three-wheel taxis that ferried passengers around the city. The *bajaj* whipped down the street, and when it turned a corner, Ethan felt sure that the back two wheels would be sheared off, and he would instantly smash into a wall. *"Ethan Figman, 36, creator of* Figland, *dead in traffic accident in Jakarta"* the headline would read.

Arriving back at the Leena Toys Factory, he was relieved to still have his pass with him, and the guard waved him through the gates, distracted. Ethan stood in the courtyard, unsure of who he should confront now and what he should say. Probably he should find Mr. Wahid again, and state his case to him forcefully, saying, You told me there was nothing more for me to see, but I don't think that's true. But he imagined he would get no satisfaction from that man. No one had admitted to anything, and they weren't going to start now. Ethan pushed through the heavy metal doors, and went back onto the hot floor. At first, he perceived only the same clatter and heat, but then he sensed that it was a little different now, a little louder and more crowded. The machines were all in use, he realized; there were no spaces between people. Beside a hunched-over man was a hunched-over smaller man, and Ethan came closer to look at the face, which was not wizened or even settled into an acceptance of a hard life. This was a teenager — thirteen? fourteen? — and he hadn't been here this morning. His head was dipped down and he was working with intensity, his hands buzzing around the machine. The man beside him looked up at Ethan with an expression of open anxiety. Busted, Ethan thought, busted. Across the way, was that a young girl? No, just an old woman with a delicate appearance. But there in the corner was a girl for certain, maybe twelve years old; it was hard to say. The underaged had not been here before when Ethan was given his tour; they had been told to come in late today, or to stay in their tiny, unlivable rooms until they were given the signal. It had all been arranged and handled brazenly, calmly, because their presence was as common as anything, was just the way it was, and because people knew Ethan Figman was some bleeding-heart liberal American animator who could put on funny voices and didn't know anything about anything — he was essentially an *infant* — and was tickled by big profits, but needed to be reassured that everything was fine. How many children were on this floor? he wondered, and he had no idea but figured it was at least a dozen. Each one had a dark face and dark eyes that were focused on holding a square of shitty fabric under the stuttering piston of a needle. It was unbearable.

He stood there surrounded, looking at the

children's faces and feeling as if he was coated in sensation, and after a while he had to close his eyes. But even with his eyes closed, he saw them; they were overrunning the factory floor, they were devoting their days to *Figland* merchandise, and he was ashamed of the smiling face of Wally Figman on all the pillows, and even ashamed of his daughter's happiness later that day when he presented her with the snow globe he'd bought. Then he thought of Mo, and knew that when he handed him the pinwheel, Mo would not be happy, would not be uplifted; but what could Ethan do? He was unable to open his own heart to his son. He felt *perverse*. He knew his detachment hadn't come about because he needed Mo to perform, the way Ash's parents had needed her to perform. Ethan and Ash had two children, a boy and a girl, like the Wolfs; and just as Goodman's lack of discipline had been intolerable to Gil Wolf, Mo's problems made Ethan feel as if the world would now see his own distorted nature, revealed through his son. Ethan had imagined his life was nearly perfect except for the flawed son; but the flaw was in the father.

He would start to atone for his detachment and emptiness. Standing in the heat and noise, facing the rows of bent heads, Ethan Figman willed himself to leave that long sleep in which you dream that the inhuman things that people do to one another on a distant continent have nothing to do with the likes of you.

The postcard didn't arrive in the Jacobson-Boyd mailbox until weeks later, having been ripped nearly in half and then taped back together. The trip from Bali to New York City had been almost too much for that oblong of stiff paper with the painting on its front of the Balinese god of love. But Ethan, when he went to visit Jules himself only a few days after his return, was in very good shape. With no warning he had called her and asked if he could come over.

"When?"

"Now."

"Now?"

It was the middle of the day on a Saturday, and Jules and Dennis's apartment was unkempt. Rory had been "learning" karate lately, and she frequently chopped the pencils and balsa wood sticks that Dennis bought her in bulk at the hardware store. The floor of the living room was littered with broken wood, and no one had the energy to clean it up. Dennis was still asleep. He'd been on yet another new antidepressant, and one of the side effects was that he was very, very sleepy. Shouldn't an antidepressant try to keep you in the world *more*? This one wasn't doing that. Jules had asked Dennis to talk to Dr.

Brazil about this, but she had no idea if he had.

"Yeah. Now," said Ethan.

"I don't have anything in the house," Jules said. "And I look like crap."

"I doubt it."

"Also, Dennis is sleeping. The place is pretty chaotic. By which I mean it's hell. I'm warning you: you would be walking into hell."

"You sure know how to entice me, you siren you," said Ethan.

It was unusual for Ethan to come over without Ash. Jules and Ethan had occasionally gone out for a meal on their own in recent years, but mostly in their thirties they saw each other in the context of being couples, then families. There used to be all those *couple* vacations, which had given Ethan and Jules a chance to sit together and talk, but after the children were born, the group vacations had mostly stopped. Now it had been a very long time since they'd seen each other alone, and it was almost as though they'd forgotten the perfection of their original, single-selves' friendship.

Jules hung up the phone in the living room and turned around. Behind her, Rory was dressed in her *gi,* with her arm raised in the air over the ledge of the table, hovering above a pencil. "Hi-*yaaaaa!*" she cried, and when the pencil cracked, she jumped in pleasure, as though there was even a chance that a

566

simple Ticonderoga no. 2 might be able to resist the side of the hand of a girl as strong as she was.

A while later, with Rory off in the bathroom doing experiments at the sink, and with Dennis still not having arisen, Jules watched the street from the living room window and saw the Town Car arrive. A driver got out and opened the back door, and Ethan appeared, scratching his head. Then the driver handed him a small bag, which Ethan took, and headed for the entrance of the walk-up building. Jules hoped he wasn't thinking of how poor the building looked, but was instead reminded that some people lived in a way that was modest but true to themselves — that some people had not entirely changed. Some people had no Town Car. What *was* a Town Car, and why did they call it that? What town did it refer to? The buzzer sounded and she let him in. Peering out the apartment door, she watched as Ethan Figman began to climb the four flights, slowing down as he rose. When he got to three and stopped for a moment, winded, she called down to him, "You're doing great! Almost at nineteen thousand feet!" He looked up at her and waved.

Once he got to five, he didn't make a show of what a big climb it had been. He seemed to know that Jules had developed a jokey attitude about living in a walk-up building only in order to deflect the comments she often heard from anyone who made the climb. Ethan put his arms around her, and Jules couldn't recall when they'd actually last embraced; in their foursome there were often kisses and hasty hugs, but because their lives were so scattered and children were always swirling and pulling, all touching had a distracted, thoughtless quality. Here, in the doorway, just the two of them, Ethan Figman hugged Jules Jacobson-Boyd with what seemed to her like undiluted and almost overwhelming feeling.

"Hi, you," he said.

"Hi, you." She pulled back and looked at him. He was mostly the same: still indisputably homely, but he now had more sun in his face, and seemed somehow less burdened than usual. "Did you sunbathe on Bali or something?" she asked.

"Nope," he said. "But I walked around Jakarta. That was interesting. Can we go in? I have things that need to be eaten."

He had brought her the best brioches in New York City. "They're as warm as baby birds," Jules said when she opened the bag. "Peep, peep, peep."

"Where is everyone?" Ethan asked.

"Dennis hasn't put in an appearance yet. Rory is making penicillin in the bathroom sink. I know she'll want to come out and see you before too long."

They sat on the living room couch, eating the small, buttery things. Neither Ash nor Dennis was a big eater; Ash was too tiny for that, and Dennis's appetite had flattened out in recent years, though he still weighed a little too much from the different drugs. Jules and Ethan, though, now sat in sated silence. She thought again of Ethan's walk-in refrigerator, which 'had survived the move from the Tribeca loft to the Charles Street brownstone; she knew how differently stocked it would be if she were the one married to him. These brioches would always be on hand, along with the brick of farm butter he had brought. You would walk into that cold room and find anything that people like Ethan and Jules liked.

How was it possible that she still related so closely to him, and he to her? There was a bit of butter dotting his lip right now, and probably there was a bit of butter dotting hers. Ethan seemed curiously happy today. The purpose of the visit, she was sure, was to once again discuss the monetary gift that he and Ash wanted to give her and Dennis. He would offer them several thousand dollars, maybe even as much as five or ten thousand, and she would feel sick at the offer, so much did they need that money, but so unwilling would she be to take it, particularly because Dennis wouldn't want them to.

It was probably for the best that Dennis

was still in bed. He didn't need to be part of this, after they'd already gone over it so uncomfortably at brunch recently. She would continue to put Ethan off, despite the fact that she and Dennis owed so much to two different credit card companies, and to the well-intentioned but mostly useless Dr. Brazil. Jules also still had student loans to pay, as well as estimated quarterly taxes. Once, they had thought of having a second child, but between her single income and Dennis's depression, it was a bad idea. Plus, you needed to have sex in order to get pregnant, and that wasn't happening very often anymore. Everything had slowed, was stopping.

"Now look," Ethan began.

"I don't want you to do this, Ethan."

"You don't know what I'm going to do," he said. "I was going to start off by telling you a story about something that happened in Indonesia."

"Oh," she said, and she sat back, a little surprised but still suspicious. "All right. Go ahead."

Ethan drank the coffee she'd served to him in a *Figland* mug that he must have given them years earlier. He held it up high now and looked at the bottom of it, then put it down. "I asked to go see a factory," he said, "where they make some of the merchandise. There are different types of factories, ones for metals or plastics; they have these molds that they use. This particular factory was for textiles, and of course what I saw there, child labor, is a really common sight, but I just couldn't tolerate it. It just screams out at you, and you have to do something. You can't just keep going on your merry way. I know that how I came to it isn't great; it's like those Republicans who are against gun control until their wives are shot in the head. But I decided that I had to pull out of this whole thing, at least to whatever degree they'll let me. I called my lawyer and asked him what he thought we could ask for, and what he thought we could get. Then we had a huge conference call on the phone with Pushkin."

"I'm assuming this isn't the Russian writer."

"Pushkin has never read Pushkin. That tells you a little bit about who he is. If you shared a name with one of the great Russian writers, wouldn't you at least try to read him? Jack Pushkin is an executive at the studio, and he's not a bad guy at all. But when my lawyer told him that we wanted to move some of the merchandising out of the factories and bring it back to the States, he got really silent really fast. Obviously. It's incredibly complicated, and what's going to happen to those kids and their families, right? Will they keep working? Will they be okay? Is there something else that can be done for them? It's a terrible, terrible situation. These questions could break your head open."

"I can see that."

"I was thinking about all of that on the phone, while Pushkin and my lawyer were fighting, and then Pushkin hung up. He called back about two seconds later, very apologetic, and everybody had to get conferenced in again, which is not so easy when one of you is in Indonesia. They continued their talks without me, and by the time I got back to New York I found out that everybody tentatively agreed on the basic idea, though they're still haggling. It's a really huge deal. My lawyer said that if they didn't just say yes, it would make them look really bad. They're losing so much money on this, not just because of labor costs but because of the overseas tax breaks, which they're going to have to sacrifice for the greater good. So they're taking a hit, but at least I'm doing something I can live with — though who knows, maybe it'll turn out worse than it had been to begin with. Anyway, they get to send out a press release saying how proud they are that we're doing this thing. A small, as-yet-to-be-determined percentage of the manufacturing moved over here, to struggling factories in upstate New York. And I've just started talking to this woman at UNICEF about bringing in money to those workers, those kids. And I asked her whether it might be possible even to start a school for them over there. She said she'd put me in touch with some people. I know I still cause harm, probably a ton of it no matter what I do. And it kills me, it just kills me, that maybe the best you can ever do is cause less harm. But there you have it."

"I'm sorry, but I think you are the least harmful person I know," said Jules.

"Oh, I'm sure that isn't true," Ethan said. "But at least now I'm a harmful person who had an epiphany. I call it the Jakarta transformation. At least when I'm talking to myself."

"So what does Ash say?"

"She's supportive. She's not one of those critical spouses," he said. "You aren't either," he added after a moment, but Jules didn't say anything. "You wouldn't do that to Dennis. You just let him be himself, and go through what he has to go through."

"Do I have a choice?" asked Jules, and it came out so sour. "It's the middle of the day, and you and I are having a conversation about actual things, and eating actual food, while Dennis lies in bed."

Ethan gave her a long, considering look. "I know it's very hard for both of you," he said.

"He's so passive," she burst out. "We used to laugh all the time, and talk a lot, and have good sex — excuse me for saying that, Ethan — and he had a lot of energy. Then everything stopped. He's taken care of Rory, which has been a huge and admirable job, and stay-at-home parents never get enough credit, and I don't want to underplay what he's done. But you know he's still not fully here. He has no *desires* for himself. It's like when my father was dying, that same kind of slow-motion loss. But now it just goes on and on. A person who's half here and half not. I don't want that, and I feel so selfish saying it. I don't want him to go through this, of course, but I also think about Rory and me."

"And there's really nothing else he can try? It seems like everyone in the world is on an antidepressant, and they're always mixing and matching. I don't mean to take this lightly, but is there really nothing that can work?"

"Oh, you know, sometimes a new drug seems to be having an effect. And we get all hopeful. But then he tells me it's not working after all. Or else the side effects are bad. I see depressed people in my practice, but his depression, even though it's supposedly 'low-level,' is just so tenacious, and hard to treat. Atypical, they call it."

"If you want to experience over-the-top depression," said Ethan, "just go to Jakarta and see how those workers live. That'll really depress you."

"Just what I want," said Jules. "More depression in my life."

Rory appeared then in the entry of the living room, still wearing her *gi,* though the sleeves were now dripping from what she'd been doing in the sink. She bowed deeply to Ethan, who stood and bowed back. "Ethan, I've gotten very good at destroying wood," Rory said.

"That's good, Rory. Wood is *evil*. That's what I tell Larkin every day."

"I know you're teasing me. Want to see me destroy a piece of wood?"

"Naturally."

Rory placed a thick piece of wood on the edge of the table and said, "Hi-*yaaaaa*!" and split the thing in half. The wood went flying, some of it landing under the radiator. It would stay there for months, years, wedged in a small space even after the Jacobson-Boyd family moved out. The wood would go unnoticed for a very long time, like the library book that had been flung under the bureau during Rory's conception. Jules often thought of that night; she remembered Dennis in black tie, and how substantial he'd looked, how full of himself. That was it: Ethan was full, and Dennis now wasn't. Depression sprang a leak. Dennis was *leaking*.

"You're a genius at karate, kiddo," Ethan said, and then he pulled Rory onto his lap.

"You can't be a genius at karate," declaimed Rory.

"No, that's true. *I* can't. But *you* can."

Rory understood the joke and laughed chestily. "Ethan Figman, THAT'S NOT WHAT I MEANT!" she said in a voice that was so sure of itself and so deep that Jules sometimes referred to her as James Earl Jones. There was no point in telling Rory that she had to use her *inside voice;* she didn't really have any idea how to modulate. She was spirited, full of herself too, the way Jules had just been thinking Ethan was.

Rory slipped off, went to destroy more wood in the front hallway. Ethan said to Jules, "Okay, I have to leave. Ash wants me to look at some set designs for that Balinese play. But before I go, you and I have to talk about the thing between us. The horrible thing about one friend helping another."

"I never get to help *you,*" Jules said. "You're always helping me and Dennis and everyone else."

"Are you kidding?" he said. "You know you help me."

"Oh," she said. "You're talking about me going with Ash to the Yale Child Study Center? I know she brought that up at brunch, but it was no big deal. And anyway, I helped her that day more than you."

"You helped both of us." He looked at her for a long, unblinking moment, and then said, "All right. I'm going to tell you something now that I really wasn't planning on telling you. But I'm just going to do it. And once I do, you're obviously free to think anything you want about me." He crossed his arms, looked away and then looked back at her. "You know how I couldn't come that day because I was in LA?"

"Yes."

"I wasn't in LA. I was hiding out at the Royalton Hotel in midtown. I just couldn't bring myself to go up there and hear them give my son a definitive diagnosis. They were the experts, and once they said what I pretty much knew they were going to say, they couldn't unsay it. I should have gone up there with Ash. But I just couldn't bear it."

Jules stared at him, her eyes first wide, then narrow. "Really?" she said. "You did that?"

"I did that."

"Wow."

"Say something," Ethan said.

"I just did. I said wow. As in, I can't believe that you did something . . . so morally bad. And that you did it to Ash." Despite herself, Jules began to laugh.

"I can't imagine why you're laughing," said Ethan, who wasn't smiling at all, but appeared very somber and still.

"What you told me is just so unlikely," said Jules. "You did something really *not good,* and I don't know what to make of it."

"I've been telling you for a long time that I'm not so good. Why doesn't anyone believe me? Did you know that I yell at people too? People I work with? I never used to do that, but everything's become so stressful. I yelled at one of the writers and called him a hack.

Then I spent the entire table read apologizing to him. My temper is short, and I've made some horrible decisions. You know the spin-off *Alpha*? The one that just got shelved? The studio lost a shitload of money on that because I insisted it would work. I sort of convinced myself that everything related to *Figland* would turn to gold. But that can't happen if it isn't good; and the spin-off was pretty lame. But I pushed it through because I got delusional about the *Figland* brand. They're all mad at me over there, but they won't say it. This has actually not been a good moment for me professionally, but I act like it is. And I hid out in a hotel room for two nights while you went up to New Haven with Ash to have Mo diagnosed."

"I really cannot believe you did that," Jules said. It was terrible what Ethan had done to Ash, abandoning her at such an important moment, but the fact that he hadn't confessed it to Ash, and had confessed it to Jules instead, gave this exchange a sudden intimacy.

He looked at her with his familiar, searching eyes, and said, miserably, "I don't even know that I love him."

Jules gave this a moment, and it seemed rude to refute it, but she felt strongly that she had to. She folded her arms and said, "I think you do."

"I'm telling you, I don't know."

"You don't have to know. Just do the right things around him. Be loving. Be attentive. Don't leave it all on Ash again, okay? Just say to yourself, This is love, even if it doesn't feel like it. And then go barreling ahead even when you feel cheated that this is how things have turned out. He's your little boy, Ethan. Love him and love him."

Ethan was silent, and then he nodded. "Okay," he said. "I will try to do that. I will really try, Jules. But Jesus, there is nothing of Old Mo in my kid. Nothing." Then he added, worriedly, "You won't tell Ash?"

"No." But Jules thought, suddenly, that if Ethan told Ash, then maybe Ash could tell him about Goodman. It was all about leverage, and Ash would have it at that moment. But Ash wouldn't want to do that; she would never want to.

Ethan said, "All right, that's enough about this. Thank you for letting me unburden myself to you. Please don't hate me, at least not overtly. I will really think about what you said. And now here's the part that's not about me; here's the part about you and Dennis. Every day, in my work life, there are people who want me to give them something because it's my job to do that, and then there are other people who want me to give them something because they think it'll advance their careers. I usually end up saying yes to everyone, regardless, because it's easier that way. When in fact the person I really want to give something to is you. You and Dennis," he amended. Ethan reached into his pocket and felt around. *"Shit,"* he said. "I know I brought it." He frisked himself. "God, where is it? Oh wait, here we go." Ethan extracted a small, folded piece of paper and smoothed it out; it was a bank check with his signature on it. He handed it to her and she saw that it was made out to her and Dennis, in the amount of one hundred thousand dollars.

"No!" Jules said. "This is a ridiculous amount. And Dennis will never let you do it."

"Is it fair to let a depressed person call the shots?" Jules didn't answer him. "This'll make life a little easier," Ethan said. "That's something that money can really do. You know I'm not really into things — but money isn't just for *things*. In my experience it also paves your life, so you don't have to think about all the constant worries and problems. It just makes everything run so much more smoothly."

"We could never pay it back."

"I don't want you to. The point is that you work really hard, you're dedicated, and New York is so tough and unforgiving. Dennis will come around eventually. Something will change for him, I know it will. But in the meantime you've got to leave this apartment, Jules. It's a step. Go put a down payment on someplace bright and modern that gives you a hopeful feeling each day. I'll cosign the mortgage. I want you to feel like you're getting a new start, even if you aren't, exactly. Sometimes you just have to trick yourself a little. Move someplace with an elevator; those stairs are a bitch. Also, give Rory her own room already. She needs it! And buy her some more pencils and wood and whatever else she wants. There's nothing worse than money anxiety. I used to hear my parents arguing about money, and I was positive they were tearing each other's flesh from their bones. I thought that in the morning they'd come out of their bedroom with their skin hanging off. Plus, constantly worrying about money is *boring.* Use your brain to think about your clients and their problems. Use it to be creative."

"There's no way I can take a hundred thousand dollars from you." Jules held out the check and tried to tuck it back into his shirt pocket.

"Hey, what are you doing?" he said, dodging her, laughing slightly. "Come on, take it, Jules, take it."

"I can't," she said.

"I'm sorry, you have to, I'm afraid it's too late," Ethan said, and he stood and backed away, as though there were nothing he could do about it now.

■ ■ ■ ■

A little while after Ethan left, Rory stormed
the bedroom where Dennis slept, climbed up
on the bed, and stood above him. When he
opened his eyes in the darkened room his
daughter was looming, one leg on either side
of his chest. "Daddy," she announced. "Guess
what? Ethan Figman gave Mom *a hundred
dollars.* And he said, 'Take it, Jules, take it.' I
heard them from the hallway. A hundred dollars," she boomed, scandalized.

Dennis got out of bed and came into the
living room. "Ethan was here?" he asked.

"Yeah," Jules said. "He called and asked if
he could come over. He brought some really
good brioches, if you want one."

"I don't want his really good brioches.
And as you already know, I don't want his
money. Was it all in twenties or one crisp
new bill? I mean, this is so pathetic, Jules,
so humiliating, I can't believe it. Why would
you *take* it? What are you, a homeless person?"

"What are you talking about, Dennis?"

"Rory told me about the hundred dollars."

"Oh, she did?" Jules laughed in a single,
hollow syllable.

"What?" he said, confused.

She brought over the check, holding it out
to him in such a way that, when discussing it

582

later, he could not say she had *thrust* it at him.

Dennis took it, looked at it, and closed his eyes. "Jesus," he said. He sat down on the couch and put his hands to his head. "I was insulted by the idea of a hundred dollars. But now I'm much more insulted. I don't know what to do anymore."

"Dennis, it's okay," Jules said.

"If you want to get out of this marriage, then just do it," he said. "You didn't ask for this."

"I'm not saying anything like that. Why are you talking about it?"

"This isn't good. I was fun to be with back before the stroke, back before they changed my meds, wasn't I?"

"Yes, of course."

"God, I hate the word 'meds.' I hate that it's something I have to think about. I try to remember, *I was fun, and I can be fun again.* But I keep finding myself unable to do that. Or else I do something all wrong. That girl from Kentucky with the liver mass — if it was malignant she's probably dead by now. Oh Jesus, now I'm going to obsess about her again. Everything is such an effort. I'm not crisp like you and Rory. And I know I'm going to lose you."

"You're not," said Jules. Here he was in the middle of the day, in soft, creased clothes. He had lost all crispness the night he ate the food

583

containing hidden stores of tyramine, and then she and everyone had continued marching through the world while he struggled. He might lose her if they stayed as they were. She saw this now, and it was like looking ahead to the very sad ending of a novel, then quickly shutting the book, as if that could keep it from happening. "Dennis, we have to get out of this moment in our lives," she said. "We have to leave this place, for starters. This apartment. You have to keep trying whatever you can try. Newer medications. More exercise. Mindfulness. Whatever. But I think, just this one time, we need to accept Ethan and Ash's help."

Dennis looked at her searchingly, and then Rory reappeared; her timing was always exact in this way, as though she was guided by electrical impulses that led her toward the heat in any given, tense moment. She stood before her parents, looking from one face to the other. "Is that the hundred dollars?" she asked her father.

"Yes."

Satisfied, Rory looked at her mother, and who knew what complexities caused her to make the request, the demand, that she then made. "Mommy, kiss Daddy," she said.

"What?" said Jules.

"Kiss Daddy. I want to see."

"A kiss is kind of private, babe," Dennis said, but Jules took him by both sides of his face and pulled him toward her; he did not resist. Their eyes were closed, but they could hear Rory laugh — a low, satisfied laugh, as if she knew the full extent of her power.

FIFTEEN

Then they were in another place half a dozen blocks north, a cleaner, brighter place, "an elevator building!" they remarked to each other with wonder, as if such a thing were unheard of. They actually owned this apartment, and on moving day, when the miracle elevator took them upstairs to their new, bright, though slapped-together rooms with the smell of paint and polished floors, they felt as if they had been saved. They weren't saved; they'd only been transplanted somewhere different and better, in a co-op whose mortgage Ethan had cosigned. And Dennis's depression was certain to hang around like a paint smell that wouldn't fade, but still it was something. The movers worked, dropping everything in the middle of the rooms. The same framed posters — *Threepenny Opera,* a Georgia O'Keeffe animal skull — which they'd outgrown but could not yet replace, would soon decorate these new walls. Ash came over to help in the afternoon, and as a joke she wore one of the moving company's red T-shirts. SHLEPPERS, it read. Who knew how she'd gotten one from them? She went right to work, tearing open cartons and helping assemble Rory's bedroom — an actual bedroom of her own, not just a corner of a living room turned into a bedroom at night. Jules could hear them, Ash's soft voice inquiring, and then Rory's loud voice intoning, "Don't put the Rollerblades away, Ash. Mom and Dad say I can wear them IN THE APARTMENT like my Indian moccasin slippers." They were in there together, the best friend and the little girl, until the room was completely unpacked. At eight in the evening Ash was still at the new apartment, and they all ate Vietnamese food from what would become their primary takeout restaurant for over twelve years, until it closed during the recession of 2008. Jules tore the plastic wrap and packing tape from the couch and they sat on it with plates and silverware they had dug up from boxes marked KITCHEN 1 and KITCHEN 2. Rory ate too many spring rolls, one after another, then belched appreciatively and went into her new room and fell asleep in her clothes. The three adults were hopeful — even, guardedly, Dennis.

"This is going to be good," Ash said. "I'm excited for you."

She sat with them, talking about the apartment and her theater company and about how great Mo's therapists were, and how he'd already shown some improvement. "He's working so hard with Jennifer and Erin. He's my hero, that boy." Ethan was in Hong Kong this week, and Ash was keeping all the parts of their lives going.

"When you have a child," she'd recently said to Jules, "it's like right away there's this grandiose fantasy about who he'll become. And then time goes on and a funnel appears. And the child gets pushed through that funnel, and shaped by it, and narrowed a little bit. So now you know he's not going to be an athlete. And now you know he's not going to be a painter. Now you know he's not going to be a linguist. All these different possibilities fall away. But with Mo, I've seen a lot of things fall away, really fast. Maybe they'll be replaced by other things I can't even imagine now; I really don't know. But I met this mother recently who said that she'd become so grateful that her child is high-functioning. She said she'd become proud of the term *high-functioning,* as if it was the same as *National Merit Scholar.*"

Jules thought about her own child, and though she had the suspicion that Rory would have a life that wasn't gilded with specialness and privilege, she knew Rory wouldn't even want that kind of life. She was happy with herself; that was apparent. And the child who was happy with herself meant the parents had won the jackpot. Rory and Larkin might well do fine; Mo, with his long, anxious face and active fingers — who knew?

On the night of the move, Ash went home at around ten, saying she was exhausted, and joking that she and the other Shleppers had a job in the morning in Queens. That night, not too far away, on the sixth floor of the Labyrinth, Ash's mother Betsy Wolf, age sixty-five, was awakened from sleep by a headache so tremendous she could only whimper "Gil," and touch her head to show him what was wrong. It was a bleed to the brain, and she died immediately. Later, after the trip to the hospital and the paperwork, Ash called Jules, barely able to speak, and the ringing phone in the night and the crying friend told the story. Ethan was in Hong Kong, Ash reminded her; could Jules come over now? Of course, Jules said, I'll be right there, and she dressed in the darkness of the new, unfamiliar apartment among the unpacked boxes, and went down in the elevator in the middle of the night to find a cab.

She had not been to the Labyrinth for years now; there had been no reason to go there anymore, and on the ride up in the gold elevator she held her arms around herself, feeling sad and full of dread as she rose. Ash opened the apartment door and fell against Jules so hard it was as if she had been flung. Having lost her mother, she appeared so different from how she'd been all afternoon and evening, helping Rory put her room together, then sitting around with everyone, eating sugarcane shrimp. "What am I going to do?" Ash said. "How can I not have a mother? How can I not have *my* mother? We just talked tonight, when I got home from your new place. And now — she doesn't exist anymore?" A fresh bout of almost assaulted-sounding weeping began.

Jules kept her arm around her and they stood together for a couple of minutes. Behind Ash, the apartment revealed itself dimly, both real and somehow like a stage set for this apartment instead of the actual place. She took in the wide foyer and then the living room, and the long hallway that led to all those bedrooms where the Wolfs had lived and slept. Jules tried to think of something to say to Ash, but all she could do was agree with her. "It's terrible," she said. "Your mother was an amazing person. She wasn't supposed to die so young." Or ever, was what Jules meant. Betsy Wolf at sixty-five had still been a beauty. She was a docent at the Met, and taught an art class there for children on Saturdays. Everyone always said how young and elegant she looked.

When Jules's father had died, that had been a tragedy too, even more of one if you thought of it in terms of age. "Forty-two," Ethan had once marveled. "So fucking unfair." Jules wanted to explain to Ash how the death of a parent is such a big and inexpressible event that all you can do against it is shut yourself down. That was what Jules — Julie — had originally done. She'd shut herself down, and she hadn't started herself up again until that summer when she first met the rest of them. Julie would have done all right on her own, Jules suddenly thought. She would have been fine, would probably have been pretty happy.

Finally Ash extricated herself and walked ahead into the living room, so Jules followed. What was it about the place now — what made it seem frayed? Maybe it could have used a paint job, or maybe it had immediately absorbed the death of Betsy Wolf, so that everything about this room and this apartment that had once been warm and glittering had now been dimmed and dulled — and even the familiar lamps and rugs and ottomans were symbols not of comfort and familiarity but of something useless, wasteful, even awful. Ash threw herself down on the loosely slipcovered couch and put her hands over her face.

Almost immediately there was a sound, and Jules turned to see Ash's father standing in the entrance of the living room. While in her new grief Ash looked like a young girl, Gil Wolf just looked old. He wore a bathrobe; his silver hair was tufted and he seemed bewildered and slow. "Oh," he said. "Jules. You're here."

She gave him a careful hug, saying, "I'm so sorry about Betsy."

"Thank you. We had a good marriage," he said. "I just thought it would be so much longer." Then he shrugged, and coughed away a sob, this thin man in his sixties with the soft androgynous face that aging seemed to bring, as though all the hormones were finally mixed up in a big coed pot because it just didn't matter anymore. He looked over at Ash and said, "That sleeping pill you gave me hasn't kicked in."

"It will, Dad. Give it a little time. Just go lie down."

"Did you call?" he asked with anxiety.

Jules didn't know what this meant, but then immediately she did: Did you call your brother?

"I'm about to." Ash helped her father down the hall to bed, and then she went into her old bedroom to make the call. Jules didn't dare follow her, not wanting to see the mausoleum bedrooms that had once belonged to Ash and Goodman. She stayed in the living room, sitting stiffly in an armchair. Ash's mother *did not exist* anymore, Ash had said. Betsy's hair, in its bun, the strays coming loose in filaments, did not exist; the New Year's Eve parties she'd overseen did not exist; the *lat-kees* she'd fried in a pan each

Chanukah did not exist. Goodman had gone into hiding, but Betsy was the one who was gone.

Ash's mother's funeral was held four days later at the Ethical Culture Society, where Jules had attended memorials for various men who had died of AIDS, and then the wedding of her teepeemate Nancy Mangiari. For Betsy's funeral they all had to wait for Ethan to return from Hong Kong on the network's private jet. Jules's own mother had said she wanted to come to the funeral. "But why, Mom?" Jules asked irritably on the phone. "You didn't really know Ash's mother. You only met her at the airport once, like a hundred years ago in 1977, when I went to Iceland with them."

"I know," said Lois. "I remember it well. They were very generous, taking you along like that. And Ash has always been so dear. I'd like to pay my respects."

So Lois Jacobson took the Long Island Railroad into the city from Underhill and attended the funeral with Jules. It was an openly emotional memorial, crowded with family friends and relatives; it seemed as if everyone connected with the Wolfs wanted to speak. Cousin Michelle, who'd gotten married in the Wolfs' living room and danced to "Nights in White Satin" and was now, incredibly, about to be a *grandmother,* spoke about Betsy's generosity. Jules herself stood and said a few stiff words about loving the sensation of being around the Wolf family, though as she spoke she realized she didn't want to go too far and hurt her own mother's feelings. With Lois in the room, she couldn't say, "When I was with them, I was happier than I'd ever thought I could be." She kept her remarks very brief, and looked right at Ash, who was having a very hard time getting through this. Ethan's arm was around her, steadying her, but Ash could barely be steadied. On her other side sat Mo, in a shirt and tie. He sat forward in his seat, both hands driving a Game Boy, as if he could steer himself away from this entire event.

After Jules, Jonah stood and spoke, handsome in his dark, tailored suit, while in his seat to the side, Robert Takahashi watched him closely. Jonah so rarely spoke in front of a gathering of people; he didn't perform, he didn't do this sort of thing. The last time might have been at Ash and Ethan's wedding. But here he was now, and everyone seemed to like looking at him, and listening to him. "I had many dinners at the Wolfs' apartment when I was young," he said. "Everyone tended to stay at the table for a long time, and there was always joking around, and really good conversation, and amazing meals. I tasted foods there that I'd never had in my life. My own mother was a vegetarian long before you could be one and actually eat well.

So our meals at home were a little . . . you know. But whenever I went over to the Wolfs' apartment, Betsy would be in the kitchen whipping something up. One night she served a new pasta, and she told us it was called orzo, and she spelled it out for me when I asked. O-R-Z-O. But I remembered the name wrong, and I kept going into supermarkets and asking, 'Do you carry ozro? O-Z-R-O.' And no one knew what I was talking about." There was laughter. "But you know, God, this was all so long ago," Jonah added. "I just . . ." He stopped, unsure of what to say. "I just want to say that I'd give anything for another one of Betsy's meals."

Finally Larkin, barely five and a half, stood and walked to the podium, tipping the microphone down, and said in a hoarse voice, "I'm going to read a poem I wrote for Grandma B." First, it was strange enough that Larkin looked almost exactly the way Ash had looked in the photos from when she was that young. Larkin's beauty had somehow been untouched by the Ethanness in her, which had revealed itself in the brain and on the surface of the skin, but not in the facial features; today Larkin wore a dress that covered her arms, and Jules thought she knew why.

The poem was very precocious and moving: "Her warm hand could always cool our fevers," was one of the lines, and Larkin cried as she read it, her nose and mouth twisting to the side. At the end she said, "Grandma B., I'll never forget you!" Her voice broke, and much of the room cried in one swoop at the sight of this overcome little girl. Jules suddenly thought of how Goodman should have been here. First he had missed his dog's death — a rehearsal, in the scheme of things — and now *this,* the real event.

Maybe everyone in the room was thinking about Goodman too. Jules wondered if he'd wanted to come to the funeral, if he'd even discussed with Ash the possibility of flying here and showing up. Jules looked toward the door in the back, as if she expected him to be lurking beneath the exit sign, taking his chances that no one here would dare to turn him in. She could see him standing with his head bowed, his shoulders set, and his hands folded, a tall middle-aged man dressed in the clothes of someone who had been traveling on a plane all night. But because Jules had not seen Goodman for nineteen years, all she could picture was his young handsome face juxtaposed with gray-stippled hair.

Goodman was lightly mentioned in the female minister's list of the people Betsy had left behind. Frequently when Jules looked at Ash and Ethan during the service, Ash was bent over, as if her mother's death had brought her near death herself. Ethan had his arm around her the entire time. He was dropping everything for a while, he'd said when he returned from Hong Kong; he was canceling a speech at Caltech, postponing meetings about the Keberhasilan School that he was trying to create in Jakarta. Finally, when the head of the Ethical Culture Society seemed to be making her way toward wrapping up, Mo, who had been absorbed in his Game Boy, threw it to the floor with a dull crash and then shrieked as if scalded and sprang up. He twisted away from his sister and mother, and there was a commotion as someone by the door blocked him from running out, and the service was hastily brought to a close.

Jules took her mother in a cab back to Penn Station after the reception. Even now, Lois Jacobson wasn't comfortable getting around the city by herself. Manhattan had never felt like a hospitable place to her; instead, it was a place where you might spend a lively but exhausting day seeing a Broadway show or shopping at Bloomingdale's, and then at the end of it you would make a break for the train as fast as you could. Jules's sister, Ellen, was the same way. She and her husband, Mark, lived in a house two towns away from Underhill and ran a party-rental company. Ellen had once remarked that she didn't need the "excitement" that Jules had always needed since she first went to Spirit-in-the-Woods, and this was probably true.

"Don't be a stranger," Lois Jacobson actually said at the entrance to the track in Penn Station that night. Beyond it, the Long Island Railroad train awaited with all its steaming, gastric sounds. They kissed cheeks, and Jules's mother, with her raincoat and pale gray hair, seemed fragile, although maybe it was just that Jules was seeing her now through the warning light of another mother's death.

That night, in the new apartment, Jules slept poorly, thinking of Ash, and Betsy, and how everyone simply had to wait patiently in order to lose the people they loved one by one, all the while acting as if they weren't waiting for that at all. Neither she nor Dennis had been able to find the mattress cover among the boxes yet, and finally one elastic corner of the bedsheet unattached itself, and Jules woke up in the morning on a bare mattress, like a political prisoner. Dennis was already in the kitchen with Rory, making breakfast. It was a school day — also an egg day, from the smell of it. She wondered if Dennis had been able to turn up a spatula from one of the still unpacked kitchen boxes, and then she thought, *Oh, Ash's mother is dead.* The spatula and the death of Betsy Wolf occupied the same part of her brain, briefly given equal weight. Jules lay on the uncovered mattress inhaling paint, and when the phone rang, her hand was on it before Dennis could get to the other extension in the kitchen. It must be

Ash, she thought. Probably Ash had been awake all night crying, and now morning was here and she would need more comfort. Jules had a client at ten a.m., a new mother who was terrified of dropping her baby. She couldn't cancel.

But after she said hello, a man's voice said, "Hey," under an ambient hiss.

Whenever a voice spoke into the phone but didn't announce its owner, Jules thought it might be a client. "Who's this?" she would ask neutrally, and so she asked it now.

"You don't recognize me," he said.

Jules gave herself an extra second to think, just the way she did in therapy sessions. The hiss of the call was a clue, but it wasn't just that. She thought she knew who it was, and she sat up, grasping the blanket around the open front of her nightgown and her freckly, sleep-warm chest. "Goodman?"

"Jacobson."

"Really?"

"Yeah. I just wanted to call you," Goodman said. "Ethan told Ash he's not going anywhere for a few weeks. He wants to be with her. So Ash said she won't be able to call me too much, even on her supersecret Batphone." Jules still didn't know what she could say; she wasn't composed, she was thrown. She heard a match being struck, and she imagined Goodman balancing a cigarette on his lip, tipping his chin up to meet the match.

"I'm so sorry about your mother," she finally said. "She was wonderful."

He said, "Yeah, thanks, she was pretty great. It's a fucking shame," and then he didn't say anything else, just smoked a little, and Jules heard ice knocking around in a glass. It was only four hours later where he was, eleven a.m., but maybe he was already drinking. Goodman asked, "So what was it like?"

"What?"

"The funeral."

"It was good," she said. "It felt like something she would have wanted. No references to God. Everyone spoke, and they were genuine. They all really loved her."

"Who's everyone."

Jules named several different people, including Jonah, and cousin Michelle, and then she said, "Larkin read a poem she wrote, really moving, really precocious. It had a line in it about how your mother's warm hand could cool a fever." As soon as she said this, she realized that Goodman had never even met his niece. Larkin was just a concept to him, a generic niece in a photograph.

"That's right, it really could," he said. "She took good care of Ash and me when we were kids. I don't get to see my parents very often, obviously. When they come over here they look more shrunken, especially my dad. I always thought he would go first. I can't believe I'll never see my mom again," he said, and his voice thickened, became froggy.

Then Goodman started to cry, and Jules's eyes responsively filled too; together they cried across an ocean, and she tried to picture the room he was in, the flat he lived in, but all she could come up with was a murky brown and gold decor, a color scheme she'd retrieved in her mind from the way the Café Benedikt had looked that night in 1977. He'd never thought to call her before; she had always been of little interest to him. He was still probably arrogant, but he was also broken up. Most recently, when Goodman's name had come up, Ash had said, "Don't ask." Goodman was described as a lost cause, "kind of a mess." Over all this time, whenever Jules intermittently thought about him, she was aware he rarely thought about her. But even with this disparity she felt tenderly toward him now. Motherly, because like his sister he was motherless. Goodman made a sound of nose blowing, and then she just heard breathing on the line. She waited it out, the way she did in therapy, being sympathetic and in no hurry. Though really, she thought, it was time to get up. She wanted to say good-bye to Rory before school; she wanted to shower. She waited for him to stop crying.

"Will you be okay?" Jules finally asked when he was quiet.

"I don't know."

"Do you have, you know, someone to talk to there?"

"Someone to talk to? Like, some Icelandic version of Dr. Spilka?" Goodman asked. "Right, Ash said you're a shrink now. So you believe in all that."

"I meant like a friend."

"A girlfriend?"

"Or a group of friends," she said. "It doesn't matter."

"Do I have a group of friends to sit around a teepee with in Reykjavik? Is that what you're asking me?" His voice was challenging now, not tearful.

"I don't know what I'm asking," Jules said. "I'm extemporizing. You can't just call me as if this is *casual.* I mean, come on."

"Some things never change, right?"

"What does that mean?"

"You were always a little into me," Goodman said. "We even had a moment once, in my parents' living room, remember? A little *tongue,* I believe." He laughed lightly, teasing her, and she heard some relaxed pouring, then more ice.

"I don't remember that," Jules said in a new, formal voice, hot-faced.

"Oh, I'm sure you remember everything from that time," he said. "I know how important it all was to you. Summers at camp. The *Interestings.*"

"It was just as important to you," she tartly

said. "You got to be a big deal at Spirit-in-the-Woods, and your father wasn't there to criticize you. You were in heaven there. It wasn't just me."

"You do have a good memory," was all he would say.

"Look, Goodman, I realize you're really upset about your mother," said Jules. "And I know it's been hard for you living so far away. But I'm sure Ash will find a way to call you soon. And you two can talk about everything. But this is too strange for me. I can't do this now. I'm sorry." Her voice stuck a little. "I think I'm going to hang up," Jules said. Goodman didn't say anything, so then she added, pointlessly, "I'm hanging up." She returned the phone to its cradle, then for two full minutes she sat in bed, waiting, hearing sounds of pans and plates, and the deep voices of Dennis and Rory, and finally she picked up the receiver again, making sure he was really gone.

Over time, the two couples continued to live their lives, sometimes separately, sometimes not, but always differently from each other. One couple traveled the world. The other couple unpacked the rest of their boxes and hammered the same old posters up on the walls, and placed the same lightweight silverware in a drawer. They became used to having an elevator, and barely remembered all those stairs they'd climbed. The apartment allowed them to breathe a little, though it seemed that always they would live with certain indignities; one day a mouse tore across the kitchen floor, and Jules insisted to Dennis that this was the *same mouse* from their previous apartment. It had followed them all the way here to their new apartment, like one of those dogs that goes out into the world searching for its master and eventually, miraculously finds him.

Ash grieved for a long time for her mother, and called Jules a lot, wanting to talk, asking her if she was being too much of a pain. "How could you be a pain?" Jules said. Ethan, following his run of bad fortune with *Alpha,* the failed spin-off of *Figland,* had a failure so big and public and expensive that it seemed to threaten the whole Figland enterprise. An article ran in the *Hollywood Reporter* called "An End to All Things Figman?" Ethan had created and written a high-budget animated feature film called *Dam It!* using animated beaver characters to tell the story of the plight of child labor. It received bad reviews and did poorly, as Jules had warned him it would when he first told her he was thinking of trying to develop it as an idea. "Are you sure you want to do that?" she'd said. "It just sort of sounds unappealing and preachy, Ethan. Just stick to the actual cause. You don't have to make it into a cartoon."

"Other people have been really encouraging about it," he'd replied. "And Ash likes it." But other people usually said yes to Ethan, and Ash was generally encouraging to him too; it was her way. "The *Ishtar* of cartoons," wrote the *Reporter.* Every failure was the *Ishtar* of something; years later, Ethan would pronounce the Iraq war was the *Ishtar* of wars. No one at the studio blamed Ethan openly, but of course it was his fault, he explained to his friends over dinner one night, because the urgent work of the Anti-Child-Labor Initiative apparently did not translate into *whimsy.* "I should have listened to you, Jules," he said moodily, looking at her across the table. "I should always listen to you."

After the movie's terrible opening weekend, Ethan took several days off and stayed in the house on Charles Street, but there he was made more aware than ever of how, when you took away work, you were left with the actual meat of your personal life: in this case, specifically, the developmental disability of his son. His young son, Mo, who was fractious and often unresponsive, and cried and cried, and was given therapy throughout the week by a rotation of teachers and therapists. Kind young women still streamed through the house, all of them lovely, all of them named Erin, Ethan joked, all of them deeply thoughtful and kind to the extent that they seemed *angelic,* and in comparison he seemed, at least to himself, cold-hearted and indifferent, or even worse.

His daughter, Larkin, was easy to love, so advanced and creative. Already she was talking about how when she was a teenager she wanted to be an apprentice at her father's studio, the Animation Shed. "I could write cartoons and draw them on paper," she said, "the way you used to do, Dad." Which killed Ethan, because of course he'd moved far away from the old pen and paper days. Ethan still did the voices for his two *Figland* characters, and he still oversaw preproduction, and he was there at table reads, and in the recording studio, and stalking the floor of the Animation Shed even at the end of the day, when the staff probably said to themselves, *Oh please, Ethan, not me; I just want to go home, I just want to have a little time to myself and my family. I'm not like you, Ethan; I can't work this much and still have a life.* Though Ethan's feature film was a calamity, and his TV spin-off a dud, the original show itself was still robust. It might go on and on forever.

Ash kept directing serious and usually feminist though somewhat uninspired plays, receiving respectful reviews from critics who were impressed by her modest but sly touch, especially in contrast with the very public, hyperkinetic work of her high-profile husband. She appeared on panels called "Women

606

in Theater," though she resented the fact that people thought such panels were still interesting or necessary. "It's *embarrassing* to have to keep being seen as this minority. Why do we keep only looking to male voices again and again for authority?" she complained to Jules. "Well, I shouldn't say 'we.' We don't do it, but 'they' do. I mean everyone else." It was astonishing and depressing to her that even now, in this enlightened age, men had the power in all worlds, even the small-potatoes world of off-Broadway theater.

Jules's practice had been reasonably populated, but like all therapists, she'd experienced an increasing thinning-out of patients. People took antidepressants now instead of going into therapy; insurance companies paid for fewer and fewer sessions; and even though she kept her fees low, some clients ended therapy quickly. The ones who stayed said they were grateful for Jules's calm, funny, kind presence. She poked and prodded at her practice as if it were kindling, supporting her family.

Rory grew bigger, and though she'd once been deeply envious of boys, she outgrew that and enjoyed herself. She was a very physical girl, needing to be in motion at all times. On weekends she played soccer in a league, and during the week Dennis took her to the park after school, the two of them smashing a ball back and forth. Dennis still talked about going back to work, though his voice was full of trepidation when he spoke about it. He read up on the latest advances in sonography, subscribing to a professional journal because it interested him, and because he hoped he could go back one day, but just not yet.

In March 1997, Jules and Dennis went to dinner at Ash and Ethan's house along with Duncan and Shyla, the portfolio manager and the literacy advocate. The prick and the cunt, Jules had once called them. Jules and Dennis had never understood why Ash and Ethan liked this couple so much, but they'd all been thrown together so many times over the years, for casual evenings and more formal celebrations, that it was too late to ask. Duncan and Shyla must have felt equally puzzled at Ash and Ethan's fidelity to their old friends the social worker and the depressive. No one said a word against anyone; everyone went to the dinners to which they were invited. Both couples knew they satisfied a different part of Ash and Ethan, but when they all came together in one place, the group made no sense.

On this night, which was unusually warm, the three couples sat at the table in the small backyard garden of the house, in torchlight. Larkin came outside with Mo to say good night to the adults; she held her brother's hand in a death grip while they stood in the orange light of the garden. The guests tried to make the moment light and felicitous, but it was forced. "Mo," said Ash, "did Rose give you dinner, honey?"

"No," said Mo.

"Do you want to try our food here at the table? There's some paella left."

Everyone stiffly waited for his answer; their smiles were tight and anticipatory even as they tried to look relaxed. But Mo just shook his hand free, broke away from his sister, and darted back inside.

"I'd better go follow him," said Larkin. "I am my brother's keeper. Good night, everybody. Oh, Mom, Dad, save me some lemon cake, please. Bring it into my room and leave it on my dresser, even if it's really, really late, okay?" Then she kissed her mother and father and danced off winningly into the house. Everyone watched her go, in silence.

"So adorable, both of them," Jules finally said, and there were noises of agreement from around the table.

The paella, prepared by an unseen cook, had been delicious; the men's and Jules's plates were now empty, all the rice gone and the juices and oils mopped up with bread, and with only a few mussel shells scattered; but Ash and Shyla's plates, in that female way that unnerved Jules, were left half full. Tonight at dinner, like at all dinners lately, everyone was talking about the World Wide Web. They all had stories to tell about websites they'd been to, and startups they'd heard about. Duncan talked about a financial website he and three partners were investing in, and he teased Ethan about going in on it with them; never as he talked did he look over to Dennis and Jules to include them in the conversation, even as a courtesy.

After Duncan was done speaking, Shyla told a story about an old friend of hers in LA, the wife of a record producer. "She and Rob had the most beautiful house in the canyon. And a place in Provence. I mean, *I* was jealous of their life."

"Oh, you were not," said Ash.

"I was. And one weekend when I was in LA I called Helena and asked if we could get together. She was very reluctant, but finally she agreed that I could come over. So I went, and she'd gotten heavy, actually, which amazed me. I hadn't seen her in years; we'd all been to the Grammys together a long time ago. I mean, if I think about who won that year, it was probably the Bee Gees. I'm joking, but it had been a while. She said she rarely left the house anymore. Nothing made her feel good, and she admitted that she was seriously thinking of taking her own life. I was very shaken. Anyway, long story short, the following week she was hospitalized at Cedars-Sinai, in some special unit where it's like a spa but with heavy meds. And they tried her on all sorts of different things, but nothing worked. The insurance company wouldn't cover it, but of course Rob did. They were going to start her on electroshock, but then a doctor came in during rounds and said that there was this new drug about to enter clinical trials at UCLA, but that it was controversial because it approached serotonin in a whole new way, and no one knew if it would do anything. There was going to be a double-blind study, and Rob was like, 'Well, let's put her in the study, but can you see that she doesn't get a placebo?' Apparently even he couldn't make that happen. These researchers are totally ethical. Well, maybe not totally, because they squeezed Helena in, and I wouldn't be surprised if they bumped someone else from the trial. Within a month she felt different. Sort of like she was a marionette that was being pulled back to life. That was her metaphor, not mine."

No kidding, Jules thought.

"But the upshot," said Duncan, "is that when Rob saw how his wife had been helped, he gave the psychiatric center the largest donation it had ever received. I know," he said, "that double-blind means double-blind, but when potential big donors' wives take part in a clinical trial, don't you think it's prudent to make sure they don't get a placebo?" Everyone laughed a little, and Jules looked over at Dennis, who to her surprise didn't seem all that interested in this story;

she would have to be interested *for* him. He could get into that trial if it was still going on, she thought. He could push to the front of the line and be accepted into the trial because of Rob and Helena and Duncan and Shyla and Ethan and Ash. Because of the wealthy people being discussed at this table or sitting here. She knew that Dennis would never ask whether there was a way he could try this drug too; he wouldn't even think it could help him. But maybe it could. As with everything, you had to know someone; you had to have connections and power and influence. LA doctors, at least some of them, were seducible by Ethan Figman and his high-end friends. When Jules called UCLA on Dennis's behalf the following day, she was told that yes, the clinical trial was ongoing, but that it was not taking any new patients. Then Jules called Ethan, who agreed to look into it.

Not long afterward, Dennis flew to LA to meet with the doctor running the study and have blood work and a physical done. A day later, he was accepted into the double-blind trial, and he and Jules hoped very hard that he hadn't received a placebo. Within a month of starting the drug, Stabilivox, he was fairly sure he hadn't. "Only the migrant farmworkers in the study have received a placebo," Jules told Ethan and Ash. Though really, she thought briefly, maybe Dennis had received a placebo too. Maybe the idea of a drug that required knowing someone powerful just to get a chance to try it was itself so suggestive that it could change your neurology. But, no, that would only have worked on Jules, not Dennis.

Everything inside him seemed to unfold a little, he told her; only then did he realize how folded he'd been all these years. "Crouched," he said to Jules. He'd previously only thought of his depression as draining him, which was how she'd seen it too, but now he saw that it had also forced him into an unnatural stance. For years he'd not only been depressed, he'd also been uneasy. The opening, the return, was slow and incremental over that spring and summer, but genuine. Jules had treated a few clients who were also taking antidepressants while in therapy with her, and she'd seen this kind of shift in them, but never in Dennis.

"My sleep is deeper," he said in wonder. Once, in the middle of the night, he woke Jules up with his head between her breasts, and then he was crying a little, and she said, alarmed, "What's wrong?" Nothing was wrong, he told her. He had awakened and felt *good*. Felt like doing things. Doing things to her. With her. Sex, which had been intermittent, returned to them like an old gift they'd once been given and which had been lost under a big pile of objects for a long time. He was unsteady at first, and one time his

fingers jammed into her in a way that made
her yelp like a dog whose tail has been
stepped on, and then he was horrified that
he'd hurt her. "I'm fine," she told him. "Just
go easy. Have a lighter touch." There were
other problems; it took him longer now, and
they made jokes about her inevitable sore-
ness later on. "You know what kind of cook-
ware I want as a gift?" she asked him once,
lying together after an episode of this new,
post-depression sex.

"What? Oh, this is a joke," Dennis said. "A
pun. Let me see . . . No, I can't think of
where you're taking this."

"A chafing dish," she said, smiling, her chin
on his chest.

By the end of the summer Dennis felt as if
he'd returned to himself almost completely
for the first time since he'd been taken off his
MAOI in 1989. Neither of them trusted it
would last forever, or even for a while. In late
August, Dennis went back to work; though
he had a black mark on his employment
record from the previous clinic, he managed
to demonstrate that his inappropriate behavior there had been due to his untreated
depression at the time, and that now he was
well. Dr. Brazil heartily backed him up. A
clinic in Chinatown, understaffed and desperate, hired Dennis at a bad starting salary, and
he began work again part-time; then, months
later, full-time.

The two families went on like this as the decade ended and the millennium began. There were fears about worldwide computers crashing, and both couples and their children and Jonah and Robert held their silly, collective breaths on New Year's Eve at the house on Charles Street, then released them. Jules felt her envy toward Ash and Ethan seem to lighten, as though it had been a kind of long, intractable depression itself. The sight of Dennis getting dressed for work in the morning seemed to be enough gratification for her for a while.

In time, small changes took place almost imperceptibly; among them was Ash's slow but noticeable acceptance of her mother's death. Her dreams about Betsy became less constant and harsh. Ash also became marginally less beautiful, and Ethan became marginally less ugly. Dennis was so relieved to be working again that his job seemed *bracing* to him, and Jules tried harder to be a good therapist to her crop of clients who hardly ever seemed to change unambiguously. But when she looked over at Ash and Ethan, she often felt a small reminder of how she herself didn't entirely change. Her envy was no longer in bloom; the lifting of Dennis's depression had lessened it. But it was still there, only closed-budded now, inactive. Because she was less inhabited by it, she tried to understand it, and she read something online about the difference between jealousy and envy. Jealousy was essentially "I want what you have," while envy was "I want what you have, but I also want to take it away so you can't have it." Sometimes in the past she'd wished that Ash and Ethan's bounty had simply been taken away from them, and then everything would have been *even*, everything would have been in balance. But Jules didn't fantasize about that now. Nothing was terrible, everything was manageable, and sometimes even better than that.

The city evolved, becoming cleaner, its homeless population pushed off the streets by a zealous mayor in crackdown mode. Everyone admitted that though the mayor and his laws were cruel, you could now walk virtually anywhere and feel safe. It was almost impossible to find an affordable place to live in Manhattan, though, and if Ethan hadn't given them that money and cosigned their mortgage, Jules and Dennis would have been gone from here like so many people they knew. Larkin attended some private girls' school her mother had also attended. Mo went to a special school in Queens that cost so much money that most parents — though of course not Ethan and Ash — had to sue the city in order to be reimbursed for much of the tuition. Rory attended the local public middle school, and that was fine for now, but there would be problems when high school arrived and she'd need to apply to one of the city's better schools. She didn't "test well," Jules said to Ash. But actually Rory wasn't interested in those tests, or even all that much in school. She longed to be a forest ranger instead, though her parents pointed out that she would still need to go to school for that. They had no idea of how much school it entailed, though, or even what *kind* of school; they really didn't know what they were talking about. The time Rory had spent in forests was primarily because of Ethan and Ash; up at their weekend house in Katonah as a little girl she'd waved a stick as she tramped through woods, and she'd also gone hiking around their ranch in Colorado. She was happy when she was slick with mud, wearing waders, doing activities that were outside the usual spheres of city life.

In 2001, the World Trade Center's destruction was an equalizer, briefly. Strangers talked to one another on the street; everyone felt similarly dazed, afraid and unprotected. Jules gave her clients her home phone number for the first time ever, and fielded frequent calls. The phone would ring at dinnertime, bedtime, even the middle of the night, and she would hear, "Jules? It's Janice Kling. I'm really sorry to bother you, but you said I could call and I'm kind of freaking out." Jules would take the phone into another room to talk to a client in private. She herself was frightened — it was a shock to see such primitive anger on such a large scale — but never hysterical. As a therapist in this crisis, she realized that she'd been given a kind of reprieve, in that she didn't have the option to become overly anxious herself. Instead, she helped her clients so they didn't fall apart. Sylvia Klein, the woman whose daughter had died of breast cancer years earlier, was very afraid now, and didn't think she could manage her anxiety. "If there's another attack, Jules," she said, "and it's the middle of the night and I wake up and hear it, I won't be able to cope. I'll just start screaming."

"So you'll call me," Jules said. "I'll expect screaming."

When Sylvia Klein called, it wasn't the middle of the night but early morning in New York City on a weekday late in September, and Sylvia, who'd been driving out to New Jersey to see her motherless grandchildren, found herself in her car, completely stopped in traffic near the exit of the Holland Tunnel. There was apparently some kind of police action ahead, according to the radio, and nothing was moving. She thought she'd be killed momentarily, and that she would soon join her poor dead daughter, Alison, and never see her husband or grandchildren again. She would die in her blue Nissan Stanza when a remote explosive device was set off by al-Qaeda in another car, suffusing the whole tunnel with fire and poison gas. But sitting trapped in her car, waiting for her own death, she took out her phone and hoped that somehow she got reception here. Fortunately she did, and she called Jules, who at the time was on the exercise bike that had been squeezed in recently next to Dennis's closet in the bedroom.

"Jules," said the voice on the phone. "I am going to die."

The last person to have said similar words to Jules was Dennis, back in the restaurant during his stroke; and now, after she had established who was calling, she said to Sylvia what she had said to him. "You're not going to die," she told her panicking client. "But I'm not getting off the phone. I'm right here, and I'll stay here, because I actually don't have to be anywhere else." So she stayed on the phone with Sylvia, chatting lightly with her about different subjects, and then, finally, when almost half an hour had passed and they seemed to have run out of conversation, she encouraged Sylvia to put a CD on in the car. "What have you got there? Anything good?"

"I don't know. My husband handles the CDs. Some of them were Alison's."

"Which ones? Any Julie Andrews?" Jules remembered how Sylvia's mood had lifted talking about her daughter's love of Julie Andrews when she was a girl.

"No, I don't think so. Oh, let me see. Wait, yes, here's one. *My Fair Lady.*"

"Crank it up," said Jules.

"I could have dawnced all night," Julie Andrews sang, and Sylvia began to sing too, and then so did Jules, the trio of voices tremulous but holding together, until finally up ahead the traffic began to move.

A few days later, near the very end of that bad month, Dennis and Jules were cleaning up one night after dinner; Rory, eleven, was slowly rolling around the apartment on her skateboard, anything so as not to turn to her homework, which she loathed. The TV was on, as it had often been on during those early weeks. Channel after channel showed the same footage. CNN had a talk show, and Dennis paused at it, then clicked past, but Jules, who'd been looking at the screen, held up a hand and said, "Wait, turn back." A blond woman in her early forties was being interviewed; she was sleekly dressed, with big, nuggety earrings and a hard but anguished face.

"It's her," Jules said, shocked.

"Who?" said Dennis. White letters were superimposed over the screen: Catherine Krause, CEO, Bayliss McColter. This was the firm that had lost 469 employees; two weeks earlier, on September 12, the CEO had made a public vow not to cut off the paychecks of the dead, or their families' health insurance.

Jules had read about her but hadn't seen her interviewed until now.

"Cathy Kiplinger," said Jules. "Oh my God. I mean, I'm not *positive,* but I think so. I wish I could call Ash!" she said. "But it would just be too weird, and I don't know how she'd react. I'm calling Jonah; I hope he's home." When she got him on the line she said, "Oh good, you're there. Turn on CNN, okay? You need to tell me if I'm right."

"What's going on?" Jonah said as he turned on his TV in the loft. A commercial was jabbering.

"Wait."

When the show resumed, Jonah watched for about fifteen seconds without saying anything, then let out a long breath and said, "It's her, right?"

In the background Jules heard Robert say, "*Who* her?"

"Yes," said Jules. "I think it is."

"Well, I do too."

Jules and Jonah stayed on the phone watching throughout the entire hour, magnetized by the image of Cathy, who had finally and dramatically emerged from her time portal. Her face was drawn, and tense and upset, but her bearing was professional; she'd learned to be composed in public, even as she was once again most likely falling apart.

"What do you say to your critics?" the aquiline-featured TV host asked her, leaning

621

forward as if he might kiss her, or hit her.

"That I'm still going to keep my promise."

"But the widows and widowers are saying you haven't done that. Their paychecks were cut off. They lost their health insurance at the worst time in their lives."

"It's just that the money's not there yet," Cathy said. "I'd thought we could get up and running again somewhere else, in some limited form, almost immediately, but it turned out not to be possible. Look, I'm asking the families to be patient. As you know, we're building a relief fund. But I really need everyone to bear with me a little longer."

"That's right," said Jonah. "I read about that — how she said she was going to give everyone all this money. But then she cut off the checks."

"She said it isn't her fault," Jules said.

The host fielded calls, mildly saying, "Go ahead, caller," and turning them over to Cathy.

"We believed you," a woman said, her voice husky, furious. "We believed what you told us. My family is in bad shape, not only because we're grieving but also because we don't have my husband's income. This is how you honor the memory of the people who worked for you? This is what you do?"

"We're going to take care of you," Cathy said evenly. "Please give us a little more time."

"You're such a hypocrite, it's unbelievable.

I mean, fu—" said the caller, before being cut off.

Cathy Kiplinger sat very still on camera. In their living room, Jules and Dennis sat very still too, and in his loft, so did Jonah. Oblivious to everything, Rory rolled around on her skateboard, trying new moves. Jules watched as Cathy stayed in her swivel chair in the TV studio, accepting the wrath of murdered employees' spouses but also accepting some mitigating support from a lawyer and a motherly if whorish psychotherapist, who regularly lent herself out to the evening news shows. Cathy stayed still, repeating the same lines about asking for patience, but by the end of the hour she'd been worn down. The last shot of her, beneath the credits, showed her lightly blowing her inflamed nose and shaking her head.

Dennis shut off the TV and went off to get Rory ready for bed. "You still there?" Jonah asked Jules on the phone.

"Yes."

"So what do you think about it?"

"I don't want to sound like that therapist, that 'Dr. Adele,' " said Jules, "but to me it's like Cathy is almost repeating what she feels was done to her."

"Explain," Jonah said.

"Well, you know, she felt that nobody came to her defense originally with Goodman. That nobody was looking out for her. So when this

623

enormous tragedy happens, it makes sense that she wants to be heroic. Except she can't be. The money isn't there yet. So she ends up doing to these families what she says Goodman did to her. And what she says we did to her too."

"And bin Laden."

"Exactly. Destroyed her."

"So do you think she's destroyed?" Jonah asked.

"Oh, I don't know," Jules said softly. "I have no way of knowing."

"Do you actually even remember Goodman all that well anymore?"

"I remember certain details. His sunburned nose. His knees. And his big feet in those sandals."

"Yeah, he was a big, sexy guy," said Jonah.

"He was."

"I must have been so attracted to him, but I couldn't even deal with it then," said Jonah. "I couldn't admit I was gay to any of you, and I could barely say it to myself, though God knows I'd been gay forever. Born queer." He was quiet. "I wonder what kind of life he has," he said. Jonah had occasionally made comments like this over the years. "And how he supports himself, wherever he is. Cathy switched gears and ended up with this huge financial career. I don't know what Goodman's talent would have been in the end.

Other than fucking up. He was very good at that."

"And being seductive," Jules said faintly.

"So what do you really think about what happened with him and Cathy?"

"Jonah," said Jules, hardly knowing what to say. It had been so long since this had come up. "We're here in New York City only weeks after this huge terrorist attack. We're all trying to keep ourselves together. You're asking me about Cathy and Goodman *now*?" She was deflecting his question, trying to bat it away, and not very believably.

"I'm sorry," Jonah said, surprised. "Don't you ever think about it anymore?"

Jules gave the question a considered, deliberate pause. "Yes," she said. "I do."

SIXTEEN

"If you had told me, in 1986, after I was first diagnosed, that I would still be alive in 2002, I would have asked you what you were smoking," Robert Takahashi told the dark gold banquet room. This was met with polite laughter and a slightly ominous, liquid cough from somewhere among the tables. "Then again," he said, "if you had told me, in 1986, that one day two towers in our city would be brought down by hijacked airliners, I would have said the same thing." Earlier that night, in Jonah's loft, when Robert was practicing this speech, Jonah had interrupted to say he didn't see the relevance of the terrorism line; including it seemed knee-jerk, he said, but Robert insisted it was required. "But as I well know, sixteen years after my diagnosis," Robert went on now, "with access to protease inhibitors and good care, HIV remains a serious disease but is no longer necessarily a death sentence. I'm grateful to Lambda Legal for providing me with a great place to work over all these years that I've remained surprisingly alive — the terrifying years, the tremendously sad years, and now this new era that I guess we could call the anxious years. I myself happen to be anxious but hopeful. And very much alive."

There was applause, then more coffee was poured, and the gelatinous roofs of unloved desserts were listlessly poked at, along with the obligatory three raspberries, then another speech was given by a French virologist, and the final speech of the night was delivered by a diminutive activist nun, who shook her fist as she leaned up toward the too-high microphone. Jonah and Robert, in their good dark suits, sat at the head table. Domenica's had been a savings and loan at the turn of the twentieth century, and now its soaring ceilings and paneled walls lent themselves well to fund-raising evenings such as this one. It was late February, and many of the winter benefits in the city had been canceled; no one had the heart or the concentration to go through with them. But the organizer of this benefit had said something about how if we weren't going to give in to AIDS, we also weren't going to give in to terrorists.

That logic didn't exactly track, but enough time had passed so that some of the generalized shakiness had gone away. Instead of feeling frightened all the time that another building would come down, or that a dirty bomb would go off in Times Square, you could also feel a little defiant, and that was the mood here tonight. Many aging men in this room had danced closely together as young men or boys in the 1980s at places like Limelight or the Saint, or Crisco Disco. Then their numbers had been thinned, and of the ones still alive, quite a few had ended up here tonight, in business dress, holding on.

Robert Takahashi was not, apparently, dying after all, at least not with certainty. He'd held on long enough for protease inhibitors to become standard protocol, and suddenly, astonishingly, if you were lucky enough to tolerate the side effects of the drugs, you might live for a very long time. No one they knew had ever thought this change would occur in their lifetimes; they'd imagined the death pileup continuing on into infinity. Still, it did often lead to death. People went unprotected, ignorant, passed it on; and in many places the drugs often weren't affordable, or weren't available at all, and so the world was still dying and AIDS was still a reason why, but in some quarters there was hope. Death was often held off, pushed back. President Reagan had left the scene long ago, and now he was an elderly, confused man who probably no longer remembered how he'd once behaved — or maybe he only remembered certain glittering, particular pieces of his long presidency: "Mr. Gorbachev, tear down this wall."

Tonight, having been the recipient of the Eugene Scharfstein Award for Political Activism Within the Legal Profession, Robert stayed on at the glossy bar of Domenica's after the ceremony and dinner had ended. Other, younger men were also still hanging around, but the new generation barely looked over at Robert and Jonah, thinking they were stylish men from another generation, which at just past forty they nearly were. Both of them had had a lot to drink; Robert wasn't supposed to do that, but tonight was a special occasion. He was fairly drunk when he tugged on Jonah's ice-blue tie and said, "You look so good in a suit. I always tell you that."

"Thank you."

"You should dress like this every day for work. You'd get your way in all the meetings. Everyone would want to do you."

"No one dresses up at my job, as you know."

"I didn't know that. You hardly talk about your job."

"You hardly ask."

In all their years together, Robert had only been to visit Jonah at Gage Systems once, and that was when the robotics firm was still at its old location. Robert had never seen Jonah's sun-filled cubicle with the drafting table and the corkboard on which he'd pinned a photo of himself and Robert, and another photo of the world's largest Lego sculpture, and one of his mother singing on a river barge with Peter, Paul and Mary about a million years ago. But to be fair, Jonah thought, he'd only been to Robert's office once, too. It was just the way they were. On the nights they were together, one of them was usually preoccupied with something that didn't include the other. Even stripped down to boxers for bed, Robert was often on his BlackBerry, tapping away, and Jonah was at the table looking over designs. Half the week Robert slept in his own apartment nearby on Spring Street.

"Well, you look good," Robert said now at the bar, and he leaned forward and kissed Jonah quickly. Jonah's recoil was imperceptible, he hoped; Robert smelled like whiskey concentrate, and even under the best circumstances Jonah Bay was not completely natural when it came to being physically demonstrative. But Robert let go of the tie and sat back on the stool, his expression readjusting itself. "Jonah," he said. "I need to talk to you."

"Okay."

"We struck a bargain back in the beginning, don't you think?"

Jonah felt himself tense down his arms and the long sides of his calves. "I'm not sure what you mean," he finally said.

"You couldn't handle too much with me. And that was okay. Because truly, I couldn't give you all that much then. I had this *diagno-*

sis. I was going to die. And we had to watch what we did, of course. And what we do. Which has been fine, really."

"Except?"

"Except now, as you know," said Robert, in deep discomfort but forcing himself to keep going, "it seems I am not necessarily going to die of this. And honestly, Jonah, as time has gone by I've been thinking that I want something more complete."

"Complete? What the hell does that mean?"

"Oh, you know — love. Sex. The full package. Someone who throws himself into me, physically and mentally."

"And where are you going to find this package, Robert? This throwing-himself-in package."

Robert looked down into his drink, the default place to look during a breakup, which this was so hideously and amazingly turning out to be. "I found him," he said.

"You found him." A sour statement.

"Yes." Robert looked up and bravely held Jonah's gaze. "At the board meeting three months ago. He's in research at Columbia. He's positive."

Not thinking, Jonah said, "He's positive he's in research?"

"He's HIV positive. Like me. We started talking. We fell into this, Jonah. It wasn't supposed to happen, I recognize that. But we found ourselves sort of . . . free. It felt amazing. I don't think there's been too much freedom in our relationship, yours and mine."

"Oh, *freedom,* that's the coveted thing? The holy grail. Fucking without protection?"

"It's not just that," said Robert. "He knows what it means to live with this."

"And me? I have lived with you all these years."

"No, not *with* me. You never even wanted me to move in. Look, I am this year's winner of the Eugene Scharfstein Award, and I think I deserve a moment of big honesty here. You always wanted to keep yourself separate, Jonah. That was your doing, not mine, and I went along with it because what else could I do?"

Each time he said Jonah's name, it got worse, as if Robert were a kindly, distant person speaking to someone who was doomed. After all this time, Robert was the survivor, while Jonah occupied a land between the ill and the well, a torturous purgatory in which he'd be forced to remain. "All right," said Jonah, gathering himself. "So what is it you want now?"

"I think I should go," Robert said.

"Go? What does that mean? Go to this guy? This 'researcher'?" He tried to give the word a sarcastic edge, but sarcasm just seemed immature now.

"Yes."

Robert took Jonah's hand, but his own

hand was so cold from the drink that it felt as far from reassuring as possible. Jonah would remember the press of fingertips of a man who had already left him, who was already thinking of his researcher and the night ahead and what would follow, now that he could live and be loved. Now that he was free. Robert Takahashi said, "It's been a very nice run. We weren't lonely. But now maybe we should see where the wind will carry us, so to speak."

The streets of lower Manhattan actually resembled a wind tunnel that night. Jonah's tie flipped over his shoulder and he stuck his hands into his coat pockets, feeling the contours of an old, fossilized tissue inside one and the linty coins and swan song subway tokens with their cut-out pentagram centers in the other. Jonah couldn't go home yet. Instead he found himself at Ash and Ethan's doorstep not too far away on Charles Street, ringing the bell, which gave a resonant sound from deep inside the house. A security camera purred and angled down on Jonah's face, then a female voice with a Jamaican accent spoke to him from an intercom. "Yes, who is it please?" This was Rose, the nanny.

"Hi, Rose," he said as lightly as he could. "Are Ash and Ethan around? It's Jonah Bay."

"Oh wait, turn a little; yes, I can see your face now. They're away, Jonah; they flew to the ranch in Colorado. But they'll be back tomorrow. Ethan has meetings. Is there anything I can help you with?"

"No," he said. "It's okay. Just tell them I was here."

"Wait a moment, all right?"

"All right." Jonah stayed on the step, not sure why he was being asked to wait, but very soon Rose opened the heavy door and asked him to come in. In the front hallway, a pale and tranquil space where the light seemed to come from a hidden source, the nanny handed Jonah a cordless telephone. Then she showed him into a sitting room that he hadn't ever been in before, and, still partly drunk and anguished, he sat on a plum velvet settee below a large painting of a vanilla ice cream cone.

"Robert left me," he said to Ash on the phone with a suppressed cry.

"He *left* you?" she said. "Are you sure? It's not just a fight?"

"We didn't fight. He's got someone else."

"I'm shocked, Jonah."

"A 'researcher.' Apparently I'm too with-holding."

"That's not true," said Ash. "You're a very loving person. I don't know what he's talking about." But of course she did know, and was just being polite. "When I come home," she said, "I'm all yours. But spend the night at our house tonight, okay? Rose and Emanuel will set you up. I wish we were there, but we flew the cast of *Hecuba* out here for rehearsals, and Ethan came too. You can have breakfast with Larkin and Mo in the morning; would that be okay? You can check on them for me. I hate to be away from Mo. He doesn't do well with change in his routine."

So Jonah spent the night in the second-floor guest room, which in his view was almost as grand as the Lincoln Bedroom in the White House. He distantly remembered that his mother had taken pictures with a Polaroid the night she'd spent there, back when Jimmy Carter was president. (Rosalynn Carter had loved "The Wind Will Carry Us," and had cried a little when Susannah sang it after dinner.) In the morning the sunlight spread across the bed where Jonah slept, and someone knocked on the door. He sat up and said, "Come in." Ash and Ethan's children walked into the room, and Jonah was startled to see how much they'd changed since he'd seen them last a few months earlier. Larkin was beautiful, poised, heading toward adolescence. Mo, poor kid, appeared uncertain and not exactly right even just standing doing nothing. The way he held himself was disconcerting. He stared at Jonah searchingly.

"Hey, you guys," Jonah said, sitting up and suddenly feeling self-conscious. He was never able to sleep with a shirt on, so he was barechested now. His hair, still long, had begun to go gray, and he worried that he appeared to these children like a menacing, effeminate gypsy. But Jonah always felt that something was wrong with him, no matter how many people exclaimed over his face or his long body or his designs for devices to aid disabled people or his "gentleness," a word that often, irritatingly, got used to describe this held-back, polite man.

"Mom and Dad said you were here, Jonah," said Larkin. "They said you should stay and have breakfast with us if you can. Emanuel is making waffles that Mom says are to die for."

"I don't want to die," Mo said with a quivering mouth. "You know that, Larkin."

"I was kidding, Mo," his sister said, putting an arm on his shoulder. "Remember? It's a joke." Then, over her brother's head, she said, "He is the most *literal person* any of us has ever met. That's the way people on the spectrum can be."

After getting dressed, Jonah followed the sound of the children's voices, which led him one flight up to a well-stocked playroom. Larkin stood at an easel, painting a skillful landscape that was apparently based on the view from her bedroom on the ranch in Colorado. Mo lay on his stomach on the carpet like a much younger boy. So many Lego pieces were scattered around him that it appeared as if there'd been a volcanic explosion and all the flung bits had cooled

and hardened. Jonah stood in awe, just looking; long ago he'd loved Lego too, and what
all those little pieces could do. In a sense,
he'd gone to MIT because of Lego, and now
he worked for Gage Systems because of his
early interest in what interlocked and what
did not.

"What are you making?" he asked.

"A garbage claw," said the boy, not looking
up.

"How does it work?" Jonah asked, and he
crouched down and let Mo Figman give him
a demonstration of the uses of his invention.
Right away he saw that Mo possessed a
visceral understanding of mechanics that
went deep and wide. Jonah questioned him
about the functionality of the garbage claw,
and asked him a series of problem-solving
questions relating to use, form, durability,
aesthetics. Mo shocked him with his cool
skill, yet he was grim about it all, too. Lego
was what he loved, but he behaved like a
worker, like one of the child laborers who
had inspired what had now become Ethan's
cause.

At the breakfast table a little later, Jonah
was tended to like the Figmans' third child,
instead of like a man who'd been broken up
with by another man only eight hours earlier.
Jonah sat with the children in the sunny
kitchen, looking out onto a garden that
featured a wall threaded so heavily with vines

it appeared like the underside of a tapestry. He ached to have lived here, to have had parents like Ash and Ethan and not like his mother, who'd been well-intentioned but unable to save him from being ripped off and diminished. Up on the farm in Dovecote, Vermont, Susannah Bay still lived with her husband, Rick, and taught guitar and prayed, and was revered in that enclosed world, famous and beloved within the membrane of the Unification Church. She assured Jonah that she liked her life there very much, and that she had no regrets about slipping from this larger world into that smaller one. In her daily life she was admired for her talent, which was so much more than he could say for himself.

"Are you okay?" Larkin suddenly asked him. Jonah was surprised, and he wasn't sure how to reply.

"Why wouldn't he be okay?" Mo asked. "He doesn't have anything *wrong* with him."

"Again, you're being really literal," Larkin said. "Remember, Mo, we talked about that?"

"I'm okay," Jonah said. "But if you're picking up something, it's just that I feel kind of sad right now."

"Sad? Why is that?" said Mo, almost barking out the words with impatience.

"Well, you've met Robert, right?"

"The Japan man," said Mo. "That's what I always call him."

"Oh, you do? Oh. Well, he doesn't want to be my partner anymore. So that was hard for me. He told me last night, which is how I wound up here." The conversation was starting to take a peculiar turn; why was he discussing his love life and his breakup with two *children*? Also, the words felt imperfect; he hadn't exactly ever been anyone's partner.

Larkin looked at her brother, fixing her gaze on him in a specific way that she had clearly done before. "Mo," she said. "Did you hear what Jonah said about being sad?"

"Yes."

"So what's the appropriate response right now?"

Mo looked around desperately, like someone searching the classroom walls for an answer on a test. "I don't know," he said, his head dropping slightly.

"Oh, it's really okay," said Jonah, putting a hand on Mo's shoulder, which was all wood, like the back of a chair.

"You do know," said Larkin softly. Her brother looked at her, waiting it out, waiting to remember, and suddenly he found the answer.

"I'm *sorry,*" Mo said.

"Say it to Jonah."

"I'm sorry." Ethan's son said it in a voice that strained for expression, though Jonah didn't have to strain to find any feeling to meet it.

Seventeen

Manny Wunderlich at eighty-four was vigorous but mostly blind. His wife, Edie, was not so vigorous, though her eyesight was decent. Together, though, they were no longer in a position to have even a partial day-to-day directors' role in their summer camp, and they both knew it. Probably they should have stopped completely years earlier. The 2010 season had just finished; Paul Wheelwright, the young man who'd been running the place for them over the past few years, had been uninspired, they felt, and attendance was way down. Yesterday they'd fired him, telling him there were no hard feelings, but they were looking to go another way with Spirit-in-the-Woods next year.

"Manny. Edie," Paul had said to them. "I actually do have hard feelings, because I tried to make this place work for you. In some ways you're both living in the past, and it's very frustrating for me. This just isn't the kind of camp that twenty-first-century kids want. Kids are all tech-savvy now. I know it's difficult for you to face that, but unless you find someone who can really bring the place into the present day, I'm worried that it's only going to get worse, and you're going to lose too much money to make it feasible to run at all. I could have done so much more with it if you'd let me."

"Computer game design," Manny said with derision. "That was your idea of so much more?"

"Well, yes, we would've had a computer lab," said Paul. "It wouldn't just have been a place to design games or check e-mail, though the kids could have done those things too. Their parents would have loved to stay in touch with them electronically. As for computers, don't forget that everywhere but here, things are completely computerized now. But all summer, for instance, some of these kids were off in the animation shed drawing on *paper.* That's got nothing to do with the real world."

"The real world?" said Edie, offended. "Tell me, Paul, how well did someone like *Ethan Figman* manage in the real world? He drew on paper too, didn't he? And yet he managed to adapt when things changed. We gave him a foundation here; that's what matters. A foundation of creativity. Does everything have to be explicitly pre-professional? In my estimation, he ended up doing just fine. Or perhaps slightly better than fine, some people might say."

"Edie, I am obviously well aware that Ethan Figman attended Spirit-in-the-Woods a very long time ago. He's mentioned it in many, many interviews, and I'm certain that you're extremely proud that he's an alum, as anyone would be. It's amazing and wonderful that he got his start here." He paused. "Why don't you hit him up? I'm sure he'd drop a bundle on this place if he knew you were struggling like this. He and his wife would probably buy the joint. She went here too, right? Didn't they meet here?"

"We would never ask him for anything," said Edie. "That's crass. Our motives are pure, Paul."

"Well, you can have all the purity you want, but if the place goes under, you know what you'll be left with? A lot of scrapbooks from old productions of *Mourning Becomes Electra* starring a bunch of fifteen-year-olds with zits."

"Now you're being rude," said Manny.

"I just think you're keeping these kids from having access to all the available tools," said Paul. "It's amazing what's out there now. The Internet has cracked open the possibilities for everyone. If a kid has always fantasized about . . . Abbey Road, now he can suddenly *be* there. On the street, or even in the recording studio. Suddenly even a certain kind of virtual time travel is possible. It's amazing what this does for the imagination."

Manny shook his head and said, "Oh, come on. You're telling me that because of the Internet, and the availability of every experience, every whim, every *tool,* suddenly everyone's an artist? But here's the thing: If everyone's an artist, then *no one* is."

"It's good to have principles, Manny, but I still think you have to adapt to the times," said Paul.

"We have adapted," Edie said. "In the 1980s, with multiculturalism, we made an executive decision to offer traditional West African drumming, and as you know, our drumming teacher Momolu has been with us ever since. We were instrumental, so to speak, in helping him get a visa."

"Yes, that's terrific, and Momolu is great," said Paul. "But multiculturalism is easy. Of course you folded it into the life of the camp, and I know it's a much more diverse place now than it used to be. But I think technology is a lot harder for you both to accept. Racists and xenophobes think multiculturalism is the enemy of America, but you guys think *technology* is the enemy of *art,* which is also not true. When Ethan Figman was a camper in, what, the mid-1970s, I guess? — the technology didn't even exist. Now it does and you can't pretend it doesn't. Artists in all fields have tremendous digital tools available.

Composers do. Even painters. Ninety percent of all writers use computers. I understand if you want to move on from me. But even without me, I think you need to make some changes across the board — not just getting computerized but also maybe branching out a bit in other directions."

"What directions?" said Manny in a defeated voice. His eyes would not let him really see the face of his tormenter; all he heard was this dispiriting barrage of doomsday reports, emanating from a hazy male figure who shook his head a lot.

"Well, like llamas. I've already told you that you could offer a workshop in llama care; a lot of camps have that these days, and it's very popular. Girls in particular seem to like taking care of them. They're smarter animals than you'd think, and quite manageable."

"Thank you for your input," said Manny.

"And, well, you could offer sports. Not just Ping-Pong or the occasional Frisbee toss. One arts camp I heard of even has a Quidditch team," he said with a light laugh. "Today's arty teenagers are more well-rounded than in the past. They want to bulk up their résumés. Speaking of which, you could also offer a community-service credit."

"For what?" cried Edie, the tougher of the two Wunderlichs. " 'They cleaned their teepees?' 'They sewed costumes for *Medea*?' 'They helped each other roll a joint?' "

"No," said Paul patiently. "For real things. And there's something else too. You need to be on social media. I recognize that phrase hurts your eardrums, but bear with me. You should not only have a page on Facebook but you should be on Twitter."

"Twitter," said Manny, waving his hand. "You know what that is? Termites with microphones."

"This is really quite enough, Paul," said Edie. "You've made your point. We appreciate all the work you've done. Your last paycheck should be in the front office. You ought to run along."

"Now who's being rude," he murmured, and he shook his head as he walked away.

On a city bus Jules Jacobson-Boyd drowsed and drifted. The night before, she and Dennis had returned from taking Rory up to the state university in Oneonta for the start of her senior year; Rory was looking forward to taking a class in a subject her parents didn't understand, Environmental Spaces. Though not stellar like Larkin Figman, Rory had emerged from childhood intact, a middling student and an antsy, enthusiastic person who knew she wanted to be in motion, to be outside in the world. Out in environmental spaces. She had moved out of the apartment smoothly and unhistrionically when she left for college, and though people said that because of the terrible economy kids didn't fully leave home until age twenty-six anymore, she showed no sign of needing or wanting to come back. Rory occasionally descended over a school vacation with a couple of friends in tow, all of them outdoorsy, jocular young women, not entirely knowable by their parents. At age fifty-one, Jules and Dennis were entering what for most people was a quieter period — a slight roll down a soft incline. Dennis remained in decent spirits from the Stabilivox, though it made him gain weight that he couldn't take off. He liked being back at the clinic, and he now subscribed to three different sonography journals and had become so knowledgeable that the staff at the clinic all came to him with questions.

Jules and Dennis had rented a car for the drive up to Oneonta; their no-nonsense daughter with the frizzy dark hair and big open face had hugged each parent hard in turn, then one of her housemates in the pink off-campus run-down Victorian had leaned way too far out an open second-floor window and called, "Rory, get your ass up here!" And now, riding the packed bus down Broadway to her office, Jules sat with her head against the window, her eyes flickering closed and then open, when she became aware of a woman sitting across from her. Soon the whole bus became aware of her too. Every few seconds the woman gave herself a severe smack in the face. Jules watched with excited shock. Then the woman accompanying this poor woman gently took her hand, whispering something to her. They actually seemed to be having a conversation, and the disturbed woman smiled and nodded. There was a moment of silence, and then the disturbed woman freed her hand and, once again, *bang,* she hit herself even harder. Again, the other woman spoke to her gently. They looked somewhat alike, and were probably sisters. Maybe they were even *twins,* but the disturbed one's face had been rearranged over time by the agonies of her condition, so the two women really didn't resemble each other all that closely.

Jules, who knew she ought to look away now, that it was indecent not to, found herself unable to do that, and she turned her rubbernecking attention to the sister who was softly speaking. Jules stared at her, and as she did, the woman's face seemed to reveal its younger self, and Jules thought, *I know you.* This was another so-called sighting. She stood up and confidently said, "Jane!"

The woman looked across the aisle at her, at once smiling and amused. "Jules!" Jane Zell, Jules's former teepeemate from Spirit-in-the-Woods, stood too, and they hugged each other. Jules suddenly remembered a late-night teepee conversation during which

647

Jane had discussed her twin sister, who she'd said had a neurological disorder that caused her to hit herself for no apparent reason. "This is my sister Nina," Jane said, and Jules said hello.

As Jules and Jane spoke, Nina continued her self-savaging. But Jane was used to it, and seemed composed and undistracted as she recounted for Jules what had happened in her life over the past thirty-plus years. "I work for a foundation in Boston that gives grants to orchestras," Jane said. "My husband's an oboist. I gave up music myself — I was good but not *that* good — but I knew I still needed to be around the arts. I'm in New York this weekend for a conference, and to visit Nina." Jane Zell at fifty-one had a brightness to her face that she'd always had; it was a relief to see that it hadn't disappeared.

"Are you in touch with anyone?" Jules asked.

"Nancy Mangiari, once in a while. Are you and Ash still friends?" said Jane.

"Oh yes." She felt a flood of pride as she said it.

"It's amazing about Ethan," Jane said. Nina suddenly smacked herself with even more ferocity, pow, pow, pow, and Jane leaned down and said a few words, then returned to the conversation. "You know who I ran into in Boston last week?" said Jane. "Manny and Edie."

"Really? We've totally been out of touch," said Jules. "Once, after I got married, my husband and I were in New England in the summer and we stopped by, but that was the last time I saw them. I always had a fantasy that when my daughter was a teenager she'd go to Spirit-in-the-Woods. But when she was fifteen she wanted to go to wilderness camp. And Ash's daughter always traveled with her parents in the summer — going to other continents, helping with the school that Ethan started."

"Edie looks the same, mostly," said Jane. "Pretty solid, like always. Manny is basically blind, which is sad. The camp still runs, but they said it's been limping along, and that they're looking for someone new to run it next summer."

Jane Zell and her sister Nina were planning to get off at the next stop, but before they did there was a sentimental embrace between the old friends, and Nina slapped herself a couple more times, and then Jules and the whole bus watched as the sisters stepped out onto Broadway. Jules closed her eyes for the final couple of stops during the slow ride in morning traffic, but the conversation with Jane had made her start to buzz and fizz. She was in her teepee; she was in the theater; she was in the dining hall, where the meal was green lasagna and a salad topped with tangled sprouts. She was sitting on the hill listening to Susannah Bay sing; she was in the animation shed, receiving the surprising pressure of Ethan Figman's mouth; she was in Boys' Teepee 3, smoking a damp joint and looking at Goodman Wolf's hairy golden legs as they hung down from an upper bunk. She was putting on a refugee's accent in Improv class; she was sitting on her narrow bed at night talking to Ash; and oh she was happy.

"Listen, there's something we need to discuss today," Jules said to her client Janice Kling late one Thursday afternoon. Nearly a month had passed since she'd run into Jane Zell on the bus, and in that time Jules had behaved like someone in a trance, following orders from an obscure source. From the moment she'd found a chance to get back to Spirit-in-the-Woods — that place where her life had opened and spilled and thrust her to the ground, delirious and changed — she'd moved fast. After the idea of applying for the job had occurred to her, she'd gone to Dennis and he'd laughed indulgently, thinking she wasn't serious. They discussed it for three days before she even called Manny and Edie. By the end of those three days, Dennis had been talked into considering it.

A few other applicants were also sentimental Spirit-in-the-Woods alumni. At the interview, held in a midtown hotel room, the Wunderlichs looked extremely old to Jules, but then again they always had, even in 1974. Edie was still thickly built and bossy, and Manny was grandfatherly, with white eyebrows that sprang out like branches you had to swerve away from. Jules felt breathless in the Wunderlichs' presence, just hearing their familiar voices talk about this person and that one from the past.

After all the reminiscing, throughout which Dennis politely listened, certainly bored, they began discussing what the job would entail, and what the challenges were. The interview lasted an hour, and it ended with effusive hugs from the Wunderlichs, which seemed like a good sign, but you never knew. Then Jules waited, and two days later the call came with the offer. She picked up the message in her office, between clients. The voice-mail was from Edie, who said, "Well, we saw everyone, but you two are the ones we want. Will you be able to move up to Belknap in the spring?"

Jules let out a little woofing sound, then immediately covered her mouth, remembering that she'd already buzzed a client in, who was now sitting in the waiting room. It was not ideal to hear one's therapist woof. That evening, Jules and Dennis accepted the offer. It was as uncertain as anything; they'd been hired provisionally, and at the end of the summer they and the Wunderlichs would "reassess" the situation and see whether it was a good fit. Dennis had been assured he'd be rehired at the Chinatown clinic if for some reason he returned to the city after the summer; the understaffed clinic needed him there. Dennis knew so much and was very valuable to them. Jules, though, had to close her practice. There was no way she could keep her clients suspended; she would have to tell them that she'd help them seek other therapists, if that was what they chose. Though the Wunderlichs were only committing to the one summer, Jules felt fairly confident. And if it worked out, running the camp would become a year-round job. She and Dennis would be required to stump aggressively for Spirit-in-the-Woods, finding prospective campers and boosting enrollment in the off-season.

So this morning she'd begun to tell her clients that she was giving up her practice and moving away from New York City in April. The next several months, she said, would be spent talking with them about whatever came up, and trying to find closure, that impossible thing that no one had ever really experienced in life, because there always seemed to be a little aperture, a slit of light. Two clients cried, including Sylvia Klein, but Sylvia often cried, so it wasn't a surprise; and a speech pathologist named Nicole asked if she could take Jules out to dinner and be her friend, now that Jules would no longer be her therapist. Jules demurred, but told her she was very touched by the offer. Most of the encounters had been like this, moving and a little mystifying. She knew these people but they didn't really know her.

Now at the end of the day here was Janice Kling, her longest-standing client, who looked forward to her sessions with religious verve, even though it seemed that the quality of her life generally stayed the same. Janice still mourned the absence of intimacy, and had not been touched in a very long time. She was alone, and went on dates with men she described as uninteresting. She was faithful to therapy, though, and to her work with Jules. It was the center of her week, maybe her life. "So I'm leaving New York this spring," Jules told Janice Kling. Suddenly she worried for Janice; wondered what would become of her, whether she would be okay. The city was hard on single people after a certain age; loneliness could be felt so sharply here, and sometimes if people weren't in twos they started to hang back, stay home. "I'm closing my practice."

"How far away will you be?" Janice asked. "Because my friend Karen, the one with lupus? Her therapist moved to Rhinebeck, and Karen takes Metro-North up there once a week. I could do that."

"I won't be doing therapy anymore."

"Are you sick?" Janice asked in anxiety.

"No, I'm fine."

"Then what is it?"

"I guess it's one of those second-acts-in-American-lives moments," Jules said.

"I don't understand."

"I'm actually going to be the director of a summer camp."

"A summer camp?" said Janice, shocked. "That's what you're giving this up for? What if it doesn't work out? What if you find out that you're bad at it?"

"I guess that's always a possibility when you try something new," said Jules. But she and Dennis had thought this through. They owned their apartment. The salary, and their low expenses in Belknap, would make it possible for them to return to the city after each summer ended, and work for the camp from their apartment until the spring. At which point they could try to sublet for a few months. Also, if the job proved to be a disaster — according to either them or the Wunderlichs — they would still have their home to return to. Jules's practice, however, would be lost.

"I can't believe you're doing this. Doesn't it feel bizarre?" asked Janice. "And, no offense, but what does running a summer camp have to do with being a therapist? It seems to me that they're completely unrelated. Don't you feel that way too? I just can't see you ringing a wake-up bell, or singing

'Kumbaya.' "

"I know the news comes out of nowhere, and I'm sure there's a lot about it that's going to keep coming up," said Jules. She saw the fierce hurt conveyed in Janice's eyes, but it had been in there for so long already, and though she wished she could make it go away, she'd never really been able to before, and now she never would.

That night, Jules lay in bed overly anxious and rustling, and beside her Dennis said, "You okay?"

"Who makes such a change at our age? No one."

"Well, we're pioneers."

"Yeah, right; in our Conestoga wagon. And I know I've let my clients down."

"You have to live your life."

"I don't only mean I let them down by leaving. I mean by having stayed all this time too. I found my way of being with them, and I was always interested in their lives and in the things that blocked them. I'll miss them; I really hate to leave them. But the reality is, I'm not all that much more talented as a therapist than I was as an actor. I wasn't what you'd call a natural." She thought about this. "Actually, back at Spirit-in-the-Woods, everything did seem to come naturally. It was all sort of *electric*. That's what I got there."

Jules rested her head on Dennis's shoulder, and would have stayed like that, falling asleep there, when he suggested they go for a walk, and maybe even go have a drink at a bar. "To celebrate," he said. "Like Rory said."

"Oh, right." On separate extensions of the phone with Rory, who was up at school, they'd told her their sudden new plan. She'd been silent at first, shocked. "Are you both shitting me?" she finally said.

"No," said Dennis. "Your parents shit you not."

"Can we move on from this lovely exchange, please?" Jules said. But she was actually a little nervous about what Rory thought. Fully grown children often had a difficult time with change in their parents' lives, she knew. They wanted everything to be the same, forever. In an ideal world, parents of grown children would never divorce, would never sell the childhood home, would never make any sudden moves to suit themselves. But this was a fairly significant sudden move, and Jules wasn't surprised that Rory was shocked.

"You're really doing this?" Rory asked.

"I think we are," said Dennis. "I guess it's pretty startling to you."

Rory laughed her familiar, chesty laugh. "Jesus, Dad, you guys don't do things like this. Big moves."

"That's true, we generally don't."

"You're sure this isn't some kind of early

dementia? I'm mostly kidding," she quickly added.

"I think we have all our faculties," said Jules.

"Well, okay then," said Rory. "I mean, it's more than okay. Congratulations, you guys."

"Will you visit us up there?" Jules asked.

"Sure. Maybe at the end of the summer. I do want to see the place. Anyway, you should celebrate, right? Even if this is just a midlife crisis or something, you should definitely celebrate."

So now, following her advice, they fished into the laundry hamper and put back on the clothes they'd only taken off an hour earlier, and headed for the elevator. Outside, walking eastward, the streets increasingly stirred. They found a little bar called Rocky's on a side street, and to their surprise it was fully populated. A couple of the men there looked familiar, though Jules couldn't figure out why. In their small red booth, she and Dennis drank their beers. "Who are these people?" he asked. "They look like people we sort of know. Like people you see in a dream."

The men's faces appeared relaxed, middle-aged and older, with the occasional set of young, sharp features. Accents drifted over, strands of Eastern Europe and maybe also Ireland, but Jules couldn't exactly place any of it or tease it apart. "I don't know who they are," she said.

"Wait," Dennis suddenly said, "I do. They're the doormen in the neighborhood. After they get off work, this is where they come." Off duty, out of their greatcoats and peaked caps, the doormen looked completely different, but, yes, it was them, members of one of the countless subcultures in the city. "We've never had a doorman," said Dennis. "And now we probably never will, which is fine with me. I wanted to say," he said to her, "that I am very impressed with you for doing this. Being impetuous. Really making us go up there and do this."

Though Dennis hadn't gone to the camp, he had willingly been educated in its lore over the decades. It sometimes seemed to her that Dennis *had* gone there; he knew three of the central, relevant figures, and he knew so much about some of the others. If he'd been given a pop quiz about his wife's summers at Spirit-in-the-Woods, he would have done well. "*Sandbox* by Edward Albee!" he would have answered correctly. "Ida Steinberg, the cook!" And he would have been able to write detailed observations about what the place had meant to his wife back then and what it had meant to her later on. Spirit-in-the-Woods was the camp that would not die, the camp that would not leave her, so instead she'd decided to go there, to become it.

Ash and Ethan and Jonah had all been excited and shocked when she told them about the job. "You'll actually be living there again?" Ethan said. "You'll be in charge of the whole place? You'll go into the animation shed? That's amazing. Take pictures."

"For selfish reasons," Ash said, "I want you to stay in the city forever. But I know that isn't fair. And it's not like I'm home so much anyway; I'm always running off on you. It's just so hard to think of you not being here. That this is maybe the end of our New York life together. That's huge."

"I know," said Jules. "It feels that way to me too."

"But it's also touching that you'll be there, carrying the torch," said Ash. "I wish we could come and visit this summer, but I'll be directing, and then we'll barely be on the East Coast. Maybe we can squeeze it in at the end, with a little luck." Jules knew that Ash and Ethan had the weeklong Mastery Seminars in Napa, during which Mo would be with them, along with a caregiver, before he had to return to boarding school. And Larkin was planning on attending a Yale summer program in Prague; her parents would visit her there after Napa. "Next summer, for sure," Ash said. "But you'll give me a detailed report about everything, a blow-by-blow. Walk around and do one of those virtual tours, telling me everything that's different and everything that's the same. Do you get to decide what plays they put on? Or do you at least get to make suggestions? I know some excellent plays with strong parts for women."

"I will take that under advisement."

Jules and Dennis finished their drinks now and went outside into the street. The city — this place that they had managed rather than conquered — had its own relentless activity even at two a.m. Somewhere, far off, someone was banging metal against metal. She linked her arm through Dennis's and they headed back to their apartment along the unremarkable streets, though already Jules was putting a lake behind them, and a mountain before them. She dotted the landscape with teenagers, and with bunches of bumblebees hanging low over wildflowers; with a crude but functional theater, and an animation shed and a dance studio and various indestructible teepees built of unfinished wood. She added llamas, for she'd been warned by the Wunderlichs that today all summer camps needed to offer llama care, for reasons unknown. No one ever loved the poor llamas, whose faces were as narrow as shoes. Here, in this green and golden world, among mountains and paths and trees, Jules and Dennis would venture out together. In the woods, she would be spirited again.

■ ■ ■ ■

PART THREE:
THE DRAMA OF THE
GIFTED CHILD

■ ■ ■ ■

EIGHTEEN

The first car arrived before nine a.m. on the last day of June, slowly slipping between the stone gates that over the decades had become breaded and then repeatedly rebreaded with moss. "Sorry we're early," sang a man, leaning his head out the window as the car pulled up in front of the main building. "The Taconic was a breeze." He was the father of a camper, and yet he looked appreciably younger than Jules and Dennis. The back door opened and a girl slid out grimly, as if saying, Take me, please take me. So Jules and Dennis took her. Soon others followed, a long line of cars with trunks strapped to roofs and back windows jammed with a mash of adolescent essentials. All over New England today, similar cars were crawling, though here on this lawn were a preponderance of cellos and bassoons and guitars and amps, and bags lumpy with dance gear. These were arty teenagers, today's model. The population was more diverse than in the 1970s, though once again, as Jules had felt the first time she'd stood here, she was on the outside. This time, the inside involved being young, and the outside involved being old. The equation was simple and clear.

Was she really old?

Relatively. But it was much stranger to admit this than it was upsetting. As long as nothing terrible happened this summer — no campers went missing or were injured in a kiln explosion or *died* (Jules had nightmares of making that phone call to parents) — she wouldn't have to worry about how much time had passed between then and now. Dennis puttered around with a clipboard, helping send everyone to the right teepee. None of the parents wanted to leave that first day. They lingered on the lawn and in the teepees, helping their children unpack each item individually from duffels and trunks. One mother said, with a wistful face, "Oh, if only I'd known about this place when I was growing up." Many photographs were snapped of smiling or unsmiling teenagers indulging their mothers and fathers one final time. The parents would post them on Facebook immediately. The day lengthened, the sun dipped, and Jules and Dennis finally asked a percussionist to stand at the top of the hill and bang the gong she'd brought, at which point Dennis called into a megaphone, "Now it's time for all families to say their farewells."

Then somehow they managed to send the parents away, and the camp looked the way it was meant to. Not empty, as it had been all spring since Jules and Dennis had moved up here and begun living in the Wunderlichs' house across the road. Running a summer camp for teenagers wasn't as challenging as running one for younger kids, Jules had been told by veterans of this world on a summer camp directors' Internet message board. Hardly anyone got homesick. There were no bullies. There was the likelihood of sexual activity and also drug use, but these would be hidden and beyond your control. Mostly, Jules thought, the kind of teenagers who came to Spirit-in-the-Woods came to do the art they loved and to be around similarly inclined teenagers. Every summer in recent years, though, enrollment had dropped further; a few of the teepees now sat empty. The Wunderlichs had sent Jules and Dennis to man a booth at several camp fairs that winter — loud, dull events held in high school gyms around the tristate area. Parents and kids gathered at other booths that promised a summer of "xtreme" sports, or "a 24/7 soccer extravaganza." Even the booth for a juvenile diabetics' camp called, almost tauntingly, Sugar Lake, had more customers than the Spirit-in-the-Woods booth did. The camp could not survive like this much longer.

"What I would love," Manny had said after

Jules and Dennis had been hired, "is for you to give the place new life not through some expensive computer lab or sports team — we'll do the llamas, but that's *it* — but through the passion you feel and the memories you hold."

Ordering raw chicken thighs and broccoli and extra-firm tofu in industrial bulk was such a new and particular task that it felt revelatory. Overseeing repairs to the theater was gratifying too, though the building itself seemed much smaller than it once had. Being onstage in 1974 had felt like appearing on Broadway; now, the performance space revealed itself as a small square with a floor that was dotted with remnants of old masking tape. As for the teepees: how could anyone bear to live in them? One day shortly before the season started, Jules had gone into Boys' Teepee 3 and sat down on the floor in the corner. All she could feel was the filth of the room and the choking musk of the years. She stood up almost immediately and went outside to get some air. Apparently you didn't require air when you were a teenager. You made your own air.

On the opening night of camp, the counselors put on a show introducing the campers to all the different classes that would be available that summer. The music counselor, a rangy guy who called himself Luca T., played piano in the rec hall while the other counselors began to sing a song they'd collectively written:

"You won't feel like a freak, if you try
  batik . . .
You can get your ass goin' with a little
  glassblowin' . . ."

At the end, the campers seemed jazzed up; no one could stay sitting anymore, and they jumped to their feet. Jules and Dennis stood at the microphone and made a few comments about what a great summer it would be. Jules told them, "I used to be a camper here myself," but she was confronted with a squeal of feedback, and even when she repeated her words, she saw that it didn't matter to them that she, a middle-aged woman with a sweater draped over her T-shirt and the kind of softened, undefined features that their mothers shared, had once been a camper here. They didn't care, or even really *believe* it. Because if they did believe it, then they would have had to think that one day they too would become softened and undefined.

"This summer will be amazing," Dennis said to them when he stood up at the mike. "Just watch." He liked being here, seeing what Jules had been talking about all these years. Also, being here reminded him of how hard the city had been, its unyielding surfaces, the relentless need for more and more money just to keep yourself vaguely afloat. The city was not a place for the contemplative or the slow. Up here in Belknap, they lived for free in the Wunderlichs' big house, and their job was straightforward. No striving was necessary.

Ash had said that she envied them the decision to live a simpler life, and, of course, the decision to return to the place they'd once loved. You almost never got an opportunity to do that in life. Of course, Ash said, Jules and Dennis *had* to take the job, even though it meant changing and reorganizing their lives around it. "Once you step on that train," Ash said, by which she meant once they had contacted the Wunderlichs and arranged an interview, "you can't get off. What are you going to do, *not* accept the offer? I wish more than anything that Ethan and I could move up there with you." This was a lie, a friendship lie. Ash was currently directing a gender-reversed *Cat on a Hot Tin Roof,* in which the terrifying central figure was now called Big Mommy. Possible new theater projects were arrayed before her. She would never give everything up to move to Spirit-in-the-Woods, and of course neither would Ethan, but she could see why Jules and Dennis might.

Now the floor of the rec hall was cleared, a DJ station was hastily set up, and music chugged through the long room. Jules recognized none of it. It was jangly, slidey techno, with an occasional human voice speaking almost accidentally. The DJ, an electric bass player named Kit Campbell, was fifteen, small, appealing, and capable. She had short spiky dark hair and pale skin. She was stylish in miniature, her shorts hanging low, her combat boots unlaced. This was her first summer here, and the other kids seemed drawn to her. By the end of the night Kit was ringed by several campers — a plain, white girl; an unplain black girl; two boys — one in eyeliner, the other stud-like and swaggering, his baseball cap on backward — and they headed out, the girls doing hip bumps, the boys with hands shoved into pockets, all of them in a puppyish, coed knot.

Jules and Dennis walked across the dark lawn with flashlights, following the campers who zigzagged and looped around and hollered. She wished she could drop her flashlight with a thud and run ahead to catch up with them. But she had no place there, and so she stayed with her husband, who she could tell was content walking slowly, just the two of them. Finally, up ahead, the girls went one way and the boys went the other. Jules wondered if some of them had arranged to meet up later, though as camp directors she and Dennis were supposed to keep that from happening. It wasn't that this place was about *sex;* it was more about the end of

669

childhood aloneness, that lone-pilgrim-in-a-bed situation you found yourself in up until adolescence, when suddenly aloneness started to become unbearable, and you needed togetherness at all hours of the day and night.

Here was Dennis now, clicking off his flashlight and pulling open the unlocked door of the Wunderlichs' house. "We will reconvene at some mutually agreeable point near the end of the summer and see where we stand," Edie had said to them before she and Manny moved to a cottage they'd rented in Maine. For now, the Wunderlichs had left all their belongings behind, and the walls of the house were a tribute to summers past, and also to a Greenwich Village folk scene that no longer existed. Campers had never been invited in here; when Jules and Dennis arrived in April, it was the first time Jules had ever seen the inside.

"Aren't you glad not to be sleeping in a teepee tonight?" Dennis asked as they walked through the dim entrance and turned on an overhead light. "You grew up, and so now you get to sleep in a real house."

"Yes, thank God," Jules said, mostly to be agreeable. She didn't want to be in one of the teepees, but she also didn't particularly want to be in this house now, either. She was restless, suddenly realizing that there was nowhere to go at night here, unless you wanted to wander around in the dark. She hadn't felt that way before tonight. The city at least gave you the option of night-crawling; if you couldn't sleep, you could find an all-night diner, not that Jules had done that many times in her life. But she and Dennis were here in the house for the night, the whole summer, perhaps years, perhaps for good. She wondered what was happening off in the teepees right now. Maybe she'd volunteer to do patrol before bed one night this week, a task that was almost always left to the counselors.

Upstairs in the bedroom, Dennis lay down on the side of the high old bed that he'd claimed in April: Manny's side, clearly. When they moved in, Manny's night table still held pieces of male paraphernalia: nail clippers, a much-squeezed tube of cream for athlete's foot. "So?" said Dennis when Jules climbed into bed and turned off the light. "It started out okay, yes?"

"Yes. That's what we'll tell people. 'It started out okay.' And then we'll segue into the terrible story."

"The kiln tragedy," he said.

"Or the sprouts tragedy."

"They looked so innocent, those sprouts," Dennis said. "The kids just piled them on their plates. If only we'd known!"

They laughed tentatively, as if they could ward off the possibility of something actually going badly wrong. Whatever happened, it

671

would be their responsibility now. Already they'd received a couple of e-mails from parents. "I'm going to call Rory," Jules said. "She told me to let her know right away how it was going."

"Tell her I liked her e-mail," said Dennis. "The one with the link to all those camp jokes. Lots of punchlines about bears and latrines."

They'd gotten a crash course in camp directorship from Manny and Edie. The word "safety" came up a lot. The property had to be a secure place, with outsiders kept out and with campers and staff operating all the equipment in the workshops correctly. Though there were endless worries, and provisions for emergencies to consider, you could delegate a lot of the menial tasks to the underpaid but cheerful counselors, who had come here from all over the United States and, for some reason, Australia. American summer camps were routinely packed with Australian counselors. Jules had had a brief but unrealistic fantasy that somehow Rory would want to join the staff, but she preferred to spend the summer with her friends in Oneonta, where she had a job in a plant nursery. She promised to visit at the end of the season, "to see your midlife crisis in action, Mom," she had written in an e-mail.

The idea of calling Rory tonight became less necessary. Rory would want her mother to be happy, and that was all. On the phone they would murmur at each other in the way they always did. Their worlds were far apart: the plant nursery and the dream of art. They didn't need to speak tonight; they could talk tomorrow. Jules and Dennis turned to each other, as much because of the oddness of their new life here as anything else. They both wanted motion and forgetting. They wanted sex because they could have it, unlike the kids across the road, who were told they had to lie separately each night, their bodies poised in a clench of anticipation, while counselors circled with an intrusion of dancing flashlights. Dennis propped himself up on an elbow and craned his head toward her. His black hair had become increasingly spattered with gray in recent months, and his body, always so hairy, now seemed like a forest floor, all silver pine needle and turning leaf. You accepted this when you were this age. Jules thought of her mother, alone in the bed in the house in Underhill. Spending her forties alone, and her fifties, and her sixties, and then her seventies! All of those decades, alone and aching, just like the teenagers across the road, but without the reassurance that all of it would probably end in a blissful sexual fusillade. Why hadn't her mother ever gone out on a date? How had she lived without sex or love? Sex could *be* love, or else, like now, it could be a very good distraction.

Dennis's mouth was opening, his head tilting, his large hand cupping Jules's breast that dropped down like a crookedly hung ornament. Isadora Topfeldt had long ago claimed that Dennis was "uncomplicated," and though this wasn't really true, what was truer was that he'd never felt as entitled as Jules did. He was here with her in Belknap because it was what she wanted, and she'd convinced him it could work. It took care of so many unmet needs. Dennis, cupping her breast, stroking her arm, said, somewhat anxiously, "You're happy?" He wished his intermittently envying wife could finally, finally be fully happy again. Happy and electric. He didn't wait for an answer, but turned her away from him, on her side, her face almost flush against Edie Wunderlich's night table, which held a very old framed photograph of a young man and a young woman, bohemians from a long-ago day whooping it up on a rooftop in the city. Behind Jules, Dennis moved into a good position, and with an indecipherable syllable of acknowledgment, and with the briefest of overtures, he began to impel himself into her. Her own immediate replies made her self-conscious, as if one of the teenagers from the camp might have stealthily slipped into the house, and was even now standing in the doorway of the darkened room, shifting from foot to foot while watching an improbably carnal scene between these two people in

their fifties. At any moment the gangly teenager would quietly say, "Um, excuse me?
Jules? Dennis? A boy in my teepee has a
nosebleed that won't stop."

But the campers were on the other side of
the road, with no interest in making the
crossing. If anything went wrong, a counselor
would call. The Wunderlichs' heavy red
rotary-dial telephone sat on Dennis's night
table, at the ready. It would certainly ring in
the night over the course of the eight weeks;
Manny and Edie had warned them that it
always rang at least once a summer, sometimes more than once, and sometimes it was
serious. For now, on the first night, no one
was calling, and they were alone in the old
groaning maple bed. Sex between these
middle-aged people — not quite the Wunderlichs but not remotely teenagers — seemed
to have no reason to be except for pleasure
or escape. She knew it excited Dennis to
think that she was fully happy, that what she
had now was acceptable, satisfying, a good
way to be. But she saw herself from the
viewpoint of the phantom teenager in the
doorway, and she was too aware of what she
and Dennis were doing, and how old they
were, and where they were. She didn't know
if she was happy yet; she really had no idea.

"Your turn," he said into her neck after his
heart had returned to a normal thump.

"No, that's okay." Her thoughts had pulled

her from him.

"Really? But this is so nice," said Dennis. "We could continue. I'd like to."

But no, she didn't want to anymore; she told him she was tired, and then, it seemed, she was. For now, though, she needed to sleep. In the morning when Jules awakened, Dennis was already off to start the day, which began with the wake-up music, Haydn's *Surprise* Symphony, a tradition that the Wunderlichs had upheld over the decades. Jules dressed and stood outside, looking across the road and beyond it to the lawn, and then she walked toward the smells of camp cooking. The dining hall was in partial bloom; half-alive teenagers carried their bowls to the tureens of oatmeal and glass canisters of muesli. Girls wanted to know where they could find soy milk. *"Latte,"* a boy whispered dramatically. *"Latte."* No one was completely awake yet. After checking to make sure the kitchen workers had all punched in their time cards and that she wasn't needed, Jules sat at a table with a group of earnest girls, all dancers.

"How are things so far?" she asked.

"Buggy," said Noelle Russo from Chevy Chase, Maryland, showing off her arm, which was already lined with a row of pink button-like bites.

"Maybe there's a hole in your screen," said Jules. "I'll have someone check that."

"My dad said there are no requirements here," Noelle's teepeemate, Samantha Cain from Pittsburgh, said. "Is that true? I don't have to take swimming lessons or anything?"

"No requirements. Just take what interests you. Sign-up's at ten. Put down your first three choices for each time slot."

They all nodded, satisfied. Jules noticed that almost none of them were eating much and that all of them had only token amounts of food on their plates. She realized she'd probably stumbled into a little nest of eating disorders. Dancers — no surprise.

"So, still happy?" Dennis asked Jules one afternoon in the second week, walking with her through the trees. They passed the animation shed, where a light was lit: a couple of kids were working after class had ended, standing around a table with the instructor, a young woman named Preeti Singh, who was today's version of Old Mo Templeton.

"I'm just relieved it's not unmanageable," Jules said. "I was really afraid we weren't going to be able to handle it somehow. That it would require too much competence, and we wouldn't be up to the task."

"We are very competent," he said.

"High praise."

They continued on through the woods and out the back gates. It was past four-thirty, the time of day when camp was mostly quiet, everyone showering or practicing instruments or lying on their backs in the grass or finishing up projects they couldn't let go of yet. Jules and Dennis walked the half-mile slope down the road to town. Belknap had barely changed since the 1970s, with a few exceptions. The first day they'd arrived here in the spring, they'd been sorry to find that the bakery that made the huckleberry crumble had closed years earlier and was now a cell phone store. But the general store was still in operation, and so was the Langton Hull Psychiatric Hospital. Dennis had come so far since he first fell apart in college, and even after the depression returned when he was taken off the MAOI, he had recovered and had stayed strong for years, not blunted. He was in no real danger of falling again, but as they passed the small white sign with the arrow pointing toward the hospital, they pretended the sign wasn't there and the hospital wasn't there and that, even if it was, it had nothing to do with them.

Dennis bought them iced coffees and they sat on a bench on Main Street, and within moments his cell phone rang and he spoke quietly into it. "They need us," he told her when he flipped the phone shut. "The generator went out, and no one seems to know what to do."

"Do *you* know what to do?"

"Manny and Edie left us that bible of phone numbers. We'll find the right person to call.

But we can't just leave the camp with no power while we sit here drinking iced coffee and thinking about life." They stood and slowly walked in the direction from which they'd just come. On the way back into camp at dusk, bugs collected in little midair tumbleweed formations, and at least two violins could be heard in a quickie predinner practice, one playing a *scherzo,* the other playing something slow and weary, while elsewhere on the grounds a drummer performed a battering solo.

Every day from then on involved small or big surprises, broken things, problems, the occasional dispute between counselors and kids. Noelle Russo, the girl with the mosquito bites, turned out to be deeply anorexic, and spent several nights in the infirmary. She was a highly talented dancer, word got around, and hard on herself, practicing until she dropped. The news traveled across the road to the house that Noelle had a fierce crush on one of the counselors, the head of the theater prop shop, whose name was Guy. Dennis sat down with Guy, a ruddy and guileless university student from Canberra with pirate rings in both ears, and came away convinced that the counselor had in no way encouraged or reciprocated the crush, nor had he acknowledged his awareness of it to Noelle or any of the other campers.

Sometimes Jules would stop in to Girls'

Teepee 4 for a visit, hoping to find Noelle there. Jules would sit on a bed for a few minutes, knowing that she'd probably shut down any meaningful conversation just by walking in. "How goes it?" she asked the teepee at large, and the girls told her about the plays they were in or the pottery they were making. Kit, the popular androgynous girl, showed her a tiny tattoo of a meerkat that she'd gotten on her ankle that spring. Noelle fretted about the camp nurse's insistence that she consume many more calories each day or else she might have to leave. "I can't go home," said Noelle. "Now that I've been here and seen it, I can't possibly *leave.* Do you have any idea of what it's like where I live? Chevy Chase, Maryland?"

"Nope. Tell me."

"Everyone is so conventional," said Noelle. "Their idea of experimental music is an a capella group doing 'Moondance.' I just cannot believe I'm expected to live there. Out of all the places in the world, that's where my parents had to settle? It just seems so arbitrary. I can't bear it there."

"Everything you do, it'll all feel really slow for a long time," Jules said. "But looking back, much later, it will have seemed like it was fast."

"That doesn't do me much good now," Noelle said.

"I suppose not."

"You're not really going to send me back there, are you, Jules?"

"Well, one day I will."

"Not before the summer is over. I love it here. If this place was a boy or a girl, I would marry it. Maybe it'll be legal to marry *places* one day. And if so, then I will marry this one."

"Noelle, stop talking," said Kit, who was lying on her stomach on the bunk above, a bare arm hanging down. "I feel like I fell down the rabbit hole. You're just running on at the mouth and I'm trying to read and/or sleep."

"I'm running on at the mouth because I want Jules to know she can't send me home. The nurse doesn't know shit about calorie consumption. I know a lot more than her."

"Well," said Jules, "there's an excellent lasagna for dinner tonight that I hope you try." Noelle made a face that seemed to indicate no lasagna would ever cross her lips.

"I'll eat what you don't," said Kit. A third girl entered lugging a kettle drum. "Where are we possibly going to put that?" Kit asked, and all the girls began a discussion about musical instruments and their proper storage places at camp.

Samantha banged in, fresh from the showers, towel-wrapped, calling out to the teepee, "Pantene conditioner is the exact consistency of *semen*!" before noticing that Jules was there. All the girls went immediately silent,

681

then laughed in horror. Jules took that moment to leave.

They needed her and didn't need her. They had formed their own society, and she was touched and unnerved seeing it in operation. What surprised her was that they didn't have trouble asking for what they needed. They frequently approached Dennis or Jules; she might be walking by herself listening to a concerto drifting up from the music barn, or just thinking about nothing much, when a voice would call out to her, "Jules?" Or more likely, "Jules!" And then the follow-up: "There's a stuffed toilet in the upper girls' bathroom. Super tampons again, we think, and no one can find the plunger."

They assumed she would be as interested in their stuffed plumbing as she would be in their creations; she was meant to be interested, concerned, at the ready. The counselors did a lot of work, but the camp directors did too. Had the Wunderlichs felt special being here for all those decades, or had they simply accepted their role as art and plumbing shepherds? She wished she could ask them, but she didn't want to disturb them up in Maine, where, according to a postcard that had arrived days earlier, they were busy "clamming" and "snoozing." They'd turned the problems of camp-running over to Jules and Dennis, and they meant to stay out of it now.

It was becoming apparent to Jules that this job had probably never been much of a creative job. It hadn't occurred to her to ask the Wunderlichs, "When you were running the camp, did you feel creatively fulfilled?" She felt irritated somehow that they hadn't told her and Dennis at the interview, "You do realize that a not-insignificant part of your job will be to make sure that bulk orders of produce from Greeley's Farms arrive on time, yes? The kitchen staff can't be trusted to handle that." But even if Manny and Edie had said this, Jules would have been positive the trade-off was worth it, and sometimes it was. Sitting in the theater watching this new production of *Marat/Sade,* she was enraptured. Dennis seemed to sense these moments, and he held her hand in the dark. She'd been swimming back to this place all this time, though she hadn't known she'd ever get back or that when she got here it would be similar to what it had been, due to the Wunderlichs' diligence. It was as though Manny and Edie had been curators of art, preservationists of a past that, if not carefully maintained, would be forgotten like a lost civilization.

That was it: the Wunderlichs were preservationists, not artists. Jules had wanted to be an artist. The difference could be felt here now in the darkness of the theater, sitting on one of the hard wooden benches among the campers and the counselors, watching the dynamic Kit Campbell onstage, a girl who in everyday life was punked out in combat boots and low-riding shorts, but onstage was regal in the bolt of material that had been fashioned into a gown just for her. People whispered to one another that she would go far, would become famous, would be *huge.* But again, who ever knew anything about what might or might not happen?

When the play ended the lights came up, and it was Dennis or Jules's role to stand onstage and make a series of dull announcements. The strange beauty of the play and the power of Kit's performance had barely been given time to be acknowledged, but the camp directors were required to come in and break the moment. "You want to do it?" Dennis asked, but Jules shook her head no. Instead she walked toward the door, and the night outside, heading alone onto the lawn as her husband climbed onstage and reminded everyone that this camp was a peanut-free environment.

NINETEEN

The Mastery Seminars had been named in a fit of desperation. Ethan Figman knew the name sounded pretentious, but back when the project was starting up, he was told he had to decide on a name immediately, and a majority of board members liked it, so he had waved his hand in resigned agreement. Now the name appeared in sans serif type all around the Strutter Oak Resort and Conference Center in Napa, California. The seminars were taking over the entire resort for a week, as they had done for the previous two years, and never in Strutter Oak's history had there been such a concentration of VIPs here at one time. The board had gotten a little punch-drunk at those organizing meetings in the early days, shouting out names, aiming higher and higher into what seemed unreachability and eventually, at midnight, even naming two people who were *dead,* but who still, in the heat of the moment, were carelessly added to the list.

Now Ethan stood in the broad corridor outside the resort's main dining room. Attendees gathered, holding the booklet that listed the events — a chapbook, really, so beautifully made was it — and surreptitiously glanced at Ethan, as well as at the elder-statesman astronaut Wick Mallard who stood facing a wall, talking quietly into his cell phone. Nearby, two assistants spoke into their headsets like astronauts themselves. Everyone here was privileged, accustomed to *access;* because all the proceeds from the Seminars went to the Anti-Child-Labor Initiative, Ethan justified this saturation in the world of the hyperrich. As he walked along the wide, elegant corridor, trailed by his assistant, Caitlin Dodge, a few participants waved shyly, and a couple of them tried to engage him in talk, but he kept going.

"Mr. Figman," said a young boy standing with his parents, who had absurdly paid full fee for their nine-year-old to attend for the week. Subtly, the parents pushed the boy into Ethan's path, and he stood with his head down, as if ashamed of his parents' frank aggressiveness.

"You can tell him," said the mother. "Go on."

"No, forget it," said the boy.

"It's okay," she said.

"I'm an animator too," the boy said quietly.

"What's that? You're an animator? Well,

that's good; keep working," Ethan said. "It's a great job. Though honestly, these days," he added for an unknown reason, "you might consider choosing a slightly different field."

"Not animation per se?" asked the mother worriedly, waiting for Ethan's answer and preparing herself to concentrate hard on whatever course correction he suggested. "Maybe something related?"

"Nah. Private equity is a much better idea."

"You're teasing him," said the mother. "I can tell." To her son she said, uncertainly, "Dylan, he was teasing you."

Ethan only smiled and wandered off. He didn't even know why he had teased that boy and mother; it had been a little mean of him. He felt that he ought to give the boy a notebook next time he saw him — just say, "Here," handing him one of those chunky numbers that Ethan was always filling with doodles. The kid would be thrilled, and the parents would be thrilled — "Don't draw in it; save it!" perhaps the mother would tell her son — and Ethan would redeem himself. He would try to remember to do this, but he knew he probably wouldn't. Instead, the whole family would leave after the week ended thinking that Ethan Figman wasn't what he seemed at all. He was nothing like Wally Figman, the boy who was bursting with ideas. Instead, he'd become a little bit like Wally's crabby father. Certainly Ethan was under pressure this week, living here in an immense suite with Ash; and with Mo and Mo's current caregiver, Heather, right across the hall. Mo had nothing to do, even here in this place where there was everything to do. Ethan had tried to send his son off to a seminar yesterday on the mechanics of animation, given by three young animators whom Ethan had mentored, but Mo had gotten restless and bolted in the middle of the session.

Ethan asked Caitlin Dodge, "Has my friend registered yet?"

"Let me see. . . . Yes, half an hour ago. He's waiting in the hospitality suite."

They turned a corner and Ethan pushed through a set of fire doors, briefly exchanging the wood-beamed rustic luxury of the conference center for the industrial ambience of the fire stairs. The hospitality suite had to be accessed with a special card; Caitlin swiped it and Ethan entered first. A former undersecretary of State sat alone in a leather wingback chair, dozing, his mouth half-open. Two servers stood at attention at the buffet table. There by the window was Jonah, who had ostensibly been sent here by his employer, Gage Systems, in order to attend a few technology lectures. Ethan had of course invited Jonah to be his guest this week, and Jonah's boss was excited that Jonah had access to Ethan Figman and the Mastery Seminars, and hoped that maybe one year someone from Gage — maybe even Jonah? — would be invited to give a presentation on innovations for the disabled.

The men hugged hard, with loving back slaps. Both of them were now fifty-two, one thick, with thinning hair, the other lean and gray-haired. "Everything to your liking?" Ethan asked.

"What did you give me, the King's Suite? The Sultan's Suite? It's very luxurious."

"It's called the Vintner's Bounty Suite. I wanted you to be comfortable."

"I'm never comfortable."

"Then we're even," said Ethan. They smiled at each other. "I'm so glad you actually came."

"It wasn't too hard to convince them at work," said Jonah. "Your name opens doors."

"Yep, I'm the original doorman," said Ethan. "Listen, Ash is up in our suite, working. She likes to get a lot done during the day but she'll join us for dinner; she's so excited you're here. Mo is here too, though the last time I looked he was outside, in the vineyard, being trailed by his saintly caregiver." Ethan went to the window and squinted out, and Jonah stood beside him. Deep in the distance, in a bolt of sun, were two figures in the rows of vines. Maybe it was only two workers, or maybe it was Mo being followed by the person looking after him; it was hard to tell from here. "Jules and Dennis can't make it," said Ethan, turning away from the window, "but I guess you know that. Spirit-in-the-Woods — how crazy is that? All roads lead to Spirit-in-the-Woods."

"I know," said Jonah. "She was so excited to go back. The camp was such a big thing for her. I wish I could go there this summer, but this is my only time off. Are you and Ash going to go? I bet it would really give you a pang."

"It would. It's slightly possible we'll go for a day at the very end. We're going to try. But we're visiting Larkin in Prague, and then I'm off to Asia for Keberhasilan — you know, the school. And of course there's the show."

Caitlin stepped forward and said, "Ethan, some Renee person said you agreed to introduce a dialogue?"

"Shit, I did say that. Will you be okay?" Ethan asked Jonah. "I do not mean in a cosmic sense."

"I'll be fine." Still Jonah looked so uncertain. "Hey, it's fucking Bambi," Goodman had once said as Jonah entered the teepee. And it was true that if you categorized people by which Disney character they were, then Jonah would always be Bambi. Motherless, graceful, unobtrusive. Ethan — Jiminy Cricket, the annoying little conscience but a more sedentary, pudgy version — wanted to give Jonah a wonderful time this week. Caitlin looped an all-access pass around Jonah's neck, then handed him a booklet that contained all the information he would need. The men agreed to meet for drinks alone later, then for dinner with Ash and a small group of presenters. During the day, Ethan said, Jonah should feel free to go to as many seminars and presentations as he liked. Or go to none. He could get a hot-stone massage in his suite if that was what he wanted, and then go home at the end and tell Gage Systems he'd learned so much.

"I'm not going to get a hot-stone massage," said Jonah. "I want to go hear Wick Mallard talk. I remember when he had to repair that space station; it was so dramatic."

"That's at two," said Caitlin Dodge. "And he's brought a virtual weightlessness chair, which is supposed to be amazing."

"Okay, I'm in," Jonah said.

They slapped backs again in that awkward way of middle-aged men who ache to hug but have already hugged too recently. The gay-straight dichotomy was always slightly stymieing to Ethan. Beauty was beauty; after all, just look at Ash. In the Disney hierarchy she was Snow White; always had been, always would be. Inscrutably sad beauty, like Jonah's, was always compelling, regardless of its gender package. Ethan loved his old friend and wished he could talk about him right then with Ash, or maybe even with Jules. He paused to wonder which Disney character

Jules was, and realized that Disney did not make women or girls or woodland animals that were like her.

It was a siren song. That was how Jonah Bay described it to himself later. He was walking without much thought toward the lecture by the astronaut Wick Mallard, and could see the long line forming outside the closed doors of the ballroom. A few staff members were talking on cell phones; the line of attendees waiting to get in seemed lively and excited. Most of this crowd was male; the idea of an astronaut telling stories of his experiences in space seemed to offer an enviable pioneer bleakness, and the presence of the supposedly amazing virtual weightlessness chair made it even more tantalizing. Jonah was about to get in line too, when he heard a sudden torrent of music from further down the hall, where someone had briefly opened the door of another ballroom. The music was acoustic and sharp and somehow familiar, even in the few seconds that the door stayed open. In curiosity he walked toward that other ballroom. The sign outside read "Reinvention: The Creation of a Second Self," and Jonah slipped inside. He didn't know why he was doing this, and he didn't even think to wonder.

The ballroom, smaller than the first one, was packed, and the hundred or so attendees sat at attention, watching a heavy old man onstage sing and play a banjo. Jonah moved deeper in, taking a seat against the wall. The old man sang into a headset mike:

". . . And the ocean belongs to me, just me
I really don't want to share this sea . . .
I know that you think I'm being selfish . . .
But whoever heard . . . of a generous . . .
    shell . . . fish?"

There was a long, canny pause, during which the audience laughed knowingly. Among the crowd of the wealthy and informed were people who had been tired young parents once; and the lyrics to this song that they'd played for their children had stayed with them over time. But really, the performer had been far more successful in his initial incarnation as a member of a sixties folk group that once sang tight, clear harmonies; after that, his solo folk effort was brief. But then, much later, he'd apparently reinvented himself — twice, actually — in two different subcultures. First there was children's music, in which, known as Big Barry, he'd had a modest run and a single hit, and then, recently, there was environmentalism. Both were subcultures whose key players — like Civil War reenactors or neo-Nazis or poets — you might never in your life be aware of if you hadn't ever lived with someone who was passionate about that world. The other participants on this panel on reinvention were a former NASCAR driver who'd been blinded in an accident and now devoted his life to promoting road safety, and a farmer running for the U.S. Senate. The singer sang on, his voice easygoing and low, and Jonah, rapidly bumping upward toward consciousness, understood who this was.

Barry Claimes had loved the idea of the Selfish Shellfish after Jonah had begun writing the song. Barry had recorded Jonah's music on his cassette tape deck and filed the tapes away for what would turn out to be the next century, a time long after the Whistlers had broken up and become obscure, and long after Barry's brief solo career, which had been propelled by his one Vietnam song, "Tell Them You Won't Go (My Lad)," which had also relied on an idea and lyrics and melody of Jonah's.

But that's mine, Jonah thought as he heard "The Selfish Shellfish" now, and perceived the nostalgic response from much of the audience. *That's mine.* Of course, he didn't even *want* it now, or care about it or think that what he was hearing was particularly good, but the fact that it had originated with him and then been stolen from him, and that as a result he'd turned away entirely from music, now took the form of a thick glottal

694

pressure. It was impossible to know, but he might have gone far as a musician, especially along with that group he'd been in at MIT, Seymour Glass, who were actually still performing sometimes thirty years later. He'd had a real talent, but what was talent without confidence, self-possession, "ownership," as people said, pompously but maybe accurately.

The strumming got harder as Barry Claimes — Big Barry — continued this song sung from the point of view of the tremendously selfish shellfish, who was apparently a non-sharer and a polluter, essentially embodying all the traits of oil-dependent, big business–loving America. Big Barry's fat hand beat down on the banjo as he wailed on and on about grotesque greed; he was throwing himself into the song, exerting himself as he acted out the part of eleven-year-old Jonah's weird and clever creation, the Selfish Shellfish. He finished with a big flourish of the banjo, and the audience responded with cheers.

Jonah was going to turn and leave right then, but the event moderator asked, "So what was the path of transformation that led you from being just a successful folksinger to being a children's singer and then an environmental activist?"

"Well, if you look back at the beginning, the sixties were a time of upheaval," said Barry Claimes. "I know that's a cliché, but it happens to be true, because I was there, and I certainly up and heaved a good lot of the time. My first group was called the Whistlers, as some of you may recall." The audience politely applauded at the memory. "And then I was off on my own," he went on, "and I had one hit in 1971, a Vietnam protest song. Can someone reach into the past and name that tune?"

" 'Tell Them You Won't Go (My Lad)'!" called a man.

"Excellent, excellent. But you know, I assumed that would be the end of it for me. I lay low for a number of years, lived on my royalties, and bummed around doing very little except practicing my banjo. I began dabbling in children's music because I've always been captivated by the natural spontaneity of kids. Plus, you can't bullshit them. And as my work with them proved rewarding, I bought myself a houseboat and traveled around, and I started seeing what was being done to the ocean, and it made me ill. I could not get over the greed of the oil companies and the politician enablers, who were all in bed together and who were all responsible for the ruination of the oceans and the deaths of those extraordinary sea creatures. And then I realized that some of my songs could have an environmental impact too. And that is how an activist is born. So if you're going to reinvent yourself for the second or even third time in your life," he said, "you have to do it for a reason. And preferably not a selfish one — like a certain *shellfish* I know."

Jonah, who had barely been breathing during this monologue, felt his throat and chest fully constrict, and he pushed out of the doors and back into the hallway, just as Barry was finishing up and the senatorial candidate was about to go on. He found a men's room further down the corridor and went into a stall and sank down onto the toilet. He stayed there for a long time, trying to recover and think. He was still in there a little later when the door to the men's room swung open, voices preceding the men who entered.

"— really great. It's all about branding. I'm involved with TEDx — you know what that is? We bring the TED conference experience right into communities. Here's my card; I'd love to tell you more about it."

"Well, thank you."

The men went to their separate urinals, and Jonah heard stereophonic urination. There were more pleasantries, some hand washing, then turbine hand dryers roared, and finally the door opened again and one man left. Jonah peered out the narrow vertical slot of the stall door. He saw part of Barry Claimes's wide back at the sink, the black silk vest and the thin white plankton layer of hair combed across the head. Big Barry picked up the banjo that was leaning on the sinks, swung it around himself on its strap, and strode out of the men's room.

Jonah followed him through the wood-beamed hallways of the Strutter Oak Resort and Conference Center, staying at a distance and trying to look like someone on his way to a seminar. Every once in a while he glanced blankly at the booklet Caitlin Dodge had handed him. Barry Claimes stepped onto the elevator and so did Jonah, but three other people stepped on too, so Jonah was hardly noticed. They all pressed different floors. Ping, went the button, and a few people exited. Ping again. At 4 Barry Claimes got off, and so did Jonah Bay. The former Whistler was actually *whistling* a little as he walked to his hotel room. He slid the key card into the door, but Jonah felt sure it wasn't necessary to stride forward quickly in that second; Barry was old and slow-moving, and would be imprecise in his card swiping. It would likely take two swipes for him to get the card in exactly right, and it did. By the time the green light popped on in the lock, Jonah was right behind him. No one was in the hall to see Jonah slip in after him before the door closed. Right inside the doorway, Barry Claimes turned, his mouth opened in old-man concavity and fear.

"What do you want?" he said, but the heavy door had sucked shut, and now Jonah reached out with both hands and pushed him deeper into the room. "I'll get my wallet," Barry said. "Are you on drugs? Meth?"

Of course Barry Claimes didn't recognize him. Though Jonah felt transfixed inside his own childhood, no one else saw him as a child. He was already over the hump of middle age, heading rapidly toward those years that no one liked to speak of. The best parts had already passed for people Jonah's age. By now you were meant to have become what you would finally be, and to gracefully and unobtrusively stay in that state for the rest of your life.

"It's me, you sick fuck," Jonah said. He shoved Big Barry against the wall in the entryway, and Big Barry shoved back, slamming him against a closet door. Jonah responded in kind, and they banged back and forth between two walls, clunking and clomping, accompanied by exerted breaths, moving further into the hotel room, and now Jonah had the advantage. He pushed Big Barry onto the bed and leapt on him, pinning him there, Jonah's lean self on all fours above the bloated sea creature that was Barry Claimes. If Barry was a shellfish, he'd be a horseshoe crab, round and ancient, washed up on the sand. His face was all rosacea and splotch; the eyes behind his little Ben Franklin frames were pale blue and teary, as they'd been even back in 1970.

"Who?" demanded Barry. He squinted in

terror for several seconds, then his face slackened and became almost thoughtful. "Oh my God. Jonah," he said. "Jonah Bay. You scared the shit out of me." He kept squinting at Jonah, and marveled softly, "Your hair got gray. Even you."

It was as if, now that he knew this was Jonah, he felt he didn't have to be afraid any longer. Immediately Jonah thought about sex with Robert Takahashi, and how one of them had sometimes been on all fours, while the other one lay resting, like the lion and the gypsy in the Rousseau painting. He didn't want Barry Claimes to have a single moment of rest; he had no compassion for him, even though Barry looked like any other old sixties survivor, anyone who might have appeared on that PBS documentary *They Came, They Saw, They Strummed,* which seemed to air around the clock, because people could not get enough of what they'd lost, even if they no longer really wanted it.

Jonah kept Barry pinned down with a knee in his gut, and Barry made a sound of deep organ pain, so Jonah probed with his knee a little deeper, feeling floating objects shift inside. But then somehow Barry was up, roaring. "I tried to be a father figure to you," Barry panted. "To teach you banjo. To encourage you. You weren't used to it."

"A father who drugs his child?" Jonah said, and he reached for anything nearby, his hand

700

coming upon the banjo, which he swung wide, smacking Barry Claimes in the face once with an awful, gongish, vibrato.

"Oh Jesus, Jonah," cried Barry in a nasal voice. Both he and Jonah were equally shocked. Barry fell back against the bed and brought his hands to his face, cupping it, for there was a little blood. The cupping was too much for Jonah. That we each need to protect what little we have, seemed, then, the truest thing, and he wouldn't deny even Barry Claimes that instinct. He'd probably broken Barry's nose, but he hadn't fractured his cheekbone or blinded him or damaged the brain that sat inside that self-involved head. A banjo wasn't the best weapon, for folk music itself wasn't all-powerful. It hadn't been able to stop a war in Southeast Asia, though the songs had kept people unified, passionate, listening with wild attention among an enormous block of bodies or all alone. And now it had maimed a man, but hadn't killed him, which was maybe just as well.

"Oh Jesus," Barry kept saying. "I'm . . . hurt here. What's *wrong* with you, Jonah?" he continued in a gravel-based, thick voice.

"What's *wrong* with me? You're really asking me that?"

"Yes. What kind of person have you become? Are you always like this?"

"Stop talking, Barry, okay? Just stop."

Jonah went to the bathroom and washed his hands with the inadequately tiny leaf-shaped soap that sat in the soap dish. There was a little blood on his sleeve, but not much. He noted Barry's Dopp kit nearby on the marble counter. The kit was unzipped, revealing the items in it that belonged to this elderly man who was on the road many weeks a year. There was a pill bottle whose label read Lipitor, 40 mg, and an asthma inhaler and, oh God, a canister of Tucks Pads, which were described as meant to temporarily relieve "the local itching and discomfort associated with hemorrhoids." All the little accoutrements of this reinvented person. No matter what you'd done in your life, no matter how forcefully antiwar you'd been or how much you'd helped preserve the oceans; no matter how many ideas you'd stolen from a young, shy boy, leaving him cerebrally scrambled and overstimulated, it all came down to the smallest details that made you *you*. Jonah left the bathroom, certain that Barry Claimes wouldn't call security. Barry wouldn't want to open this up; not now, when he had managed to transform himself one last time and remain viable long past the reign of mainstream folk music and into the twenty-first century, where it was usually so hard to make money from your own creations. In the nineties when all kinds of famous pop songs had become available to use on commercials, art and advertising became forever entwined. But folk music, the do-gooding underdog, had been preserved more often than not, and now it was back again, in a way. It wasn't the dominant genre, but its seedlings had blown all around; and like all music now, even folk songs were file shared and showed up on YouTube and went everywhere they could go. Most folksingers, like all singers, made very little money, and that was hideously unfair, and was even often criminal, but for what it was worth, their work got played. He wished his mother knew about some of this; he hoped she did. He planned to tell her.

Barry was sitting on the bed looking at himself in the dresser mirror. "Look at me, my nose is going to swell up. I can't be seen like this; I'm going to have to leave." He turned to Jonah in annoyance, then appeared to become reflective. "You were such a creative kid. So free. It was a magnificent thing to witness."

"Oh, stop talking."

"I did what I could for you," said Barry. "You didn't know anything about being taken care of or being encouraged; it wasn't your fault. Your mother had a great voice, but it's sad what happened to her."

"No it isn't," said Jonah. He didn't want to hear another word spoken by Barry Claimes, and he had nothing more to say to him either, so he started to walk out of the hotel room. But at the door, where the walls were scuffed, he turned back and impulsively seized the banjo, and then he was out of there. Jonah's head and his hands shook as he rode the elevator to his own floor. Pacing the Vintner's Bounty Suite to try and calm his uncalm self, he felt his cell phone vibrate against his groin. He reached down and saw that it was an unfamiliar number, so he answered tentatively, hearing a female voice say, "Hey, Jonah, it's Caitlin Dodge. Ethan thought you might meet him at Blue Horse Vineyard for a drink. If that works, someone will pick you up in twenty minutes. Sound okay?"

Jonah agreed, though this was probably a mistake. He showered quickly, then made his way out to the front entrance of the conference center, and within minutes a black Prius had pulled up at the curb. A driver got out and opened the back door, and Jonah slipped in. He was still shaking so much that he leaned hard against the door to anchor himself.

"How was your day, sir?" the driver asked. "You get to see any of those talks?"

"Yes."

"There was that astronaut who came with a virtual weightlessness chair. You get to try it?"

Jonah paused. "Yes, I did."

"What's it feel like?"

Jonah sat up a little. "At first it's terrifying," he said. "Like you have no idea of what's going to happen to you."

"Oh, that makes sense," said the driver, nodding. "The anticipation."

"But then after a while you remember that it's virtual, and you sort of go along with it. And somehow it changes you a little," Jonah said.

"You still feeling the effects right now?" asked the driver.

"Yes, I still am."

On the patio of the Blue Horse Vineyard, everyone but Ethan Figman sat in the generous sunshine with their big wineglasses and their small plates of pecorino and olives, but Ethan had commandeered the shade beneath an umbrella. All around, conference attendees discreetly glanced over, but no one approached his table. Jonah took a seat across from Ethan, still trembling; it had to be noticeable, didn't it? When the wine arrived, "a mischievous Syrah," the wine steward said before mercifully disappearing, Jonah began to drink a glass of it without stopping, pausing in the middle only because he realized that Ethan was staring at him.

"What?" said Jonah.

"Slow down, you're not supposed to drink like that. Man, you're like a kid with *milk*. You've practically got a wine mustache."

Jonah obediently slowed down, then took an olive and tried to show interest in it. But his hand was unsteady, and the slippery olive fell to the patio and bounced off into the shrubs like a Super Ball. "Sorry," Jonah said, and he put a hand over his face and let loose a single wretched sob. Ethan, shocked, stood and moved to the seat beside him. They were side by side now, facing away from all the other people on the patio; they looked out upon calm, sunlit acres of grapes and spindly sticks.

"Tell me," Ethan said.

"I can't."

"Oh, just tell me."

"I did something that I can't undo, okay? It was very much not like me. Though really, you're probably thinking you don't even know what's *like* me or *not* like me. You've never made me tell you things. You've never made me confess anything."

"Why would I do that?" Ethan asked. "I'm no Catholic, I'm a big Jew. But I know that you don't have to feel like this, Jonah. If you're unhappy, or if you think you're lost —"

"Yes, lost. That's right."

"Then you can do something about it. You've been in that situation before. Your Holy Father, Reverend Moon, remember him? 'Reverend Moon Will Carry Us'?" Jonah was able to smile a little, wincingly. "I don't

know what you think you've done," said
Ethan, "but I can't believe it's irreparable."
He stewed for a few seconds. "Is this about a
relationship?" he asked.

"No. I don't do those," said Jonah. "Don't
you know that I'm a monk?"

"No, I didn't know that," said Ethan. "I
only know what you tell me. After you and
Robert broke up, Ash and I worried a lot. We
didn't want you to be alone. But you'd never
go out with any of those guys she knew, those
actors."

"I haven't wanted to be in a real relationship since Robert," Jonah said. "There have
been occasional things — you know — but
they tend to overwhelm me. And if you really
want to know, it's just not as urgent anymore,
as I get older. The sex part. I've mostly
focused on my work, just to stay busy."

"Sometimes I think work is the great excuse
for everything," said Ethan. "But then I think,
maybe it's not an excuse at all. Maybe it
really *is* more interesting than everything
else. Than relationships."

"Oh, I find it hard to believe that you think
your work is more interesting than Ash and
your kids."

Ethan poked his fingers among some cubes
of pecorino, and dislodged two of them and
indelicately worked them into his mouth at
the same time. "I love my family. Obviously I
do. Ash and Larkin and Mo," he said, giving

each name deliberate, equal weight. "Though I think about work all the time. For me, it's not just to stay busy. I mean, partly it's a distraction from what I can't change. They need me at the studio. When I'm gone, like this week, they all . . . flail. But mostly it's because work is just so great to think about. It's sort of endlessly replenishing." He peered across the table at Jonah and said, "If you can't have a good relationship with somebody, then you should at least have a good relationship with your work. Your work should feel like . . . an incredible person lying next to you in bed."

Jonah laughed sharply and said, "Well, my work doesn't feel that way at all. I put the time in, but it doesn't interest me enough."

"How can that be? You showed me those designs you were working on, and then I went to the website and started clicking, looking at everything going on there; there's just so much, so many things happening. And you always liked building things; you'd talk about that, back at MIT, and I didn't know what the hell you were saying, it was so far beyond me. And what you do now, creating devices for really disabled people, it seems meaningful, no? Making people's lives bearable, so they want to get up in the morning and live in the world and not have to be despairing — or even wish they weren't alive or something?"

"I would've liked to be a musician," Jonah said curtly. He was shocked that he'd said this.

"So why didn't you?" Ethan said. "What was the deal with that?"

Jonah looked downward, not able to meet Ethan's eyes, which were just too sympathetic to tolerate right now. "Something happened," Jonah said. "When I was really young, before you knew me, there was this guy, it doesn't matter who, and he gave me drugs and tried to get me to come up with lyrics for songs, and little tunes, little musical phrases, that kind of thing. I didn't know what was happening. He stole my ideas, my music, and used it himself and made money off it. I spent a long time feeling like I was neurologically a mess. Actually seeing things. That went away, which was a relief, and I kept playing my guitar, mostly because there it was, and I was good. But there was no way music was going to be my life. I mean, it had been taken from me."

"That's a terrible story," said Ethan. "I am really sorry, and I'm sorry I never knew about it. I hardly know what to say."

Jonah shrugged. "It was a long time ago," he said.

"I don't want to sound insensitive here," said Ethan, "but you could still do some music anyway, right?"

"What do you mean?"

709

"Well, couldn't you just play?"

"Just play?"

"On your own, or with friends. You know, the way Dennis and his friends play football in the park, and they're not in shape, right? But they enjoy it, and some of them are good, some of them worship the game. People do that all the time with music. They sit around playing whenever they get together. Does it have to be a job? And as for your actual job, you do like mechanical engineering, robotics. Do you have to think of your job as a consolation prize? What if you played on your own, Jonah? Not during the workday, not getting famous, not finding a manager, not heading in that direction. What if you just *played*? Isn't it possible that then you'd also like your job more, because you wouldn't think of it as something that's secretly had to replace this other thing? Am I completely off base here?"

"He *stole* my *music* from me, Ethan. He stole it; he took it away."

"He didn't steal all of it," said Ethan. "He stole some. It's not this finite thing. I think there's probably more."

An hour later, Jonah lay down for a rest on the bed of his suite in a stunned, winey state, looking around at the enormous flat screen TV, the view of Napa, the robe with its Mastery Seminars insignia. Then he remembered the banjo, and he stood up, got it from where it leaned against a wall, and sat on the edge of the bed with it in his arms. The strings were as sharp as weapons, and sharply responsive. He played until it was time for dinner, summoning up songs that went way back into the dinosaur brain, songs he had no memory of ever learning, but which, it seemed, he knew.

TWENTY

By the midpoint of the camp season, nothing terrible had happened, and for this Jules and Dennis congratulated themselves, but only very quietly, for fear of jinxing it. One afternoon a couple of serious, hushed violists came back from a walk in the woods saying that they'd seen someone there. The swimming counselor and the pottery counselor were dispatched to see if there were trespassers, and they reported meeting up with two young hikers, a man and a woman, who had wandered out of the mountains and were stopping to rest, which sometimes happened on the grounds of the camp. The outer edges of the woods, although camp property, had always been lightly shared, and unless there was trouble, generally no one really complained. Occasionally, the Wunderlichs had said, they'd called the local police to have a look around, because you could never take chances when you were dealing with the safety of minors.

The summer bore on, with its quotidian demands. Only one camper had defected, a French horn player from the city, who simply hated everything about the program and did not want to stay here a day longer. No one was sorry to see him go. But when, early in August, the dancer Noelle Russo was discovered behind the dance studio after dinner with her finger down her throat, throwing up loudly into the bushes, the local doctor affiliated with the camp was called in for a consult, and together he and the camp nurse agreed that Noelle ought to go home.

The night before she was to leave, there was much drama in her teepee, with the other girls apparently sitting around her as if she were being sent to prison or damned to hell. Noelle, her belongings hastily packed in her trunk, cried and said, "Why are they doing this to me? I'm fine. Whoever ratted me out is totally exaggerating." Her friends came to the front office and begged Jules and Dennis to let Noelle stay, but they had to say no, regretfully. "It's not safe," the camp nurse had said. "She needs more supervision."

In bed that night, Jules heard a sound from somewhere in the distance, probably on the camp property, but she couldn't make it out. Even Dennis heard it from his sleep. She expected that one of the counselors would call now, and as she thought this, the red phone on Dennis's night table sounded its raw ring. This was the first middle-of-the-night phone call all summer; they'd been waiting for it. Preeti Singh, who was in charge of both animation and llama care, was on the line. "Something's happened to the llamas," Preeti said. "Can you get down here?" Dennis and Jules put coats on over their pajamas and hurried outside with flashlights.

Both llamas had vanished from their pen; Preeti had learned this when she went to check on them before lights-out. "But who would want them?" she said. "Only some kind of sick vivisectionist."

The counselors were all sent off in different directions to look for the animals. The campers quickly heard what was going on and came out of their teepees in pajamas and shorts and T-shirts to join the search party. It was midnight now, with a nearly full yellow moon, and the entire camp was on the lawn and in the field and by the lake and the pool. "Over here!" came a girl's voice, and they ran toward it. In the light from twenty different flashlights, the two llamas were located, huddled together on the path that led down to the art studios. They both had signs draped around their long, poignant necks: NOELLE SHOULD STAY, one read. THIS IS SO FUCKING UNFAIR, read the other.

The frightened llamas were gently led back to their pen. Someone noticed then that Noelle was missing too, and as the search for her began, Jules felt a sharp bolt of fear. She was in charge, she and Dennis. "Noelle!" she called, her throat tight, and she pictured the lake, and how it could take a person, and suddenly she was hysterical.

"Noelle!" hollered Dennis.

"Noelle! Noelle!" called the campers. All the flashlights went on again, and the teenagers were excited and thrilled at the drama that had unexpectedly collected around them twice in one night. Guy, the counselor with the pirate earrings, whom Noelle had such a crush on, stood in the middle of a path and called out in the loudest voice of anyone, distinctive with its strong Australian accent, "Noelle! Where the hell are you? It's Guy here! Come on, Noelle, give it up!"

Everyone was quiet, thinking that Guy would somehow smoke her out. And he did. She rustled tentatively out of the woods; Jules and Dennis watched as the birdlike, fragile girl went directly to this counselor, and he took her in his arms and spoke to her, and after a moment he looked up toward Dennis and Jules, whose job it was to take her. Later, Jules sat on the edge of Noelle's bed while the other girls lingered nearby, excited, listening.

"It's just that I wanted this summer to be so good," said Noelle, still crying a little.

"There were good parts for you, weren't there?" asked Jules.

She nodded. "Oh yes. I got to dance," she said. "I danced more than I ever get to dance in the entire school year. They're always making me do things I hate there, which have nothing to do with the rest of my life."

"I know," said Jules. "I really know."

Noelle lay back on her pillow and closed her eyes. "I'm sorry about the llamas," she said. "I just wanted to make a point. I went to put the signs on them for everyone to see in the morning, but they got out of the pen, and I couldn't get them back in. I didn't want to hurt them."

"They're not hurt."

"I hope they'll be okay, and that you don't think that, you know, they shouldn't be here anymore. They're a part of this place."

"Yeah," echoed Samantha. "The llamas are completely a part of this place."

No they're not, Jules wanted to say, but of course yes they were. When these girls thought back on this summer, they would see, among everything else, llamas. Forever they would have a specific association to llamas, whose bland faces would represent a moment in their lives that would be like no other. A first moment, art filled, friend filled, boy filled, llama filled. The teepee was as small as a thimble, but it fit these girls. Jules left them there to comfort their friend who was being driven to Logan Airport in Boston tomorrow, where she would fly home to her waiting, worried parents. A summer emergency had taken place, but no one had died.

The following morning, Noelle was gone. Dennis played the *Surprise* Symphony and the music drifted out, but the camp roused itself slowly, tired from the excitement of the late-night adventure and already aware, even in sleep, that the day was going to be hot. So far the summer had been mild, but the forecast called for a succession of very hot days, and this would be the first of them. The heat hit the nineties by noon, causing a mandatory interruption of classes, and extra pool time. These kids were not big swimmers; they hung in the water like eels.

The cook made raspberry milk sherbet in long metal tubs. The campers staggered into the dining hall, and already the heat had turned them listless, and no one ate very much. That first afternoon, off in the woods with their drama class to rehearse *A Midsummer Night's Dream,* the boy and girl playing Puck and Hermia told their drama teacher they'd seen a man urinating against a tree. By the time the drama teacher went to find the man, he was gone, so Dennis said that he and Jules would go check out the situation. It was an unpleasant task on such a damp, hot day, and there was a mosquito drone like a soundtrack over the entire woods. Dennis and Jules were both tired from the night, and they split up and walked around slowly in the heat.

Jules soon saw the hiker. "Hello!" she called in what she hoped was a casual voice. He was leaning against a tree drinking from a beer bottle. He was young, early twenties, his face possessing a feral alertness. He looked unclean, and Jules suddenly thought to be cautious. Dennis was elsewhere, but certainly not too far away. "You've been hiking?" she asked, though there was no sign of any gear.

"I'm staying in the area," the young man said neutrally.

"This is actually the property of a summer camp," Jules said in as easy and cheerful a voice as she could manage. "A lot of people end up here, not knowing. I think we need to mark it a little better."

"A lot better," he said. "I thought it was just a place we could go. A place we could go and spend a few days and nights."

She knew something was wrong with him, and she remembered once feeling afraid of a patient at the psychiatric hospital where she used to work, an agitated young man who'd sliced the air with vertical chops as he spoke about his mother. "No harm done," said Jules now. "It's not public property, though. There's a public campground a few miles south. I think you need a permit to spend the night, but you can ask at the visitors' bureau downtown, and they should be able to point you in the right direction."

Branches broke and a second man came through, looking unperturbed. He was much older, gray-bristle-haired, tall, stooped, creased. He had a face like something in a woodcut, a smoker's face. He seemed about to say something, his mouth opening, and she saw his gold incisor. Father and son? she wondered, then thought, no.

She still didn't recognize him yet. The beauty had been cut away from the face as if through multiple cruel procedures. He looked wrecked, as if he hadn't been taking care of himself for a long time. She thought: *This is a moment of strangeness,* but she didn't even know why she thought that; and then, seeing how he looked at her, languid and unsurprised, though perhaps very faintly entertained, she knew, but she hardly believed it until he spoke, and then she was certain. "Jacobson?" he said. "I wondered when I'd see you."

She stared at Goodman Wolf, as if he were a lost animal that had stumbled into woods where he shouldn't have gone. Both of them were lost animals in the woods. Neither of them had any business being here, but they were.

The younger man looked back and forth between them, and then finally he said, "John, you know her?"

"Yes, I do."

"Ash told you I was living here?" Jules

asked Goodman.

"Oh yeah." He squinted slightly and tilted his head a little. "Oh, you thought *that's* why I came? Because you're here? That's sweet," he said. "But actually I haven't come across an ocean on account of you, Jacobson. Security's pretty tight since you know what. And I didn't even tell Ash I was coming. She doesn't know. But I made an executive decision."

Goodman formed the words as though they were witty, but they weren't. Jules felt her face heating up fast, the heat moving up toward the hairline, giving everything away, not letting her keep her dignity. A man like Goodman would never be attracted to a woman like Jules, but finally they were even: she wasn't attracted to him either. His gold tooth reasserted itself as his lip drew back, and she wondered how it was he thought this was a good look. It was actually a terrible look, seedy and truculent. He held himself as though he was still handsome, though his handsomeness was entirely gone from him. Goodman seemed not to know it, though; no one had told him. Maybe no one had had the heart to. Or maybe he hardly knew anyone anymore who had known him then. He kicked at the dirt; she looked down and saw his scuffed sandals. A toenail poked out, a thick yellow horn.

"But why did you suddenly want to come?"

Jules asked. "I don't get this."

Goodman said, with quiet feeling, "It wasn't sudden. I've always thought about moving to one of the hill towns."

"But how could you?" Jules said. "How could that be possible?"

Goodman shrugged. "I don't know," he said. "I kept thinking about it. I kept going to these real estate sites on the Internet and I saw all these properties — real cheap pieces of shit. It was just a fantasy, that's all. But suddenly Ash tells me *you've* moved back here, and I'm thinking maybe it's the thing to do. The zeitgeist thing, you know? And maybe, if I get my act together, Lady Figman could be convinced to help me."

"I'm just amazed by this," Jules said.

"I could say the same thing about you."

"It's not the same," she said sharply. "Not at all. So were you going to come by? Like, through the front entrance?"

"I actually was there this morning, just sort of going past and looking in, but I didn't see you. I didn't see anyone I knew," he said, as if bewildered. "It was all new people." Then he looked at her and said, "So how's it been for you? Is it everything you've dreamed of, and more?"

"It doesn't matter," Jules said. She didn't want him to know anything about her life, how it felt to be back, or why she'd come.

"But look, you're really not supposed to be here."

"You mean 'here' here?" Goodman said. "Or here more generally."

"Come on, you know what I mean." She looked toward his friend, who appeared completely confused by all of this, but then she understood that they barely knew each other.

"John," said the young man. "You said we'd get something to eat."

"We will; take it easy."

"Where did you two meet each other?" Jules asked, curious. "And when?"

"Downtown yesterday. His name's Martin," Goodman said. "He's a fucking great artist. A printmaker. I've been giving him advice. People will try and use him; I told him he should be wary, not sell himself to the lowest bidder. He should take time to let his talent unscroll — isn't that what I said, Martin?" Goodman Wolf, the gold-toothed fugitive, was now an art consultant?

"Yes," said the young man.

"It's fucking good advice," Goodman added. "Don't forget it."

Bushes crackled with the sound of another approach, and Jules turned to see Dennis pushing through, big as a bear; she wanted to rush over to him, but she felt she shouldn't register too much right now. "Hello," said Dennis, looking them over, taking this in.

"What's going on?"

Goodman looked him over as well, overtly, taking in the convexity of Dennis's thick middle-aged gut in a T-shirt, and his bramble-haired legs, and his work boots with white socks and shorts. The nerd camp-director look, not bohemian the way Manny Wunderlich had looked when he ran this place, but a different look that was Dennis's own: more of a husband look.

"You're the husband," Goodman said.

"What's happening?" Dennis asked.

"I've had a *sighting*," said Jules. She sent Dennis a message, pulsing with telekinesis, but still he could not understand, and he just appeared baffled. "This is Ash's brother," she said, somehow still not wanting to say Goodman's name aloud and expose him.

"For real?" said Dennis.

"For real," said Goodman.

Dennis had no allegiance to the past, or to this man who seemed like someone you knew enough to dislike, even as you saw he was mostly pathetic. "You shouldn't be here," Dennis said to him.

"Yeah, that's what your wife said too," said Goodman Wolf.

"Okay, I'm not kidding," said Dennis. "From what I understand, there's a warrant."

"Whoa, whoa," said Goodman. "You're talking ancient history."

"You want to get into a thing?" Dennis said.

"Because we can do that. I am really ready."

"Dennis," said Jules in the blandest voice she could manage.

Her husband took out his cell phone and said, "Verizon sucks, but we get service in the woods. I'm going to call."

"All right, stop," said Goodman, his eyes brighter, and Martin looked at him with equal intensity.

"What's going on?" Martin said. "I don't understand this at *all*."

"Apparently I've got to go, man," said Goodman, and he came forward and gripped Martin's arm in a handshake and an embrace.

"But we were going to get some food."

"Good luck with your artwork. Don't sell out."

"Get the fuck out of here, Goodman," said Dennis. "Not just the camp. Go back to where you live. Go back to your life there. I am really not kidding."

Goodman nodded at him, then looked at Jules and said, "Jacobson, you got yourself a man." The tooth shone one last time, but when he turned and walked off, his steps quickened, and then he became like an animal leaping away from hunters — a wounded deer that had once been a boy who had drunk from an enchanted, unlucky stream. Jules crossed her arms hard around herself, and she would have liked Dennis to come over to her and throw his big arm

across her shoulder, but he wasn't even looking at her yet; he was talking to Martin.

"Where do you live?" he asked.

"Rindge, New Hampshire."

"And what brought you down here?" Dennis's voice was tender and deep; Jules thought
he might put an arm around Martin, not her.

"I had some problems," Martin said in an
indistinct voice. "There's a hospital here."

Dennis nodded quickly. "Langton Hull."

"But they weren't doing anything for me.
Too many drugs, so I walked out. It was
entirely my choice," he added.

"Okay, you walked out," said Dennis. "And
then you met that guy?"

"John. Yeah, at the bus station. I was going
to go somewhere, maybe home. He started
talking to me; he showed like a real interest.
He'd just gotten off a bus. So I went with
him to this place. He said it was for artists."

"It is," Jules felt she had to say.

"Look, I've stayed at Langton Hull," said
Dennis. "They'll help you, okay? You should
go back and let them try."

Martin considered this. "I *am* very hungry,"
he finally said, as though that made the decision.

Dennis dropped his cell phone back into
his pocket and said to Jules, "I'm going to
take him there. You go back by yourself, okay?
They're going to wonder where we are."

She watched as the two men headed off in

the other direction, away from camp and toward town. Goodman was already somewhere far ahead, getting smaller, getting on a bus soon, then a plane, leaving and going home. Maybe he would eat one last big American meal in the airport — a bloody hamburger and fries, looking around at all the travelers, most of whom probably had people waiting for them somewhere. Jules's heart was beating so hard, and she checked her own cell phone and saw that she had two bars of reception, which was probably enough. Ash's cell phone was on Jules's phone's speed-dial; so many times Jules had called it over the years when Ash was traveling with Ethan, or traveling alone for work and meeting up with Goodman in Europe. Now Ash and Ethan were visiting Larkin in Prague at her Yale summer program. It was evening there; the phone rang in that international way, loud and quick and stern.

Ash answered, her voice revealed through a hiss like water in pipes. "It's me," Jules said.

"Jules? Oh, wait a sec, I'm in the car. I'll put —" Her voice cut out for a second. "— phone," she said.

"What? You're breaking up. I just heard 'phone.'"

"Sorry. Is this better? Is everything okay?" Ash asked.

"Look, I have to tell you something. I saw Goodman!" she said in a rush. "He's here at *camp,* he traveled here from Iceland, wanting to look at houses here. He said he hadn't told you he was coming. It's just crazy. Dennis started yelling at him, and Goodman ran off. I think he's going back to Reykjavik. It was horrible. He looks so different, Ash," she said. "You didn't tell me that." Still she heard nothing. "Are you all right?" Jules asked. "I know it's all pretty wild. Ash?"

There was more silence on the line, followed by some muted background talking. Jules heard, "No, I will *tell* you. Yes, *Iceland,*" and then a male voice spoke to Ash, agitated, but all of it took place under that international hiss, and Jules couldn't make anything else out.

"Hello?" Jules said. "Hello?"

But Ash was talking to Ethan, not her. "Give me a second," Ash was saying to him, strained, "and I'll tell you. Yes," she said. "Goodman. Jules was talking about Goodman. All right, Ethan, all right. Please just stop." Her voice was pleading, and then she came back on the phone and began to cry. "I have to go, Jules," she said. "You were on speakerphone and Ethan's right here."

"Oh God," Jules said before she could stop herself. And then the call was over.

She hurried out of the woods, walking fast, then running, finding her way back instinctively and emerging onto the lawn in the middle of a hot, ordinary afternoon. Several teenagers were lolling under trees playing instruments, and they waved to her. That night, Jules sat through an evening of one-act plays written by campers, and the next day she tolerated a lunchtime barbecue, at which a hammer dulcimer trio played Nirvana songs on homemade instruments. She had her phone in her pocket at all times, waiting for it to vibrate and for Ash to be on the other end. When Ash did call, during breakfast the following day, she said, "Jules? Can you talk?"

The hiss on the line was back. Jules abruptly stood up from the table where she'd been sitting with two boys, actors, who seemed to be falling in love right in front of her. "Yes," Jules said into the phone, walking through the dining hall and out the screen door to the patio, where it was quiet and she could be alone. "Where are you?"

"I'm at the Prague airport. I'm going home alone. Ethan and I broke up."

"What?"

"Yeah, I know. After we got back to the hotel we just got into everything. The whole marriage. He says that it isn't only the actual lie that gets to him, it's also the implications."

"Which are what?"

"Oh, that in keeping this promise to my parents, I basically chose them over him. He says he's always felt that anyway, and this just confirms it. Like I'm still a little girl. He was so condescending, Jules! And I told him that, too."

"It sounds awful," Jules said.

"It was. I apologized to him about Goodman over and over, and he just ignored me and kept going on about my family. Finally I told him that he never tries to see things my way, and that he has no idea what it's like being married to him."

"What did you mean?"

"Everyone fawning all over him. And how much space he takes up in the world; it's just exhausting. And he said, 'Oh, I'm sorry it's such torture flying on company jets and not thinking about all the little boring details of running a life; and also having more money than anyone we know.' And I said, 'Is that what you think I care about?' He backed down really fast, because he knows I'm not like that. By now we were just saying all kinds of deranged things to each other." Ash's voice was increasingly manic, and Jules just listened. "I told him I knew he never really liked my work. And in the middle of this fight he basically stops the action and feels he has to refute that point and actually compliment me. He says, 'You know I like what you did with the staging in that evening of one-acts.' And I said, 'God, Ethan, stop it! Stop saying something nice but vague, trying to show that you respect me.' And he admitted that I was right. I know he's bored with me, Jules, and he's too polite to say so. Him finding out about Goodman just cracked everything open that's been there in front of us. Like, even though Ethan spends so little time with Mo, I know it really bothers him how involved I am in Mo's education and treatment and vocational plan; can you believe that? Someone has to take charge of Mo's schedule, and it's sure not going to be Ethan Figman. But he also gets jealous, I swear he does, because I'm paying so much attention to Mo, and I know how to do it, and he doesn't. He practically admitted this. We were standing in this Prague hotel room screaming at each other. And now we're broken up. We reached that decision at about sunrise, when we were both so exhausted we were practically falling on the floor. But it was mutual." Suddenly she was silent.

"Come on, Ash, you can't be serious," said Jules, gesticulating, and a few campers looked out at her through the windows in curiosity or concern.

"I am," Ash said. "We just said too many things."

"But you love each other. You're this huge couple, and you belong together, and that can't just change."

There was a tiny sound, when crying is so great that it can't even be released. Finally Ash composed herself, and said, "It's done now, Jules. It's done."

■ ■ ■ ■

When you have inadvertently been responsible for ending the marriage of your oldest and closest friends, it is impossible to think of much else. Jules discovered this in the final weeks of Spirit-in-the-Woods, as she was forced back into the daily needs of the camp but felt herself only partly available. Ethan and Ash were really separated; Ash wasn't going to go with him on their planned trip to Asia. When she returned from Prague she stayed in New York for a few days, but couldn't stand being in the house alone, and instead she flew to the ranch in Colorado in the middle of August, taking Mo with her and the cast of her next production, surrounding herself with her son and actors and scripts and work.

"I have to lie low for a while," Ash explained. "I can't think about the things that remind me of everything." The people, she meant. "I'll call you," she said vaguely, but she didn't, and she swore it had nothing to do with Jules having accidentally let Ethan know about Goodman. Ash wasn't angry with Jules, she promised her; not at all. She just had to go somewhere alone. Ash was in such distress, and though it was unlike her not to rely on Jules, she stayed away.

Jules thought about how she and Dennis

had actually managed to come back up to Belknap, Massachusetts, to the bursting, splendid place of her early life, but the catch seemed to be that she could never again see the people she'd loved when she had first been here. "Call Ethan," Dennis said one night when they were sitting in the Wunderlichs' house answering e-mails from parents, which came in at a far greater volume than they could have imagined. If Jules's mother had ever called the camp when Jules was a camper, she would have been mortified and furious. But today's parents could not stay away. They wanted to know what classes their children were taking and whether they were being cast in plays. "Talk to him," said Dennis, not looking up from his laptop. There were nine days left in the camp season, and the Wunderlichs were driving down from Maine the next day to have the planned end-of-summer discussion. Jules didn't know what they were going to say; someone at the camp would surely tell them about what had happened with the llamas, and they had already been informed about Noelle's unhappy departure. Who knew what they would think about the job that Jules and Dennis had done, but Jules was so upset by Ash and Ethan's breakup and her own role in it, that she could barely think about camp right now.

"I can't call Ethan," she said. "I'm sure he's very angry at me for knowing about Goodman and not telling him."

"He can't be that angry at you. Not for long."

"And why is that?"

"You know," said Dennis.

The Wunderlichs arrived the next afternoon during free period, and Jules and Dennis walked them around the grounds, showing them all the healthy, fertile activity taking place. You barely had to do anything to get the kids split up into groups, sewing costumes, planning events. "We haven't run the place into the ground," Dennis said easily. "Yet." Manny, with his anarchic eyebrows, and Edie in her big straw summer hat, seemed like benevolent grandparents who'd come to visit their grandchildren, and they nodded and smiled in approval of everything they saw.

During lunchtime, the four of them sat at their own table by the windows in the dining hall. "It all looks good," Manny said. "It seems that we weren't wrong to turn it over to you."

"No, we weren't," Edie echoed. "We'd thought about going in a different direction, but we're glad we went with you."

"Whew," said Dennis, and he and Jules laughed self-consciously. There was a pause, and no one spoke.

"We think it's going so well," said Manny, "that we want to make you another offer."

"Oh boy," said Dennis. "Okay." He was pleased to have been praised. He'd rarely been praised for work he did, and Jules could see him almost leaning into it. Praise could be more gratifying than work itself.

"We'd like to ask you to make a five-year commitment to the camp," Manny said. "A five-year contract. We've written down the terms. With five years, you can bring the camp along in the way that you see fit. One year is *nothing*. You're just getting your feet wet now. With five years, not only can you make the camp become the place you'd like it to be, but we also won't have to worry about it. We can back off completely. That sounds like a relief to us, if you must know. We've been so invested in every last detail all these years; we've been very hands-on. Maybe now we might do a little something else with ourselves. Like sleep, for a start."

"Or I might finally have surgery on my bunions," Edie said. "I've let them go a very long time. My feet don't even look human right now. They look like hooves," she said.

"It's true," he said. "They do."

"Thank you, darling," said Edie, and they smiled at each other.

"When we started this place we thought we could make a utopia," said Manny. "And for a long time we did. When you were here as a camper, Jules, it was still pretty great, wasn't it? But already it was long past the heyday."

"I'm curious, Manny, what would you say the heyday was?" asked Edie, and for a moment it was just the two of them mulling it over. "Nineteen sixty-one?"

"Or maybe nineteen sixty-two," said Manny. "Yes, that was a good year."

"It was," said Edie, and they nodded together at the distant image of that year.

"And the late sixties were very exciting here too, naturally," Manny said. "A couple of kids actually tried to take over the front office. They called themselves SDS. 'Spirit-in-the-Woods for a Democratic Society.' Cracked me up. And we did have all that trouble for a while with LSD, remember that?"

"That harp player on the diving board at three a.m.," Edie said, and the couple nodded at each other again, in a reflective, knowing way.

"By the time the eighties came around," said Manny, turning back to the table, "the main thing the kids wanted to do was shoot those damn music videos. And every time something new came along, we had to fight it off with a stick."

"Five years sounds good," Dennis said suddenly, and Jules turned to him in surprise. "No?" he said to her. "It doesn't?"

"Dennis, we'll have to talk about it," she said. He gave her a perplexed, glowering look, then returned to the Wunderlichs.

"I personally feel honored that you're so

pleased with how we've handled the camp this summer," Dennis said to them.

Jules felt her face grow warm as she said, "Yes, thank you, Manny, Edie. We'll get back to you about this."

Later, when the Wunderlichs were gone, and the whole camp was in the rec hall for the poetry slam, Dennis and Jules stood together on the buggy hill at dusk. "I don't know what you're thinking anymore," he said to her. "First you want to come up here, and I say yes, fine, you can return to your roots, let's give it a whirl. And then you get a chance to make it happen, to make it *stick,* and suddenly you realize this isn't what you want to do after all. Because all you're thinking about is your friends. What about us? We gave up our jobs, Jules. You quit your practice. We left the city and came up here for this idea of yours."

"It's not what I thought it would be," she said.

"And what did you think? You were going to get to have funny parts in plays? And everyone would pay attention to you all over again?"

"No," she said.

"I think that's exactly what you thought," said Dennis. "I knew that going into this. But you seemed so excited, and I didn't think I should interrupt that."

"What do you want from me, Dennis?" she

said. "My friends have broken up because of me. Can't I be upset?"

"It's not because of you," he said. "It's because of them. And you are here now. You're running a summer camp. You're supposed to do the budget with me, and write the newsletter, and send e-mails to parents about their brilliant sons and daughters. And instead you're off in some deep, lost place in your brain, some pathetic place."

"Oh, pathetic?"

"Definitely. Look at you. You should have seen the way you were blushing when that loser brother of Ash was in the woods."

"It was just a reflex," Jules said.

"*That's* who you've been talking about all this time? When I took that kid back to the hospital I heard all about how Goodman — I mean *John* — was going to advise him about his artwork. Give me a fucking break! What did the Wolf parents tell their kids: You are so special that the normal rules don't apply to you? Well, you know what? Everybody's grown-up, everybody's old, and the normal rules do apply."

"Why are you so mad at me?" Jules said. "Because I don't want to sign on for five years? You're just thrilled that someone wants you," she said, knowing this was mean but unable to stop herself. "That someone is saying, yes, yes, you can do this job and we're happy with your performance. That you're not in danger of falling into a depression and telling some poor woman she might be dying of a tumor on her liver."

"Yes, that's right," Dennis said. "I haven't had people telling me how great I am. And the truth of it is that none of you were all that great. Your friends: Mr. loser gold tooth, and his lying sister with her precious plays that I have never understood, and Ethan the magnificent, all of whom you've always worshipped beyond anything or anyone else on earth. And the thing is: *They're not that interesting.*"

"I never said they were."

"That's all you said. That's all you said. And I was the good-natured husband. And it's still not enough for you, you're still there with them, so much more invested in their story than you are in ours."

"Not true."

"You wanted to come back here," Dennis said, "but it turned out to be hard work. And none of you ever had to really work when you were here. Everything was fun. And you know why? Because what was so great about this place wasn't *this place.* It's perfectly fine. We have plays! We have dance! We nurture the inner glassblower in your kids! I'm sending e-mails to parents who demand that their kids get into the glassblowing workshop. Parents love glassblowing children, right? But good luck to the glassblowing adult. If those same kids ended up blowing glass at thirty, their parents would feel they'd *failed.*" He was panting, raging. "This camp is a perfectly fine place, Jules, but there are a lot of other places like it, or at least there used to be. And if you'd gone to another one, you would've met an entirely different group of people and become friends with *them.* That's just the way it is. Yeah, you were lucky you got to come here when you did. But what was most exciting about it when you were here was the fact that you were young. That was the best part."

"No. It wasn't only that," Jules said. "You weren't here then. It did something to me. *This* place — this particular place — did something to me."

"All right," Dennis said. "So it did. It made you feel special. What do I know — maybe it actually *made you* special. And specialness — everyone wants it. But Jesus, is it the most essential thing there is? Most people aren't talented. So what are they supposed to do — kill themselves? Is that what *I* should do? I'm an ultrasound technician, and for about a minute I was the director of a summer camp. I'm a quick study. I learn skills and I read up on things to compensate for my absolute lack of specialness."

"Stop it," said Jules. "Don't say you're not special."

"You don't treat me like I am," he said. His

face burned; together, both their faces burned. She tried to touch him, but he twisted away and didn't look back at her.

That night Dennis slept downstairs on the old mildewed couch in the living room, and the following day they formally declined the Wunderlichs' offer. "You tell them, I don't want to," Dennis said. Manny and Edie were shocked and disappointed, but not destroyed. Apparently other Spirit-in-the-Woods alumni were eager for a chance at this job; many people wanted a way to return here. A woman who used to do elaborate mosaics at the camp in the 1980s really wanted the directorship, and they would offer it to her and her female partner, who had both been the Wunderlichs' close second choice.

The camp would go on in its own fashion, and teenagers would continue to be shepherded through the gates, and then shepherded back out again at the end of the summer, weeping, stronger. They would blow glass and dance and sing for as long as they could, and then the ones who weren't very good at it would likely stop doing it, or only keep doing it once in a while, and maybe only for themselves. The ones who kept up with it — or maybe the *one* who kept up with it — would be the exception. Exuberance burned away, and the small, hot glowing bulb of talent remained, and was raised high in the air to show the world.

TWENTY-ONE

The clinic in Chinatown was relieved to have Dennis back in September, as they were still badly understaffed, but Jules had no job to return to. The social worker whose office she'd shared offered to help her with referrals, and Jules thanked her, but she dreaded trying to build a practice all over again; she didn't have the energy for it or the belief. She missed her clients, but they wouldn't be back. They were off, some of them with new therapists, others with no one. Janice Kling had written Jules a nice note about how much she liked the woman she was working with, someone Jules had referred her to. A colleague urged Jules to advertise on a few psychotherapy websites, and when she did, describing herself as "a caring, nonjudgmental therapist with a special interest in creativity," she felt uneasy, as though she was lying.

The ads did nothing, and her practice did not refill. She would have to think of something else. At night Jules and Dennis sat across from each other at the small kitchen table in the apartment, often eating some form of takeout. They'd made a patched-up peace by the time they left Belknap, for both of them were too weary to take up the fight again. As Jules's work dwindled, Dennis worked overtime. He knew his field very well, and after his disaster at MetroCare, he'd become highly vigilant; by now, his vigilance had transformed into expertise, and he was in demand. Needing more income because Jules wasn't working, Dennis asked for a significant raise and was startled to receive it.

In a marriage, they both knew, sometimes there was a period in which one partner faltered, and the other partner held everything together. Jules had been the one to hold everything together after Dennis's stroke and during his depression. Now he took on that role, and didn't complain. Jules was so worried about finding work, but what remained just as pressing to her was the breakup of Ethan and Ash. She'd sent more e-mails to Ash, who was still living on the ranch in Colorado. Jules had implored her to at least talk to her on the phone, and they'd spoken a few times, but the calls were flat, because Ash was so unhappy.

Rory, who didn't really understand why her mother had given up the job at the camp, and was now concerned about whether she would find another job in New York, called more often than usual. "Don't worry," Jules said. "We'll still be able to pay your tuition, in case you were wondering."

"I wasn't thinking about that," said Rory. "I was thinking about you, Mom. It's weird with you not working. You always had a client to see. No matter what was going on, you were thinking about your clients."

"I thought about you too, honey."

"I know you did. I didn't mean that. I just meant that you were really involved in your work, and it seems so weird now that you're just kind of . . . between things."

"Yes, that's a good way to put it," said Jules.

"Well, I'd better go," said Rory apologetically. "There's a house party."

"There's always a house party," said her mother. Someone shrieked in the background up in Oneonta, and then Rory laughed and hung up before Jules could finish telling her to have fun and be safe.

One day, in that strange and fallow time, Jules's mother called and said, "Well, I have some news. I'm selling the house." It was time for her to move to a condo in Underhill — actually, it had been time for years, Lois Jacobson said, but she hadn't wanted to deal with it until now. Could Jules come and help her clean out the basement? Her sister, Ellen, would come too.

Jules took the Long Island Railroad out to Underhill on a weekday morning, and when

743

she stood on the platform she saw her mother in the parking lot, waving from beside her little compact car. Her mother had gotten small, losing a couple of inches of spinal height. She'd also let her hair go dove white, and still had it styled each week at the same beauty shop where she'd always gone, and where Jules had once gotten that dreadful perm. There was Lois now with her swirled, newly set white hair and her raincoat, looking like someone's grandmother, which she also was. Jules clattered down the stairs to the car, and when she embraced her mother she refrained from picking her up like a doll.

Ellen was in the backseat, and the sisters reached toward each other in some approximation of an embrace. In middle age, Ellen and Jules looked more alike now than they ever had. Ellen, who lived only twenty minutes away with her husband, Mark, saw their mother all the time. They were close, and Jules was the one who had left the family, going off into the city, which could seem sometimes like another country. Neither Lois nor Ellen went into the city very often themselves. Underhill had improved greatly, and there were now two Thai restaurants and a bookstore/café. Lois Jacobson had kept up the house on Cindy Drive as best she could all these years, but it needed a paint job, and the mailbox still hung at a slant. Thinking about her mother coming into the house alone, evening after evening, was enough to make Jules want to sweep her mother up in her arms for real and ask her how she'd done it. But now they were in the kitchen, and Lois was making them lunch with ingredients from an organic market that had just moved into town, "thank God," said Lois.

"Mom, you buy organic now?" asked Jules.

"Yes. Is that so surprising?"

"Yes!" said both daughters — both *girls,* they thought of themselves in the infrequent times they were together.

"Who are you?" said Jules. "Give me back my real mother. The one who served us Green Giant frozen corn when we were growing up."

"And Libby's canned peaches," said Ellen, and they looked at each other and laughed. After lunch, their mother was already down in the basement getting to work, and Jules and Ellen stood in the kitchen clearing the dishes. Ellen and Mark had a close marriage. No children, their choice; a small, pretty house; a Caribbean cruise each year. "So what will you do now if you don't have a therapy practice anymore?" Ellen asked Jules.

"I don't know. I'm sending out feelers. But I'm going to have to figure it out soon."

"I'm sorry the camp didn't work out," Ellen said. "I remember that place. The sight of all those kids running around."

"At the end of the first summer I went

there, I returned all show-offy, I think," said Jules. "I'm sorry if I was a jerk," she added, unexpectedly emotional. "If I bragged a lot. I'm sorry if I made you jealous."

Ellen picked a dish up from the table and slipped it into a slot in the avocado-colored, apparently indestructible dishwasher of their girlhood. "Why would I have been jealous?" she said.

"Oh, because I always went on and on about my friends, and the camp, and the Wolf family and everything. I thought that was why you, you know, treated me kind of coldly."

Ellen said, "No, I treated you kind of coldly because I was kind of a bitch. I treated everyone that way, didn't you notice? Mom was thrilled when I finally moved out of the house after college. Mark sometimes teases me and tells me I'm in 'bitch royale' mode, so then I try and rein it in. But it's just who I am; I can't really help it. No, don't worry, Jules, I was never jealous of you."

The streets around the Animation Shed's midtown Manhattan office building were purposeful by day, and then quiet and characterless at night. Almost everyone fled at the end of the workday, and now, at seven p.m. on a Thursday in December, Jules walked into the enormous, chilled lobby, with its roped-off elevators and skeleton-crew security guards. Ethan's assistant, Caitlin Dodge, had

746

called a few days earlier, to say that Ethan wondered if Jules was free for dinner this week. The call had come in the wet heart of winter, when Jules was spending her days answering ads for part-time clinical social workers. Only from one did she receive an interview; at over fifty, it was rare to be a first-choice hire. She and Dennis barely discussed what she would do now, though the urgency of finding work was upon them, bearing down. He'd come home at night and there she'd be at her computer, answering ads or rearranging items on her résumé. She was friendless, she felt, with Ash still very separate in Colorado, and Jonah busy with work and apparently now informally playing guitar every Saturday night with a group of musicians — one of the guys from Seymour Glass and three of his friends. A couple of social workers e-mailed Jules, wanting to get together, and she went once; at the bar, the women talked about how managed care was ruining everything, and then they all drank much too much and left feeling defeated.

So when Caitlin Dodge suddenly called, Jules felt like shouting into the phone. Someone needed to rescue her, though she had never dared to hope it would be Ethan. She'd worried that he wouldn't want anything to do with her ever again. But for some reason, here he was.

In the hallway outside the animation studio

after hours, Jules spoke her name into an intercom and waited beside a glass wall until an assistant came to get her. The place was dim but still discreetly active at this hour. All she could see was busyness, industry, motion.

Behind the glass wall of his large office, Ethan was at his desk. She hadn't seen him since the spring, before she and Dennis had made the move up to Belknap. His hair didn't look particularly combed now, and he was staring into a computer screen and might have already been staring into it for hours. On his couch sat Mo, bent over a banjo and studiously playing. Adolescence had claimed Mo Figman unhappily; he'd been a bony boy, all heightened sensitivity and irritability, and now at age nineteen he had a man's body but a restless, awkward demeanor.

Jules walked up to the office and tapped lightly on the glass. "Hello," she said.

Mo stopped playing, then stood quickly, as if she'd scared him. "It's Jules, Dad," he said in his thin voice.

"I see that," said Ethan. He stood up behind the wide plane of battered copper that served as his desk.

She wasn't sure which of them to greet first, and so she went to Mo, who didn't want to either shake hands or be hugged. They nodded to each other, almost bowing a little. "Hi, Mo, how are you? How's boarding school?"

she asked.

"I'm home for a break," he said. Then he added, as if he'd rehearsed it, "I don't like school, but what else am I going to do."

"Oh," she said. "I'm sorry you don't like it. I didn't like school either. I liked camp. Hey, I didn't know you played the banjo."

"Jonah Bay started giving me lessons on Skype," said Mo with sudden force. "He gave me this." He held out the instrument, and Jules admired the faded rainbow on the worn surface.

Mo smiled quickly, and then a stylish young woman entered the office and said, "Are you about ready to go, Mo?"

"Ready," he said. He zipped the banjo into a case and started to leave with her, but Ethan said, "Wait, wait. You're just going to leave like that?"

"Sorry, Dad." Mo sighed, rearranging his shoulder bones, oddly stretching his neck, and then he turned to Jules and made eye contact, which seemed to take all his effort. "Good-bye, it was nice to see you," he said to her. Then he turned again, toward Ethan, and said, "See you later, Dad. Is that better?"

"So much better," said Ethan. He reached out to hug Mo, who tolerated the touch, his eyes closed as if he were heading downhill on a sled, awaiting a soft collision at the bottom.

When he was gone, Ethan turned to Jules and their embrace was no less awkward; she also closed her eyes against it. Then she pulled back and had a good look at him, and it was almost worse to see that he didn't appear angry. "Hi," she said.

"Hi."

"I didn't know when I'd hear from you," said Jules. "I assumed you were furious."

"Nah. Just upset about everything. I needed to calm down."

"And you're calm now?"

"I'm the Dalai Lama," he said. "Can't you tell?" But it was hard to conclude anything about him, really; he mostly looked disheveled and morose. "Let's go get dinner," Ethan said, and instead of leaving the building they walked up a shuddering metal spiral staircase that led to a space she hadn't known about.

"This place is like something in a dream, when you find out there's an extra room in your apartment," she said as they stood in the dislocating, loftlike space that had been designed expressly for Ethan upstairs. He told her that sometimes over the years when he was working late he would simply spend the night there instead of going home, even though technically he wasn't supposed to, because this was an office building.

A winter stew had been left in a slow cooker in the open kitchen, and Ethan brought two bowls of it over to the dining table. He and Jules sat across from each other, with a row of dark windows behind him. "I haven't seen

Mo in almost a year, I think," she said as they ate. "He's getting so handsome. And he has a lot of Ash in him."

"They both do, physically. I'm glad for them. Mo usually likes being home on break from school, but now, with Ash and me living apart, it's been really difficult for him. He just doesn't understand why we're doing this. I've tried to keep him busy, tried putting him to work here, but he gets very agitated. I had him sorting mail, putting it in people's boxes, but sometimes he would actually open the letters, and once he threw a whole stack out. Everyone's very nice about it, of course, but he's just too disruptive. He can live at the boarding school until he's twenty-three, and then who knows what we'll do. It terrifies me not to know."

"Twenty-three is a long time from now," Jules said. "You don't have to figure it out yet."

"I have to figure everything out."

"You really don't."

"I am all fucked up, Jules. Everything just sort of fell into a hole. The end of marriage hole. It was kind of building up, I guess."

"Wait," Jules said. "Before we get into that, can we talk about me in all of this? Me knowing about Goodman too? Let's get that out right away."

Ethan waved a hand at her. "What else were you supposed to do? You promised the family, and there was just one of you versus all of them. I get it. I'm sure Ash gave you a blow by blow of our fight that night," he went on, "and I hardly remember what I said, but I know I talked about her choosing them over me. Did she tell you that?"

"Yes."

"And, you know, she had a few things to say about me too. She didn't exactly hold back. Since then, dealing with the kids and everything, we've tried to be cordial, and not get into everything all over again. But here's one thing I keep thinking about: Ash is this big feminist director, and yet she never seriously considered Cathy Kiplinger's version of what happened with Goodman. And that was never a contradiction for her. Her brother was separate, and he was in a category all his own. She's able to compartmentalize like that. But what can I say? In other instances, it's kind of great. She's an amazing mother to Mo, whereas I have been a failure as a father. She shows delight when he comes into a room; she never loses her temper with him. Why does that irritate me? Am I really such a baby that I need all the attention? Or is it just that it reminds me of my horribleness? Ash has many amazing qualities, she truly does. She put together a thoughtful, beautiful home for us, and everyone always wanted to be in it. It's hard not to fall in love with her. She makes such an effort with everything.

She was raised to do that. Her mother was like that too, with all her meals," he said. "Poor Betsy."

"Poor Betsy," Jules echoed. "I think of her so often."

The death of Betsy Wolf stayed between them for a moment. "I know that Ash feels her parents put all this pressure on her, demanding art plus achievement," Ethan said. "Meanwhile, it's not like they were arty themselves. Drexel Burnham was about making money. But all her complaining about the pressure — I mean, enough already, right? I kind of feel these days that unless your life has included *torture* — unless you've practically been raped, or kept in a cellar, or you're twelve or thirteen and forced to work in a factory — well, in the absence of any of that, I feel a little bit, like, *get over yourself.* When I started in with child labor, Ash saw what I saw — I showed her — and she was really shaken. But in a lot of ways she could never leave her family drama, and I get that. The past is so tenacious. It's just as true for me. Everyone basically has one aria to sing over their entire life, and this one is hers. She was so into the whole idea of being the good child, the producing child, the gratifying child, which also in this case meant the lying child. The one who protects her horrible brother."

"You think he's horrible? You think he

raped Cathy?" said Jules, her voice rising.

"Well, he definitely got too aggressive with her," Ethan said. "He couldn't imagine that she didn't want to keep doing what they were doing. No one ever felt that way about him; everyone was charmed, at least at camp they were. It was that, plus maybe Cathy's neediness. A bad combination. So, yeah, I would safely say he did something. I think he did it." He paused and corrected himself, saying, "My adult self thinks that." Then he looked at Jules, as if waiting for her to catch up with him, to leave her passive teenaged self that had waited for too long in overlapping states of knowing and not knowing.

"But none of it even exists anymore," said Jules. "That's the unreal part."

"I know," said Ethan. "Those two detectives are gone, remember them? The older one retired. And the younger one, Manfredo? Died of a heart attack. I googled him sort of compulsively over the years, wanting to see if he was still on the force, still somehow quietly working on the Goodman Wolf case. Maybe googling people *kills* them," Ethan said. "Did you ever consider that? You keep looking them up to see where they are, until one day you look them up and they're dead."

"Even Tavern on the Green is gone," said Jules.

"Right. And Goodman is ruined, I gather." Ethan paused and collected himself. "Is he still, you know, attractive to you?" he asked in a suddenly formal voice. "Did you still feel something when you saw him in the woods?"

"God, no. Nothing. Just shame."

Ethan nodded, as if relieved to have this information. "As for Cathy," he said, "I think she's actually doing okay now."

"How do you know?"

"Because I've seen her."

"You *have*? When? Does Ash know?"

Ethan shook his head. "No. I first got back in touch with her after September eleventh, when she was being crucified in the news. I'd seen one of those interviews with her — people phoning in to the TV show to yell at her, and I knew it was her; I'd followed her life a little bit, and I knew she'd married this German guy, Krause. On TV she just sat there *taking* it, and it was very upsetting. I got her e-mail address and privately wrote to her, just saying hey, I'm so sorry about this, and letting her know I was thinking about her. She wrote back immediately, and we got together. But she seemed traumatized all over again. At some point she was talking about the relief fund for the families, and I ended up writing a check."

"I'll bet you did."

"I think I felt guilty. The way we all just let everything drop; let *her* drop."

"I read the profile of her on the ten-year anniversary of the attacks," said Jules. "I hate saying that: 'the attacks.' It's just so jargony. But she finally got the families their health insurance, right? Through bonuses or something? And some of them apologized for being so hostile."

"It took a few years," said Ethan, "and it was obviously complicated, but, yeah, she did it."

"Do you still see her?"

He shook his head. "We e-mailed each other a bunch more times, and I wrote to her when the families' health insurance worked out. As I said, I think she's doing okay. She told me she has a very good husband. I asked her about her and Troy, and she said that they'd broken up for good when she was eighteen. And she told me that many years after camp, when she was around thirty, she went to see him dance. She just sat there in the audience at Alvin Ailey, and he was magnificent. And instead of feeling upset about her life and her problems and how she hadn't been able to dance professionally, it actually made her not think about herself at all. She said it did something else that art is supposed to do. Absorb you. The thing with Goodman, that definitely was a trauma for her. So yeah, I think it was a rape. But a lot of time finally passed. That's mostly what happened: time."

"Maybe that's what you and Ash need," Jules said. "To let time pass. I know everybody always says that; I'm not saying anything groundbreaking or original." Ethan didn't say anything at all. They sat for a while, then he stood with a loud shriek of his chair, and walked to a cabinet and produced a bottle of dessert wine. Jules followed him to the long gray couch, where they drank the wine, which was sweet and golden; it had the kind of taste that would have also appealed to their teen-aged selves — a wine for people who were just starting to enter the adult world.

"So," he said, "he's back in Iceland, you know. Ash told me that much."

"I didn't know, but I assumed it. Ethan, you should see him. It's just really awful; he looks so *marginal.* I wanted to talk to Ash about him, about all of this. But she doesn't want to talk to me now. I've been pretty isolated."

"Well, you have Dennis." Jules shrugged and made a face, and Ethan said, "What? You don't have Dennis? What's that face?"

"We're not so great. First I made us give up our jobs, then I made us give up the camp. I liked being around teenagers, but he was right — I didn't want to be there and not be one of them. Actually, it was the fucked-up ones I liked working with most. And now we're back here in the city and I'm jobless and Dennis is basically supporting us. I'm just sort of lumbering along, trying to figure out what to do now. I feel like I sort of missed the boat in a lot of ways."

"You always underestimate yourself," he said. "Why would you do that? I saw what you were like. I saw it that very first night in the boys' teepee. You were wry."

"And awkward."

"Okay, fine, wry and awkward. Awkward and wry. A combination I happen to have a soft spot for. But maybe it's an easier combination for a boy."

"Yes," she said. "It definitely is. Awkward and wry does not usually work for a girl. It makes everything hard."

"I don't want things to be hard for you." He came closer on the couch and touched her hair, which didn't seem at all strange. She felt that whatever he would do now, it wouldn't be strange. Leaning forward, Ethan kissed her on the mouth, and as he did, Jules's girl self flew up to meet her middle-aged-woman self. She recalled the way Ethan had long ago tried to upset her about her father's death, hoping her sadness would lead to arousal. This time the moment was softened by golden wine, and it took place not in the animation shed but in the Animation Shed. He was rich and she wasn't; he did what he loved and she did what she could, but they were alike: awkward and wry. The kiss would seal them and keep them alike; now their mouths were moving on each other, creating the seal. First there was only a sensation of gentle pressure, and it didn't feel bad. But then Jules realized she'd become aware, in this new iteration of the kiss, that Ethan tasted and smelled a little sour, as if the sugars in the wine were already breaking down. Or maybe it was mostly that his mouth was an unknown interior, and she knew she shouldn't be there, that this wasn't hers, that she didn't want to be there. How amazing to come this far and get an opportunity for a *do-over,* as Rory always used to say, but to feel it as if this were the same moment as the first one. Not a similar moment, but the very same one.

Pulling back from him, the anti-magnetism of their mouths making the lightest sound, a creak, a sigh — *straw-sound,* she thought. Jules looked away, and without speaking they each retreated to a far corner of the couch. She could not kiss Ethan Figman, or touch his body, or fuck him, or do anything at all physical with him. He was always trying to work his way back to her, always seeing how far he could go. He was like the mouse that Jules had told Dennis had followed them from one apartment to another. But she still wouldn't let him, because he wasn't hers.

Dennis, she thought, sometimes smelled a little toxic from the Stabilivox yet appealing, with a yeasty overlay. So he wasn't whirling with irony and speed and creativity. She wondered what Dennis was doing right now, late on this cold weeknight. They'd been remote and cordial since the summer. There had been almost no sex, almost no kissing, but a good deal of polite, neutral-territoried conversation. He was still angry at her for making them turn around and leave Belknap when the camp season had actually run smoothly. He was probably sitting in bed with ESPN on now and a *Journal of Diagnostic Medical Sonography* in his lap. Here, in a loft space improbably located inside an office building, late at night, Jules and Ethan looked at each other across the expanse of the long couch.

"I've got to go," she said.

"I tried," said Ethan. "It's just that these days I don't really know the best way to live. I honestly just don't know."

"It's always complicated."

"No," he said. "This is different. Jules, I have something."

"What does that mean, something?"

"A melanoma," he said.

She looked hard at him. "Where?" she demanded, and she sounded almost angry, disbelieving. She uneasily remembered her father coming into her room one night and telling her he was sick, and he needed to be in the hospital. She'd been sitting at her little white rolltop desk, writing a book report, and all at once the desk, the looseleaf paper, the pen in her hand, seemed absurd, as weightless as objects in space.

"It doesn't really matter," Ethan said. "But for what it's worth, it's up here." He tapped the top of his head, and then tipped his head down and parted his hair so she could see the small bandage on his skull. "It's also in the lymph nodes, apparently."

"When did you discover it?" she said, and her voice was suddenly nearly inaudible.

"In the fall. I had an itch on my head and I scratched it. There was a little blood. It scabbed over. I thought it was nothing, but it turned out to be a mole that had been there for a long time, except I never saw it."

"You were living on your own when you found it," she said. "Who was there with you? Who did you tell?"

"No one," he said. "I've kept it very quiet."

"Ash doesn't know?" He shook his head. "Ethan, you have to tell her."

"Why?" he asked. "Apparently you're allowed to keep critical information from your spouse."

"She has to help you."

"Maybe you can do that. Because frankly," he said with a willed little smile, "it's partly your fault, Jules. You made me take off my floppy denim hat that first summer, saying I looked like Paddington Bear. So the sun beat down all these years —"

"Shut up, that is really not funny." He saw at once that he'd been in error teasing her. It seemed cruel, and he certainly would never want to be cruel to her. "There's treatment, right?" she asked. "You've been doing things, chemotherapy?"

"Yes," he said. "Two rounds. Hasn't been effective yet, but they're hopeful."

"So what's next?"

"A different drug," he said. "I'm going to start Monday."

"Ethan, you need to get Ash involved with this. She'll want to take charge. She'll want to take care of you. That's what she does."

Ethan's face was unmoved. "I don't think so," he said. Then, softer, he told her, "You're the one."

"I'm not the one."

"You are."

She couldn't continue the volley, and she thought: Okay, I am the one. I am the one and I have always been the one. This life was here for me, pulsing, waiting, and I didn't take it.

But, she knew, you didn't have to marry your soulmate, and you didn't even have to marry an Interesting. You didn't always need to be the dazzler, the firecracker, the one who cracked everyone up, or made everyone want to sleep with you, or be the one who wrote and starred in the play that got the standing ovation. You could cease to be obsessed with the idea of being interesting. Anyway, she knew, the definition could change; it had changed, for her.

Once, stepping out on a stage had been the greatest tonic for a fifteen-year-old girl whose father had died. Julie Jacobson, the poodle-headed girl from Underhill, New York, had been slapped into life at Spirit-in-the-Woods. But that was so many generations away from these middle-aged people in their soft skins, up late and talking. "Ethan, I'll go with you wherever you want me to go," she said. "I'm not working these days, so I have the time. I'll be there for your appointments and your treatments. Is that what you'd like?"

He nodded and closed his eyes, relieved. "Yes, very much. Thank you."

"All right," Jules said. "But you have to call Ash and tell her things."

"What things?"

"She can't be the only one who *did something.* I recognize that not telling you about Goodman set off a lot of things between you. But she's Ash, and you love her, and you have to tell her about, you know, how you hid out in that hotel room instead of going with her and Mo to the Yale Child Study Center."

"Oh my God."

"And also, if it seems appropriate, you might even tell her you've been in touch with Cathy, and gave her money. And, obviously, you have to tell her about being sick."

"That is some conversation, Jules."

"Yes. And you have to have it with her, not me."

Dennis had fallen asleep before Jules got home, though he denied it in that strange way that people often deny they've been sleeping. But his face appeared lined with a pattern that was an exact match with the ribbed velour of the old sofa in the living room, and Jules imagined him lying with his face smashed down, solidly asleep but still near enough to the surface to become snortingly attentive upon hearing her key in the lock. It was nearly midnight. She hadn't accepted the offer of a ride in Ethan's car uptown but had instead said she'd wanted to walk a little. The night was cold, with snow persistently falling, on a slant, and it was a relief to walk for at least a few blocks on the deserted streets before getting on the subway.

"What happened?" Dennis said, looking at her peculiarly. "Something happened."

"Your face is all creased," said Jules. She took off her snowy coat and sat on the sofa, which was still warm from where he'd lain.

"You're not going to tell me?" he asked.

"I'll tell you," she said. "Even though I don't really want to." Then, with as little intonation as possible, keeping it all at a slight distance for self-preservation, just as Ethan had done with her, she told him about Ethan's melanoma. She didn't tell him about the kiss, for it had already inverted itself and disappeared. Dennis sat passively listening, then he said, "Oh shit. Well, it's Ethan, so he'll get himself the best treatment. He'll do whatever he has to do."

"I know that."

"What about you?" Dennis said. "Are you going to be okay?"

He reached out and touched her hair, just as Ethan had done; it was one of the basic moves in the male playbook, coming as naturally to them as anything. Jules let herself fall with a thud against her husband's wide chest, and Dennis willed himself into full presence again. He willed the marriage back, and pulled his wife toward him. Dennis was present, still present, and this, she thought as she stayed landed against him, was no small talent.

TWENTY-TWO

The two couples met for dinner twice more
that winter; Jonah joined them for the first
one. They went to the same easy, muted
restaurant both times, and they ate very early
because Ethan got too tired from his chemotherapy. He was high from the medical
marijuana he'd been smoking for nausea, and
he smiled loopily at Jules from across the
table. The first time she'd spoken to him in
her life he'd been rolling a terrible, wet joint.
These days his joints were tightly rolled by
someone else, and they were uniformly thin
and powerful. He smoked often lately, Jules
knew. They were all slow-moving and cautious, closed up into a small, private bloom
of friends. Ash, having reconciled with Ethan
that winter, still seemed afraid her marriage
would fall apart again, and she sat beside him
with her hand on his. She and Jules didn't
see each other alone very often. The leisureliness of a girlhood friendship — or even of a
friendship between two women, in which

they'd talked about sex and marriage and art and children and the election and what would happen *next* — was enviable, but not what either of them wanted right now. They hadn't known in advance that leisureliness would be something they would lose, and would mourn. When Jonah came to dinner, Ash told everyone about how he'd been teaching Mo to play banjo. "I don't know if he's actually going to learn that much," Ash qualified, "but he seems to really want to try."

"He's definitely learning," said Jonah. He'd only come to their house for two in-person lessons when Mo was home from boarding school, but he was still working with him on Skype; the distance was reassuring to Mo, and so was the filtering presence of the screen. Jonah had his guitar with him at dinner in the restaurant, and he made an apologetic exit before coffee; he was meeting up with a couple of musicians in Greenpoint, Brooklyn, and he didn't want to be late.

Ethan began dying early that spring, though no one except Ash recognized this until it was really upon them. He'd lost some weight, and he was pale, but it was subtle. Because he had so many projects going, they didn't understand what was happening. He had been away from the studio so much, but the staff worked around his absence. From the house on Charles Street he'd been shooting out e-mails liberally, and sometimes indiscriminately, trying to make arrangements for next year's Mastery Seminars and recording his lines for the show with a highly sensitive voice recorder that he'd had installed. He dictated a memo to the network about a minor dustup over some supposedly controversial material on a recent episode of *Figland* that had caused an energy drink company to threaten to pull advertising.

There were stories, out there in the world, that Ethan Figman was ill, but no one knew the extent of his illness. Everyone had cancer; that was the consensus. Cancer wasn't shocking anymore, and melanoma didn't seem so bad, the way, say, pancreatic cancer did. Ethan had always maintained that doing projects kept you in the world, and kept you alive. Work, he'd once said, was the anti-death. Jules, who realized she agreed with this, somehow had managed to return to work too. The adolescent groups at the Child and Family Center in northern Manhattan were held in one of those drab all-purpose rooms where folding chairs were stacked at the side and an ancient piñata still hung overhead, bashed in and excavated of its loot. The light in the room was poor, and the teenagers sat slumped in their circle at the beginning, but as the hour progressed they were enlivened; and by the end one of them was weeping about her alcoholic father, another was hugging the weeper, and a boy stood on a chair and pulled down the useless piñata once and for all. The motherly supervisor, Mrs. Kalb, who had hired Jules on a trial basis, sat in a corner on her own folding chair, taking notes.

Afterward, in her office, Mrs. Kalb remarked that Jules seemed to have "an enormous affection for the young and troubled," and Jules readily said yes, this was true. So now she was running three groups that each met twice a week for two hours. Two more groups would be added by the end of the year. The pay here was lousy, but Jules and Dennis's expenses weren't all that high. Rory's state school tuition was manageable, and soon enough she'd be out of college, though God knew if there was a job for her out there; that was what all parents of college-age students said to one another. Everyone was terrified that their kids would be unemployable, just another statistic, living at home forever in their childhood bedrooms, among their posters and trophies. People dissuaded their kids from going into the arts, knowing that there was no longer a future there. Once, a few years earlier, Jules had gone to see a play at Ash's theater, and afterward, during the "talkback," when the audience asked questions of the playwright and of Ash, who'd directed the production, a woman stood up and said, "This one is for Ms. Wolf. My daughter wants to be a director too. She's applying to graduate school in directing, but I know very well that there are no jobs, and that she's probably only going to have her dreams dashed. Shouldn't I encourage her to do something else, to find some other field she can get into before too much time goes by?" And Ash had said to that mother, "Well, if she's thinking about going into directing, she has to really, really want it. That's the first thing. Because if she doesn't, then there's no point in putting herself through all of this, because it's incredibly hard and dispiriting. But if she does really, really want it, and if she seems to have a talent for it, then I think you should tell her, 'That's wonderful.' Because the truth is, the world will probably whittle your daughter down. But a mother never should."

The audience had spontaneously applauded, and Ash had looked very pleased, and so had the mother. Jules wondered what had happened to that daughter; had she tried to be a director? You could feel a little smug with a daughter like Rory, who wanted to work for the national parks and wasn't one of those kids who needed to be creative but ended up working behind the counter at Chipotle.

Ethan was glad to hear that Jules had a new job that she liked. "I wish I could come to your group and eavesdrop," he said. "I want to see you in action. I could pretend I was one of the teenagers."

Across the table at the second of the two dinners that year, in the low light of the candles, Ethan said something to Jules that she didn't hear. She put her hand to her ear, but at that moment Dennis put his own hand on top of Jules's other hand, and each of them returned to the relevant partner.

After the latest round of chemotherapy proved "disappointing," Ethan and Ash decided to seek alternative treatment, and so they traveled to a clinic in Geneva, Switzerland, which had been recommended to them through another friend of Duncan and Shyla's. "The Toblerone cure," Ethan said on the phone to Jules the night before the trip, sarcastic but resigned. In Switzerland Ethan felt so poisoned by the harsh, untried drugs that he quit five days into the twenty-one-day protocol. Home again, he and Ash stayed in the house, not wanting to see friends, not even Jules, who became very agitated by the lack of communication. "Let me know the next phase of the battle plan," she wrote to Ash. "Will do," Ash wrote back, but she was unconvincing. Jules sent e-mails directly to Ethan, telling him what had happened in her "children of divorce" group that day. "Actually, you could join that group," she wrote to him. "You're a child of divorce. Plus, the *Times* Science section said there's a new cutoff age for when adolescence officially ends. Fifty-two! You just made it!!!" She liberally threw out exclamation marks, each one more desperate and manic than the last.

No one told you that in moments of crisis, family was allowed to trump friendship. Ethan and Ash's children were summoned by their mother in the middle of the week; Larkin, at home, was almost hysterical with anxiety, needing Klonopin, which Ash fed her bits of over the course of the day, then fed the rest to herself. Larkin had gotten a tattoo in New Haven that crawled across her shoulder and down the length of her left arm. It was a compendium of *Figland* characters, and was meant as a tribute to her father, but all he could say when he saw it was, "Jesus, what were you *thinking*?" Which made Larkin start crying that her parents never cared about what she wanted, only what they wanted. "That isn't true," said Ash, who'd been a tremendous mother to both of her children. Then Larkin collapsed, saying that of course Ash had been a good mother; she didn't know what she was saying. Ash cried too, and Mo, who had been driven home only hours earlier from his boarding school, became so anxious by all the untamed emotion that he slammed into his bedroom and stayed in there.

Later, his parents could hear him playing banjo through the door. "Mo," said Ethan, standing outside the room but wanting nothing more than to go back down the hall and get into bed. "Please come out." He tried the knob, but it wouldn't turn.

"I don't want to, Dad. I don't like what's going on here."

"Nothing's going on," Ethan said. "I got angry at your sister because of the tattoo, but it's her body, and she was trying to do something loving. I shouldn't have yelled at her. Come on out. I'm your dad and I want to be with you." He forced himself to say these words, and forced himself to mean them, the way Jules had always explicitly told him to try to do. For a few seconds the door didn't open, and then it did. Mo stood in the doorway, flesh of Ethan Figman's flesh. *Love your son,* Jules always told him. *Love him and love him.* She had sent love messages for Ethan to pour into Mo, and now, still feeling so sick from this recent experimental drug, Ethan said, "Can I come in?" Mo was surprised, because his father rarely came to him. But Ethan entered the room and sat at the foot of Mo's bed. "What were you playing?" he asked.

"A song. I'll show you," said Mo. And then, stopping and starting as he needed, making errors but continuing on, he slowly worked his way through a recognizable instrumental version of "The Wind Will Carry Us," the strings lifting and coming together like individual chimes banging. When he was finished, Mo said, "Dad, didn't you like it? Dad, are you *crying*?"

The family stayed together in the house for a full week. Meals were prepared for them; packages arrived and were signed for; an oncological nurse visited twice; and still very few other people understood what was happening. Even Jules, uptown in her own apartment with Dennis, could not make herself understand. "Do you think they'll figure something out?" she asked Dennis.

"I don't know," he said.

"Yes, you do. You deal with cancer at work all the time. You read those journals. Tell me. Tell me what you think."

Dennis looked at her, unblinking. It was morning and they were both awake and in the one bathroom they shared, side by side at the sink. She'd never gotten her own bathroom in marriage, though it had been something she'd always longed for. Dennis was shaving, drawing a path through the field of dark hair on his cheek. By the time he returned from work it would already have grown back. He looked mournful with his half beard and thatches of shaving cream. He put down the razor on the side of the sink and said, "If it's in both lungs now, as you say it is, then, no, I don't think there's anything more they can do for him. At least, not that I'm aware of. I'm only an ultrasound technician," he felt compelled to add. "I'm not a doctor."

"Oh, but you know a lot by now, Dennis," said Jules. "And here's what I keep thinking. I keep obsessing over the idea that he might never get a chance to be known as Old Ethan Figman."

"What?"

"Like Old Mo Templeton," she said in what almost sounded like a wail.

"Right. Disney's tenth Old Man."

Dennis went to work that morning, and Jules went to work, and it was a regular day, with spring trying to crack through everywhere and the adolescents in Jules's recently released inpatient group particularly rambunctious and flirtatious with one another. An air of good cheer infused the grim room at the mental health center; and a boy named JT, who had body dysmorphia, had brought in a box of Entenmann's raspberry Danish, saying that if you microwaved it for twenty seconds, no more and no less, it was "ambrosia." JT and two girls ran down the hall to use the microwave in the kitchenette, and in the brief lull before group resumed, Jules recalled the huckleberry crumble that she'd eaten in her teepee, and how it had supposedly tasted like sex, whatever that meant. The group reassembled, and the kids talked about their meds; their parents; their boyfriends; their cutting; their bulimia; and mostly their tender, hectic lives.

At lunch with her supervisor, Mrs. Kalb, at the one place in the bad neighborhood where the food was okay, and where all the mental health workers went to eat Caesar salads, Jules's cell phone pulsed and it was Ash calling. Even as Jules answered the phone in that crowded, dark green–walled restaurant with the TV playing overhead, she wasn't afraid, because it was daytime, and a cell phone pulsing in daylight was benign. But Ash, on the phone, her voice very soft but audible, said, "Jules? It's me. Oh, listen. Ethan had a heart attack this morning, and they couldn't revive him."

And even then, for a few seconds, Jules thought he could still recover. She remembered that when her mother had come home from the hospital on Long Island late at night and dropped her purse heavily to the floor, and said to Jules and Ellen, "Oh girls, Dad didn't make it," Jules had cried, "Can't they try something else?"

There was nothing else to try for this long chain of bodies, souls. Ethan's heart had stopped, possibly because of the drug he'd tried in Switzerland, or the accumulation of drugs he'd taken before. He'd had a massive heart attack sitting up in bed eating breakfast, and had died in the ambulance. After Jules talked to Ash for a few minutes, standing outside the restaurant coatless in the cold, she came back in and flatly repeated to Mrs. Kalb what she'd been told. Mrs. Kalb said, "Let me go cancel your group for you, honey. You're too upset for that. Just go home," but Jules wanted to go back to the group.

The kids, when she told them her friend had died, gathered around their therapist as if she were a maypole. A big, phobic Hispanic boy named Hector put his arms around her, and a tiny girl with a face so heavily pierced it looked like a bulletin board with old staples all over it, started to cry too, saying, "Jules! Jules! You must have loved your friend so much."

All the kids kept saying, "We're so sorry about your friend!" and she realized eventually that they thought *friend* was a euphemism, and maybe it was. Because *friend* was encompassing, and here it encompassed so much, including the contradictions. She hadn't seen Ethan's penis; he hadn't seen her breasts. Big deal, she thought, though she wished somehow that she could show herself to him and say, "You see? You didn't miss that much."

That evening she and Dennis went to the house on Charles Street and stayed the night. The household was awake into the morning, the lights blazing. "What am I going to do?" Ash said in her nightgown at four a.m., sitting on the stairs smoking. "When we were separated for those months, I just couldn't bear it. I was so lonely. And I'm so lonely again already now."

"I'll help you," Jules said.

"You will?" asked Ash, grateful like a child, and Jules said yes, she would, she always would, and though neither of them knew what this meant, it already seemed to have some effect.

Ash's father came over in the morning. Though he himself now appeared frail, and walked with a cane because of bad knees, he hugged his crying daughter to him as if keeping her grounded in a very strong wind. And then Ethan's long-divorced parents coincidentally arrived at the same time, each one furious with the other, both of them round-bodied and disheveled. They promptly began to cry, then argue, and then they quickly left. Jonah came over too, and in the hurtling toward the funeral and then the plans for the larger memorial that would take place a month from now, it seemed that there were many details to address. Larkin and Mo needed attention, and, in Larkin's case, sedation. Jules periodically observed, often in her peripheral vision, what Dennis was doing. Now he was making a series of phone calls to Ash's friends, at Ash's request; now he was sitting and watching Jonah and Mo play guitar and banjo; now he was bringing coffee to everyone; he was making himself useful in whatever ways he could. The house felt like a little insulated if exhausted environment free of outside clamor.

The next night, the night before the funeral, Duncan and Shyla appeared on the front doorstep. Oh, why were they here? Jules thought. The prick and the cunt! Even now, after Ethan's death, she would have to share him and Ash with these people. But Duncan and Shyla were as broken up as everyone else; Duncan's face kept screwing up into an expression of shocked, ongoing misery, and in the end they all stayed up very late drinking and trying unsuccessfully to comfort one another. Finally they fell asleep in chairs and on couches, and in the morning the house staff quietly came in, tiptoeing around them and picking up bottles and glasses and wadded-up tissues. Someone wiped down a surface that was unaccountably coated with a substance that no one could name.

Everyone wondered eventually about Ethan's money, who it would go to, and how much of it there was. His family would be taken care of forever, of course. After Mo became too old for his boarding school, he would live in a community where he would not be overwhelmed and where he could do some work that interested him. Larkin would be allowed to flail for a while, then settle down to graduate school or to write a precocious and angry autobiographical novel. Much of Ethan's money would certainly go to the Anti-Child-Labor Initiative and to other charities.

But then, regarding his money, there was also the question of his closest friends, and no one knew what his plans were for them. Two months before his death, Ethan had made an opaque joke to his estate lawyer, Larry Braff. "I don't know," Ethan had said as they sat together going over papers for several hours. "I think there are probably dangers in leaving your friends a lot of money."

"I imagine that's true."

"You could call it *The Drama of the Gifted Adult,*" said Ethan. "And I'm using *gifted* in a different way here. As in, *having received a gift.* Maybe the gifted adult becomes a child, and then stays a child forever because of the gift. In your experience, Larry, is that the case? Is that what happens?"

The lawyer regarded Ethan through his rimless glasses and said, "Forgive my ignorance, Ethan, but this 'drama' thing — I actually don't know what you're referring to. Is it a specific reference? Can you explain?"

"It's all right," Ethan said. "I was just thinking out loud. Not to worry. I'll figure it out." So no one knew yet what he had decided, and no one asked; it would be dealt with in time.

A month after Ethan died, Ash, who Jules

once again spoke to every day, called and said she'd finally been able to begin cleaning out Ethan's office in the house, and that she was messengering over something she'd found that she thought Jules' might like to have. "I don't actually know how you'll feel about it," Ash said, "but it belongs to you more than me."

The package arrived, a big brown paper square. Jules was home alone when the messenger came; Dennis was out in the park, kicking around a ball, "kicking around death," he'd said. Tonight, very late, Rory was returning home from school upstate by bus and would stay for a week. "I just like being with you guys," she'd explained to her parents; but they knew that for her, coming in from the outdoors and the world of her friends to be with her mother and father was something of a sacrifice, and she was doing it to cheer them up, to be kind. They awaited her return as if she were Jesus and would set them right.

In the front hallway, after signing for the package, Jules stood and opened it. Inside were some faded folded papers stapled together, and she opened them up to see they were a storyboard from an animated short that had never gotten made. Right away she recognized how old the drawings were. It wasn't just that the paper looked delicate. Ethan's style had also changed over the years, the faces taking on very particular qualities;

but here, back in the beginning, the pencil strokes were wild and loose, as though his hand was in a race with his brain. The first frame, carefully drawn, was of a boy and a girl, immediately recognizable as Ethan and Jules at around age fifteen, standing under pine trees in moonlight that flooded down on their homely, goofy faces. The boy gazed upon the girl in rapture.

"So what do you think?" he wanted to know. "Any chance you might reconsider?"

And the girl said, "Can we *pleeeeze* talk about something else?"

The next frame showed them trudging up a hill together. "All right, so what do you want to talk about?" he asked her.

"Did you ever notice the way pencils look like collie dogs?" she said, and a big no. 2 pencil with the face of a dog appeared, its mouth open and yipping.

"Nope, I never did," Ethan said in the next frame. The two figures reached the top of the hill and walked together through the trees. *Oh tragedy, oh tragedy,* the boy said to himself, but he was smiling a little. *Oh joy, oh joy.* Hearts and stars exploded in the darkness above their heads.

The stapled sheets lay on the front hall table of the Jacobson-Boyds' apartment for a couple of days, the same place where the Christmas letter from Ash and Ethan lingered for a while each year. Jules stood and looked at Ethan's drawings again. Finally she placed them in the chest in the living room where she kept the few things that corresponded to that time in her life. There were the signed, spiral-bound Spirit-in-the-Woods yearbooks from three summers in a row and the aerial photograph of everyone at camp the second summer. In it, Ethan's feet were planted on Jules's head, and Jules's feet were planted on Goodman's head, and so on and so on. And didn't it always go like that — body parts not quite lining up the way you wanted them to, all of it a little bit *off,* as if the world itself were an animated sequence of longing and envy and self-hatred and grandiosity and failure and success, a strange and endless cartoon loop that you couldn't stop watching, because, despite all you knew by now, it was still so interesting.

ACKNOWLEDGMENTS

Various people — friends, experts, and often both — shared their knowledge and observations with me, and I am grateful to them all. They include Debra Solomon, Greg Hodes of WME, Lisa Ferentz, LCSW-C, Sandra Leong, M.D., Kent Sepkowitz, M.D., David France, and Jay Weiner. Sheree Fitch, Jennifer Gilmore, Adam Gopnik, Mary Gordon, Gabriel Panek, Suzzy Roche, Stacy Schiff, Peter Smith, and Rebecca Traister are all sensitive readers whose advice I am lucky to have. I also owe a great deal of gratitude to my stellar agent, Suzanne Gluck. And I am once again indebted to my profoundly wise, generous editor, Sarah McGrath, as well as to Jynne Martin, Sarah Stein, and everyone else at Riverhead, including its excellent and, yes, feminist publisher, Geoffrey Kloske. As always, many thanks to Ilene Young. And, of course, my thanks and love to Richard.

ABOUT THE AUTHOR

Meg Wolitzer's previous novels include *The Wife, The Position, The Ten-Year Nap,* and *The Uncoupling.* She lives in New York City.

megwolitzer.com
facebook.com/meg.wolitzer